GILIAN THE

NEIL MUNRO was born in 1863, the illegitimate son of an Inveraray kitchen-maid. After leaving school, he worked for a time in a lawyer's office, before leaving the Highlands for a career in journalism, eventually editing the *Glasgow Evening News*. However, it was his work as a poet and novelist that established Munro as one of Scotland's finest writers. His historical novels, such as *The New Road* and *John Splendid*, were acknowledged as masterpieces of the genre; but he also achieved great success with the *Para Handy* tales and other light-hearted stories he wrote under the pseudonym Hugh Foulis. Neil Munro died in 1930.

Other B&W titles by Neil Munro

JOHN SPLENDID
DOOM CASTLE
THE NEW ROAD

NEIL MUNRO

Gilian the Dreamer

INTRODUCED BY
DOUGLAS GIFFORD

B&W PUBLISHING

First published 1899
This edition published 2000
by B&W Publishing, Edinburgh
Introduction © Douglas Gifford 2000

ISBN 1 903265 02 9

British Library Cataloguing in Publication Data:
A catalogue record for this book is available
from the British Library

Cover design by *Winfortune & Co*

Cover illustration:
Detail from *Self Portrait* by Archibald Skirving (1749-1819)
reproduced by kind permission of the
National Galleries of Scotland

Printed by WS Bookwell

CONTENTS

PART I

PART II

INTRODUCTION

Douglas Gifford

DIAGNOSING THE HIGHLANDS:
THE HISTORICAL FICTION OF NEIL MUNRO

The last two decades have seen a remarkable revaluation of
Scottish literature as having its own themes and historical
contexts, within which the work of hitherto undervalued writers,
such as Robert Fergusson or James Hogg, is now appreciated
as the major achievement it is. It is not only the work of
authors such as these, however; established authors like Scott and
Stevenson are being re-read in ways that reveal their sub-texts,
their ironic, symbolic, and often deeply critical commentaries on
Scotland's history and culture.

The work of Neil Munro comes somewhere between these
categories, and is a supreme example of how Scottish criticism
allowed a major writer to disappear from the canon of Scottish
literature. His historical novels especially were valued in their
time as comparable with the work of Stevenson and Scott—but
in the second half of the twentieth century it was of course his
Para Handy tales which kept his name alive. Quite simply, literary
historians failed to look beyond the apparent romance and colour
of Munro's great historical novels to see the darker themes and
satires which lay behind. As with the Scottish novels of Scott

and Stevenson, with whom Munro forms a great triumvirate, romance and ironic realism are kept in continual tension, in ways which exploit conventional views of Scottish character, landscape and history, only to ask fundamental questions regarding their truth and worth. Munro's *John Splendid*, *Gilian the Dreamer*, and *The New Road* belong with the great tradition of historical romance-satires of Scott, Hogg, Galt and Stevenson, in novels such as *Waverley*, *The Brownie of Bodsbeck*, *Ringan Gilhaize* and *The Master of Ballantrae* respectively; while Gilian in particular belongs also to a tradition which Scott began in *Waverley* when he portrayed an insipid hero whose failures stemmed from a destructive intensity of imagination which paralysed heroic action. Such a 'hero' recurs in Scottish fiction till the present day, and is arguably as much an ironic criticism of the society which fails to find a place for creative imagination as criticism of the flawed protagonist himself. In Gilian, a figure whose lonely and unusual childhood held many parallels with his own, Munro was scathing about Inveraray and Scotland's male-dominated culture and its treatment of creative genius, its historical tendency to allow its poets and artists to be marginalised.

Munro was born in Inveraray in 1863, the illegitimate son of a kitchen-maid in the castle—and reputedly son of a great Argyll. The equivocal nature of his birth informs all his life and all his best fiction, resulting in an ambivalence towards his country's history and its leaders which is very much in the great tradition of nineteenth-century Scottish fiction. On one hand lies Munro's identification with the great house of Argyll, Inveraray, and the West Highlands as representative of the best of Gaeldom, and leading it from barbarism to a new future in which it would bond with the Lowlands. But opposed to this lies a contrary dissociation, in which the absence at the core of his life of a father, together with his sensitivity towards the limitations of clan inheritance, leads to a coded portrayal of a series of Argyll father-chieftains and Campbell aristocrats as apparently noble, but fatally flawed and recurrently bombastic, pretentious, anachronistic and representative of the failure of the Clan Highlands to come to terms with an inevitable new world order where mercenary and clan military values were outmoded. There is throughout his work a tension between, on the one hand, an instinctive admiration for martial Gaeldom, brilliantly evoked in scenes of battle, such as his treatment of Montrose's devastation of Argyll in 1644—and, on the other, a reflective distaste for wanton slaughter, which comes out in a rare sensitivity to the aftermath of such destruction, in the descriptions of smoking ruins and families destroyed. His complex exposure of ancient attitudes culminated in his greatest attack on Highland military anachronism, his last and greatest novel, *The New Road*, in which General Wade's opening up of the old Highlands to trade with the Lowlands is triumphantly endorsed, and most of all for its satiric attack on the bloated black spiders at the heart of Highland anachronistic corruption, like the bubbly-jock strutting double-dealing blackmailer Barisdale or the treacherous MacShimi, Simon, Lord Lovat, symbol of all that Munro sees as the endless and endemic betrayals and treacheries of the Northern clans.

And Munro is profoundly important for this reorientation. Hostile to the Kailyard from the beginning, his first desire was to interpret the Highlands from the inside, since he felt that all previous literary evocations had been Lowland distortions. The result was the pioneering collection of short stories, *The Lost Pibroch* of 1896, in the same year as Barrie's satire on Scotland's repression of imagination and art, *Sentimental Tommy*, which may have provided inspiration for Gilian, with its similar theme of genius in an unsympathetic community. It is important to realise that Munro's first volume of stories combines parody with a cunning exploitation of the nostalgic self-indulgence and pseudo-Celtic mannerisms of 'Fiona Macleod' (William Sharp), the doyenne of the Celtic Twilight movement. These stories are essentially tragic, elegiac, and satiric. They draw in style from the great collections of West Highland folktales of J. F. Campbell (1860–1862), but they consciously underweave a dark sub-text which can easily be missed, given the strength of their narratives, their cruel and often shocking twists of fate, and their seemingly sincere but deceptively mannered Celticism. The title story tells of a haunting and ancient pipe tune which must not be played; if it is—and it is played—a blight will descend on the dear green places of the Highlands, and villages will lose their young men to emigration and war, following a nameless yearning. Story after story has the sly, tongue in saturnine cheek sub-text; a jealous second wife slashes the piping hand of her stepson, who threatens to outplay his father; a son kills his unknown father as a result of a pointless, long-drawn blood feud, jealous brothers drive a French lover from their enchanted sister, and always neighbouring communities and clans are mutually distrustful and ready to find the insult that leads to bloodshed. Romance is a deceit, the traditional artist an anachronism,—blind, crippled, or pushed outside community to wander. The last pibroch has indeed been played.

Three stories carry Munro's recurrent, lifelong thrust against the weak heart of his Highlands; 'Boboon's Children', 'Castle Dark', and 'War'. The first tells of how John Fine Macdonald, leader of an ancient nomadic tribe, at one with season and landscape, perhaps the ur-Highlander himself, is 'civilised' by the Campbell Captain of Inveraray; a pseudo-father who aims to destroy these original and natural Highlanders, with his clanship enclosure of their ancient and nomadic simplicity of spirit. Boboon hears his tribe calling at night to him from outside the castle walls, and eventually succumbs to their temptations of salmon and deer and freedom—but his daughter dies as the captain's prisoner-wife. 'Castle Dark' is even more revealing of Munro's sense that something ancient and good in Highland tradition has been corrupted by castle dominance; in this fable three periods of the Highlands are evoked, as the adventurer journeys three times to the mysterious heartland of Gaeldom; on his first journey the heartland is harmonious and fertile; in the second the chief's war-lust threatens his family and community; and in the third the land is broken, a wasteland. Here are the roots of the Golden Age mythology which the Scottish Renaissance would place at its centre.

If Munro's developing and satiric vision of his Highlands can be found in these tales, perhaps as important is his movement towards the characterisation and psychological analysis of what he is discovering as the archetypal Hollow Highlander, the vaunting, unreliable, deceitful and flattering Jaunty Jock who represents the tragic flaw at the core of clanship—not, it must be stressed, at the core of what the Highlands were before clanship, but emerging with a system of clan feuding and approved despoliation, a social system which finds ultimate value in stealing cattle and killing women and children in the name of tribal honour, and in which the supposed traditional equality of blood kinship (found with Boboon and his children) now sits very uneasily with the claims of the clan chief, Marquis or Earl or Duke, of whatever period. In 'War', one of Munro's starkest and most effective tragedies, Rob Donn follows Duke Archibald to Culloden and the boastful, satisfied killing of fellow-Highlanders—leaving his wife and child with no money, but with pretentious promises of his returning glory. Months pass; the restless soldier thoughtlessly spends the money he took from his wife; glutted with killing, he returns just as his wife, her own milk long dry, in last extremity of famine draining some blood from her cow for her dwining child, hears its death-cry. Here is the prototype for the John Splendids, the Jaunty Jocks and the bubbly-Jocks, the 'John Hielan'men'—and ultimately the Dukes themselves, who are their jaunty clan unreliables writ large. Munro will play with endless cunning with the many variations of the name of Highland Jock, and always the play is satiric and symbolic, a sign of weakness and pretension. A kindlier and later mood will see Munro reshape them into the crew of *The Vital Spark*, slipping in and out of Highland and Lowland ports with all the unreliability and shiftiness of their forebears, generally avoiding any claims of duty and responsibility, and covering their tracks with the relics of older self-inflating importance. But in

1898, with *John Splendid*, Munro was out to change Lowland perceptions of the Highlands with a subtle but deadly undermining of the House of Argyll from within.

For this is the strangest of historical romances—indeed, it is closer to the anti-romance of Lowlander James Hogg in his *Tales of the Wars of Montrose*, and particularly the parody of historical romance of *An Edinburgh Bailie* (1835). The two 'heroes', ex-soldiers of European fortune John McIver (*alias* John Splendid, so called because of his vain but taking demeanour) and 'sobersides' Colin Elrigmore, are amongst The Marquis of Argyll's right-hand men. The events are set amidst Montrose-Macdonald's ravaging of Argyllshire in 1644, and the consequent pursuit of Montrose by Argyll, in which the hunted became the hunter. After his legendary mountain march Montrose surprised and destroyed Argyll's army at Inverlochy, and—for the second time—Argyll fled from him, leaving his men to death and disgrace.

Argyll's double shame hangs over the book; and virtually all the narrative shares this overall feeling. For John and Colin achieve nothing for their side, apart from saving their own and some of their friends' skins—as far as battle goes, they are strangely ineffective, getting caught by their enemies as they carelessly dispute Highland poetry with the cranky bard Ian Lom Macdonald before Inverlochy. They are on the run constantly; slouching like thieves, begging from poor women in lonely cottages, lost on Rannoch Moor, inglorious in their company and their cause. The sensitive reader realises that this is a parodic extension of Scott's complex protagonists, and even more of Stevenson's *Kidnapped*, with its apparently similar but essentially different Breck-Balfour relationship. The Scottish novel's sly use of dramatic monologue from the work of Galt and Hogg down to *The Master of Ballantrae*, in which the suspect teller of the tale reveals more about his limitations than he knows, is maintained here in Colin Elrigmore's obtuse unawareness throughout the novel that his idolised Betty, the Provost's daughter, loves, and is being wooed by, his apparent boon companion John

Splendid. Little is as it claims to be in this novel; Highland honour is exposed as sham bragging, shallow loyalty, and male egocentricity, as John wheedles, struts, manipulates, up to the edge of murder, with Colin his rather dull Sancho Panza.

These nasty little wars of Lorn, with their rival leaders Montrose and Argyll seen as hardly in control of their armies, are strangely detached from what is going on in the bigger British world. Munro deliberately leaves out any account of what Argyll is up to in the bigger world, and nothing of how he plays his much greater game with Covenanters, King Charles, and Westminster parliamentarians—the Highlands interested in the larger picture—and Munro thus shows their limited and disconnected mindset. And nowhere is Munro's point about reductive Highland insularity made more clear than in the treatment by his Campbell adherents of Archibald the Grim, Gillespie Gruamach, Marquis of Argyll. Their failure to understand his new world vision, and their insistence on fawning upon his least wish, is summed up in his relationship with John Splendid. Here is the key to Munro's psychological analysis of the destructive mindset of Gaeldom, and it is a critical assessment the more trenchant because it comes from within, from the heart of Inveraray—or at least from a Inveraray exile moved by love and profound disillusion.

Argyll can be read as representing the beginning of the third phase of Highland development as predicted and welcomed by Munro; namely, that move away from clan identification and ethos to acceptance of the values of a bigger world. Argyll plays his part—whatever his failings in this bigger world; it will lead him to execution in Edinburgh ten years after Montrose. John Splendid will have none of Argyll's bookish and civilising tendencies—freedom to war, at home against Macdonalds or the Athole men, or abroad as mercenary, never judging the morality of the cause, is John the Hielan'man's way, as long as the good figure is cut, and fair speech given to friends. As the novel develops, Munro shows the Lowlands changing Inveraray. The new shopkeepers, the vessels from Glasgow and Ayr, and the new 'English' church with its dour minister Gordon seem to sleepy Colin at first an intrusion, but by the end of the book he accepts the need for Lowland influence and change, and even decides—to Splendid's discomfiture—that the most courageous soldier and the best man throughout the sorry wars of Lorn has been minister Gordon, the dour and inflexible Lowlander, the only man to speak plain and honest, without Highland flattery and face-saving and boasting—especially to Argyll. The most impressive part of this strange treatment of what could so easily be the subject for romance lies at the end, when Argyll lies sick in his castle after Inverlochy. John Splendid and Argyll's leaders had at the beginning advised him to quit Inveraray—and then again Inverlochy—to lead the clan another day. Their subservient and face-saving advice has brought about the spiritual demoralisation of the Campbells. Now at last Argyll begs his cousin John to speak true. To tell him what he thinks of his chief. And at last John speaks out, in a scene as powerful as anything in Scottish literature, in a denunciation of his chief's cowardice which is the more savage since it is a complete and shocking reversal of his previous flattery—although even now it will appear afterwards that his apparent final frankness has been calculated roleplaying, and his dramatic declaration to abandon Argyll for European wars was for effect only.

This is a subtle novel, and a superficial reading will miss the ambivalences and qualifications which are Munro's way of expressing his love and hate for the way the essential early and natural goodness of Highland culture has been warped into time-serving deceit and arrogance. John must not be read solely as Highland deceiver; he has much of the old virtues—the skills of a scout, the loyalty to immediate comrades, an instinctive protectiveness to women and children. He may deceive Colin in love, but he relinquishes his chances for love to the younger man, and does indeed go off to Europe, leaving as the end of the novel the realisation by Betty that she has lost the man she really loves through misunderstanding, and the possible realisation—for he is dense!—by Colin that the woman he will marry will always love another—hardly the conventional romantic finale!

If John Splendid is important as Munro's fusion and summation of all he deprecates and values in a period of Highland culture which has lost its way into a single figure, then *Gilian the Dreamer* (1899) is its counterpart, an assessment of the nineteenth-century Highlands at the tail-end of the Napoleonic wars, when innumerable half-pay Cornals and Major-Generals returned to rot in Inveraray and the small Highland towns, in a dwam of bloody and glorious memories of the foreign wars of Empire. It is the era of an even more illustrious and by now remote grandee Duke John, McCailean Mor, and these washed-up soldiers are the heirs of John Splendid. Munro mercilessly anatomizes them, and their repressive and malign influence on a burgh struggling to enter modernity. A superficial reading will miss the deadliness of Munro's satire on these pensioned-off relics, boorish to their women and nurturing old feuds. Munro was never more acidic than in his picture of the three Campbells of Keil— the old general Dugald, virtually dead apart from his memories in his dull room in a dark tenement; his brothers, Cornal John and the bull-necked Paymaster Captain John Campbell, another version of Jaunty Jock, and perhaps the least attractive. A nasty picture which was to lead to Douglas Brown's merchant-tyrant Gourlay in *The House with the Green Shutters* three years later, and to the Highland merchant-tyrant in Hay's novel *Gillespie* of 1914, set in Tarbert, further down Loch Fyne. These men are in varying degrees bullies, philistines, anachronisms, unquestioning killers for Empire. Munro leaves some of them—like the decent general, John Turner—respectability and a place to fulfil in the world; but in the main this town has become a place of drunken ex-soldiers roistering in its taverns while women do the work.

But Munro has deeper issues to fathom—and now he articulates a crucial Scottish predicament, which illustrates how he transcends Highland limitations to speak, like Gunn after him, for Scottish culture and its failings. Gilian—the name a mocking echo of Gilian-of-the-Axe, one of the great Celtic folk heroes—is a fatherless boy of twelve whose grandmother has died. From the start we realise he is an unusual and perhaps not entirely healthy child; utterly alone at her death in Ladyfield, a small farm outside Inveraray, he plays on his imagination as to how he will tell his sad news in the town—suddenly, for maximum impact? Leading up slowly, for other, more complex effect? Gilian plays with his grief, genuine enough, but dearer still to him for its imaginative and emotional effects. This is fine natural awareness and sensibility gone wrong through marginalisation.

For this boy is in his way a genius, with an imagination which cannot be fulfilled in this repressive burgh, with its lack of any aesthetic nourishment. Munro is in fact asking the question Scott posed in *Waverley* in 1814, a question posed again in 1896 by Stevenson in his portrayal of hyper-sensitive Archie in *Weir of Hermiston*, and again in the same year—and just three years before Gilian—by James Barrie in his study of imaginative genius in an equally repressive environment, in *Sentimental Tommy*. Clearly this recurrent focus on socially thwarted Scottish creativity stems from a recurrent and highly significant preoccupation of serious Scottish writers, for it too returns again, juxtaposed with the figure of the brutal father, in George Douglas Brown's portrait of the excessively sensitive and imaginative John Gourlay junior in his repressive small town, and is repeated by MacDougall Hay in *Gillespie* thirteen years later, in his evocation of the disturbed mind of young Eochan Strang, sensitive to his environment and family pressures to the point of his destruction.

In *Gilian the Dreamer* and these counterparts Scottish writers pose a fundamental question. It is simply this; what happens to creative genius in a culture and country which cannot and will not provide nourishment for it? And the answer, from all these writers—and Linklater, Jenkins and Crichton Smith thereafter, to name but a few—is that creative imagination becomes sick when its community denies it, forcing it inward into roleplaying to the point where it is an irrelevance, even a danger to the community and society outside.

It is important to realise that this novel is not just about the loss of ancient bardic involvement in Highland community. Munro's perception of the Highlands is beginning to merge with a more general perception of the overall problems of Scottish culture generally, problems of Anglicisation, neglect of native language and genius, and a hardening of philistine attitudes towards local talent and subject-matter. (The problem will remain at the forefront of Scottish culture, whether urban or rural, till the 'seventies, as shown in novels like Archie Hind's *The Dear Green Place* and Iain Crichton Smith's *Consider the Lilies*—one set in Glasgow, the other set in Strathnaver, but both deploring the repression of the natural and creative in a repressive society. And nowhere in Scottish literature is re-assessment more needed than in this area in which the treatment of this Scottish central theme through ironic parody brings together such a mixture of writers for so long wrongly labelled as 'kailyard' or 'romantic escapist' or 'over-blackly realist'.)

Gilian is no John Splendid. Indeed, he is closer to Munro himself, and this novel is surely a working out of Munro's own troubled awareness of his possible Campbell fatherhood as well as his recognition that Inveraray could never be a complete home to him. We never learn who Gilian's father is;—is it the Paymaster, who owns Ladyfield? Gilian is a misfit who will fail all but the few who see his buried qualities. To his adoptive Campbells he is a playacting fool; to his contemporaries at school a wild and unpredictable solitary; to his friend Nan, merely a foil to her real love interests. Yet again Munro introduces parody of the conventional love narrative of romance, as Gilian woos Nan Turner—only to lose her to the genuine boy of action, young Islay Campbell, who saves her from shipwreck when, like the dreamer-hero of Conrad's *Lord Jim*, Gilian is frozen at the moment of truth into thinking too precisely on the events. Imagination is divorced from action, argues Munro—the predicament of the Highlands as well as Gilian. (It is fascinating to speculate that Conrad—whom Munro knew and liked, having met him in Glasgow—might have borrowed Munro's psychological analysis of the dreamer who cannot act, for his novel, a year later.) Once again a superficial reading will miss the parody of romance, as Gilian, utterly at home with birds, animals and all nature, finds himself trapped between the ancient and natural Highlands of landscape and tradition, the world of Boboon's Children, and this ugly, contradictory and deeply unsatisfying modern world which has no respect for Art, whether it be legendary tale or traditional song—a Highland world, but now very like its Lowland counterparts, in its absorption into Empire and Britain.

An introduction such as this cannot do justice to the entire and neglected output of this writer. Other Highland-and-island novels, such as *Doom Castle* (1901) and *Children of Tempest* (1903) followed, together with Lowland work like *The Shoes of Fortune* (1901) and of course the Para Handy, Jimmy Swan and Erchie stories running from 1904 to the 'twenties. Always the dark undercurrent remained, together with the sense of a writer seeking new, parodic ways of handling old romances or comic stories of the new, urban Scotland. And always the John Splendid figure recurs, in different guises—as the magnificient villain Sim McTaggart, Argyll's Chamberlain, in *Doom Castle*, a spy on the Jacobites in France who has fled home from his betrayals, but a charmer whose flute playing hypnotises the reader into disbelief that he can be such an evil sham. In *The Shoes of Fortune*, Lowlander Paul Grieg, exiled from Scotland, falls in with Highland intrigue in France with Prince Charles and Clementina Walkinshaw—and discovers that the lady is formidable, if decent, while the prince—the ultimate John Splendid?—and his adherents are utterly vain and corrupt. This novel lead directly to Violet Jacob's masterpiece of historical deconstruction of Jacobitism in her novel *Flemington* (1911), recently rediscovered and edited by Carol Anderson, while *Children of Tempest* inspired Neil Gunn to produce *The Gray Coast* and *The Lost Glen* in the 'twenties. And then there are two experimental and highly theoretical novels which, if not as successful as these others, break entirely new ground in their speculations regarding future

Highland development. *The Daft Days* (1907) shocks Inveraray with a girl-Gilian, the contemporary American child Bud, whose fresh thinking sweeps cobwebs out of the old town—Munro said that he loved Americans 'because they beat that stupid old King George and laughed at dynasties'; while *Fancy Farm* (1910) unsuccessfully tried to recreate a Highlander of the old natural order in the unbelievable Sir Andrew Schaw—but successfully presented a picture of the New Woman ruthlessly sweeping out Highland prejudice.

Munro was writing now as the Lowland editor; his perspectives had greatly changed. He was now the sophisticated art critic, whose discussions of Whistler, French impressionism and Mackintosh richly deserve republication, as do the dozen or so unpublished volumes of commentary on war, the changing and shipbuilding Clyde, the fascinating new technologies of the Empire exhibitions, the New Glasgow—Munro would certainly have laughed at MacDiarmid's ideas that Glasgow, at any rate, needed a Renaissance, since he viewed Glasgow life as a vibrant mixture of art and commerce. But for all this relocation, he was deep down still developing his final view, to find articulation in his greatest and last historical novel, *The New Road* of 1914, of what he saw as the central transition in Highland culture, that of the period between the 'fifteen and the 'forty-five, when Wade's roads would drain away what he now clearly saw as the poison at the heart of the Highlands.

But at the same time he was also was trying out other ways of expressing this sense of the flawed Highland inheritance than in his final masterpiece. Perhaps we have not always read Munro's presentation of Para Handy and his crew—especially Hurricane Jack—as the derogatory and ironic portrayals which in essence they are. Munro himself grew somewhat disgusted with their immense popularity; and while he may simply have felt fed up and perhaps ashamed of prolonging their shelf-life, it may be also that he felt mis-read. For all the hilarity of Para's hilarious escapades should not blind us to two deeper, if typically ambivalent messages. The first of these sub-texts is that the crew are a feckless, squabbling lot, who will neither work nor want, who slip in and out of Highland and Lowland harbours with equal disrespect, who would literally sell each other down the river, with the possible exception of Sunny Jim, who does not last long, and is replaced by the most clay-footed Jaunty Jock of them all, Hurricane Jack.

The second sub-text is less satirically damaging—and here we may invoke the current fashion for citing Michel Bakhtin as a source of revaluation of the subversive, the lowlife and the bawdily irreverent in our literature from the Makars to Ramsay, Fergusson, and the Jolly Beggars of Burns. Are the crew not their descendants, as they mock the pretentious, refuse to be located in any system, and generally ape their betters with their parodic and pompous philosophising? In any event, they are the heirs of the mixed qualities of John Splendid; and the kindlier displacement of them into a territory neither sea nor land, neither ocean nor river, neither Highland or Lowland, marks Munro's joining the development of Scottish literature and culture into a single entity, where no part of the whole can any longer claim separate vitality.

All of Munro's development to this point goes into his last great historical novel, clearly separated from the earlier Highland work by ten years. *The New Road* is his final masterpiece, with its detached irony, which runs alongside a more generous and affectionate recognition of the survival of that original and natural spirit of the Highlands as exemplified in his vivid and affirmative picture of Ninian Macgregor Campbell, who takes his place between Scott's Rob Roy and John Splendid at his best. Inveraray and the house of Argyll are finally seen as the bridge between old Highlands and new Lowlands, fulfilling Gillespie Gruamach's dream. It is a novel in the grand tradition of Scott and Scottish mythic regeneration in fiction, taking its place alongside the best of Scott, Gunn, and Mitchison.

It begins in 1733. Aeneas Macmaster is a tutor in Drimdorran house to Black Sandy Duncanson, agent supreme of London-and Edinburgh-based Duke Red John. Aeneas's father Paul, rashly out in the later Glenshiel rising of 1719, is presumed drowned, and Black Sandy has taken over the forfeited estate. Fears are growing of another rebellion; arms are being smuggled from Holland, and the feared Chief of Clan Fraser, the dreaded MacShimi, Simon Lovat, is plotting in his fastness in Inverness. Against this movement into typical Highland unrest, however, is The Road; Wade's regiments are toiling without cease to drive the first-ever passage for troops and commerce through the glens.

These two counter-movements are echoed in subtle patterns of juxtaposition throughout the novel. And here the debt of Munro to Scott must be acknowledged, for Munro is once again reworking an earlier fiction—this time that most misunderstood of Scott novels, *Rob Roy*. Scott's great oppositions of past and present, disorder and order, Highland and Lowland, are reworked here to bring Scott's predictions of the triumph of order to fulfilment. The oppositions are rich; here is the Inveraray Bailie Alan Iain Alain Og Macmaster, reformed Highlander, the modern Bailie Nicol Jarvie who relishes the impact that the Road will have on his wild countrymen; and set beside him, his friend—a subtle joke here—a cousin of Rob Roy's in the form of Iain Beachdair, John the Scout, Ninian Macgregor Campbell, who can be read almost as Rob Roy himself, if more socially accept-able, since he is in the Duke's service as his Messenger-at-arms, and since he has all Rob's cunning and natural skills. The connection with John Splendid through name is also intentional; for, if the Bailie is the future, third phase of Highland integration with the Lowlands, then Ninian is descendant of Boboon, child of the mist (a motif which runs through the novel), chanter of ancient and pagan prayers and absolutely at home in wild nature.

As in Scott's novel, this pairing of opposites is symbolic. Ancient and modern will destroy the corruption which came with the Clans—of MacShimi, of all the petty chieftains, and of Black Sandy, who turns out not to be serving his Duke, but to be the murderer of Aeneas's father and in league with MacShimi and his treacherous chieftains. And with another unlikely pairing, Munro returns to exploit *Kidnapped* again, this time by setting Aeneas on a journey with Ninian, with two aims. Aeneas is to learn the new trading skills, while Ninian is to seek out the arms smugglers and the plotters of rebellion. The journey will finally destroy all Aeneas's romantic notions of the Highlands; he finds the giant Highland brigand Col Barisdale to be a hollow drum, a huge bullying bubbly-jock; he finds Inverness haggling like fishwives over salmon and salt and pickled beef; he finds the lairds planning to cut down woods to feed their new furnaces. He vows never to wear the kilt again, and, says Munro, 'his dream dispelled of a poetic world surviving in the hills, he got malicious and secret joy from stripping every rag of false heroics from such gentry'—like Munro himself!

At the heart of the novel lie potent symbols. On one hand, Munro places in opposition two kinds of Highland movers—the black Highland spider, MacShimi, rotten to the core, with his kidnappings, his flattery of his fawning clansmen with the old lie of equality, his lust for total power; on the other, Duke John, accepted now as a force for improvement—but never allowed the dignity and status given to Duncan Forbes of Culloden as the real new peace-maker of the Highlands. And, most powerful symbol of all, the Road; a nightmare construction for Wade's men, threatened by winter, flood and attack by the clans, who see all too well what it spells for them. Its epic, steady movement north is brilliantly evoked by Munro, a vision of the future Scotland, its internal boundaries broken down. Munro has regrets; Ninian will lament the loss of open landscape and freedom, and the decline of the Gael's sinewy athleticism—but, like Scott, his reason sees these losses as secondary to necessary integration.

The treatment of boundaries is one of the most intriguing features of this novel. Aeneas may at times feel Inveraray a Gaelic-speaking, Highland place; but frequently its status as a gateway to the Lowlands is emphasised, and roads south from it are main routes, stripped to the rock by passing commerce. And conversely, as Aeneas and Ninian move north, they encounter boundaries as real to them as any separating Inveraray from the Lowlands. Several times Ninian will indicate to Aeneas that they are crossing another boundary—at Glenorchy, at Kingshouse near Glencoe and Rannoch Moor, and—most of all—as they approach Inverness, where Ninian warns Aeneas of 'The Wicked Bounds' —the boundaries of MacShimi's power. Is Munro not making a fundamental point? That boundaries are not fixed in nature, but man-made? That Highland-Lowland separations mean as little as these internal Highland separations of greed and violence?

Nothing Munro wrote after this is as good. He had made his point about the reconciliation of Scotlands, and while he continued to write fine short stories based on his two beloved territories, north and south of the Clyde, he was by now more than anything else the accomplished war correspondent, the editor, the commentator on Scotland as a whole who had said goodbye to his ancient, pre-clan Highlands. The Scottish Renaissance which began in his later years owes a huge debt to him which has yet to be acknowledged.

Douglas Gifford
September 1999

PART I

I

WHEN THE GEAN-TREE BLOSSOMED

RAIN was beating on the open leaf of plane and beech, and rapping at the black doors of the ashbud, and the scent of the gean-tree flourish hung round the road by the river, vague, sweet, haunting, like a recollection of the magic and forgotten gardens of youth. Over the high and numerous hills, mountains of deer and antique forest, went the mist, a slattern, trailing a ragged gown. The river sucked below the banks and clamoured on the cascades, drawn unwillingly to the sea, the old gluttonous sea that must ever be robbing the glens of their gathered waters. And the birds were at their loving, or the building of their homes, flying among the bushes, trolling upon the bough. One with an eye, as the saying goes, could scarcely pass among this travail of the new year without some pleasure in the spectacle, though the rain might drench him to the skin. He could not but joy in the thrusting crook of the fern and bracken; what sort of heart was his if it did not lift and swell to see the new fresh green blown upon the grey parks, to see the hedges burst, the young firs of the Blaranbui prick up among the slower elder pines and oaks?

Some of the soul and rapture of the day fell with the rain upon the boy. He hurried with bare feet along the riverside from the glen to the town, a bearer of news, old news of its kind, yet great news too, but now and then he would linger in the odour of the bloom that sprayed the gean-tree like a fall of snow, or he would cast an eye admiring upon the turgid river, washing from bank to bank, and feel the strange uneasiness of wonder and surmise, the same that comes from mists that swirl in gorges of the hills or haunt old ancient woods. The sigh of the wind seemed to be for his peculiar ear. The nod of the saugh leaf on the banks was a salutation. There is, in a flutter of the tree's young plumage, some hint of communication whose secret we lose as we age, and the boy, among it, felt the warmth of companionship. But the sights were for the errant moments of his mind; his thoughts, most of the way, were on his message.

He was a boy with a timid and wondering eye, a type to be seen often in those parts, and his hair blew from under his bonnet, a toss of white and gold, as it blew below the helms of the old sea-rovers. He was from Ladyfield, hastening as I say with great news though common news enough of its kind—the news that the goodwife of Ladyfield was dead.

If this were a tale of the imagination, and my task was not a work of history but to pleasure common people about a hearth, who ever love the familiar emotions in their heroes, I would credit my hero with grief. For here was his last friend gone, here was he orphaned for ever. The door of Ladyfield, where he was born and where he had slept without an absent night since first his cry rose there, a coronach in the ears of his dying mother, would be shut against him; the stranger would bar the gates at evening, the sheep upon the hills would have another keel-mark than the old one on their fleecy sides. Surely the sobs that sometimes rose up in his throat were the utter surrender of sorrow; were the tears that mingled with the raindrops on his cheek not grief's most bitter essence? For indeed he had loved the old shrunk woman, wrinkled and brown like a nut, with a love that our race makes no parade of, but feels to the very core.

But in truth, as he went sobbing in his loneliness down the riverside, a regard for the manner of his message busied him more than the matter of it. It was not every Friday a boy had a task so momentous, had the chance to come upon households

4

with intelligence so unsettling. They would be sitting about the table, perhaps, or spinning by the fire, the goodwife of Ladyfield still for them a living, breathing body, home among her herds, and he would come in among them and in a word bring her to their notice in all death's great monopoly. It was a duty to be done with care if he would avail himself of the whole value of so rare a chance. A mere clod would be for entering with a weeping face, to blurt his secret in shaking sentences, or would let it slip out in an indifferent tone, as one might speak of some common occurrence. But Gilian, as he went, busied himself on how he should convey most tellingly the story he brought down the glen. Should he lead up to his news by gradual steps or give it forth like an alarum? It would be a fine and rare experience to watch them for a little, as they looked and spoke with common cheerfulness, never guessing why he was there, then shock them with the intelligence, but he dare not let them think he felt so little the weightiness of his message that his mind was ready to dwell on trivialities. Should it be in Gaelic or in English he should tell them? Their first salutations would be in the speech of the glens; it would be, "Oh Gilian, little hero! fair fellow! there you are! sit down and have town bread, and sugar on its butter," and if he followed the usual custom he would answer in the same tongue. But between *"Tha bean Lecknamban air falbh"* and "The wife of Ladyfield is gone," there must be some careful choice. The Gaelic of it was closer on the feelings of the event; the words some way seemed to make plain the emptiness of the farmhouse. When he said them, the people would think all at once of the little brown wrinkled dame, no more to be bustling about the kitchen, of her wheel silent, of her foot no more upon the blue flagstones of the milk-house, of her voice no more in the chamber where they had so often known her hospitality. The English, indeed, when he thought of it with its phrase a mere borrowing from the Gaelic, seemed an affectation. No, it must be in the natural tongue his tidings should be told. He would rap at the door hurriedly, lift the sneck before any response came, go in with his bonnet in his hand, and say *"Tha bean Lecknamban air falbh"* with a great simplicity.

And thus as he debated and determined in his mind, he was hastening through a country that in another mood would be demanding his attention almost at every step of the way. Ladyfield is at the barren end of the glen—barren of trees, but rich in heather and myrtle, and grass—surrounded by full and swelling hills. The river, but for the gluttonous sea that must be sucking it down, would choose, if it might, to linger in the valley here for ever, and in summer it loiters on many pretences, twining out and in, hiding behind Baracaldine and the bushes of Tom-an-Dearc, and pretending to doze in the long broad levels of Kincreggan, so that it may not too soon lose its freedom in so magic a place. But the glen opens out anon, woods and parks cluster, and the Duke's gardens and multitudes of roads come into view. The deer stamp and flee among the grasses, flowers grow in more profusion than up the glen where no woods shelter. There are trim houses by the wayside, with men about the doors talking with loud cheerfulness, and laughing in the way of inn-frequenters. A gateway from solitude, an entrance to a region where the most startling and varied things were ever happening, to a boy from the glen this town end of the valley is a sample of Paradise for beauty and interest. Gilian went through it with his blue eyes blurred today, but for wont he found it full of charms and fancies. To go under its white-harled archways on a market day was to come upon a new world, and yet not all a new world, for its spectacles of life and movement—the busy street, the clanging pavement, the noisy closes, the quay ever sounding with the high calls of mariners and fishers—seemed sometimes to strike a chord of memory. At the first experience of this busy community, the innumerable children playing before the school, and the women with wide flowing clothes, and flowered bonnets on their heads, though so different from the children of the glen and its familiar dames with piped caps, or maids with snooded locks—all was pleasant to his wondering view. He seemed to know and understand them at the first glance, deeper even than he knew or understood the common surroundings of his life in Ladyfield; he felt at times more comfort in the air of those lanes and closes though unpleasantly they might smell (if it was the curing season and the gut-pots reeked at the quay) than in the winds of the place he came from, the winds of the wilds, so indifferent to mankind, the winds of the woods, sacred to the ghosts, among whom a boy in a kilt was an intruder, the winds of the hills, that come blowing from round the universe and on the most peaceful days are but momentary visitors, stopping but to tap with a branch at the window, or whistle mockingly in a vent.

In spite of their mockery of him, Gilian always loved the children of the town. At first when they used to see him come through the arches walking hurriedly, feeling his feet in unaccustomed shoes awkward and unmanageable, and the polish of his face a thing unbearable, they would come up in wonder on his heels and guess at his identity, then taunt him for the rustic nature of his clothing.

"Crotal-coat, crotal-coat, there are peats in your brogues!" they would cry; or "Hielan'man, hielan'man, go home for your *fuarag* and brose!"

They were strange new creatures to him, foreigners quite, and cruel, speaking freely a tongue he knew not but in broken parts, yet deep in his innermost there was a strange feeling that he was of their kind. He wished he could join them in their English play, or better far, that he might take them to the eagle's nest in Stob Bhan, or the badgers' hamlet in Blaranbui, or show them his skill to fetch the deer at a call, in the rutting time, from the mud-wallows above Carnus. But even yet, he was only a stranger to the boys of the town, and as he went down the street in the drenching rain that filled the syvers to overflowing and rose in a smoke from the calm waters of the bay, they cried "Crotal-coat, crotal-coat," after him.

"Ah," said he to himself, inly pleased at their ignorance, "if I cared, could I not make them ashamed, by telling them they were mocking a boy without a home?"

7

Kept by the rain closer than usual to the shelter of the closes, the scamps today went further than ever in their efforts to annoy the stranger; they rolled stones along the causey so that they caught him on the heels, and they ran out at the back ends of their closes as he passed, and into others still before him, so that his progress down the town was to run a gauntlet of jeers. But he paid no heed; he was of that gifted nature that at times can treat the most bitter insults with indifference, and his mind was taken up with the manner of his message.

When he came to the Crosshouses he cast about for the right close in a place where they were so numerous that they had always confused him, and a middle-aged woman with bare thick arms came out to help him.

"You'll be looking for someone?" said she in Gaelic, knowing him no town boy.

He was standing as she spoke to him in a close that had seemed the one he sought, and he turned to tell her where he was going.

"Oh yes," said the woman, "I know her well. And you'll be from the glen, and what's your errand in the town today? You are from Drimfern? No, Ladyfield! It is a fine place Ladyfield; and how is the goodwife there?"

"She is dead," said Gilian hurriedly.

"God, and that is a pity too!" said the woman, content now that the news was hers. "You are in the very close you are looking for," and she turned and hurried up the street to spread the news as fast as could be.

The boy turned away, angry with himself to have blurted out his news to the first stranger with the curiosity to question him, and halfway up the stairs he had to pause a little to get in the right mood for his errand. Then he went up the remaining steps and rapped at the door.

"Come in," cried a frank and hearty woman's voice. He put down the sneck with his thumb and pushed in the door and followed.

A little window facing the sea gave light to the interior, that would have been dull and mean but for the brilliant delf upon

8

the dresser rack and the cleanliness of all things and the smiling faces of Jean Clerk and her sister. The hum of Jean's wheel had filled the chamber as he entered; now it was stilled and the spinner sat with the wool pinched in her fingers, as she welcomed her little relative. Her sister—Aliset Dhu they called her, and if black she was, it had been long ago, for now her hair was like the drifted snow—stood behind her, looking up from her girdle where oaten bannocks toasted.

He stood with his bonnet in his hand. Against his will the grief of his loss swept over him more masterfully than it had yet done, for those two sisters had never been seen by him before except in the company of their relative the little old woman with a face like a nut, and the sobs that shook him were checked by no reflection of the play-actor. He was incapable of utterance.

"O my boy, my boy!" cried Jean Clerk. "Do I not know your story? I dreamed last night I saw a white horse galloping over Tombreck to Ladyfield and the rider of him had his face in his plaid. Peace with her, and her share of Paradise!"

And thus my hero, who thought so much upon the way of this message, had no need to convey it any way at all.

II

THE PENSIONERS

"GO round," said Jean Clerk, and tell the Paymaster; he'll be the sorry man to lose his manager."

"Will he be in his house?" asked Gilian, eating the last of his town bread with butter and sugar.

"In his house indeed!" cried Jean, her eyes still red with weeping. "It is easy to see you are from the glen, when at this time of day you would be for seeking a gentleman soldier in his own house in this town. No! no! go round to Sergeant More's changehouse, at the quay head, and you'll find the Captain there with his cronies."

So round went Gilian, and there he came upon the pensioners, with Captain John Campbell, late Paymaster of his Majesty's 46th Foot, at their head.

The pensioners, the officers, ah! when I look up the silent street of the town nowadays and see the old houses empty but for weavers, and merchants, and mechanics, people of useful purposes but little manly interest, and know that all we have of martial glory is a dust under a score of tombstones in the yard, I find it ill to believe that ever wars were bringing trade for youth and valour to our midst. The warriors are gone; they do not fight their battles over any more at a meridian dram, or late sitting about the bowl where the Trinidad lemon floated in slices on the philtre of joy. They are up bye yonder in the shadow of the rock with the sea grumbling constantly beside them, and their names and offices, and the dignities of their battles, and the long number of their years, are carved deeply, but not deeply enough, for what is there of their fame and valour to the fore when the threshing rain and the crumbling frost have worn the legend off the freestone slab? We are left stranded high and dry upon times of peace, but the old war-dogs, old heroes, old gentles of the stock and cane—they had seen the glories of life, and felt the zest of it. Bustling times! the drums beat at the Cross in those days, the trumpeters playing alluringly up the lanes to young hearts to come away; pipers squeezed out upon their instruments the fine tunes that in the time I speak of no lad of Gaelic blood could hear but he must down with the flail or sheephook and on with the philabeg and up with the sword. Gentlemen were for ever going to wars or coming from them; were they not of the clan, was not the Duke their cousin, as the way of putting it was, and by his gracious offices many a pock-pudding English corps got a colonel with a touch of the Gaelic in his word of command as well as in his temper. They went away ensigns—some of them indeed went to the very tail of the rank and file with Mistress Musket the brown besom—and they came back Majors-General, with wounds and pensions. "Is not this a proud day for the town with three Generals standing at the Cross?" said the Paymaster once, looking with pride at his brother and Turner of Maam and Campbell of Strachur standing together leaning on their rattans at a market. It was in the Indies I think that this same brother the General, parading his command before a battle, came upon John, an ensign newly to the front with a draft from the sea.

"Who sent you here, brother John?" said he, when the parade was over. "You would be better at home in the Highlands feeding your mother's hens."

In one way it might have been better, in another way it was well enough for John Campbell to be there. He might have had the luck to see more battles in busier parts of the world, as

General Dugald did, or Colin, who led the Royal Scots at Salamanca, Vittoria, and Waterloo; but he might have done worse, for he of all those gallants came home at the end a hale man, with neither sabre-cut nor bullet. To give him his due he was willing enough to risk them all. It bittered his life at the last, that behind his back his townspeople should call him "Old Mars", in an irony he was keen enough to feel the thrust of.

> Captain Mars, Captain Mars,
> Who never saw wars,

said Evan MacColl, the bard of the parish, and the name stuck as the bye-names of that wonderful town have a way of doing.

"Old Mars", Paymaster, sat among the pensioners in the change-house of the Sergeant More when Gilian came to the door. His neck overflowed in waves of fat upon a silk stock that might have throttled a man who had not worn the King's stock in hot lands over sea; his stockings fitted tightly on as neat a leg as ever a kilt displayed, though the kilt was not nowadays John Campbell's wear but kerseymore knee-breeches. He had a fig-ured vest strewn deep with snuff that he kept loose in a pocket (the regiment's gold mull was his purse), and a scratch wig of brown sat askew on his bullet head, raking with a soldier's swagger. He had his long rattan on the table before him, and now and then he would lift its tasselled head and beat time lightly to the chorus of Dugald MacNicol's song. Dugald was Major once of the 1st Royals; he had carried the sword in the Indies, East and West, and in the bloody Peninsula, and came home with a sabre-slash on the side of the head, so that he was a little weak-witted. When he would be leaving his sister's door to go for the meridian dram at the quayhead he would dart for cover to the Cross, then creep from close to close, and round the church, and up the Ferry Land, in a dread of lurking enemies; yet no one jeered at his want, no boy failed to touch his bonnet to him, for he was the gentleman in the very weakest moment of his disease. He had but one song in his budget:

O come and gather round me, lads, and help
the chorus through,
When I tell you how we fought the French
on the plains of Waterloo.

He sang it in a high quavering voice with curious lapses in the
vigour of his singing and cloudings in the fire of his eyes, so that
now and then the company would have to jolt him awake to
give the air more lustily. Colonel Hall was there (of St John's)
and Captain Sandy Campbell of the Marines, Bob MacGibbon,
old Lochgair, the Fiscal with a ruffled shirt, and Dr Anderson.
The Paymaster's brothers were not there, for though he was the
brother with the money they were field-officers and they never
forgot it.

The chorus was ringing, the glasses and the Paymaster's stick
were rapping on the table, the Sergeant More, with a blue brattie
tied tight across his paunch to lessen its unsoldierly amplitude,
went out and in with the gill-stoups, pausing now and then on
the errand to lean against the door of the room with the empty
tray in his hand, drumming on it with his fingertips and joining
in the officers' owercome.

He turned in the middle of a chorus, for the boy was standing
abashed in the entry, his natural fears at meeting the Paymaster
greatly increased by the sound of revelry.

"Well, little hero," said the Sergeant More, in friendly Gaelic,
"are you seeking anyone?"

"I was sent to see the Paymaster, if it's your will," said Gilian,
with his eyes falling below the scrutiny of this swarthy old sergeant.

"The Paymaster!" cried the landlord, shutting the door of the
room ere he said it, and uplifting alarmed hands. "God's grace!
do not talk of the Paymaster here! He is Captain Campbell, mind,
late of his Majesty's 46th Foot, with a pension of £4 a week,
and a great deal of money it is for the country to be paying to
a gentleman who never saw of wars but skirmish with the Syke.

Nothing but Captain, mind you, and do not forget the salute, so, with the right hand up and thumb on a line with the right eyebrow. But could your business not be waiting? If it is Miss Mary who sent for him it is not very reasonable of her, for he is here no longer than twenty minutes, and it is not sheepshead broth day, I know, because I saw her servant lass down at the quay for herrings an hour ago. Captain, mind, it must be that for him even with old soldiers like myself. I would not dare Paymaster him, it is a name that has a trade ring about it that suits ill with his Highland dignity. Captain, Captain!"

Gilian stood in front of this spate of talk, becoming more diffident and fearful every moment. He had never had any thought as to how he should tell the Paymaster that the goodwife of Ladyfield was dead, that was a task he had expected to be left to someone else, but Jean Clerk and her sister had a cunning enough purpose in making him the bearer of the news.

"I am to tell him the goodwife of Ladyfield is dead," he explained, stammering, to the Sergeant More.

"Dead!" said John More. "Now is not that wonderful?" He leaned against the door as he had leaned many a time against sentry-box and barrack wall, and dwelled a little upon memory. "Is not that wonderful? The first time I saw her was at a wedding in Kames, Lochow, and she was the handsomest woman in the room, and there were sixty people at the wedding from all parts, and sixty-nine roasted hens at the supper. Well, well— dead! blessings with her; did I not know her well? Yes, and I knew her husband too, Long Angus, since the first day he came to Ladyfield for Old Mar—for the Paymaster—till the last day he came down the glen in a cart, and he was the only sober body in the funeral, perhaps because it was his own. Many a time I wondered that the widow did so well in the farm for Captain Campbell, with no man to help her, the sowing and the shearing, the dipping and the clipping, ploughmen and herds to keep an eye on, and bargains to make with wool merchants and drovers. Oh! she was a clever woman, your grandmother. And now she's dead. Well, it's a way they have at her age! And the

Paymaster must be told, though I know it will vex him greatly, because he is a sort of man who does not relish changes. Mind now you say Captain; you need not say Captain Campbell, but just Captain, and maybe a 'sir' now and then. I suppose you could not put off telling him for a half-hour or thereabouts longer, when he would be going home for dinner anyway; it is a pity to spoil an old gentleman's meridian dram with melancholy news. No. You were just told to come straight away and tell him— well, it is the good soldier who makes no deviation from the word of command. Come away in then and—Captain mind— and the salute."

The Sergeant More threw open the door of the room, filled up the space a second and gave a sort of free-and-easy salute. "A message for you, Captain," said he.

The singing was done. The Major's mind was wandering over the plains of Waterloo to guess by the vacancy of his gaze; on his left Bob MacGibbon smoked a black segar, the others talked of townsmen still in the army and of others buried under the walls of Badajos. They all turned when the Sergeant More spoke, and they saw him push before him into the room the little boy of Ladyfield with his bonnet in his hand and his eyes restless and timid like pigeons at a strange gate fluttering.

"Ho! Gilian, it is you?" said the Paymaster, with a very hearty voice; then he seemed to guess the nature of the message, for his voice softened from the loud and bumptious tone it had for ordinary. "How is it in Lecknamban?" he asked in the Gaelic, and Gilian told him, minding duly his "sir" and his "Captain" and his salute.

"Dead!" said the Paymaster. "Blessings with her!" Then he turned to his companions and in English—"The best woman in the three parishes and the cleverest. She could put her hand to anything and now she's no more. I think that's the last of Lady-field for me. I liked to go up now and then and go about the hill and do a little bargaining at a wool market, or haggle over a pound with a drover at the fair, but the farm did little more than pay me and I had almost given it up when her husband died."

He looked flushed and uncomfortable. His stock seemed to fit him more tightly than before and his wig sat more askew than ever upon his bald head. For a little he seemed to forget the young messenger still standing in the room, no higher than the table whereon the glasses ranged. Gilian turned his bonnet about in his hand and twisted the ribbons till they tore, then he thought with a shock of the scolding he would get for spoiling his Sunday bonnet, but the thought was quickly followed by the recollection that she who would have scolded him would chide no more.

The pensioners shared their attention between the Paymaster and the boy. While the Paymaster gave them the state of his gentleman farming (about which the town was always curious), they looked at him and wondered at a man who had seen the world and had £4 a week of a pension wasting life with a paltry three-hundred sheep farm instead of spending his money royally with a bang. When his confidence seemed likely to carry their knowledge of his affairs no further than the town's gossip had already brought it, they lost their interest in his reflections and had time to feel sorry for the boy. None of them but knew he was an orphan in the most grievous sense of the term, without a relative in the wide world, and that his future was something of a problem.

Bob MacGibbon—he was Captain in the 79th—leaned forward and tried to put his hand upon the child's shoulder, not unkindly, but with a rough playfulness of the soldier. Gilian shrank back, his face flushing crimson, then he realised the stupidity of his shyness and tried to amend it by coming a little further into the room and awkwardly attempting the salute in which the Sergeant More had tutored him.

The company was amused at the courtesy, but no one laughed. In a low voice the Paymaster swore. He was a man given to swearing with no great variety in his oaths, that were merely a camp phrase or two at the most, repeated over and over again, till they had lost all their original meanings and could be uttered in front of Dr Colin himself without any objection to them. In print they would look wicked, so they must be fancied by such as would have the complete picture of the elderly soldier with the thick neck and the scratch wig. The Sergeant More had gently withdrawn himself and shut the door behind him the more conveniently to hear what reception the messenger's tidings would meet with from the Paymaster. And the boy felt himself cut off most helplessly from escape out of that fearful new surrounding. It haunted him for many a day, the strong smell of the spirits and the sharp odour of the slices floating in the glasses, for our pensioners were extravagant enough to flavour even the cold midday drams of the Abercrombie with the lemon's juice. Gilian shifted from leg to leg and turned his bonnet continuously, and through his mind there darted many thoughts about this curious place and company that he had happened upon. As they looked at him he felt the darting tremor of the fawn in the thicket, but alas he was trapped! How old they were! How odd they looked in their high collars and those bands wound round their necks! They were not farmers, nor shepherds, nor fishermen, nor even shopkeepers; they were people with some manner of life beyond his guessing. The Paymaster of course he knew; he had seen him often come up to Ladyfield, to talk to the goodwife about the farm and the clipping, to pay her money twice yearly that was called wages, and was so little that it was scarcely worth the name. Six men in a room, all gentle (by their clothes), all with nothing better to do than stare at a boy who could not stare back! How many things they had seen; how many thoughts they must share between them! He wished himself on the other side of Aora river in the stillness of Kincreggan wood, or on the hill among the sheep—anywhere away from the presence of those old men with the keen scrutiny in their eyes, doubtless knowing all about him and seeing his very thoughts. Had they been shepherds, or even the clever gillies that sometimes came to the kitchen of Ladyfield on nights of *ceilidh* or gossip, he would have felt himself their equal. He would have been comfortable in feeling that however much they might know about the hills, and woods, and wild beasts, it was likely enough better known to himself, who lived among them and loved them. And the thoughts of the gillie, and the shepherd, were rarely beyond his shrewd guess as he looked at them; they had but to say a word or two, and he knew the end of their story from the beginning. But these old gentlemen were as far beyond his understanding as Gillesbeg Aotram, the wanderer who came about the glens and was called daft by the people who did not know, as Gilian did, that he was wiser than themselves.

The Paymaster took his rattan and knocked noisily on the table for the landlord.

The Sergeant More stepped softly on his tiptoes six steps into the kitchen, then six steps noisily back again and put his head in.

"What's your will, Captain?" said he, polishing a tray with the corner of his brattie.

"Give this boy some dinner, for me," said the Paymaster. "There is nothing at our place today but herrings, and it's the poorest of meals for melancholy. Miss Mary would make it all the more melancholy with her weeping over the goodwife of Ladyfield."

Gilian went out with the Sergeant More and made a feeble pretence at eating his second dinner that day.

III

THE FUNERAL

ALL the glen came to the funeral, and people of Lochowside on either side from Stronmealachan to Eredine, and many of the folk of Glen Shira and the town. A day of pleasant weather, with a warm wind from the west, full of wholesome dryness for the soil that was still clogged with the rains of spring. It filled the wood of Kincreggan with sounds, with the rasping and creaking of branches and the rustle of leaves, and the road by the river under the gean-trees was strewn with the broken blossom.

The burial ground of Kilmalieu lies at the foot of a tall hill beside the sea, a hill grown thick with ancient wood. The roots come sometimes under the walls and below the old tombstones and set them ajee upon their bases, but wanting those tall and overhanging companions, the yard, I feel, would be ugly and incomplete. It is in a soothing melancholy one may hear the tide lapping on the rocks below and the wood-bird call in the trees above. They have been doing so in the ears of Kilmalieu for numberless generations, those voices everlasting but unheard by the quiet folk sleeping snug and sound among the clods. Sun shines there and rain falls on it till it soaks to the very bones of the old Parson, first to lie there, and in sun or rain there grow the laurel-bushes that have the smell of death, and the gay flowers cluster in a profusion found nowhere else in the parish except it be in the garden of the Duke. The lily nods in the wind, the columbine hangs its bell, there the snowdrop first appears and the hip-rose shows her richest blossoms. On Sundays the children go up and walk among the stones over the graves of their grandfathers and they smell the flowers they would not pluck. Sometimes they will put a cap on the side of a cherub head that tops a stone and the humour of the grinning face will create a moment's laughter, but it is soon checked and they walk among the graves in a more seemly peace.

They buried the goodwife of Ladyfield in her appointed place beside her husband and her only child, Gilian taking a cord at the head of the coffin as it was lowered into the red jaws of the grave prepared for it. The earth thudded on the lid, the spades patted the mould, the people moved off, and he was standing yet, listening to the bird that shook a song of passionate melody from its little throat as it becked upon a table tombstone. It was a simple song, he had heard it a thousand times before and wondered at the hidden meaning of it, and now it puzzled him anew that it should encroach upon so solemn an hour in thoughtless love or merriment.

The men were on their way home over the New Bridge, treading heavily, and yet light-headed, for they had the Paymaster's dram at the "lifting" at Ladyfield in them, and the Paymaster himself was narrating to old Rixa, the Sheriff, and Donacha Breck his story, told a hundred times before, of Long Dan MacIntyre, who never came up past the New Bridge, except at the tail of a funeral, for fear the weight should some day bring the massive masonry down. "Ha! ha! is that not good?" demanded the Paymaster, laughing till his jowl purpled over his stock. "I told him he would cross the bridge to Kilmalieu one day and instead of being last he would be first."

The Fiscal hirpled along in his tight knee-breeches looking down with vain satisfaction now and then at the ruffles of his shirt and the box-pleated frills that were dressed very snodly and cunningly by Bell Macniven, who had been in the Forty-second with her husband the sergeant, and had dressed the shirts of the Marquis of Huntly, who was Colonel.

"I have seldom, sir, seen a better dressed shirt," said Mr William Spencer, of the New Inn, who was a citizen of London and anxious to make his way among the people here. "It is quite the style, quite the style, sir."

"Do you think so, now?" asked the Fiscal, pleased at the compliment.

"I do, indeed," said Mr Spencer, "it is very genteel and just as the gentry like it."

The Fiscal coloured, turned and paused and fixed him with an angry eye.

"Do you speak to me of gentry, Mr Spencer," he asked, "with any idea of making distinctions? You are a poor Sassenach person, I daresay, and do not know that my people have been in Blarinarn for three hundred years and I am the first man of business in the family."

The innkeeper begged pardon. Poor man! he had much to learn of Highland punctilio. He might be wanting in delicacy of this kind perhaps, but he had the heart, and it was he, as they came in front of the glee'd gun that stands on the castle lawn, who stopped to look back at a boy far behind them, alone on the top of the bridge.

"Is there no one with the boy?" he asked. "And where is he to stay now that his grandmother is dead?"

The Paymaster drew up as if he had been shot, and swore warmly to himself.

"Am not I the *golan*?" said he. "I forgot about the fellow, and I told the shepherd at Ladyfield to lock up the house till Whitsunday. I'm putting the poor boy out in the world without a roof for his head. It must be seen to, it must be seen to."

Rixa pompously blew out his cheeks and put back his shoulders in a way he had to convince himself he was not getting old and round-backed. "Oh," said he, "Jean Clerk's a relative; he'll be going to bide there."

They stood in a cluster in the middle of the road, the Paymaster with his black coat so tight upon his stomach it looked as if every brass button would burst with a crack like a gun; Rixa puffing and stretching himself; Major Dugald ducking his head and darting his glance about from side to side looking for the enemy; Mr Spencer, tall, thin, with the new strapped breeches and a London hat, blowing his nose with much noise in a Barcelona silk handkerchief. All the way before them the crowd went straggling down in blacks with as much hurry as the look of the thing would permit, to reach the schoolhouse where the Paymaster had laid out the last service of meat and drink for the mourners. The tide was out; a sandy beach strewn with stones and clumps of seaweed gave its saline odour to the air; lank herons came sweeping down from the trees over Croitivile, and stalked about the water's edge. There was only one sound in nature beyond the soughing of the wind in the shrubbery of the Duke's garden, it was the plaintive call of a curlew as it flew over the stable park. A stopped and stagnant world, full of old men and old plaints, the dead of the yard behind, the solemn and sleepy town before.

The boy was the only person left in the rear of the Paymaster and his friends; he was standing on the bridge, fair in the middle of the way. Though the Paymaster cried he was not heard, so he walked back and up to the boy while the others went on their way to the schoolhouse, where old Brooks the dominie was waiting among the jars and oatcakes and funeral biscuits with currants and carvie in them.

Gilian was standing with the weepers off his cuffs and the crape off his bonnet; he had divested himself of the hateful things whenever he found himself alone, and he was listening with a rapt and inexpressive face to the pensive call of the curlew as it rose over the fields, and the tears were dropping down his cheeks.

"Oh! 'ille, what's the matter with you?" asked the Paymaster in Gaelic, struck that sorrow should so long remain with a child.

Gilian started guiltily, flushed to the nape of his neck and stammered an explanation or excuse.

"The bird, the bird!" said he, turning and looking at the dolorous piper of the marsh.

"Man!" said the Paymaster in English, looking whimsically at this childish expression of surprise. "Man! you're a queer callant too. Are there no curlews about Ladyfield that you should be in such a wonder at this one? Just a plain, long-nebbed, useless bird, not worth powder and shot, very douce in the plumage, and always at the same song like MacNicol the Major."

The little fellow broke into a stammering torrent of Gaelic. "What does it say, what does it say?" he asked: "it is calling, calling, calling, and no one will answer it; it is telling something, and I cannot understand. Oh, I am sorry for it, and—"

"You must be very hungry, poor boy," said the Paymaster. "Come away down, and Miss Mary will give you dinner. Did you ever taste rhubarb tart with cream to it? I have seen you making umbrellas with the rhubarb up the glen, but I'm sure the goodwife did not know the real use of it."

Gilian paid no heed to the speaker, but listened with streaming eyes to the wearied note of the bird that still cried over the field. Then the Paymaster swore a fiery oath most mildly, and clutched the boy by the jacket sleeve and led him homeward.

"Come along," said he, "come along. You're the daftest creature ever came out of the glen, and what's the wonder of it, born and bred among stirks and sheep on a lee-lone countryside with only the birds to speak to?"

The two went down the road together, the Paymaster a little wearied with his years and weight or lazied by his own drams, leaning in the least degree upon the shoulder of the boy. They made an odd-looking couple—dawn and the declining day, Spring and ripe Autumn, illusion and an elderly half-pay officer in a stock and a brown scratch wig upon a head that would harbour no more the dreams, the poignancies of youth. Some of the mourners hastening to their liquor turned at the Cross and looked up the road to see if they were following, and they were struck vaguely by the significance of the thing.

"Dear me," said the Fiscal, "is not Old Mars getting very bent and ancient?"

"He is, that!" said Rixa, who was Sheriff Maclachlan to his face. "I notice a glass or two makes a wonderful difference on him this year back ever since he had his little bit towt. That's a nice-looking boy; I like the aspect of him; it's unusual. What a pity the Paymaster never had a wife or sons of his own."

"You say what is very true, Sheriff," said Mr Spencer. "I think there is something very sad in the spectacle, sir, of an old gentleman with plenty of the world in his possession going down to the bourne with not a face beside him to mind of his youth."

But indeed the Paymaster was not even reminded of his own youth by this queer child on whom he leaned. He had never been like this, a shy frightened dreaming child taken up with fancies and finding omens and stories in the piping of a fowl. Oh! no, he had been a bluff, hearty, hungry boy, hot-headed, red-legged, short-kilted, stirring, a bit of a bully, a loud talker, a dour lad with his head and his fists. This boy beside him made him think of neither man nor boy, but of his sister Jennet, who died in the plague year, a wide-eyed, shrinking, clever girl, with a nerve that a harsh word set thrilling.

"Did Jean Clerk say anything about where you are to sleep tonight?" he asked him, still speaking the Gaelic in which he knew the little fellow was most at home.

"I suppose I'll just stay in my own bed in Ladyfield," said Gilian, apparently little exercised by the thought of his future, and dividing some of his attention to the Paymaster with the sounds and sights of nature by the way, the thrust of the bracken crook between the crannies of the Duke's dykes, the gummy buds of the limes and chestnuts, the straw-gathering birds on the road, the heron so serenely stalking on the shore, and the running of the tiny streams upon the beach that smoked now in the heat of the sun.

The Paymaster seemed confounded. He swelled his neck more fully in the stock, cleared his throat with a loud noise, took a great pinch of snuff from his waistcoat pocket and spent a long time in disposing of it. Gilian was in a dream far off from the elderly companion and the smoking shore; his spirit floated over the glen and sometimes further still, among the hill gorges that were always so full of mystery to him, or further still to the remote unknown places, foreign lands, cities, towns, where giants and fairies roamed and outrage happened and kings were, in the tales the shepherds told about the peat fires on *ceilidh* nights.

"I'm afraid you'll have to sleep in the town tonight," said the Paymaster, at last somewhat relieved of his confusion by the boy's indifference; "the truth is we are shutting up Ladyfield for a little. You could not stay alone in it at any rate, and did Jean Clerk not arrange that you were to stay with her after this?"

"No," said Gilian simply, even yet getting no grasp of his homelessness.

"And where are you going to stay?" asked the Paymaster testily.

"I don't know," said the boy.

The Paymaster spoke in strange words under his breath and put on a quicker pace and went through the town, even past the schoolhouse, where old Brooks stood at the door in his long surtout saying a Latin declension over to himself as if it were a song, and into the Crosshouses past the tanned women standing with their hands rolled up in their aprons, and up to Jean Clerk's door. He rapped loudly with his rattan. He rapped so loudly that the inmates knew this was no common messenger, and instead of crying out their invitation they came together and opened the door. The faces of the sisters grew rosy red at the sight of the man and the boy before him.

"Come away in, Captain," said Jean, assuming an air of briskness the confusion of her face belied. "Come away in, I am proud to see you at my door."

The Paymaster stepped in, still gripping the boy by the shoulder, but refused to sit down. He spoke very short and dry in his best travelled English.

"Did you lock up the Ladyfield house as I told you?" he asked.

"I did, that!" said Jean Clerk, lifting her brattie and preparing to weep, "and it'll be the last time I'll ever be inside its hospitable door."

"And you gave the key to Cameron the shepherd?"

"I did," said Jean, wondering what was to come next.

The Paymaster changed his look and his accent, and spoke again with something of a pawky humour that those who knew him best were well aware was a sign that his temper was at its worst.

"Ay," said he, "and you forgot about the boy. What's to be done with him? I suppose you would leave him to rout with the kye he was bred among, or haunt the rocks with the sheep. I was thinking myself coming down the road there, and this little fellow with me without a friend in the world, that the sky is a damp ceiling sometimes, and the grass of the field a poor meal for a boy's stomach. Eh! what say you, Mistress Clerk?" And the old soldier heaved a thumbful of snuff from his waistcoat pocket.

"The boy's no kith nor kin of mine," said Jean Clerk, "except a very far-out cousin's son." She turned her face away from both of them and pretended to be very busy folding up her plaid, which, as is well known, can only be done neatly with the aid of the teeth and thus demands some concealment of the face. The sister passed behind the Paymaster and the boy and startled the latter with a sly squeeze of the wrist as she did so.

"Do you tell me, my good woman," demanded the Paymaster, "that you would set him out on the road homeless on so poor an excuse as that? Far-out cousin here or far-out cousin there, he has no kin closer than yourself between the two stones of the parish. Where's your Hielan' heart, woman?"

"There's nothing wrong with my heart, Captain Campbell," said Jean tartly, "but my pocket's empty. If you think the boy's neglected you have a house of your own to take him into; it would be all the better for a young one in it, and you have the money to spend that Jean Clerk has not." All this with a very brave show of spirit, but with something uncommonly moist about the eyes.

26

The Paymaster, still clutching the boy at the shoulder, turned on his heel to go, but a side glance at Jean Clerk's face again showed him something different from avarice or anger.

"You auld besom you!" said he, dunting the door with his rattan. "I see through you now; you think you'll get him put off on me. I suppose if I refused to take him in, you would be the first to make of him."

The woman laughed through her tears. "Oh, but you are the gleg-eyed one, Captain. You may be sure I would not see my cousin's grandchild starving, and I'll not deny I put him in your way, because I never knew a Campbell of Kiels, one of the old bold race, who had not a kind heart for the poor, and I thought you and your sister could do better than two old maiden women in a garret could do by him."

"You randy!" said he, "and that's the way you would portion your poor relations about the countryside. As if I had not plenty of poor friends of my own! And what in all the world am I to make of the youth?"

"You'll have nothing to do with the making of him, Captain Campbell," said Jean Clerk, now safe and certain that the boy's future was assured. "It'll be Miss Mary will have the making of him, and I ken the lady well enough—with my humble duty to her—to know she'll make him a gentleman at the very least."

"Tuts," said the Paymaster, "Sister Mary's like the rest of you; she would make a milksop of the boy if I was foolish enough to take him home to her. He'll want smeddum and manly discipline; that's the stuff to make the soldier. The uneasy bed to sleep on, the day's task to be done to the uttermost. I'll make him the smartest ensign ever put baldrick on—that's if I was taking him in hand," he added hastily, realising from the look of the woman that he was making a complete capitulation.

"And of course you'll take him, Captain Campbell," cried Jean Clerk in triumph. "I'm sure you would sooner take him and make a soldier of him than leave him with me—though before God he was welcome—to grow up harvester or herd."

The Paymaster took a ponderous snuff, snorted, and went off

down the stair with the boy still by the hand, the boy wide-eyed wondering, unable to realise very clearly whether he was to be made a soldier or a herd there and then. And when the door closed behind them Jean Clerk and her sister sat down and wept and laughed in a curious mingling of sorrow and joy—sorrow that the child had to be turned from their door and out of their lives with even the pretence at inhospitality, and joy that their device had secured for him a home and future more comfortable than the best their straitened circumstances could afford.

IV

MISS MARY

THE Paymaster and his two brothers lived with sister Mary on the upper flats of the biggest house of the burgh. The lower part was leased to an honest merchant whose regular payment of his rent did not prevent the Paymaster, every time he stepped through the close, from dunting with his cane on the stones with the insolence of a man whose birth and his father's acres gave him a place high above such as earned their living behind a counter.

"There you are, Sandy!" he would call, "doing no trade as usual; you'll not have sold a parcel of pins or a bolt of tape today, I suppose. Where am I to get my rent, I wonder, next Martinmas?"

The merchant would remonstrate. "I've done very well today, Captain," he would say. "I have six bolls of meal and seven yards of wincey going up the glen in the Salachary cart."

"Pooh, pooh, what's that to the time of war? I'll tell you this, Sandy, I'll have to roup out for my rent yet." And by he would sail, as red in the face as a bubbly-jock, swelling his neck over his stock more largely than ever, and swinging his rattan by its tassel or whacking with it on his calves, satisfied once more to have put this merchant-body in his own place.

Today he paid no heed to the merchant, when, having just

keeked in at the schoolroom to tell Dr Colin and old Brooks he would be back in a minute to join the dregy, he went up the stairs with Gilian. "I'm going to leave you with my sister Mary," he explained. "You'll think her a droll woman, but all women have their tiravees, and my sister is a well-meaning creature."

Gilian thought no one could be more droll than this old man himself. Before indifferent to him, he had, in the past hour, grown to be afraid of him as a new mysterious agent who had his future in his hands. And to go up the stairs of this great high house, with its myriad windows looking out upon the busiest part of the street, and others gazing over the garden and the sea, was an experience new and bewildering. The dwelling abounded in lobbies and corridors, in queer corners where the gloom lurked, and in doors that gave glimpses of sombre bedsteads and high-backed austere chairs, of china painted with the most wonderful designs (loot of the old Indian palaces), of swords and sabretaches hung on walls, and tables polished to such degree that they reflected their surroundings.

They went into a parlour with its window open, upon the windowsill a pigeon mourning among pots of wallflowers and southernwood that filled the entering air with sweetness. A room with thin-legged chairs, with cupboards whose lozens gave view to punch-bowls and rummers and silver ladles, a room where the two brothers would convene at night while John was elsewhere, and in a wan candlelight sit silent by the hour before cooling spirits, musing on other parlours elsewhere in which spurs had jingled under the board, musing on comrades departed. It was hung around with dark pictures in broad black frames, for the most part pictures of battles, *Fontenoy*, *Stemming the Rout at Steinkirk*, *Blenheim Field*, and—a new one—*Vittoria*. There were pictures of men too, all with soldier collars high upon the nape of the neck, and epaulettes on their shoulders, whiskered, keen-eyed young men—they were the brothers in their prime when girls used to look after them as they went by on their horses. And upon the mantelbrace, flanked by tall silver candlesticks, was an engraving of John, Duke of Argyll, Field-Marshal.

"Look at that man there," said the Paymaster, pointing to the noble and arrogant head between the candles, "that was a soldier's soldier. There is not his like in these days. If you should take arms for your king, boy, copy the precept and practice of Duke John. I myself modelled me on his example, and that, mind you, calls for dignity and valour and education and every manly part and—"

"Is that you blethering away in there, John?" cried a high female voice from the spence.

The Paymaster's voice surrendered half its confidence and pride, for he never liked to be found vaunting before his sister, who knew his qualities and had a sense of irony.

"Ay! it's just me, Mary," he cried back, hastening to the door. "I have brought a laddie up here to see you."

"It would be wiser like to bring me a man," cried the lady, coming into the room. "I'm wearied of washing sheets and blankets for a corps of wrunkled old brothers that have no gratitude for my sisterly slavery. Keep me! whose *ballachan* is that?"

She was a little thin woman, of middle age, with a lowland cap of lace that went a little oddly with the apron covering the front of the merino gown from top to toe. She had eyes like sloes, and teeth like pearls that gleamed when she smiled, and by constant trying to keep herself from smiling at things, she had worn two lines up and down between her eyebrows. A dear fond heart, a darling hypocrite, a foolish bounteous mother-soul without chick or child of her own, and yet with tenement for the loves of a large family. She fended, and mended, and tended for her soldier brothers, and they in the selfish blindness of their sex never realised her devotion. They sat, and over punch would talk of war, and valour, and devotion, and never thought that here, within their very doors, was a constant war in their behalf against circumstances, in their interest an unending valour that kept the little woman bustling on her feet, and shrewd-eyed over her stew-pans, while weariness and pain itself, and the hopeless unresponse and ingratitude of the surroundings, rendered her more appropriate place between the bed-sheets.

"What *ballachan* is this?" she asked, relaxing the affected acidity of her manner and smoothing out the lines upon her brow at the sight of the little fellow in a rough kilt, standing in a shy unrest upon the spotless drugget of her parlour floor. She waited no answer, but went forward as she spoke, as one who would take all youth to her heart, put a hand on his head and stroked his fair hair. It was a touch wholly new to the boy; he had never felt before that tingling feeling that a woman's hand, in love upon his head, sent through all his being. At the message of it, the caress of it, he shivered and looked up at her face in surprise.

"What do you think of him, Mary?" asked the brother. "Not a very stout chap, I think, but hale enough, and if you stuck his head in a pail of cream once a day you might put meat on him. He's the *oe* from Ladyfield; surely you might know him even with his boots on."

"Dear, dear," she said; "you're the Gilian I never saw but at a distance, the boy who always ran to the hill when I went to Ladyfield. O little hero, am I not sorry for the goodwife? You have come for your pick of the dinner—"

"Do you think we could make a soldier of him?" broke in the Paymaster, carrying his rattan like a sword and throwing back his shoulders.

"A soldier!" she said, casting a shrewd glance at the boy in a red confusion. "We might make a decenter man of him. Weary be on the soldiering! I'm looking about the countryside and I see but a horde of lameter privatemen and half-pay officers maimed in limb or mind sitting about the dram bottle, hoved up with their vainglory, blustering and blowing, instead of being honest, eident lairds and farmers. I never saw good in a soldier yet, except when he was away fighting and his name was in the *Courier* as dead or wounded. Soldiers, indeed! sitting round there in the Sergeant More's tavern, drinking, and roaring, and gossiping like women—that I should miscall my sex! No, no, if I had a son—"

"Well, well, Mary," said the Paymaster, breaking in again upon this tirade, "here's one to you. If you'll make the man of him I'll try to make him the soldier."

She understood in a flash! "And is he coming here?" she asked in an accent the most pleased and motherly. A flush came over her cheeks and her eyes grew and danced. It was as if some rare new thought had come to her, a sentiment of poetry, the sound of a forgotten strain of once familiar song.

"I'm sure I am very glad," she said simply. She took the boy by the hand, she led him into the kitchen, she cried "Peggy, Peggy," and when her servant appeared she said, "Here's our new young gentleman, Peggy," and stroked his hair again, and Peggy smiled widely and looked about for something to give him, and put a bowl of milk to his lips.

"Tuts!" cried Miss Mary, "it's not a calf we have; we will not spoil his dinner. But you may skim it and give him a cup of cream."

The Paymaster, left in the parlour among the prints of war and warriors, stood a moment with his head bent and his fingers among the snuff listening to the talk of the kitchen that came along the spence and through the open doors.

"She's a queer body, Mary," said he to himself, "but she's taking to the brat I think—oh yes, she's taking to him." And then he hurried down the stair and up round the church corner to the schoolhouse where the company, wearied waiting on his presence, were already partaking of his viands. It was a company to whom the goodwife of Ladyfield, the quiet douce widow, had been more or less a stranger, and its solemnity on this occasion of her burial was not too much insisted on. They were there not so much mourners as the guests of Captain Campbell, nigh on a dozen of half-pay officers who had escaped the shambles of Europe, with the merchants of the place, and some of the farmers of the glen, the banker, the Sheriff, the Fiscal and the writers of whom the town has ever had more than a fair share. Dr Colin had blessed the viands and gone away; he was a new kind of minister and a surprising one, who had odd views about the drinking customs of the people, and when his coat skirts had disappeared round the corner of the church there was a feeling of relief, and old Baldy Bain, "Copenhagen" as they called him, who was precentor in the Gaelic end of the church, was emboldened to fill his glass up to more generous height than he had ever cared to do in the presence of the clergyman. The food and drink were spread on two long tables; the men stood round or sat upon the forms their children occupied in school hours. The room was clamant with the voices of the company. Gathered in groups, they discussed everything under heaven except the object of their meeting—the French, the sowing, the condition of the hogs, the Duke's approaching departure for London, the storm, the fishing. They wore their preposterous tall hats on the backs of their heads with the crape bows over the ears, they lifted up the skirts of their swallow-tail coats and hung them on their arms with their hands in their breeches pockets. And about them was the odour of musty, mildewed broadcloth, taken out of damp presses only on such occasions.

Mr Spencer, standing very straight and tall and thin, so that his trousers at the foot strained tightly at the straps under his insteps, looked over the assembly, and with a stranger's eye could not but be struck by its oddity. He was seeing—lucky man to have the chance!—the last of the old Highland burgh life and the raw beginnings of the new; he was seeing the real *doaineuasail*, gentry of ancient family, colloguing with the common merchants whose day was coming in; he was seeing the embers of the war in a grey ash, officers, merchants, bonnet lairds and tenants now safe and snug and secure in their places because the old warriors had fought Boney. The schoolroom was perfumed with the smoke of peat, for it was the landward pupils' week of the fuelling, and they were accustomed to bring each his own peat under his arm every morning. The smoke swirled and eddied out into the room and hung about the ochred walls, and made more umber than it was before the map of Europe over the fireplace. Looking at this map and sipping now and then a glass of spirits in his hand, was a gentleman humming away to himself "Merrily danced the Quaker's wife." He wore a queue tied with a broad black ribbon that reached well down on his waist, and the rest of his attire was conform in its antiquity, but the man

34

himself was little more than in his prime, straight set up like the soldier he was till he died of the Yellow in Sierra Leone, where the name of Turner, Governor, is still upon his peninsula.

"You are at your studies?" said Mr Spencer to him, going up to his side with a little deference for the General, and a little familiarity for the son of a plain Portioner of Glen Shira who was to be seen any day coming down the glen in his cart, with a mangy sporran flapping rather emptily in front of his kilt.

Charlie Turner stopped his tune and turned upon the inn-keeper.

"I scarcely need to study the map of Europe, Mr Spencer," said he, "I know it by heart—all of it of any interest at least. I have but to shut my eyes and the panorama of it is before me. My brothers and I saw some of it, Mr Spencer, from Torres Vedras to the Pyrenees, and I'm but looking at it now to amaze myself with seeing Albuera and Vittoria, Salamanca and Talavera and Quatre Bras, put on this map merely as black dots no more kenspeckle than the township of Carnus up the glen. Wars, wars, bloody wars! have we indeed got to the last of them?"

"Indeed I hope so, sir," said the innkeeper, "for my wife has become very costly and very gaudy in her Waterloo blue silks since the rejoicings, and if every war set a woman's mind running to extravagance in clothing, the fewer we have the better."

"If I had a wife, Mr Spencer (and alas! it's my fate to have lost mine), I should make her sit down in weeds or scarlet, after wars, the colour of the blood that ran. What do you say to that, General?"

He turned, as he spoke, to Dugald Campbell, who came to dregies* because it was the fashion of the country, but never ate nor drank at them.

"You were speaking, General Turner?" said Campbell.

Turner fingered the seal upon his fob, with its motto "*Tu ne cede malis,*" and smiled blandly, as he always did when it was

---

* Dregy: the Scots equivalent of the old English *Dirge-ale*, or funeral feast. From the first word of the antiphon in the office for the dead, "*Dirige, Domine meus*".

brought to his recollection that he had won more than soldiers' battles when the odds against him were three to one.

"I was just telling Mr Spencer that Waterloo looks like being the last of the battles, General, and that one bit of Brooks' map here is just as well known to some of us as the paths and woods and waters of Glen Shira."

"I'm not very well acquaint with Glen Shira myself," was all the General said, looking at the map for a moment with eyes that plainly had no interest in the thing before them, and then he turned to a nudge of the Paymaster's arm.

Turner smiled again knowingly to Mr Spencer. "I put my brogues in it that time," said he in a discreet tone. "I forgot that the old gentleman and his brothers were far better acquaint with Glen Shira in my wife's maiden days than I was myself. But that's an old story, Mr Spencer, that you are too recent an incomer to know the shades and meanings of."

"I daresay, sir, I daresay," said Mr Spencer gravely. "You are a most interesting and sensitive people, and I find myself often making the most unhappy blunders."

"Interesting is not the word, I think, Mr Spencer," said General Turner coldly; "we refuse to be interesting to any simple Sassenach." Then he saw the confusion in the innkeeper's face and laughed. "Upon my word," he said, "here I'm as touchy as a bard upon a mere phrase. This is very good drink, Mr. Spencer; your purveyance, I suppose?"

"I had the privilege, sir," said the innkeeper. "Captain Campbell gave the order—"

"Captain Campbell!" said the General, putting down his glass and drinking no more. "I was not aware that he was at the costs of this dregy. Still, no matter, you'll find the Campbells a good family to have dealings with of any commercial kind, pernicketty and proud a bit, like all the rest of us, with their bark worse than their bite."

"I find them quite the gentlemen," said the innkeeper.

Turner laughed again.

"Man!" said he, "take care you do not put your compliment

36

just exactly that way to them; you might as well tell Dr Colin he was a surprisingly good Christian."

Old Brooks, out of sheer custom, sat on the high stool at his desk and hummed his declensions to himself, or the sing-song *Arma virumque cano* that was almost all his Latin pupils remembered of his classics when they had left school. The noise of the assembly a little distressed him; at times he would fancy it was his scholars who were clamouring before him, and he checked on his lips a high peremptory challenge for silence, flushing to think how nearly he had made himself ridiculous. From his stool he could see over the frosted glass of the lower window sash into the playground where it lay bathed in a yellow light, and bare-legged children played at shinty, with loud shouts and violent rushes after a little wooden ball. The town's cows were wandering in for the night from the common muir, with their milkmaids behind them in vast wide petticoats of two breadths, and their blue or lilac short-gowns tucked well up at their arms. Behind, the windows revealed the avenue, the road overhung with the fresh leaves of the beeches, the sunlight filtering through in lighter splashes on the shade. Within, the drink was running to its dregs, and piles of oatcake farls lay yet untouched. One by one the company departed. The glen folks solemnly shook hands with the Paymaster, as donor of the feast, and subdued their faces to a sad regret for this "melancholy occasion, Captain Campbell"; then went over to the taverns in the tenements and kept up their drinking and their singing till late in the evening; the merchants and writers had gone earlier, and now but the officers and Brooks were left, and Mr Spencer, superintending the removal of his vessels and fragments to the inn. The afternoon was sinking into the calm it ever has in this place, drowsing, mellowing; an air of trance lay all about, and even the pensioners, gathered at the head of the schoolroom near the door, seemed silent as his scholars to the ear of Brooks. He lifted the flap of his desk and kept it up with his head while he surveyed the interior. Grammars and copy-books, pens in long tin boxes, the terrible black tawse he never used but reluctantly, and the confiscated playthings of the children who had been guilty of encroaching upon the hours of study with the trifles of leisure, were heaped within. They were for the most part the common toys of the countryside, and among them was a whistle made of young ash, after the fashion practised by children, who tap upon the bark to release it from its wood, slip off the bark entire upon its sap, and cut the vent or blow-hole. Old Brooks took it in his hand and a smile went over his visage.

"General Turner," he cried up the room, "here's an oddity I would like to show you," and he balanced the pipe upon his long fingers, and the smile played about his lips as he looked at it.

Turner came up, and "A whistle," said he. "What's the story?"

"Do you know who owns it?" asked Brooks.

"Sandy, I suppose," said the General, who knew the ingenuities of his only son. "At least, I taught him myself to make an ash whistle, and this may very well be the rogue's contrivance." He took the pipe in hand and turned it over and shrilled it at his lip. "Man," said he, "that makes me young again! I wish I was still at the age when that would pipe me to romance."

The schoolmaster smiled still. "It is not Master Sandy's," said he. "Did you never teach the facture of it to your daughter Nan? She made it yesterday before my very eyes that she thought were not on her at the time, and she had it done in time to pipe Amen to my morning prayer."

"Ah! the witch!" cried the General, his face showing affection and annoyance. "That's the most hoyden jade I'm sure you ever gave the ferule to."

"I never did that," said the schoolmaster.

"Well, at least she's the worst that ever deserved it. The wind is not more variable, nor the sea less careless of constraint. She takes it off her mother, no doubt, who was the dearest madcap, the most darling wretch ever kept a sergeant's section of lovers at her skirts. I wish you could do something with her, Mr Brooks. I do not ask high schooling, though there you have every qualification. I only ask some sobriety put in her so that she may not always be the filly on the meadow."

Old Brooks sighed. He took the whistle from the General and thought a moment, and put it to his lips and piped upon it once or twice as the moor-fowl pipes in spring. "Do you hear that?" he asked. "It is all, my General, we get from life and knowledge—a very thin and apparently meaningless and altogether monotonous squeak upon a sappy stem. Some of us make it out and some of us do not, because, as it happens, we are not so happily constituted. You would have your daughter a patient Martha of the household, and she will be playing in spite of you upon a wooden whistle of her own contrivance. What you want of me, I think, General, is that I should make her like her neighbours to pleasure you and earn my fees and Queen Anne's Bounty. I might try, yet I am not sure but what your girl will become by her sunny nature what I could not make her by my craft as a teacher. And this, sir, I would tell you: there is one mischief I am loth to punish in my school, and that's the music that may be inopportune, even when it takes the poor form of a shrill with an ashen stick made by the performer during the morning's sacred exercise."

The whistle had brought two or three of the company back to see what old Brooks was doing, and among them was the Paymaster. He was redder in the face than ever, and his wig was almost off his head, it was so slewed aside.

"Giving the General a lesson?" he asked with some show at geniality. He leaned a hand upon a desk, and remembered that just on that corner he leaned on he had placed many a shilling as Candlemas and Han'sel Monday offerings when he was a schoolboy, before the farming, before the army and India, and those long years at home on the upper flat of the house up the street where Miss Mary sat the lee-lone homester among her wanderers returned.

"I was but showing him the handiwork of his daughter Miss Nan," said Old Brooks pleasantly. "A somewhat healthy and boisterous lady, I assure you."

"Oh, I have heard of her," said the Paymaster, taking a pinch of maccabaw from his pocket, and leisurely lifting it to his nostril with the indifference of one with little interest in the subject. There was insult in the contempt of the action. The General saw it and flamed very hotly.

"And you have heard of a very handsome little lady," said he, "remarkably like her handsome mother, and a very good large-hearted daughter."

The Paymaster had an unpleasant little laugh that when he chose he could use with the sting of a whip though accompanied by never a word. He flicked the surplus of his snuff from his stock and gave this annoying little laugh, but he did not allow it to go unaccompanied, for he had overheard the General's speech to Mr Spencer.

"No doubt she's all you say or think," said he dryly, "I'm sure I'm no judge, but there's a rumour abroad that she's a big handful. A want of discipline perhaps, no more than that—"

"You know the old saying, Captain," said the General, "bachelors' bairns are aye well trained."

The Paymaster started in a temper, and "I have a son," said he, "and—"

The General smiled with meaning.

"A son; at least I'll make him that, and I'll show you something of training—"

Turner smiled anew, with a mock little bow and a wave of the fingers, a trick picked up abroad and maddening in its influence on a man with the feeling that it meant he was too small to have words with.

"I'll train him—I'll train him to hate your very name," said the Paymaster with an oath.

"I'm obliged for your cake and wine," said the General, still smiling, "and I wish you all good day." He lifted his hat and bowed and left the room.

"This is a most unfortunate contretemps," said Brooks, all trembling. "If I had thought a little whistle, a mere *tibia* of ash, had power to precipitate this unlucky and unseemly belligerence I would never have opened my desk."

The great bell upon the roof of the church swung upon its

arms like an acrobat in petticoats, and loudly pealed the hour of seven. Its hammer boomed against the brassy gown, the town rang from end to end with the clamour of the curfew, and its tale of another day gone rumoured up the glens. Near at hand the air of the playground and of the street was tossed by the sound into tumultuous waves, so that even in the schoolroom the ear throbbed to the loud proclamation. Into the avenue streamed the schools of crows from their wanderings on the braes of Shira, and the children ceased their shinty play and looked up at the flying companies, and called a noisy song—

> Crow, crow, fly away home,
> Your fires are out and your children gone.

"That's a most haughty upsetting crew, and the queue-haired rover the worst of the lot!" said the Paymaster, still red and angry. "What I say's true, Brooks; it's true I tell you! You'll not for your life put it out of the boy's head when you have the teaching of him; he must hate the Turners like poison. Mind that now, mind that now!"

And turning quickly on his heels, the Paymaster went out of the schoolroom.

V

THE BROTHERS

GILIAN, meanwhile, sat on a high chair in Miss Mary's room. She gave him soup till her ladle scraped against the bottom of the tureen; she cut for him the tenderest portions of the hen; she gave him most generously of cheese—not the plain skim-milk curd cheese of Ladyfield, the leavings of the dairy, but the Saturday kebboch as it was called, made of the overnight and morning's milk, poured cream and all into the yearning-tub. And as she served him, her tongue went constantly upon themes of many varieties, but the background of them all, the conclusion of them all, was the greatness of her brothers. Ah! she was a strange little woman with the foolish Gaelic notion that an affection bluntly displayed to its object is an affection discreditable.

"You will go far," said she to Gilian, "before you will come on finer men. They are getting old and done, but once I knew them tall and strong and strapping, not their equals in all the armies. And what they have seen of wars, my dear! They were ever going or coming from them, and sometimes I would not know where they were out in the quarrelsome world but for a line in the *Saturday Post* or the *Courier* or maybe an old hint in the General Almanack itself. Perhaps when you become acquainted with the General and the Cornal you will wonder that they are never at any time jocular, and maybe you will think that they are soured at life and that all their kindness is turned to lappered cream. I knew them nearly jocular, I knew them tall, light-footed laddies, running about the pastures there gallivanting with the girls. But that, my dear, was long ago, and I feel myself the old woman indeed when I see them so stiff and solemn sitting in there over their evening glass."

"I have never seen them; were they at the funeral?" asked Gilian, his interest roused in such survivals of the past.

"That they were," said Miss Mary; "a funeral now is their only recreation. But perhaps you would not know them because they are not at all like the Captain. He was a soldier too, in a way, but they were the ancient warriors. Come into the room here and I will show you, if you have finished your dinner."

Gilian went with her into the parlour again among the prints and the hanging swords, that now he knew the trade and story of the men who sat among them, were imbued with new interests.

Miss Mary pointed to the portraits. "That was Colin and Dugald before they went away the second time," she said. "We had one of James too—he died at Corunna—but it was the only one, and we gave it to a lady of the place who was chief with him before he went away, and dwined a great deal after his death. And that's his sword. When it came home from Spain by MacFarlane, the carrier round from Dumbarton, I took it out and it was clagged in the scabbard with a red glut. It was a sore memorial to an only sister."

The boy stood in the middle of the floor feeling himself very much older than he had done in the morning. The woman's confidences made him almost a man, for before he had been spoken to but as a child, though his thoughts were far older than his years. Those relics of war, especially the sheath that had the glut of life in it corrupting when it came back with the dead man's chest, touched him inwardly to a brief delirium. The room all at once seemed to fill with the tramping of men and the shrilling of pipers, with ships, quays, tumultuous towns, camps, and all the wonders of the shepherds' battle stories round the fire,

43

and he was in a field, and it was the afternoon with a blood-red sky beyond the fir-trees, dense smoke floating across it and the cries of men cutting each other down. He saw—so it seemed as he stood in the middle of the floor of the little parlour with the crumbs of his dinner still upon his vest—the stiff figure of a fallen man in a high collar like the man portrayed upon the wall, and his hand was still in the hilt of a reddened sword and about him were the people he had slain. That did not much move the boy, but he was stirred profoundly when he saw the sword come home. He saw Miss Mary open out the chest in the kitchen and pull hard upon the hilt of the weapon, and he saw her face when the terrible life-glut revealed itself like a rust upon the blade. His nostrils expanded, his eyes glistened; Miss Mary hurriedly looked at him with curiosity, for his breath suddenly quickened and strained till it was the loudest sound in the room.

"What is it, dear?" she said kindly, putting a hand upon his shoulder, speaking the Gaelic that any moment of special fondness brought always to her lips.

"I do not know," said he, ashamed. "I was just thinking of your brother who did not come home, and of your taking out his sword."

She looked more closely at him, at the flush that crept below the fair skin of his neck and more than common paleness of his cheek. "I think," said she, "I am going to like you very much. I might be telling my poor story of a sword to Captain John there a hundred times, and he could not once get at the innermost meaning of it for a woman's heart."

"I saw the battle," said he, encouraged by a sympathy he had never known before.

"I know you did," said she.

"And I saw him dead."

"*Ochanie!*"

"And I saw you dropping the sword when you tugged it from the scabbard, and you cried out and ran and washed your hands, though they were quite clean."

"Indeed I did!" said Miss Mary, all trembling as the past was so plainly set before her. "You are uncanny—no, no, you are not uncanny, you are only ready-witted, and you know how a sister would feel when her dead brother's sword was brought back to her, and the blood of the brothers of other sisters was on its blade. That's my only grievance with those soldier brothers of mine. I said I did not think much of the soldiers; oh! boy, I love them all. I sometimes grieve that God made me a woman that I might not be putting on the red coat too, and following the drum. And still and on, I would have no son of mine a soldier. Three fozy, foggy brothers—what did the armies do for them? They never sharpened their wits, but they sit and dover and dream, dream, even-on, never knowing all that's in their sister Mary's mind. And here you are, a boy, yet you get to my thoughts in a flash. Oh! I think I am going to be very fond of you."

Gilian was amazed that at last someone understood him. No one ever did at Ladyfield; his dreams, his fancies, his spectacles of the inner eye were things that he had grown ashamed of. But here was a shrewd little lady who seemed to think his fancy and confidence nothing discreditable. He was encouraged greatly to let her into his vagrant mind, so sometimes in passionate outbursts, when the words ran over the heels of each other, sometimes in shrinking, stammering, reluctant sentences he told her how the seasons affected him, and the morning and the night, the smells of things, the sounds of woods and the splash of waters, and the mists streaming along the ravines. He told her—or rather he made her understand, for his language was simple—how at sudden outer influences his whole being fired, and from so trivial a thing as a cast-off horseshoe on the highway he was compelled to picture the rider, and set him upon the saddle and go riding with him to the King of Erin's court that is in the story of the third son of Easadh Ruadh in the winter tale. How the joy of the swallow was his in its first darting flights among the eaves of the old barn, and how when it sped at the summer's end he went with it across shires and towns, along the surface of winding rivers, even over the seas to the land of everlasting sun.

How the sound of the wave on the rock moved him and set him with the ships and galleys, the great venturers whipping and creaking and tossing in the night-time under the stars. How the dark appalled or soothed as the humour was, and the sight of a first flower upon a tree would sometimes make him weep at the notion of the brevity of its period.

All the time Miss Mary listened patient and understanding. The high-backed chair compassed her figure so fully that she seemed to shrink to a child's size. It was a twelve-window house, and so among the highest taxed in all the town, but in the parlour there were two blind windows and only one gave light to the interior, so that as she sat in her chair with her back to the window, her face in the shadow, leaning against the chair haffits with the aspect of weariness her brothers never had revealed to them, it seemed to Gilian the little figure and the ruddy face of a companion. She was silent for a moment after his confessions were completed, as if she had been wandering with him in the realm of fancy, and with wings less practised had taken longer to fly back to the narrow actual world. The boy had realised how much he had forgotten himself, and how strange all this story of his must be even to a child-companion with her face in the shadow of the chair haffits, and his eyes were faltering with shame.

"You are very thin, sweetheart," said she, with the two lines darkly pencilled between her eyebrows. "You are far too white for a country boy; upon my word we must be taking the Captain's word for it and putting your head in the cream."

At this Gilian's confusion increased. Here was another to misunderstand, and he had thought she was shivering to his fancy as he was himself. He turned to hide his disappointment. At once the lines disappeared. She rose and put an arm over his shoulder and stooped the little that was necessary to whisper in his ear.

"I know, I think I know," said she; "but look, I'm very old and ancient. Oh, dear! I once had my own fancies, but I think they must have been sweat out of me in my constancy to my brothers' oven-grate and roasting-jack. It must be the old, darling, foolish Highlands in us, my dear, the old people and the old stupid stories they are telling for generations round the fire, and it must be the hills about us, and the constant complaint of the sea—tuts! am not I foolish to be weeping because a boy from Glen Aray has not learned to keep his lips closed on his innermost thought?"

Gilian looked up, and behold! she was in a little rain of tears, at least her eyes swam soft in moisture. It comforted him exceedingly, for it showed that after all she understood.

"If you were a little older," she said, "so old as the merchants of the town that are all too much on the hunt for the bawbees and the world to sit down and commune with themselves, or if you were so old as my brothers there and so hardened, I would be the last to say my thoughts ever stirred an ell-length out of the customary track of breakfast, beds, dinner and supper. Do not think I do not love and reverence my brothers, mind you!" she added almost fiercely, rubbing with her lustre apron the table there was nothing to rub from save its polish. "Oh! they are big men and far-travelled men, and they have seen the wonderful sights. They used to get great thick letters franked from the Government with every post, and the Duke will be calling on them now and then in his chariot. They speak to me of nothing but the poorest, simplest, meanest transactions of the day because they think I cannot comprehend nor feel. Gilian, do you know I am afraid of them? Not of John the Captain, for he is different, with a tongue that goes, but I'm frightened when the General and the Cornal sit and look at me saying nothing because I am a woman."

"I do not like people to sit looking at me saying nothing," said Gilian "because when I sit and look at people without saying anything I am reading them far in. But mostly I would sooner be making up things in my mind."

"Ah!" said she, "that is because your mind is young and spacious; theirs, poor dears, are full of things that have actually happened, and they need not fancy the orra any more."

They moved together out of the parlour and along the lobby that lighted it. With a low sill it looked upon the street that now was thronged with the funeral people passing home or among the shops, or from tavern to tavern. The funeral had given the town a holiday air, and baxters and dealers stood at their doors gossiping with their customers or by-goers. Country carts rumbled past, the horses moving slowly, reluctant to go back from this place of oats and stall to the furrows where the collar pressed constantly upon the shoulder. One or two gentlemen went by on horses—Achnatra and Major Hall and the through-other son of Lorn Campbell. The sun, westering, turned the clean rain-washed sand in the gutters of the street to gold, and there the children played and their calls and rhymes and laughter made so merry a world that the boy at the window, looking out upon it, felt a glow. He was now to be always with these fortunate children whom he knew so well ere ever he had changed words with them. He had a little dread of the magnitude and corners of this dwelling that was to be his in the future, and of the old men who sat in it all day saying nothing, but it was strange indeed (thought he) if with Miss Mary within, and the sunshine and the throng and the children playing in the syver sand without, he should not find life more full and pleasant than it had been in the glen. All these thoughts made warp for the woof of his attention to the street as he stood at the window. And by and by there came a regret for the things lost with the death of the little old woman of Ladyfield—what they were his mind did not pause to make definite, but there was the sense of chances gone with no recalling, of a calm, of a solitude, of a more intimate communion with the animals of the wilds and the voices of the woods and hills.

The woman as well as the boy must have been lost in thought, for neither of them noted the step upon the stair when the General and Cornal came back from the dregy. The brothers were in the lobby beside them before Miss Mary realised their presence. She turned with a flushed face and, as it were, put herself a little in front of the boy, so that half his figure found the shelter of a wing. The two brothers between them filled the width of the lobby, and yet they were not wide. But they were broad at the shoulders and once, no doubt, they filled their funeral suits that of their own stiffness seemed to stand out in all their old amplitude. The General was a white-faced rash of a man with bushy eyebrows, a clean-shaven parchment jowl, and a tremulous hand upon the knob of his malacca rattan; his brother the Cornal was less tall; he was of a purpled visage, and a crimson scar, the record of a wound from Corunna, slanted from his chin to the corner of his left eye.

"What wean is that?" he asked, standing in the lobby and casting a suspicious eye upon the boy, his voice as high as in a barrack yard. The General stood at his shoulder, saying nothing, but looking at Gilian from under his pent brows.

Into Miss Mary's demeanour there had come as great a change as that which came upon the Paymaster when she broke in upon his vaunting. The lines dashed to her brow; when she spoke it was in a cold constrained accent utterly different from that the boy had grown accustomed to.

"It is the *oe* from Ladyfield," she explained.

"He'll be making a noise in the house," said the Cornal with a touch of annoyance. "I cannot stand boys; he'll break things, I'm sure. When is he going away?"

"Are you one of the boys who cry after Major MacNicol, my old friend and comrade?" asked the General in a high squeaking voice. "If I had my stick at some of you, tormenting a gallant old soldier!" And as he spoke he lifted his cane by the middle and shook it at the limbs of the affrighted youth.

"O Dugald, Dugald, you know none of the children of this town ever annoyed the Major; it is only the keelies from the low-country who do so. And this is not the boy to make a mock of any old gentleman, I am sure."

"I know he'll make a noise and start me when I am thinking," said the Cornal, still troubled. "Is it not very strange, Dugald, that women must be aye bringing in useless weans off the street to make noise and annoyance for their brothers?" He

49

poked as he spoke with his stick at Gilian's feet as he would at an animal crossing his path.

"It is a strange cantrip, Mary," said the General; "I suppose you'll be going to give him something. It is give, give all the day in this house like Sergeant Scott's cantiniers."

"Indeed and you need not complain of the giving," said Miss Mary: "there was nobody gave with a greater extravagance than yourself when you had it to give, and nobody sends more gangrels about the house than you."

"Give the boy his meat and let him go," said the Cornal roughly.

"He's not going," said Miss Mary, turning quite white and taking the pin carefully out of her shawl and as carefully putting it in again. And having done this quite unnecessary thing she slipped her hand down and warmly clasped unseen the fingers of the boy in the folds of her bombazine gown.

"Not going? I do not understand you, Mary; as you grow older you grow stupider. Does she not grow stupider, Dugald?" said the Cornal.

"She does," said the General. "I think she does it to torment us, just." He was tired by this discussion; he turned and walked to the parlour.

Miss Mary mustered all her courage, and speaking with great rapidity explained the situation. The boy was the Ladyfield boy; the Paymaster was going to keep him hereafter.

The Cornal stood listening to the story as one in a trance. There was a little silence when she had done, and he broke it with a harsh laugh.

"Ah! and what is he going to make of this one?" he asked.

"That's to be seen," said Miss Mary; "he spoke of the army."

"Fancy that now!" said the Cornal with contempt. "Let me see him," he added suddenly. "Let me see the seeds of soldiery." He put out a hand and—not roughly but still with more force than Gilian relished—drew him from the protection of the gown and turned his face to the window. He put his hand under the boy's chin; Gilian in the touch felt an abhorrence of the hard, clammy fingers that had made dead men, but his eyes never quailed as he looked up in the scarred face. He saw a mask; there was no getting to the secrets behind that purple visage. Experience and trial, emotions and passions had set lines there wholly new to him, and his fancy refused to go further than just this one thought of the fingers that had made dead men.

The Cornal looked him deeply in the eyes, caught him by the ear, and with a twist made him wince, pushed him on the shoulders and made his knees bend. Then he released him with a flout of contempt.

"Man! Jock's the daft recruiter," he said coarsely with an oath. "What's this but a clerk? There's not the spirit in the boy to make a drummer of him. There's no stuff for sogering here."

Miss Mary drew Gilian to her again and stiffened her lips. "You have nothing to do with it, Colin; it's John's house and if he wants to keep the boy he'll do it. And I'm sure if you but took the trouble to think that he is a poor orphan with no kith nor kin in the world, you would be the first to take him in at the door."

The Cornal's face visibly relaxed its sternness. He looked again more closely at the boy.

"Come away into our parlour here, and the General and I will have a crack with you," said he, leading the way.

Miss Mary gave the boy's hand a gentle squeeze, and softly pushed him in after her brother, shut the door behind them, and turned and went down to the kitchen.

VI

COURT-MARTIAL

GILIAN was in a great dread, but revealed none of it in the half dusk of the room where he faced the two brothers as they sat at either side of the table. The General took out a bottle of spirits and placed it with scrupulous care in the very centre of the table; his brother lifted two tumblers from the corner cupboard and put them on each side of the bottle, fastidious to a hair's breadth as if he had been laying out columns of troops. It was the formula of the afternoon; sometimes they never put a lip to the glass, but it was always necessary that the bottle should be in the party. For a space that seemed terribly long to the boy they said no word but looked at him. The eyes of the Cornal seemed to pierce him through; the General in a while seemed to forget his presence, turning upon him a flat, vacant eye. Gilian leaned upon his other foot and was on the verge of crying at his situation. The day had been far too crowded with strangers and new experience for his comfort; he felt himself cruelly plucked out of his own sufficient company and jarred by contact with a very complex world.

With a rude loud sound that shook the toddy ladles in the cupboard the Cornal cleared his throat.

"How old are you?" he asked, and this roused the General, who came back from his musings with a convulsive start, and repeated his brother's question.

"Twelve," said Gilian, first in Gaelic out of instinct, and hurriedly repeating it in English lest he should offend the gentlemen.

"Twelve," said the Cornal, thinking hard. "You are not very bulky for your age. Is he now, Dugald?"

"He is not very bulky for his age," said the General, after a moment's pause as if he were recalling all the boys he knew of that age, or remitting himself to the days before his teens.

"And now, between ourselves," said the Cornal, leaning over with a show of intimacy and even friendliness, "have you any notion yourself of being a soger?"

"I never thought anything about it," Gilian confessed in a low tone. "I can be anything the Captain would like me to be."

"Did you ever hear the like?" cried the Cornal, looking in amazement at his brother. "He never thought anything about it, but he can be anything he likes. Is not that a good one? Anything he likes!" And he laughed with a choked and heavy effort till the scar upon his face fired like blood, and Gilian seemed to see it gape and flow as it did when the sword-slash struck it open in Corunna.

"Anything he likes!" echoed the General, laughing huskily till he coughed and choked. They both sat smiling grimly with no more sound till it seemed to the boy he must be in a dream, looking at the creations of his brain. The step of a fly could have been heard in the room almost, so sunk was it in silence, but outside, as in another world, a band of children filled the street with the chant of "Pity be"—chant of the trumpeters of the Lords.

Gilian never before heard that song with which the children were used to accompany the fanfare of the scarlet-coated musicians who preceded the Lords Justiciary on their circuit twice a year; but the words came distinctly to him in by the open window where the wallflower nodded, and he joined silently in his mind the dolorous chorus and felt himself the prisoner, deserving of every pity.

"Sit ye down there," at last said the Cornal, "with my brother the General's leave." And he waved to the high-backed haffit

53

chair Miss Mary had so sparely filled an hour ago. Then he withdrew the stopper of the bottle, poured a tiny drop of the spirits into both tumblers, and drank "The King and his Arms," a sentiment the General joined in with his hand tremulous around the glass.

"Listen to me," said the Cornal, "and here I speak, I think, for my brother the General, who has too much to be thinking about to be troubling with these little affairs. Listen to me. I fought in Corunna, in Salamanca, Vittoria and Waterloo, and at Waterloo I led the Royals up against the yetts of hell. Did I not, Dugald?"

"You did that," said Dugald, withdrawing himself again from a muse over the records of victory. And then he bent a lustreless eye upon his own portrait, so sombre and gallant upon the wall, with the gold of the lace and epaulettes a little tarnished.

"I make no brag of it, mind you," said the Cornal, waving his hand as if he would be excused for mentioning it. "I am but saying it to show that I ken a little of bloody wars, and the art and trade of sogering. There are gifts demanded for the same that seriatim I would enumerate. First there is natural strength and will. All other trades have their limits, when a man may tell himself, 'That's the best I can do,' and shut his book or set down the tool with no disgrace in the relinquishment. But a soger's is a different ploy; he must stand stark against all encountering, nor cry a parley even with the lance at his throat. Oh, man! man! I had a delight in it in my time for all its trials. I carried claymore (so to name it, ours was a less handsome weapon, you'll observe), in the ranting, roving humour of a boy; I sailed and marched; it was fine to touch at foreign ports; it was sweet to hear the drums beat revally under the vines; the camp-fire, the—"

"And it would be on the edge of a wood," broke in the boy in Gaelic; "the logs would roar and hiss. The fires would be in yellow dots along the countryside, and the heather would be like a pillow so soft and springy under the arm. Round about, the soldiers would be standing, looking at the glow, their faces red and flickering, and behind would be the black dark of the wood like the inside of a pot, a wood with ghosts and eerie sounds and—"

He stammered and broke down under the astounded gaze of the Cornal and the General, who stood to their feet facing his tense and thrilled small figure. A wave of shame-heat swept over him at his own boldness.

Outside, the children's voices were fading in the distance as they turned the corner of the church singing "Pity be".

Pity be on poor prisoners, pity be on them:
Pity be on poor prisoners, if they come back again,

they sang; the air softened into a fairy lullaby heard by an ear at eve against the grassy hillock, full of charm, instinct with dream, and the sentiment of it was as much the boy's within as the performers' without.

"This is the kind of play-actor John would make a soldier of," said the Cornal, turning almost piteously to his brother. "It beats all! Where did you learn all that?" he demanded harshly, scowling at the youth and sitting down again.

"He has the picture of it very true, now, has he not?" said the General. "I mind of many camps just like that, with the cork-trees behind and old Sir George ramping and cursing in his tent because the pickets hailed, and the corncrake would be rasping, rasping, a cannon-carriage badly oiled, among the grass."

Gilian sank into the chair again, his face in shadow.

"Discipline and reverence for your elders and superiors are the first lesson you would need, my boy," said the Cornal, taking a tiny drop of the spirits again and touching the glass of his brother, who had done likewise. "Discipline and reverence; discipline and reverence. I was once cocky and putting in my tongue like you where something of sense would have made me keep it between my teeth. Once in Spain, an ensign, I found myself in a wine-shop or change-house, drinking as I should never have been doing if I had as muckle sense as a clabbie-doo, with a dragoon major old enough to be my father. He was a pock-pudding Englishman, a great hash of a man with the chest of him slipped down below his belt, and what was he but bragging about the rich people he came of, and the rich soil they flourished on, its apple-orchards and honey-flowers and its grass knee-deep in June. 'Do you know,' said I, 'I would not give a yard's breadth of the shire of Argyll anywhere north of Knapdale at its rockiest for all your lush straths, and if it comes to antique pedigrees here am I, Clan Diarmid, with my tree going down to Donacha Dhu of Lochow.' That was insolence, ill-considered, unnecessary, for this major of dragoons, as I tell you, might be my father and I was but a raw ensign."

"I'll warrant you were homesick when you said it," said the General.

"Was I not?" cried the brother. "'Twas that urged me on. For one of my company, just a minute before, had been singing Donacha Ban's songs of 'Ben Dorain', and no prospect in the world seemed so alluring to me then as a swath of the land I came from."

"I know 'Ben Dorain'," said Gilian timidly, "and I think I could tell just the way you felt when you heard the man singing it in a foreign place."

"Come away, then, my twelve-year-old warlock," said the Cornal, mockingly, yet wondering too.

"This is a real oddity," said the General, drawing his chair a little nearer the boy.

"I heard a forester sing 'Ben Dorain' last Hogmanay at home— I mean in Ladyfield; he was not a good singer, and he forgot bits of the words here and there, but when he was singing it I saw the sun rise on the hill, not a slow grey, but suddenly in a smother of gold, and the hillside moved with deer. Birds whirred from the heather and the cuckoo was in the wood."

"That was very unlucky about the cuckoo before breakfast," said the Cornal, and he quoted a Gaelic proverb.

"Oh! if I was in a foreign place and someone sang that song I would be very, very sick for home. I would be full of thoughts about the lochs and the hunting roads, the slope of the braes and stripes of black fir on them; the crying of cattle, the sound of burn and *eas* and the voices of people I knew would be dragging my heart home. I would be saying, 'Oh! you strangers, you do not understand. You have not the want at your hearts,' and there would be one little bit of the place at home as plain to my view as that picture."

As he spoke, Gilian pointed at *The Battle of Vittoria*. The brothers turned and looked as if it was something quite new and strange to them. Up rose the Cornal and went closer to peer at it.

"Confound it!" said he. "You're there with your tale of a ballant, and you point at the one picture ever I saw that gave me the day-dreaming. I never see that smudgy old print but I'm crying on the cavalry that made the Frenchmen rout."

From where he sat the boy could make out the picture in every detail. It was a scene of flying and broken troops, of men on the wings of terror and dragoons riding them down. There was at the very front of the picture in a corner, among the flying Frenchmen pursued by the horses, the presentment of a Scottish soldier, wounded, lying upon his back with his elbows propped beneath him so that he had his head up, looking at the action, a soldier of a thin long habit of body, a hollow face and high cheekbones.

Gilian forgot the two old men in the room with him when he looked intently on this soldier in the throes; he stood up from the chair, went forward and put a finger as high as he could to point out the particular thing he referred to. "That's a man," said he, "and he's afraid. He does not hear the guns, nor the people crying, but he hears the horses' feet thudding on the grass, and he thinks they will go over him and crush his bones."

"Curse me," cried the Cornal, "but you have the thing to a nicety. That's the man's notion, for a guinea, for I have been in his case myself, and the thud of horses was a sound that filled the world. Sit down, sit down!" he went on sharply, as if he had of a sudden found something to reproach himself with in any complacent recognition of this child's images. "You are not canny; how old are you?"

Gilian was trembling and parched at the lips now, aware to the enormity of his forwardness. "I am twelve," he repeated.

"It is a cursed lie," said the Cornal hotly; "you're a hundred; don't tell me!"

He was actually a little afraid of those manifestations, so unusual and so remarkable. His excitement could with difficulty be concealed. Very restlessly he moved about in his chair, and turned his look from the General to the boy and back again, but the General sat with his chin in his breast, his mind a vacancy.

"Look at the General there; you're fairly scunnering him with your notions," said the Cornal. "I must speak to John about this. A soldier indeed! You're not fit for it, lad; you have only the makings of a dominie. Sit you there, and we'll see what John has to say about this when he comes in: it is going on seven, and he'll be back from the dregy in time for his supper."

Gilian sat trembling in his chair; the brothers leaned back in theirs and breathed heavily and said no word, and never even stretched a hand to the bottle of spirits. A solemn quiet again took possession of the house, but for a door that slammed in the lower flat, shaking the dwelling; the lulled sound of women's conversation at the oven-grate was utterly stilled. The pigeons came to the sill a moment, mourned and flew away; the carts did not rumble any more in the street; the children's chorus was altogether lost. A feeling came over the boy that he had been here or somewhere like it before, and he was fascinated, wondering what next would happen. A tall old clock in the lobby, whose pendulum swung so slowly that at first he had never realised its presence, at last took advantage of the silence and swung itself into his notice with a tick—tack. The silence seemed to thicken and press upon his ears; no striving after fancy could bring the boy far enough off from that strange convention, and try as he might to realise himself back in his familiar places by the riverside at Ladyfield, the wings of his imagining failed in

58

their flight and he tumbled again into that austere parlour sitting with two men utterly beyond his comprehension.

There was, at last, one sound that gave a little comfort, and checked the tears that had begun to gather on the edges of his eyes. It came from the direction of the kitchen; it was a creaking of the wooden stairs; it was a faint shuffle of slippers in the lobby; then there was a hush outside the door deeper even than the stillness within. Gilian knew, as if he could see through the brown panelling, that a woman was standing out there listening with her breath caught up and wondering at the quiet within, yet afraid to open a door upon the mystery. The brothers did not observe it; all this was too faint for their old ears, though plainly heard by a child of the fields whose ear against the grass could detect the marching of insects and the tunnelling of worms. But for that he would have screamed—but for the magic air of friendship and sympathy that flowed to him through chink and keyhole from the good heart loud-beating outside; in that kind air of fond companionship (even with a door between) there was comfort. In a little the slippers sped back along the lobby, the stair creaked, in the lower flat a door slammed. Gilian felt himself more deserted and friendless than ever, and a few moments more would have found him break upon the appalling still with sobs of cowardly surrender, but the church bell rang. It was the first time he had heard its evening clamour, that, however far it might search up the glens, never reached Ladyfield, so deep among the hills, and he had no more than recovered from the bewildering influence of its unexpected alarm when the foot of the Paymaster sounded heavily on the stair.

"You're here at last," said the Cornal, without looking at him.

"I was a thought later than I intended," said the Paymaster quickly, putting his cane softly into a corner. "I had a little encounter with that fellow Turner and it put by the time."

"What—Jamie?"

"No; Charlie."

"Man! I wonder at you, John," said the Cornal with a contempt

59

in his utterance and a tightening of the corner of his lips. "I wonder at you changing words with him. What was it you were on?"

The Paymaster explained shortly, guardedly, because of Gilian's presence, and as he spoke the purple of the Cornal's face turned to livid and the scar became a sickly yellow. He rose and thumped his fist upon the table.

"That was his defiance, was it?" he cried. "We are the old sonless bachelors, are we, and the name's dead with the last of us? And you argued with him about that! I would have put a hand on his cravat and throttled him."

The Paymaster was abashed, but "Just consider, Colin," he pleaded. "I am not so young as I was, and a bonny-like thing it would be to throttle him on the ground he gave."

"Old Mars!" cried the Cornal, with a sneer. "Man! but MacColl hit your character when he made his song; you were always well supplied by luck with excuses for not fighting."

To the General the Paymaster turned with piteous appeal. "Dugald," said he, "I'll leave it to you if Colin's acting fairly. Did ever I disgrace the name of Campbell, or Gael, or soger?"

"I never said you did," cried the Cornal. "All I said was that fate was a scurvy friend to you and seldom put you face to face with your foe on any clear issue. Perhaps I said too much; I'm hot-tempered, I know; never mind my taunt, John. But you'll allow it's galling to have a beggarly upstart like Turner throwing our bachelorhood in our teeth. Now if we had sons, or a son, one of us, I'll warrant we could bring him up with more credit than Turner brings up his long-lugged Sandy, or that randy lass of his."

"Isn't that what I told him?" said the Paymaster, scooping a great heap of dust into his nostrils, and feverishly rubbing down the front of his vest with a large handkerchief. "I wish—"

He stopped suddenly; he looked hard at Gilian, whose presence in the shadow of the big chair he had seemingly forgotten; seeing him gaze thus and pause, the Cornal turned too and looked at the youth, and the General shrugged himself into some interest in the same object. Before the gaze of the three brothers, the boy's skin burned; his eyes dropped.

"This is a queer callant you've brought us here," said the Cornal, nudging his brother and nodding in Gilian's direction. "I've seen some real diverts in my time, but he beats all. And you have a notion to make a soger of him, they tell me. You heard that yourself, didn't you, General?"

The General made no reply, for he was looking at the portrait of himself when he was thirty-five, and to sit doing nothing in a house would have been torture.

"I only said it in the by-going to Mary," explained the Paymaster humbly. "The nature for sogering is the gift of God, and the boy may have it or he may not; it is too soon to say."

"There's no more of the soger in him than there is of the writer in me!" cried the Cornal; "but there's something by-ordinar in him all the same. It's your affair, John, but—" He stopped short and looked again at Gilian and hummed and ha'd a little and fingered his stock. "Man, do you know I would not say but here's your son for you."

"That's what I thought myself," said the Paymaster, "and that's what I said. I'll make him a soger if I can, and I'll make him hate the name of Turner whether or not."

And all this time Gilian sat silently by, piecing out those scraps of old men's passion with his child's fancy. He found this new world into which he had been dragged, noisy, perplexing, interested apparently in the most vague trifles. That they should lay out his future for warfare and for hate, without any regard for his own wishes, was a little alarming. Soldiering—with the man before him in the picture, sitting propped up on his arms, frantic lest the horses should trample on him—seemed the last trade on earth; as for hate, that might be easier and due to his benefactor, but it would depend very much on the Turners.

When the brothers released him from their den, and he went to Miss Mary, standing at the kitchen door, eager for his company, with a flush on her cheek and a bright new ribbon at her neck, he laid those points before her.

"Tuts!" said she, pressing food on him—her motherhood's only cure for all a child's complaints—"they're only haverils. They cannot make a soger of you against your will. As for the Turners—well, they're no very likeable race, most of them in my mind. A dour, sour, upsetting clan of no parentage. Perhaps that does not much matter, so long as people are honest and well-doing; we are all equals before God except in head and heart, but there's something too in our old Hielan' notion that the closest kith of the King are aye most kindly, because the habit is born in them to be freehanded and unafraid. Am not I the *oinseach* to be sticking up for pedigrees? Perhaps it is because our own is so good. Kiels was ours three hundred years, and my grandfather was goodbrother to an earl—a not very good nor honest lord they say—and the Turners were only portioners and tenants as far back as we ken."

"I liked the look of the one with his hair in a tail," said Gilian, and he wondered if she was angry at his admiration of the enemy, when he saw her face grow red.

"Oh! the General!" she exclaimed, but never a word more, good or ill.

VII

THE MAN ON THE QUAY

IT has always happened that the first steps of a boy from the glen have been to the quay. There the ships lie clumsily on their bulging sides in the ebb till the tar steams and blisters in the sun, or at the full they lift and fall heavily like a sigh for the ocean's expanse as they feel themselves prisoners to the rings and pawls. Their chains jerk and ease upon the granite edges of the wall or twang tight across the quay so that the mariners and fishermen moving about their business on this stone-thrust to the sea must lift their clumping boots high to step across those tethers of romance. At a full tide one walking down the quay has beside him the dark aspiring bulwarks of the little but brave adventurers, their seams gazing to the heat, their carvel timbers striped by the ooze and brine of many oceans and the scum of ports. Upon their poops their den-fire chimneys breathe a faint blue reek; the iron of bilge-pump and pin is rust red; the companions are portals to smelling depths where the bunks are in a perpetual gloom and the seamen lie at night or in the heat of the day discontent with this period of no roaming and remembering the tumbling waters and the far-off harbours that must ever be more alluring than the harbours where we be. From the ivy of the church the little birds come chaffering and twittering among the shrouds, and the pigeon will perch upon a spar, so that the seagull, the far-searcher, must wonder as he passes on a slant of silent feathers at its daring thus to utilise the defier of the outermost seas and the most vehement storms. And side by side with these, the adventurers, are the skiffs and smacks of the fishermen, drilled in rows, brought bow up, taut on their anchors with their lug-sails down on their masts to make deck tents for shelter from sun or rain. With those sturdy black gabbarts and barques and those bronze fishers, the bay from the quay to the walls of the Duke's garden, in its season, stirs with life.

More than once when he had come to the town Gilian looked a little way off from the Cross upon this busy concourse in the bay and wished that he might venture on the quay, but the throng of tall, dark-shirted fishermen and seafarers frightened him so that he must stand aloof guessing at the nearer interest of the spectacle. Now that he was a town boy with whole days in which to muster courage, he spurred himself up to walk upon the quay at the first opportunity. It was the afternoon, the tide lapped high upon the slips and stairs, a heaving, lazy roll of water so clear that the starfish on the sandy bottom might plainly be seen through great depths. The gunnles of the ships o'ertopped by many feet the quay-wall and their chains rose slanting, tight from the rings. The fishermen and their boats were far down on Cowal after signs of herring; the bay was given up to barque and gabbart alone. For once a slumber seemed to lie upon the place for ordinary so throng and cheerful; the quay was Gilian's alone as he stepped wonderingly upon it and turned an eye to the square ports open for an airing to the dens. In all the company of the ships thus swaying at the quayside there was no sign of life beyond the smoke that rose from the stunted funnels. The boy's fancy played among the masts like the birds from the ivy. These were the galleys of Inishtore, that rode upon the seven seas for a king's son with a hauberk of gold. The spicy isles, the silver sands, the songs the *graugach* sang below the prows when the sea dashed—they came all into his vision of those little tarred hulks of commerce. He thought how fine it would be to set foot upon those decks and loose the fastenings, and drop down the sea-slope of the shepherds' stories till he came upon Ibrisail, happy isle of play and laughter, where the sun never drops below the ocean's marge.

In one of the vessels behind him, as he mused, a seaman noiselessly thrust his head out at a companion to look the hour upon the town's clock, and the boy, pale, fair-haired, pondering, with eyes upon the shrouds of a gabbart, forced himself by his stillness and inaction upon the man's notice. He was a little, stout, well-built man, with a face tanned by sunshine and salt air to the semblance of Spanish mahogany, with wide and searching eyes and long curled hair of the deepest black. His dress was singularly perjink, cut trim and tight from a blue cloth, the collar of a red shirt rolled over on the bosom, a pair of simple gold rings pierced the ears. As he looked at the boy, he was humming very softly to himself a Skye song, and he stopped in the midst of it with "So 'ille, have you lost your ship?" A playful scamp was revealed in his smile.

Gilian turned round with a start of alarm, for he had been on some coracle of fancy, sailing upon magic seas, and thus to break upon his reverie with the high Gaelic of Skye was to plunge him in chilling waters.

"Thig an so—come here," said the seaman, beckoning, setting an easy foot upon the deck.

Gilian went slowly forward. He was amazed and fascinated by this wondrous seaman come upon the stillness of the harbour without warning, a traveller so important yet so affable in his invitation. Black Duncan that day was in a good humour, for his owners had released him at last from his weeks of tethering to the quay and this dull town and he was to depart tomorrow with his cargo of timber. In a little he had Gilian's history, and they were comrades. He took him round the deck and showed its simple furniture, then in the den he told him mariners' tales of the sea.

A Carron stove burned in the cabin, dimly, yet enough to throw at times a flicker of light upon the black beams overhead, the vessel's ribs, the bunks that hung upon them. Sitting on a

65

sea-chest, Gilian felt the floor lift and fall below him, a steady motion wholly new, yet confirming every guess he had made in dreams of life upon the wave. A ceaseless sound of water came through the wood, of the tide glucking along the bows, surely to the mariner the sweetest of all sounds when he lies in benign weather moving home upon the sigh of God.

Black Duncan but wanted a good listener. He was not quite the world's traveller he would have Gilian believe; but he had voyaged in many outlandish parts and a Skyeman's memory is long and his is the isle where fancy riots. He made his simple ventures round the coast voyages terrible and unending. The bays, the water-mouths, the rocks, the bosky isles—he clothed them with delights, and made them float in the haze wherein a boy untravelled would envelop them.

"There's a story I know," said Gilian, "of a young son who went to a town where the King of Erin bides, and he found it full of music from end to end, every street humming with song."

"Oh, lad, I have been there," said the seaman, unabashed, his teeth very white in the brown of his smiling face. "You sail and sail in winds and drift in calms, and there is a place called Erin's Eye and a mountain rock behind it, and there you come upon the town of the King's daughter. It is a town reeling with music; some people without the ears would miss it, you and Black Duncan would be jigging to the sound of it. The world, 'ille (and here's the sailorman who has sailed the seven seas and knows its worst and best), is a very grand place to such as understand and allow. I was born with a caul as we say; I know that I'll never drown, so that when winds crack I feel safe in the most staggering ship. I have gone into foreign ports in the dead of night, our hail for light but answered by Sir Echo, and we would be waiting for light, with the smell of flowers and trees about us, and—"

"That would be worth sailing for," said Gilian, looking hard at the embers in the Carron stove.

"Or the beast of the wood might come roaring and bellowing to the shore."

"That would be very frightsome," said Gilian with a shiver. "I have made believe the hum of the bee in the heather at my ear as I lay on it in the summer was the roar of the wild beast a long way off; it was uncanny and I could make myself afraid of it, but when I liked it was the bee again and the heather was no higher than my knee."

The seaman laughed till the den rang. He poked the fire and the flame thrust out and made the boy and the man and the timbers and bunks dance and shake in the world between light and shadow. "You are the sharpest boy ever I conversed with," said he.

A run of the merriest, the sweetest, the most unconstrained laughter broke overhead like a bird's song. They looked up and found the square of blue sky broken at the hatch by a girl's head. A roguish face in a toss of brown hair, seen thus above them against the sky, seemed to Gilian the face of one of the fairies with which he had peopled the seaman's isle.

"There you go!" cried Black Duncan, noway astonished. "Did I not tell you never to come on board without halloo?"

"I cried," said the girl in a most pretty English that sounded all the sweeter beside the seaman's broken and harsh accent in a language foreign to him. "I cried 'O Duncan' twice and you never heard, so I knew you were asleep in your dingy old den." She swung herself down as she spoke and stood at the foot of the companion with the laugh renewed upon her lips, a gush of happy heart.

"Indeed, Miss Nan, and I was not sleeping at all," said Black Duncan, standing up and facing her; "if I was sleeping would there be a boy with me here listening to the stories of the times when I was scouring the oceans and not between here and the Clyde in your father's vessel?"

"Oh! a boy!" cried the girl, taken a little aback. "I did not know there was a boy."

"And a glen boy, too," said the seaman, speaking in a language wherein he knew himself more the equal of his master's daughter. "I told him of Erin O and the music in its streets and he does not make fun of my telling like you, Miss Nan, because he understands."

The girl peered into the dark of the cabin at the face of Gilian that seemed unwontedly long and pallid in the half light, with eyes burning in sepulchral pits, repeating the flash of the embers. She was about his own age—at most no more than a month or two younger, but with a glance bold and assured that spoke of an early maturity.

"Oh! a Glen Aray boy," said she. "I never much care for them. You would be telling him some of the tales there is no word of truth in."

"The finest tales in the world are like that!" said Black Duncan.

She sat on the edge of a bunk and swung a little drab jean shoe. The glamour of Black Duncan's stories fled for Gilian before this presence like mist before a morning wind. So healthy, so ruddy, so abrupt, she was so much in the actual world that for him to be dreaming of others seemed a child's weakness.

"I was in the town with uncle," she said, "and I heard you were sailing away tomorrow, and I thought I would come and say good-bye."

She spoke as prettily in her Gaelic as in her English.

"Ah, *mo run*," said the seaman, putting out his arms as to embrace her, "am not I pleased that you should have Black Duncan in your mind so much as to come and say 'fair wind to your sail'?"

"And you'll bring me the beads next time?" she said hastily.

"That will I," said he, smiling; "but you must sing me a song now or I might forget them."

"Oh, I'll sing if—" She paused and looked doubtfully at Gilian, who was still open-mouthed at her breezy vehemence.

"Never mind the boy," said the seaman, stretching himself to enjoy the music at his ease; "if you make it 'The Rover' he will understand."

The afternoon was speeding. The sun had passed the trees that round the Tolbooth walls and a beam from his majesty came boldly into the den by the companion. It struck a slanting passage on the floor and revealed the figure of a girl at her ease dangling her feet upon a water anker with her hair a flood of spate-brown fallen back upon its fastening band. And the boy saw her again as it were quite differently from before, still the robust woman-child, but rich, ripe, blooded at the plump inviting lip, warm at the throbbing neck. About her hung a searching odour that overcame the common and vulgar odours of the ship, its bilge, its tar, its oak-bark tan, its herring scale, an odour he knew of woods in the wet spring weather. It made him think of short grasses and the dewdrop glittering in the wet leaf; then the sky shone blue against a tremble of airy leaf. The birch, the birch, he had it! And having it he knew the secret of the odour. She had already the woman's trick of washing her hair in the young birch brewings.

"I will sing 'The Rover' and I will sing 'The Man with the Coat of Green'," said she, with the generosity of one with many gifts. And she started upon her ditty. She had a voice that as yet was only in its making; it was but a promise of the future splendour, yet to Gilian, the hearer, it brought a new and potent joy. With "The Rover", he lived in the woods, and set foot upon foreign wharves; "The Man with the Coat of Green" had his company upon the morning adventures in the islands of fairydom. It was then, as in after years she was the woman serious, when her own songs moved her, with her dalliance and indifference gone. A tear trembled at her eyes at the trials of the folk she sang.

"You sing—you sing—you sing like the wind in the trees," said the seaman, stirred to unaccustomed passion. The little cabin, when she was done, seemed to shrink from the limitless width of the world to the narrowness of a cell, and Gilian sat stunned. He had followed her song in a rapture she had seen and delighted in for all the apparent surrender of her emotion; she saw now the depth to which she had touched him, and was greatly pleased with this conquest of her art. Clearly he was no common Glen Aray boy, so she sang one or two more songs to show the variety of her budget, and the tears he could not restrain were her sweetest triumph. At last, "I must be going," said she.

"Goodbye, Duncan, and do not be forgetting my beads." Then she dashed on deck, waiting no answer to that or to the friendly nod of parting to Gilian.

"Now isn't she a wonder?" asked the seaman, amused, astonished, proud. "Did you ever hear singing like it?"

"I never did," said Gilian.

"Ah, she is almost as fine as a piper!" said the seaman. "She comes down here every time I am at the quay and she will be singing here till the timbers strain themselves to listen."

"I like her very much," said Gilian.

"Of course you do," the seaman cried, with a thump of his hard hand on the edge of his bunk, "and would it not be very curious indeed if you did not like her. I have heard women sing in many places—bold ones in Amsterdam, and the shy dancers of Bermuda, but never her equal, and she only a child. How she does it is the beat of me."

"I know," said Gilian, reddening a little to say so much to the seaman, but emboldened by the shadows he sat among. "The birds sing that way and the winds and the tide, because they have the feeling of it and they must. And when she sings she is 'The Rover', or she is 'The Man with the Green Coat'."

"Indeed, and it is very easy too when you explain," said the seaman, whether in earnest or in fun the boy could not make out. "She is the strange one anyway, and they say General Turner, who's her father and the man this ship belongs to, is not knowing very well what to make of her. What is the matter with you?" For the boy's face was crimson as he looked up the quay after the girl from the deck where now they stood.

"Oh," said Gilian, "I was just wondering if that would be the family the Paymaster is not friendly with."

The seaman laughed. "That same!" said he. "And are you in the family feud too? If that is so you'll hear little of Miss Nan's songs, I'm thinking, and that is the folly of feuds. If I was you I would say nothing about the *Jean*, and the lass who sang in her."

VIII

THE SHERIFF'S SUPPER PARTY

BUT Gilian was soon to hear the lass again.

It was a great town for supper parties. To make up, as it were, for the lost peat-side parliaments or supper nights that for their fore-folk made tolerable the quiet glens, the town people had many occasions of social intercourse in each other's homes, where the winter nights, that otherwise had been long and dreary, passed in harmless gaiety. The women would put on their green josephs and gaudiest quilted petticoats or their tabinet gowns of Waterloo whose splendour kirk or market poorly revealed for the shawls that must cover them. The men donned their best figured waistcoats and their newest stocks, and cursed the fashions that took them from their pipes and cards, but solaced themselves mightily with the bottle in the host's bedroom. From those friendly convocations, jealousies innumerable bred. It was not only that each other's gowns raised unchristian thoughts in the bosoms of the women, but in a community where each knew her neighbour and many were on equality, there must be selections, and rancour rose. And it was the true Highland rancour, concealing itself under a front of indifference and even politeness, though the latter might be ice-cold in degree but burning fiercely at the core.

A few days after Gilian came to town Miss Mary and her

brothers were submitted to a slight there could be no mistaking. It came from the wife of the Sheriff, who was a half-sister of the Turners. The Sheriff's servant had come up to the shop below the Paymaster's house early in the forenoon for candles and Miss Mary chanced to be in the shop when this purchase was made. It could signify nothing but festivity, for even in the Sheriff's the home-made candle was good enough for all but festive nights.

Miss Mary went upstairs disturbed, curious, annoyed. She had got no invitation to the Sheriff's, and yet here was the hint of some convivial gathering such as she and her brothers had hitherto always been welcome to.

"What do you think it will be, John?" she asked the Paymaster, telling him what she had seen.

"Tuts," said he, "they'll just be out of dips. Or maybe the Sheriff has an extra hard case at avizandum, not to be seen clearly through with a common creesh flame."

"That's aye you," cried Miss Mary, indignant. "People might slap you in the face and you would have no interest."

She hastened to Peggy in the kitchen and Peggy shared her wonder, though she was not permitted to see her annoyance. A plan was devised to find out what this extravagance of candle might portend.

The maid took her water-stoups and went up to the Cross well, where women were busy at that hour of the day plying for the water of Bealloch-an-uarain, that bubbles up deep in the heart of the hills, and brings the coolness and refreshment of the shady wood into the burgh street in the most intense days of summer warmth. She filled her stoups composedly, set them down and gossiped, upset them as by accident, and waited patiently her turn to fill them anew. Thus by twenty minutes' skilful loitering she secured from the baxter's daughter the news that there was a supper at the Sheriff's that very night, and that very large tarts were at the firing in the baxter's oven.

"Oh, indeed!" cried Miss Mary, when her emissary brought to her those tidings. "Then it seems the Campbells of Keil are not good enough company for Sheriff Maclachlan's supper parties!

72

My brother the Cornal, and my brother the Major-General, would have their own idea about that if so small a trifle as Madam's tart supper and green tea was worth their notice or annoyance."

She was visibly disturbed, yet put on a certain air of indifference that scarcely deceived even Peggy. The worst of it was there was no one with whom she could share her annoyance, for, if the Paymaster had no sympathy, the other two brothers were unapproachable. Gilian found her in a little rain of tears. She started with shame at his discovery, and set herself to a noisy handling of dinner dishes that by this time he knew well enough were not in her daily office of industry. And she said never a word—she that never heard his foot upon the stair without a smile of pleasure, or saw his face at the door without a mother's challenge to his appetite.

"What is wrong, auntie?" he said in the Gaelic, using the term it had been agreed would best suit the new relationship.

"Just nothing at all, my dear," she said without looking round. "What would be wrong?"

"But you are crying," protested Gilian, alarmed lest he in some way should have been the cause of her distress.

"Am I?" said Miss Mary. "And if I am, it is just for a silly thing only a woman would mind, a slight from people not worth heeding." And then she told, still shamefacedly, her story.

Gilian was amazed.

"I did not think you cared for suppers and teas," he said. "The last time you went to the Sheriff's you said you would far sooner be at home, and—"

"Did I?" said she. Then she smiled to find someone who knew it was not the outing she immediately prized. "Indeed, what you say is true, Gilian. I'm an old done dame, and it was wiser for the like of me to be sitting knitting at the fire than going on diverts to their bohea parties and clashing supper tables. But it's not myself I'm angry for. Oh, no! they might leave me alone for ever and a day and I would care not a pin-head, but it's Dugald I'm thinking of—a Major-General—one of the only three in the shire, and Colin—a Cornal—and both of Keils. The Sheriff's lady might leave me out of her routs if she pleasured it, but she has no cause to put my brothers to an insult like this." She said "my brothers" with a high hard sound of stern and proud possession that was very fine to hear. Even Gilian, as yet only beginning to know the love and pride of this little woman, had, at her accent, a sudden deep revealing of her devoted heart.

"It is the Turners' doing," she said, feverishly rubbing a warming pan whose carved lid from Zaandam blinked and gleamed like the shining face of a Dutch skipper over his dram. "I know them; because my brother must be quarrelling with them, their half-sister must be taking up the quarrel and shutting her door in our faces."

"The Turners! Then I hate them too," cried Gilian, won to the Paymaster's side by the sorrow of Miss Mary.

"Oh, you must not say that, my dear," she cried, appalled. "It is not your affair at all, and the Turners are not to blame because the Sheriff is under the thumb of his madam. The Turners have their good points as well as the rest of us, and—"

"They have a daughter," said Gilian, almost unconsciously, for there had come flooding into his mind a vision of the sombre vessel's cabin, shot over by a ray of sunshine, wherein a fairy sang of love and wandering. And then he regretted he had spoke of hate for any of her name, for surely (he thought) there should be no hate in the world for any that had her blood and shared her home. Surely in her people, knowing her so warm, so lovely, so kind, so gifted, there could be no cruelty and wrong.

"I would not say I hated anyone if I were you, my dear," said Miss Mary; "but I would keep a cool side to the Turners, father, or daughter, or son. Their daughter that you speak of was the cause of this new quarrel. The Captain miscalled her to her father, which was not right, for indeed she's a bonny lassie, and they tell me she sings—"

"Like the mavis," cried Gilian, still in his Gaelic and in a transport of recollection.

"Where did you hear her?" asked Miss Mary.

Gilian, flushed and uneasy, told her of the performance in the ship. Finding a listener neither inattentive nor without sympathy, he went further still and told of the song's effect upon him, and that the sweetness of it still abiding made his hatred of her people impossible.

"She'll do for looks too," said Miss Mary. "She takes them with her singing from her mother, who was my dear companion before this trouble rose."

"Oh! she looks like—like—like the *gruagach* girl in the story," said Gilian, remembering the tale of the sea-maiden who sat on the shore and dressed her hair with a comb of gold.

"I hope she's not so uncanny," said Miss Mary with a laugh, "for the *gruagach* combed till a sweetheart came (that I should be talking of such daft-like things!), and he was drowned and that was the end of him."

"Still—still," said Gilian, "the *gruagach* was worth the drowning for."

Miss Mary looked at him with a sigh for a spirit so much to be envied.

"This may be but a chapter in a very old tale," said she. "It was with a lass the feud came in." A saying full of mystery to the boy. Then she changed the conversation back to her own affairs. "We'll take a walk out in the gloaming and see all the Sheriff's friends," said she, "and all the Sheriff's friends in this supper are Turner's friends and the Paymaster's enemies."

The night of the Sheriff's supper party came with heavy showers and a sky swept by clouds that let through glimpse of moon nor star. The town lay in pitch darkness, all silent except for the plash of the sea upon the shore or its long roll on the Ramparts. A deserted and windswept street, its white walls streaming with waters, its outer shutters on the ground flats barred to darkness, its gutters running over—it was the last night on which anyone with finery and a notion for comfort would choose for going abroad to parties. Miss Mary, sitting high at her parlour window with Gilian, looked out through the blurred pane with satisfaction upon all this inclemency.

"Faith," said she, "I wish them joy of their party whoever they be that share it!" Then all at once her mood changed to one of pity as the solitary street showed a moving light upon its footway. "Oh!" she cried. "There's Donacha Breck's lantern and his wife will be with him. And today she was at me for my jelly for a cold! I wish—I wish she was not over the door this night; it will be the death of her. Tomorrow I must send her over the last of my Ladyfield honey."

From the window and in the darkness of the night, it was impossible to tell who were for the Sheriff's party, so Miss Mary in the excess of her curiosity must be out after a time and into the dripping darkness, with Gilian by her side for companionship. It was an adventure altogether to his liking. As he walked up and down the street on its darker side he could think upon the things that were happening behind the drawn blinds and bolted shutters. It was as if he was the single tenant of a sleeping star and guessing at the mysteries of a universe. Stories were happening behind the walls, fires were glimmering, suppers were set, each family for the time being was in a world of its own, split off from its neighbours by the darkness.

A few shops lay open, throwing faint radiance on the footpath that swam in water.

Miss Mary went to the window of two sisters who made caps on the Lady Charlotte model and mantuas inspired by a visit to Edinburgh five years ago. She scanned the contents of the window carefully.

"It's gone; I knew it would be gone," she said in a whisper to Gilian, withdrawing hastily from the revelation of the window as a footstep sounded a little way down the street.

He awaited her explanation, not greatly interested, for the blank expanse of the moaning sea round the corner of a tall tenement filled him with new and moving emotions.

"There has been a cap there for a week with lilac trimmings for Rixa's sister, and now it has gone. It was there this morning, and I saw her lassie going by with a bandbox in the middle of the day. That's two pair at least for the Sheriff's party."

"Would it not be easier tomorrow to ask someone who were all there?" said Gilian.

She shook his arm with startled affright.

"Ask! ask!" she exclaimed. "If you dared let on to anyone we even heard there was a party, I would—I would—be terribly vexed. No, Gilian, we must hold our heads a bit higher than that."

She passed with the boy from tenement to tenement.

"Major Hall and his sister are there," she said, showing darkened windows. "And the Camerons and the Frasers," she added later, informed by the same signs of absence.

Out came the late merchants and shuttered their little windows and bolted up their doors, then retreated to their homes behind. More dark than ever became the world, though the rain had ceased. Only a few windows shone wanly in the upper flats and garrets. The wind moaning in the through-going closes expressed a sense of desolation.

And yet the town was not all asleep but for the Sheriff's party and Miss Mary and the Paymaster's boy, for there came from the Abercrombie, though the door was shut discreetly, a muffled sound of carousal. It was not, this time, the old half-pay officers but a lower plane of the burgh's manhood, the salvage and the wreckage of the wars, privatemen and sergeants, by a period of strife and travel made in some degree unfit for the tame ways of peace in a stagnant burgh. They told the old tales of the bivouac; they sang its naughty or swaggering songs. By a plain deal door and some glasses of spirit they removed themselves from the dull town drowsing in the night, and in the light of the Sergeant More's cruisie moved again in the sacked towns of Ciudad Rodrigo, Badajos and San Sebastian, gorged anew, perhaps, with blood and lust.

Miss Mary and Gilian passed the door of the Sergeant More hurriedly, she deaf to its carousal, he remembering all at once and finding wake anew his first feelings when he stood in the same room before the half-pay officers at their midday drams. He had become a little tired of this quest all to gratify an old maid's curiosity, he wished he could be home again and in his attic room with his candle and his story book, or his abundant and lively thoughts. But there was one other task before Miss Mary. She could not forbear so little as a glance at the exterior of the Sheriff's dwelling where the enemies of her home (as so she now must fancy them) were trying to be happy without the company of the Campbells of Keils. When they were in front of it every window shone across the grass-plot, some of them open so that the sound of gaiety came clearly to the woman and the boy. Miss Mary stood woebegone, suffused in tears.

"And there are my dear brothers at home yonder, their lee-lone, silent, sitting in a parlour! Oh! it is shameful, it is shameful! And all for a hasty word about a lass!"

Gilian before this curious sorrow was dumb. Silently he tried to lead the little lady away from the place, but she would not go, and would not be comforted. Then there came from the open windows the beginning of a song. At the first note Gilian thrilled in every nerve.

"Fancy that now!" said Miss Mary, checking her tears. "No more than a wean and here she must be singing at supper parties as brave as the mother before her. It's a scandal! And it shows the bitterness of the quarrel to have her here, for she was never here at supper before."

"But is she not fine?" said Gilian, with a passion in his utterance.

Nan it was, singing a Scots song, a song of sad and familiar mood, a song of old loves, old summers, and into the darkness it came with a sweetness almost magic.

"Is she not fine?" he said again, clutching with eager hands at the rail and leaning over as far as he could to lose no single note of that alluring melody.

"Oh, the dear! the dear!" sobbed Miss Mary, moved to her inmost by the strain. "When I heard her first I thought it was her mother, and that too was her favourite song! Oh, the dear! the dear! And I to be the sinful woman here on any quarrel for her!"

The song ceased, a window noisily closed, and Gilian fell back with a shock upon a wet world with roads full of mire and a salt wind from the sea moaning in the trees behind the town.

"What—what—what are we here for?" said he, beholding for the first time the impropriety of this eavesdropping on the part of so genteel and sensitive a dame.

She blushed in the dark with the shame the query roused. She had thought him too young to understand the outrage this must be on her every sense of Highland decency, and yet he could reprove her in a single sentence!

"You may well ask," she said, moving away from that alluring house-front with its inmates so indifferent to the passions in the dark without. And her sobs were not yet finished. "Because I prize my brothers," said she, "and grieve at any slight upon them, must I be spy upon my dead companion's child?" She hurried her pace away from that house whose windows stared in a dumb censure upon her humiliation. Gilian trudged reluctantly at her side, confounded, but she seemed almost unconscious that he was there, till he tugged with a shy sympathy at her gown. Then she looked and beamed upon him with the mother-face.

"Do you like that girl?" said she.

"I like her—when she sings," said he.

"Oh! it was always that," she went on helplessly. "My poor brothers! They were not to blame, and she was not to blame, at least, not very much perhaps; if blame there was, it lay with the providence that brought them together." Then she stopped a moment with a pitiful exclamation: "Oh! I was the instrument of providence in their case; but for me, that loved them all, it might never have been. What am I doing here with you? She may have her mother's nature as well as her mother's songs."

For once Gilian found himself with many pieces of a tale he could not put together, for all his ingenuity. He said nothing, but fumbled in many trials at the pieces as he and the little lady walked up the street, now deserted but for themselves and a man's footsteps sounding on the flags. The man was on them before Miss Mary realised his coming. It was Mr Spencer of the

New Inn. He stopped with a salutation, coming upon them, as it happened, in the light of the oil-lamp at the Cross well, and a discreet surprise was in his visage.

"It is an inclement evening, Miss Campbell," he said, in a shrill high dainty accent that made him seem a foreigner when in converse among the guttural Highland burghers.

She answered in some confusion, and by this time he had found a reason for her late hour abroad in the wet deserted street.

"You have left the Sheriff's early tonight," said he. "I was asked, but I find myself something of the awkward stranger from the big world when I come into the kind and homely gatherings of the clans here."

"I think we are not altogether out of the big world you speak of," said Miss Mary in a chilly tone. "The mantua-maker tells me the latest fashions are here from London sooner than they are in Edinburgh." She saw in his face the innkeeper's apology for his common sin against the Gaelic vanity. "We were just out for an airing," she added, taking Gilian's hand in hers and squeezing it with meaning.

"I thought, ma'am, you were at the Sheriff's," said Mr Spencer.

"Oh, there is a party in the Sheriff's, is there?" she said. "That is very nice; they have a hospitable house and many friends. I must hurry home to my brothers, who, like all old gentlemen, are a little troublesome and care neither to move out at night, nor to let me leave them to go out myself."

She smiled up in his face with just a hint of a little coquette that died in her twenty years before. She said "Good-night," and then she was gone.

Mr Spencer's footsteps sounded more slowly on the flagstone as he resumed his accustomed evening walk, in which for once his mind was not on London town, and old friends there, but upon the odd thing that while this old maid had smiled upon him, there was a tear very plain upon her cheek.

IX

ACADEMIA

IN the fullness of time, Gilian attained to the highest class in old Brooks' school, pushed up thereto by no honest application of his own, but by the luck that attends on such as have God's gift to begin with. And now that he was among the children of the town he found them lovable, but yet no more lovable than the children of the glen. The magic he had fancied theirs as he surveyed them from a distance, the fascination they had before, even when they had mocked with cries of "Crotal-coat, Crotal-coat," did not very bravely stand a close trial. He was not dismayed at this; he did as we must all be doing through life and changed one illusion for another. It is a wonderful rich world for dreams, and he had a different one every day, as he sat in the peaty odour of instruction.

Old Brooks would perch high on his three-legged stool conning over some exercise while his scholars in their rows behind the knife-hewn inky desks hummed like bees upon their tasks. The hornbooks of the little ones at the bottom of the room would sometimes fall from their hands in the languor of that stagnant atmosphere, but the boys of the upper forms were ever awake for mischief. To the teaching of the dominie they would come with pockets full of playthings, sometimes animals from the woods and fields about the town—frogs, moles, hedgehogs, or fledgeling birds. Brooks rarely suspected the presence of these distractions in his sacred grove, for he was dull of vision and preferred to see his scholars about him in a vague mist rather than wear in their presence the great horn spectacles that were privy to his room in Crombie's Land. The town's clock staring frankly in at the school windows conveyed to him no knowledge of the passing enemy, and, as his watch had been for a generation but a bulge upon his vest, he must wait till the hour struck ere he knew it was meridian and time to cross the playground and into Kate Bell's for his glass of waters. "Silence till I return!" he would say, whipping on his better coat and making for the door that had no sooner shut on him than tumult reigned.

On his way back from the tavern he would meet, perhaps, the Paymaster making for the house of the Sergeant More. "I cannot understood," would the Paymaster say, "what makes you take your drams in so common a civilian house as that. A man and a soldier keeps the Abercrombie, a fellow who fought for his country. And look at the company! MacNicol and Major Hall—and—and—myself, and some of the best in the burgh; yet you must be frequenting a low tavern with only merchants and mechanics and fisherman to say 'Good health' to."

Master Brooks had always his answer very pat.

"I get a great abundance of old war tales in my books," he would say dryly. "And told with a greater ingenuity—not to mention veracity—than pertain to the legends and histories of you old campaigners. Between ourselves, I'm not for war at all, but for the far finer and more wholesome rarity called peace. Captain, Captain!" (and here would he grasp the Paymaster by the coat lapels with the friendly freedom of an old acquaintance) "Captain, Captain! it is not a world for war though we are the fools to be fancying so, but a world for good-fellowship, so short the period we have of it, so wonderful the mind of them about us, so kind with all their faults! I find more of the natural human in the back room of Kate's there where the merchants discourse upon their bales and accompts than I would among your half-pay gentry who would have the country knee-deep in blood every day in the calendar if they had their way of it."

"It's aye the old story with you," the Paymaster would say tolerantly. "You cannot see that if this country has not its wars and rumours of wars, its marchings-off and weedings-out, it would die of a rot. I hope you are not putting too many notions of that clerkly kind in the boy's head. Eh? I would be vexed to have my plans for him spoiled and a possible good soldier turned into a swindling writer."

"The boy's made, Captain Campbell," said the schoolmaster one day at this. "He was made and his end appointed ere ever he came to your house or felt my ferule-end. He is of the dream nature and he will be what he will be. I can no more fashion him to the common standard than I can make the fir-tree like unto the juniper. I've had many a curious student yonder, wild and tame, dunce and genius, but this one baffles me. He was a while up in the glen school, they tell me, and he learned there such rudiments as he has, but what he knows best was never learned anywhere but as the tinkler learns—by the roadside and in the wood."

"I know he's a droll one," said the Paymaster, uneasily, with a thoughtful brow, "but you have the reputation, Mr Brooks, you have turned out lads who were a credit to you. If it is not in him, thwack it in with your tawse."

The dominie flushed a little. He never cared to have the tawse mentioned; it was an ally he felt ashamed of in his fight with ignorance and he used it rarely, though custom and the natural perverseness of youth made its presence necessary in his desk.

"Captain Campbell," said he, "it is not the tawse that ever put wisdom into a head like yon. The boy is unco, the boy is a *lusus naturae*, that is all; as sharp as a needle when his interest is aroused, as absent as an idiot when it is not, and then no tawse or ferule will avail."

And while the Paymaster and the dominie were thus discussing Gilian, the school would be in a tumult whereof he was sometimes the leader. To him the restraints were galling shackles. When the classes would be humming in the drowsy afternoon and the sharp high voice of old Brooks rose above the murmur as he taught some little class in the upper corner, the boy would be gazing with vacant eyes at the whitewashed wall in front of him, or looking out at the beech branches that tapped in faint breezes at the back windows, or listening with an ecstatic ear to the crisp contact of stone and scythe as the mowers in the fields behind put a new edge on their instruments. Oh! the outer world was ever the world of charm for him, winter or summer, as he sat in that constrained and humming school. That sound of scythes a-sharping was more pleasing to his ear than the poetry Mr Brooks imposed upon his scholars, showing, himself, how to read it with a fierce high limping accent as if it were a thing offensive. When hail or rain rattled on the branches, when snow in great flakes settled down or droves of cattle for distant markets went bellowing through the street, it was with difficulty the boy kept himself to his seat and did not rise and run out where his fancy so peremptorily called.

If he learned from books at all, it was from the wonderful, dusty, mildewed volumes that Marget Maclean had on her shelves behind the post office. She was one of three sisters and they were all so much alike that Gilian, with many other boys, never learned to know one from the other, so it was ever Marget who was behind the counter, a thin old lady of carefully nurtured gentility, with cheeks like a winter apple for hue, with eyebrows arching high in a perpetual surprise at so hurried and ridiculous a world, and a curled brown wig that was suspected of doing duty for the three sisters who were never seen but one at a time. Marget Maclean's little shop was the dullest in the street, but it was the anteroom of fairydom for Gilian who borrowed books there with the pence cozened from Miss Mary. In the choosing of them he had no voice. He had but to pay his penny and Marget would peer through her glasses at the short rows of volumes until she came upon the book she thought most suited for her customer.

"You will find that a good one," she would say. "The one you mention is not at all good; it was very fashionable last spring, but it is not asked for now at all." And in proof that the volume she recommended was quite genteel, she would add: "That one was up at the Castle last Saturday. Lady Charlotte's maid, you will notice, wet all the pages crying over the places where the lover went to sea another voyage. It is a very clever book, my dear, and I think there is a moral, I do not remember what the moral is, but I know there is one or else I would not recommend it. It is in large black type you see, and there is a great deal of speaking in parlours in it, which is always informing and nice in a book."

"You have none of Mr Scott's poetry?" asked Gilian one day, moved thereto by an extract read by Brooks to his scholars.

"Scott, Scott," said Miss Marget. "Now let me think, my dear."

She turned her odd thin figure and her borrowed curls bobbed behind her ears as she tilted up her head and glanced along the shelves for what she knew was not there.

"No, my boy," she said. "We have none of Mr Scott's works at present. There is a demand among some people for Mr Scott I believe, but," here she frowned slightly, "I do not think you are old enough for poetry. It is too romantic, and—it lingers in the memory. I have not read him myself though I hear he is clever—in a way. I would not say that I object to Mr Scott, but I do not recommend him to my young customers."

So off Gilian would go with his book under his arm to the Ramparts. The Ramparts were about the old Tolbooth and kept crime within and the sea without. Up would the tide come in certain weathers thrashing on the granite cubes, beating as it might be for freedom to the misunderstood within, beating and hissing and falling back and dashing in again and streaming out between the joints of masonry in briny jets. Halfway up the Ramparts was a foot-wide ledge, and here the boy would walk round the bastions and in the square face to the sea would sit upon the ledge with his legs dangling over the water and read his volume. It might be the *Mysteries of Udolpho*, *Thaddeus of Warsaw*, *Moll Flanders*, or *Belinda*, the story of one Random, a wandering vagabond, or Crusoe, but no matter where the story led, the boy whose feet dangled over the sea was there. And long though the tale might be Gilian pieced it out in fancy by many pages. His situation on the Ramparts was an aid to his imagination, for as he sat there the sea would be sluggishly rolling below or beating in petulant waves and he floated, as it were, between sea and sky, as free from earth's clogging influence as the gannet that soared above.

He sought the Ramparts because for a boy of his age to read in books, except as a task of the school, was something shameful; and he had been long accustomed to the mid-air trip upon the walls ere some other boys discovered him guilty, flushing and trembling with a story book in his hand. They looked with astonishment at their discovery and were prepared to jeer when his wits came to his rescue. He tore out one or two leaves of the book, twisted them into a rough semblance of a boat and cast them in the water.

"Watch," said he, "you'll see the big ones are sunk sooner than the little ones."

"Do not tear the good book," said one of the boys, Young Islay, shocked, or pretending to be so, at the destruction.

"Oh! it's only a stupid story," said Gilian, tearing again at the treasure, with an agony that could have been no greater had it been his heart. He had to forego many books from Marget Maclean to make up for this one, but at least he had escaped the irony of his companions.

Yet not books were his first lovers and friends and teachers, so much as the creatures of the wild, and the aspects of nature. Often the dominie missed him from his accustomed place at the foot of the class, and there was no explanation to offer when he returned. He had suffered again the wood's fascination. In the upper part of the glen he had been content with little clumps and plantings, the caldine woods of Kincreggan or the hazels whereof the shepherds made their crooks. But the forest lay for miles behind the town, a great land of shade and pillars where the winds roved and tangled. It abounded in wild life, and sounded ever in spring and summer with songs and cries. Into its glades he would wander and stand delirious to the solitude, tingling to the wild. The dim vistas about him had no affrights; he was at home, he was the child of the tranquil, the loving mother, whose lap is the pasture-land and forest. Autumn fills those woods with the very breath of melancholy, no birds will sing in the multitudinous cloisters except the birds of the night whose melody is one doleful and mocking note. The bracken burns and withers, lush grass rots and whitens above the fir-roots, the birds flit from shade to shade with no carolling. And over all will stand the trees sleeping with their heads a-nod.

He would walk among the noisy fallen leaves, posturing the heroes of his reading or his own imagination about him in the landscape—a pleasant recreation. He would set Bruce the King himself sitting at a cave-mouth, a young gentleman with a queue like Turner's, pondering upon freedom, while the spiders wrought for his instruction; deer breaking from covert to dash away, or moving in stately herds across the forest openings, became a foreign cavalry. Sometimes he would take a book to the upper hunting-roads, where rarely any intrusion came except from some gillie or fisher of the lochs far back in the moors, and stretched on dry bracken he would read and dream for hours.

It was in such an attitude Young Islay found him on the Saturday after the episode on the Ramparts. Gilian was in the midst of the same book, trying hard to fill up the gaps that his sacrifice of leaves had brought into the narrative, and Young Islay going a-fishing in the moor-lochs, a keen sportsman all alone, stood over him a very much surprised discoverer.

He gave an halloo that brought Gilian to his feet alarmed, for it happened to fit in with some passage in his mind where foes cried. In vain the book went behind the Paymaster's boy; Islay saw the ragged pages.

"Oh!" he cried, "you'll not cheat me this time; you're reading." An annoying contempt was in his manner, and as he stood with his basket slung upon his back, and his rod in the crook of an arm, like a gun, a straight, sturdy lad of neat limb, a handsome face, and short black curls, he was, for a moment, more admirable in Gilian's eyes than the hero of the book he was ashamed to show.

"I had it in my pocket," said Gilian, in a poor, ineffective explanation, relinquishing the volume with a grudge to the examination of this cynic.

"You pretended on the Ramparts you were tearing it up like any other boy," said Young Islay, "and I was sure you were doing nothing of the kind." He turned over the pages with scornful fingers. "It's not a school-book, there's not a picture in it, it's full of talking—fancy being here with that rubbish, when you might be fishing with me!"

Gilian snatched the volume from him. "You don't know anything about it!" he cried.

"I know you at any rate!" said Young Islay craftily. "You were ashamed of your book; you come here often with books; you do nothing like anybody else; you should have been a girl!"

All the resentment of the Paymaster's boy sprung to his head at this taunt; he threw the book down and dashed a small fist in Young Islay's face. There he found a youth not slow to reply. Down went the rod and the book, and with the fishing-basket swinging and beating at his back, Young Islay fell upon the zealous student. Gilian's arms, as he defended or aimed futile blows, felt, in a little, as heavy as lead. Between each blow he aimed there seemed to be a great space of time, and yet his enemy was striking with rapidity.

"Are you beaten?" at last cried Young Islay, drawing back for a truce.

"No," said Gilian, gasping. "I'm only tired," but he looked bloody and vanquished.

"It's the same thing," said Young Islay, picking up his rod. "You can do nothing with your hands; I—I can do anything." And he drew up with a bantam's vanity. He moved off. The torn book was in his path. He kicked it before him like a football until he reached the ditch beside the hunting road, and there he left it. A little later Gilian saw him in a distant vista of the trees as an old hunter of the wood, with a gun in his hand and his spoil upon his back, breasting the brae with long strides, a figure of achievement altogether admirable.

X

ON HIS MAJESTY'S SERVICE

MARGET MACLEAN (or one of her sisters) was accustomed
when the mails contained a letter on His Majesty's Service
for the Paymaster, to put on a bonnet, and in a mild flurry cross
the street, feeling herself a sharer in the great matters of State.
So important was the mission that she had been known even to
shut her shop door for the time of her absence upon eager and
numerous youths waiting the purchase of her superior "black
man", a comfit more succulent with her than with Jenny
Anderson in Crombie's Land, or on older patrons seeking the
hire of the new sensation in literature—something with a tomb
by Mrs Radcliffe.

"Tell your mistress I wish to see her," she would say on these
occasions with great pomp to Peggy, but even Miss Mary was
not sufficiently close to State to be entrusted with the missive.

"Good day, Miss Campbell! I called to see Captain John on
important business," and the blue document with its legend and
seal would be clutched with mittened hands tight to the faded
bodice.

Miss Mary shared some of this awe for State documents; at
least she helped out the illusion that they were worth all this
anxiety on the part of the post office, and she would call the
Paymaster from his breakfast. His part on the other hand was to

depreciate their importance. He would take the most weighty and portentous with an air of contempt.

"What's this, Miss Maclean?" he would say impatiently with the snuff-pinch suspended between his pocket and his nose. "A king's letter. Confound the man! what can he be wanting now?" Then with a careless forefinger he would break the seal and turn the paper outside in, heedless (to all appearance) as if it were an old copy of the *Courier*.

One day such a letter sent his face flaming as he returned to the breakfast table. He looked at Miss Mary, sitting subdued behind her urn and Gilian at her side, and then at his brothers, hardly yet awake in the early morning, whose breakfasts in that small-windowed room it needed two or three candles to illuminate.

"The county corps is coming south this way," said he, with a great restraint upon his feelings.

Cornal Colin turned on him a lustreless eye.

"What havers are you on now, John?" said he, with no pause in the supping of his porridge. Dugald paid no heed. With a hand a little palsied he buttered a scone, and his lower lip was dropped and his eyes were vacant, showing him far absent in the spirit. Conversation was never very rife at the Paymaster's breakfast table.

"I'm telling you the county corps is coming south," said Mars, with what for him to the field officer was almost testiness. "Here's a command for billeting three hundred men on Friday night on their way to Dumbarton."

Up stood the Cornal with a face transfigured. He stretched across the table and almost rudely clutched the paper from his brother's hand, cast a fast glance at the contents and superscription, then sat again and gave a little choked cheer, the hurrah of spent youth and joyfulness.

"Curse me! but it's true," he cried to the General. "The old 91st under Crawford—Jiggy Crawford we called him for his dance in the ken at Madrid before he exchanged—Friday, Friday; where's my uniform, Mary? They'll be raw recruits, I'll warrant, not the old stuff, but—are you hearing, Dugald? Oh! the army, the army! Let me see—yes, it says six pipers and thirty band. My medals, Mary, are they in the shottle of my kist yet? The 91st— God! I wish it was our own; would I not show them! You are not hearing a word I am saying, Dugald."

He paused in a feverish movement in his chair, thrust off from him with a clatter of dishes and a spilling of milk the breakfast still unfinished, and stared with annoyance at the General. Dugald picked at his fish with no appetite, seeing nothing, hearing nothing, a silent old man palsied on one side, with a high bald head full of visions. "What's that about the Argylls?" he said at last, with a start, brought to by the tone and accent of his brother.

Cornal Colin cleared his throat, and read the notification of the billet.

"Friday, did you say Friday?" asked Dugald, all abstraction gone.

"This very Friday."

The old man rose and threw back his shoulders with some of the gallantry of his prime. He walked without a word to the window and looked at the deserted street. Ten—fifteen—twenty years fell from his back as thus he stood in the mingled light of the wan reluctant morning and the guttering candles on the table. To Miss Mary, looking at him there against the morning light, his figure—black and indefinite—was the figure that went to Spain, the strong figure, the straight figure, the figure that filled its clothes with manliness. There was but the oval of the bald high head to spoil the illusion. He turned again and looked into the candle-lit room, but seeing nothing there, for all his mind was elsewhere.

"I thought," he muttered, brokenly, "I thought I would never see red-coat again." Then he straightened his shoulders anew, and flexed the sinews of his knees, and pressed the palsied hand against the breeches' seam. The exertion brought a cough to his throat, a choking resistless cough of age and clogging humours. It was Time's mocking reminder that the morning parade was over for ever, and now the soldier must be at ease. He gasped and spluttered, his figure lost its tenseness, and from the fit of coughing he came back again an old and feeble man. He looked at his hand trembling against his waist, at his feet in their large and clumsy slippers; he looked at the picture of himself upon the wall, then quitted the room with something like a sob upon his lip.

"Man! he's in a droll key about it!" said the Paymaster, breaking the silence. "What in all the world is his vexation?"

Miss Mary put down her handkerchief impatiently and loaded Gilian at her side with embarrassing attentions.

"What—in—all—the—world—is—his vexation?" mocked the Cornal in the Captain's high and squeaking voice, reddening at the face and his scar purpling. "That's a terribly stupid question to put, Jock. What—in—all—the—world—is—his—vexation? If you had the soger's heart and your brother's past you would not be asking what an ancient's sorrow at his own lost strength might mean. Oh, man, man! make a pretence at spirit even if the Almighty denied it to you!"

He tossed the letter from him, almost in his brother's face.

The Paymaster held his anger in leash. He was incapable of comprehending and he was, too, afraid. With a forced laugh, he pressed the creases from the document.

"Oh, I'm glad enough to see the corps," said he, "if that's what you mean. If I have not your honours from the army, I'm as fond of Geordie's uniform as any man of my years. I'll get the best billets in the town for—"

The Cornal scowled and interjected, "Ay, ay, and you'll make all the fraca that need be about the lads, and cock your hat to the fife, and march and act the veteran as if you were Moore himself, but you'll be far away from knowing what of their pomp and youth is stirring the hearts of your brother Dugald and me. The army is all bye for us, Jock, Boney's by the heels; there's younger men upon the roster if the foreign route is called again in the barrack yard."

His glance fell upon Gilian, wide-eyed, wonderful, in the shade beside Miss Mary's chair, and he turned to him with a different accent.

"There *you* are!" said he, "my wan-faced warlock. What would Colin Campbell, Commander of the Bath, not give to be your age again and all the world before him? Do you say your prayers at night, laddie, before you go to your naked bed in the garret? I'll warrant Mary taught you that if she taught you nothing else. Pray every night then that heaven may give you thew and heart and a touch of the old Hielan' glory that this mechanic body by my side has got through the world wanting. Oh, laddie, laddie, what a chance is yours! To hear the drum in the morning and see the sun glint on the line; to sail away and march with pipe or bugle in foreign countries; to have a thousand good companions round about the same camp-fires and know the lift and splendour of parades in captured towns. It's all bye for me; I'm an old pensioner rotting to the tomb in a landward burgh packed with relics like myself, and as God's in heaven, I often wish I was with brother Jamie yonder fallen in my prime with a clod stopping the youth and spirit in my throat."

"Tut, tut, now we're in our flights!" said the Paymaster, not very audibly, so that in his transport the Cornal never heard.

"*Are* you for the army?" asked the Cornal, like a recruiting sergeant bringing the question home to a lad at a country fair; and he fixed Gilian with an eye there was no baffling.

"I would—I would like it fine," said Gilian stammering, "if it was all like that."

"Like what?" asked the Cornal, subdued, and a hand behind his ear to listen.

"Like that—" repeated the boy, trembling though Miss Mary's fingers were on his. "All the morning time, all with trumpets and the same friends about the camp-fire. Always the life inside and the notion to go on and on and—"

He stopped for want of English words to tell the sentiment completely.

The Cornal looked at him now wistfully.

"I would not say, Gilian," said he, "but what there might be the makings of a soger in you yet. If you have not the sinews for it you have the sense. You'll see a swatch on Friday of what I talked about and we'll—Come away this minute, Mary, and look me out my uniform. Jiggy Crawford! Young Jiggy that danced in the booze-house in Madrid! He was Ensign then and now he has his spurs and handles tartan. He is at the very topmost of the thing and I am going down, down, down, out, out, out, like this, and this, and this," and so saying he pinched out the candle flames one by one. The morning swept into the room, no longer with a rival, lighting up this parlour of old people, showing the wrinkles and the grey hairs and the parchment-covered knuckles, and in its midst the Paymaster's boy with a transfigured face and a head full of martial glory.

XI

THE SOUND OF THE DRUM

AND the same spirit, martial, poetic, make-believe, stayed
with Gilian up till the Friday. It was hard indeed to escape
it, for was not the town about him in a ferment of anticipation?
In our sleeping community we know no longer what of zest the
very name of the army had for the people now asleep in the rank
grasses of Kilmalieu. The old war-dogs made more lingering
sederunts in the change-houses, the low taverns in the back lands
sounded with bragging chorus and debate, and in the room of
the Sergeant More the half-pay gentlemen mixed more potently
their midday drams. The burgh ceased its industry, and the Duke,
coming down the street upon his horse, saw most of the people
who should be working for his wages leaning upon the gables
indolent or sitting at the open windows with the tumblers at
their hands, singing naughty songs.

He leaned over, and with his crop rapped upon the factor's
door. Old Islay came out with a quill behind his ear and a finger
to his brow.

"What is wrong in the place today?" asked his Grace with a
flourish of his crop about him to the lounging rascals and the
groups at the tavern doors. "Am I paying good day's wages for
the like of that?"

Islay Campbell bobbed and smirked. "It's the coming of the

army," said he. "The county corps comes tomorrow and your men are all dukes today. They would not do a hand's turn for an emperor."

"Humph!" said Duke George. "I wish I could throw off life's responsibilities so easily. The rogues! the rogues!" he mused, soothing his horse's neck with a fine and kindly hand. "I suppose it's in them, this unrest and liability to uproar under the circumstances. My father—well, well, let them be." His heels turned the horse in a graceful curvet. "I'm saying, Islay," he cried over his shoulder, "have a free cask or two at the Cross in the morning."

But it was in the Paymaster's house that the fullest stress, the most nervous restlessness of anticipation were apparent. The Paymaster's snuff was now in two vest-pockets and even then was insufficient, as he went about the town from morning till night babbling in excited half-sentences of war, and the fields he had never fought in, to men who smiled behind his back. His brothers' slumbers in the silent parlour had been utterly destroyed till "Me-the-day!" Miss Mary had to cry at last when her maid brought back untasted viands, "I wish the army was never to darken our gates, for two daft men up there have never taken a respectable meal since the billet order came. Dugald will be none the better for this."

All this excitement sustained the tremulous feeling at the boy's heart. There must be something after all, he thought, in the soldier's experience that is precious and lasting when those old men could find in a rumour the spark to set the smouldering fire in a blaze. He wondered to see the heavy eyelids of the General open and the pupils fill as he had never seen them do before, to hear a quite new accent, though sometimes a melancholy, in his voice, and behold a distaste to his familiar chair with its stuffed and lazy arms. The Cornal's character suffered a change too. He that had been gruff and indifferent took on a pleasing though awkward geniality. He would jest with Miss Mary till she cried "The man's doited!" though she clearly liked it; to Gilian he began the narration of an unending series of campaign tales.

Listening to those old chronicles, Gilian made himself ever their hero. It was he who took the flag at Fuentes d'Onoro, cutting the Frenchman to the chin; it was he who rode at Busaco and heard the Marshal cry "Well done!"; when the shots were threshing like rain out of a black cloud at Ciudad Rodrigo, and the soldiers were falling to it like ripe grain in thunderplumps, he was in the front with every "whe—e—et" of the bullets at his ear bringing the moment's alarm to his teeth in a checked sucking-in of air. Back to the school he went, a head full of dreams, to sit dumb before his books with unwinking eyes fixed upon the battle-lines upon the page—the unbroken ranks of letters, or upon the blistered and bruised plaster of the wall to see horsemen at the charge and flags flying. Then in the absence of Brooks at the tavern of Kate Bell, Gilian led the school in a charge of cavalry, shouting, commanding, cheering, weeping for the desertion of his men at deadly embrasures till the schoolboys stood back amazed at his reality, and he was left to come to himself with a shiver, alone on the lid of the master's desk in the middle of the floor, utterly ashamed before the vexed but sadly tolerant gaze of the dominie.

Old Brooks took him by the ear, not painfully, when he had scrambled down from the crumbled battlements where his troops had left him.

"At the play-acting again, Master Gilian?" said the dominie a little bitterly, a little humorously. "And what might it be this time?"

"Sogers," said the boy most red and awkward.

"Ay, ay," said Brooks, releasing his ear and turning his face to him with a kind enough hand on his shoulder. "Soldiers is it? And the playground and the play-hour are not enough for a play of that kind. Soldiers! H'm! So the lessons of the gentlemen up-bye are not to be in vain. I thought different, could I be wrong now? And you're going to meet Captain Campbell's most darling wish. Eh? You have begun the trade early, and I could well desire you had a better head for the counts. Give me the mathematician and I will make something of him; give me a boy like yourself,

97

with his head stuffed with feathers and the airs of heaven blowing them about through the lug-holes and—my work's hopeless. Laddie, laddie, go to your task! If you become the soldier you play-act today you'll please the Paymaster; I could scarcely wish for better and—and—I maybe wished for worse."

That night Gilian went to bed in his garret while yet the daylight was abroad and the birds were still chattering in the pear-trees in the garden. He wished the night to pass quickly that the morrow and the soldiers should find him still in his fine anticipation.

He woke in the dark. The house was still. A rumour of the sea came up to his window and a faint wind sighed in the garden. Suddenly, as he lay guessing at the hour and tossing, there sounded something far-off and unusual that must have wakened half the sleeping town. The boy sat up and listened with breath caught and straining ears. No, no, it was nothing; the breeze had gone round; the night was wholly still; what he had heard was but in the fringes of his dream. But stay! there it was again, the throb of a drum far-off in the night. It faded again in veering currents of the wind, then woke more robust and unmistakable. The drums! the drums! the drums! The rumour of the sea was lost, no more the wind sighed in the pears, all the voices of nature were dumb to that throb of war. It came nearer and nearer and still the boy was all in darkness in a house betraying no other waking than his own, quivering to an emotion the most passionate of his life. For with the call of the approaching drums there entered to him all the sentiment of the family of that house, the sentiment of the soldier, the full proclamation of his connection with a thousand years of warrior clans.

The drums, the drums, the drums! Up he got and dressed and silently down the stair and through a sleeping household to the street. He of all that dwelling had heard the drums that to ancient soldiers surely should have been more startling, but the town was in a tumult ere he reached the Cross. The windows flared up in the topmost of the tall lands, and the doors stood open to the street while men and women swept along the causeway. The drums, the drums, the drums! Oh! the terror and the joy of them, the wonder, the alarm, the sweet wild thrill of them for Gilian as he ran bare-legged, bare-headed, to the factor's corner there to stand awaiting the troops now marching on the highway through the wood! There was but a star or two of light in all the grudging sky, and the sea, a beast of blackness, growled and crunched upon the shore. The drums, the drums, the drums! Fronting that monotonous but pregnant music by the drummers of the regiment still unseen, the people of the burgh waited whispering, afraid like the Paymaster's boy to shatter the charm of that delightful terror. Then of a sudden the town roared and shook to a twofold rattle of the skins and the shrill of fifes as the corps from the north, forced by their jocular Colonel to a night march, swept through the arches and wheeled upon the grassy esplanade. Was it a trick of the soldier who in youth had danced in the ken in Madrid that he should thus startle the hosts of his regiment, and that passing through the town, he should for a little make his men move like ghosts, saying no word to any one of the aghast natives, but moving mechanically in the darkness to the rattle of the drums? The drums, the drums, the drums! Gilian stood entranced as they passed, looming large and innumerable in the darkness, unchallenged and uncheered by the bewildered citizens. It was the very entrance he could have chosen. For now they were ghosts, legions of the air in borrowed boots of the earth, shades of some army cut down in swathes and pitted in the fashion of the Cornal's bloodiest stories. And now they were the foreign invader, dumb because they did not know the native language, pitying this doomed community but moving in to strike it at the vitals.

XII

ILLUSION

HE followed them to the square, still with the drums pounding and the fifes shrilling, and now the town was awake in every window. At a word the Colonel on his horse dispelled the illusion. "Halt!" he cried; the drum and fife ceased, the arms grounded, the soldiers clamoured for their billets. Over the hill of Strone the morning paled, out of the gloom the phantom body came, a corps most human, thirsty, hungry, travel-strained.

Gilian ran home and found the household awake but unconscious of the great doings in the town.

"What!" cried the Cornal, when he heard the news. "They came here this morning and this is the first we have of it." He was in a fever of annoyance. "Dugald, Dugald, are you hearing? The army's in the town, it moved in when we were snoring and only the boy heard it. I hope Jiggy Crawford does not make it out a black affront to him that we were not there to welcome him. My uniform, Mary, my uniform, it should be aired and ironed, and here at my hand, and I'll warrant it's never out of the press yet. It was the boy that heard the drums; it was you that heard the drums, Gilian. Curse me, but I believe you'll make a soger yet!"

For the next few days, Gilian felt he must indeed be the soldier the Paymaster would make him, for soldiering was in the air. The red-coats gaily filled the street; parade and exercise, evening dance and the continuous sound of pipe and drum left no room for any other interest in life. Heretofore there was ever for the boy in his visions of the army a background of unable years and a palsied hand, slow decay in a parlour, with every zest and glamour gone. But here in the men who stepped always to melody there was youth, seemingly a singular enjoyment of life, and watching them he was filled with envy.

When the day came that they must go he was inconsolable though he made no complaint. They went in the afternoon by the lowlands road that bends about the upper bay skirting the Duke's flower gardens, and with the Cornal and the Paymaster he went to see them depart, the General left at home in his parlour, unaccountably unwilling to say good-bye. The companies moved in a splendour of sunshine with their arms bedazzling to look upon, their pipers playing "Bundle and Go".

"Look at the young one!" whispered the Cornal in his brother's ear, nudging him to attention. Gilian was walking in step to the corps, his shoulders back, his head erect, a hazel switch shouldered like a musket. But it was the face of him that most compelled attention for it revealed a multitude of emotions. His fancy ran far ahead of the tramping force thudding the dust on the highway. He was now the army's child indeed, stepping round the world to a lilt of the bagpipes, with the *currachd*—the caul of safety—as surely his as it was Black Duncan the seaman's. There were battles in the open, and leaguering of towns, but his was the enchanted corps moving from country to country through victory, and always the same comrades were about the camp-fire at night. Now he was the footman, obedient, marching, marching, marching, all day, while the wayside cottars wondered and admired; now he was the fugleman, set before his company as the example of good and honest and handsome soldiery; now he was Captain—Colonel—General, with a horse between his knees, his easy body swaying in the saddle as he rode among the villages and towns. The friendly people ran (so his fancy continued) to their close-mouths to look upon his regiment passing to the roll and thunder of the drums and the cheery music of the pipes. Long days of march and battle, numerous nights of wearied ease upon the heather, if heather there should be, the applause of citadels, the smile of girls. The smile of girls! It came on him, that, with a rush of blood to his face and a strange tingling at the heart as the one true influence to make the soldier. For what should the soldier wander but to come again home triumphant, and find on the doorstep of his native place the smiling girls?

"Look at him, look at him!" cried the Cornal again with a nudge at his brother's arm. They were walking over the bridge and the pipes still were at their melody. Jiggy Crawford's braid shone like moving torches at his shoulder as the sun smote hot upon his horse and him. The trees upon the left leaned before the breeze to share this glory; far-off the lonely hills, the great and barren hills, were melancholy that they could not touch closer on the grandeur of man. As it were in a story of the shealings, the little ones of the town and wayside houses pattered in the rear of the troops, enchanted, their bare legs stretching to the rhythm of the soldiers' footsteps, the children of hope, the children of illusion and desire, and behind them, sad, weary, everything accomplished, the men who had seen the big wars and had many times marched thus gaily and were now no more capable.

"It is the last we'll ever see of it, John," said the Cornal. "Oh, man, man, if I were young again!" His foot was very heavy and slow as he followed the last he would witness of what had been his pride; his staff, that he tried to carry like a sword, must go down now and then to seek a firmness in the sandy footway. Not for long at a time but in frequent flashes of remembrance he would throw back his shoulders and lift high his head and step out in time to the music.

The Paymaster walked between him and Gilian, a little more robust and youthful, altogether in a different key, a key critical, jealous of the soldier lads that now he could not emulate. They were smart enough, he confessed, but they were not what the

46th had been; Crawford had a good carriage on his horse but—but—he was not—

"Oh, do not haver, Jock," said the Cornal, angrily at last; "do not haver! They are stout lads, good lads enough, like what we were ourselves when first the wars summoned us, and Crawford, as he sits there, might very well be Dugald as I saw him ride about the bend of the road at San Sebastian and look across the sandy bay to see the rock we had to conquer. Let you and me say nothing that is not kind, Colin; have we not had our own day of it with the best? and no doubt when we were at the marching there were ancients on the roadside to swear we were never their equal. They are in there in the grass and bracken where you and I must some day join them and young lads still will be marching out to glory."

"In there among the grass and bracken," thought Gilian, turning a moment to look up the slope that leads to Kilmalieu. The laurel drugged the air with death's odour. "In the grasses and the bracken," said Gilian, singing it to himself as if it were a coronach. Was that indeed the end of it all, of the hope, the lilt, the glory? And then he had a great pity for the dead that in their own time had been on many a march like this. Their tombs are thick in Kilmalieu. It seemed so cruel, so heedless, so taunting thus to march past them with no obeisance or remembrance, that to them, the dead soldiers, all his heart went out, and he hated the quick who marched upon the highway.

But Crawford, like the best that have humour, had pity and pathos too. "Slow march!" he cried to his men, and the pipers played "Lochaber No More".

"He's punctilious in his forms," said the Paymaster, "but it's thoughtful of him too."

"There was never but true *duine uasail* put on the tartan of Argyll," said the Cornal.

The pipes ceased; the drums beat again, echoing from the Sgornach rock and the woody caverns of Blaranbui, Glenshira filled to the lip with rolling thunder, the sea lulled to a whisper on the shore. Gilian and the children were now all that were left to follow the soldiers, for the oldsters had cheered feebly and gone back. And as he walked close up on the rear of the troops, his mind was again on the good fortune of those that from warfare must return. To come home after long years, and go up the street so well acquaint, sitting bravely on his horse, paled in the complexion somewhat from a wound, perhaps with the scar of it as perpetual memorial, and to behold pity and pride in the look of them that saw him! It would be such a day as this, he chose, with the sun upon his braid and the sheen upon his horse's neck. The pipers would play merrily and yet with a melancholy too, and so crowded the causeways by the waiting community that even the windows must be open to their overflowing.

And as thus he walked and dreamed saying no word to any of the chattering bairns about him he was truly the army's child. The Paymaster was right, and generous to choose for him so fine a calling; the Cornal made no error, the soldier's was the life for youth and spirit. He had no objection now to all their plans for his future, the army was his choice.

It was then at the Boshang Gate that leads to Dhuloch, Maam, Kilblaan and all the loveliness of Shira Glen, that even his dreaming eyes found Nan the girl within the gates watching the soldiers pass. Her face was flushed with transport, her little shoes beat time to the tread of the soldiers. They passed with a smile compelled upon their sunburned faces, to see her so sweet, so beautiful, so sensible to their glory. And there was among them an ensign, young, slim, and blue-eyed; he wafted a vagabond kiss as he passed, blowing it from his fingertips as he marched in the rear of his company. She tossed her hair from her temples as the moon throws the cloud apart and beamed brightly and merrily and sent him back his symbol with a daring charm.

Gilian's dream of the army fled. At the sight of Nan behind the Boshang Gate he was startled to recognise that the girls he had thought of as smiling on the soldier's return had all the smile of this one, the nut-brown hair of this one, her glance so fearless and withal so kind and tender. At once the roll of the drums lost its magic for his ear; a caprice of sun behind a fleck of cloud dulled the splendour of the Colonel's braid; Gilian lingered at the gate and let the soldiers go their way.

For a little the girl never looked at him as he stood there with the world (all but her, perhaps) so commonplace and dull after the splendours of his mind. Her eyes were fixed upon the marching soldiers now nearing the Gearron and about her lips played the smile of wonder and pleasure.

At last the drumming ceased as the soldiers entered the wood of Strone, still followed by the children. In the silence that fell so suddenly, the countryside seemed solitary and sad. The great distant melancholy hills were themselves again with no jealousy of the wayside trees dreaming on their feet as they swayed in the lullaby wind. Nan turned with a look yet enraptured and seemed for the first time to know the boy was there on the other side of the gate alone.

"Oh!" she said, with the shudder of a woman's delight in her accent. "I wish I were a soldier."

"It might be good enough to be one," he answered in the same native tongue her feeling had made her choose unconsciously to express itself.

"But this is the worst of it," she said, pitifully; "I am a girl, and Sandy is to be the soldier though he was too lazy to come down the glen today to see them away, and I must stay at home and work at samplers and seams and bake bannocks."

With wanton petulant fingers she pulled the haws from the hedge beside her, and took a strand of her hair between her teeth and bit it in her reverie of wilfulness.

"Perhaps," said Gilian, coming closer, "it is better to be at home and soldiering in your mind instead of marching and fighting." It was a thought that came to him in a flash and must find words, but somehow he felt ashamed when he had uttered them.

"I do not understand you a bit," said Nan, with a puzzled look in her face. "Oh, you mean to pretend to yourself," she added immediately. "That might be good enough for a girl, but surely it would not be good enough for you. You are to be a soldier, my father says, and he laughs as if it were something droll."

"It is not droll at all," said Gilian stammering, very much put out. "There are three old soldiers in our house and—"

"One of them

Captain Mars, Captain Mars,
Who never saw scars!"

said the girl mischievously, familiar with the town's song. "I hope you do not think of being a soldier like Mars. Perhaps that is what my father laughs at when he says the Paymaster is to make you a soldier."

"Oh that!" said Gilian, a little relieved. "I thought you were thinking I would not be man enough for a soldier."

Nan opened the gate and came out to measure herself beside him. "You're a little bigger than I am," said she, somewhat regretfully. "Perhaps you will be big enough for a soldier. But what about that when you think you would sooner stay at home and pretend, than go with the army? Did you see the soldier who kissed his hand to me? The liberty!" And she laughed with odd gaiety as if her mood resented the soldier's freedom.

"He was very thin and little," said Gilian, enviously.

"I thought he was quite big enough," said Nan promptly, "and he was so good-looking!"

"Was he?" asked Gilian gloomily. "Well, he was not like the Cornal or the General. They were real soldiers and have seen tremendous wars."

"I daresay," said Nan, "but no more than my father. I cannot but wonder at you; with the chance to be a soldier like my father or—or the General, being willing to sit at home pretending or play-acting it in school or—"

"I did not say I would prefer it," said the boy; "I only said it could be done."

"I believe you would sooner do it that way than the other," she said, standing back from him, and looking with shrewd scrutiny. "Oh, I don't like the kind of boy you are."

"Except when you are singing, and then you like to have me

listening because I understand," said Gilian, smiling with pleasure at his own astuteness.

She reddened at his discovery and then laughed in some confusion. "You are thinking of the time I sang in the cabin to Black Duncan. You looked so white and curious sitting yonder in the dark, I could have stopped my song and laughed."

"You could not," he answered quite boldly, "because your eyes were—"

"Never mind that," said she abruptly. "I was not speaking of singing or of eyes, but I'm telling you I like men, men, men, the kind of men who do things, brave things, hard things like soldiers. Oh, I wish I was the soldier who kissed his hand to me! What is pretending and thinking? I can do that in a way at home over my sampler or my white seam. But to be commanding, and fighting the enemies of the country, to be good with the sword and the gun and strong with a horse, like my father!"

"I have seen your father," said Gilian. "That is the kind of soldier I would like to be." He said so, generously, with some of the Highland flattery; he said so meaning it, for Turner the bold, the handsome, the adventurer, the man with years of foreign life in mystery, was always the ideal soldier of Brooks' school.

"You are a far nicer boy than I thought you were," said she enjoying the compliment. "Only—only—I think when you can pretend so much to yourself you cannot so well do the things you pretend. You can be soldiering in your mind so like the real thing that you may never go soldiering at all. And of course that would not be the sort of soldier my father is."

A mellowed wail of the bagpipe came from Strone, the last farewell of the departing soldiers; it was but a moment, then was gone. The wind changed from the land, suddenly the odours of the traffics of peace blew familiarly, the scents of gathered hay and the more elusive perfume of yellowing corn. A myriad birds! among them the noisy rooks the blackest and most numerous, sped home. In the bay the skiffs spread out their pinions, the halyards singing in the blocks, the men ye-hoing. For a space the bows rose and fell, lazy, reluctant to be moving in their weary wrestle with the seal then tore into the blue and made a feather of white. Gilian looked at them and saw them the birds of night and sea, the birds of prey, the howlets of the brine, flying large and powerful throughout the under-sky that is salt and swinging and never lit by moon or star. And as the boats followed each other out of the bay, a gallant company, the crews leaned on tiller or on mast and sang their Gaelic *iorrams* that ever have the zest of the oar, the melancholy of the wave.

As it were in a pious surrender to the influence of the hour, he and the girl walked slowly, silently, by the wayside, busy with their own imaginings. They were all alone.

Beyond the Boshang Gate is an entrance to the policies, the parks, the gardens, of the Duke, standing open with a welcome, a trim roadway edged with bush and tree. Into it Nan and Gilian walked, almost heedless, it might seem, of each other's presence, she plucking wild flowers as she went from bush to bush, humming the refrain of the fishers' songs, he with his eyes wide open looking straight before him yet with some vague content to have her there for his companion.

When they spoke again they were in the cloistered wood, the sea hidden by the massive trees.

"I will show you my heron's nest," said Gilian, anxious to add to the riches the ramble would confer on her.

She was delighted. Gilian at school had the reputation of knowing the most wonderful things of the woods, and few were taken into his confidence.

He led her a little from the path to the base of a tall tree with its trunk for many yards up as bare as a pillar.

"There it is," he said, pointing upward to a knot of gathered twigs swaying in the upper branches.

"Oh! is it so high as that?" she cried, with disappointment. "What is the use of showing me that? I cannot see the inside and the birds."

"But there are no birds now," said Gilian; "they are flown long ago. Still I'm sure you can easily fancy them there. I see them quite plainly. There are three eggs, green-blue like the sky

108

up the glen, and now—now there are three grey hairy little birds with tufts on their heads. Do you not see their beaks opening?"

"Of course I don't," said Nan impatiently, straining her eyes for the tree-top. "If they are all flown how can I see them?"

Gilian was disappointed with her. "But you think you see them, you think very hard," he said, "and if you think very hard they will be there quite true."

Nan stamped her foot angrily. "You are daft," said she. "I don't believe you ever saw them yourself."

"I tell you I did," he protested hotly.

"Were you up the tree?" she pressed, looking him through with eyes that then and always wrenched the prosaic truth from him.

He flushed more redly than in his eagerness of showing the nest, his eyes fell, he stammered.

"Well," said he, "I did not climb the tree. What is the good when I know what is there? It is a heron's nest."

"But there might have been no eggs and no birds in it at all," she argued.

"That's just it," said he eagerly. "Lots of boys would be for climbing and finding that out, and think how vexatious it would be after all that trouble! I just made the eggs and the young ones out of my own mind, and that is far better."

At the innocence of the explanation Nan laughed till the woods rang. Her brown hair fell upon her neck and brow, the flowers tumbled at her feet all mingled and beautiful as if summer has been raining on its queen. A bird rose from the thicket, chuck-chucking in alarm, then fled, trailing behind him a golden chain of melody.

XIII

A GHOST

I THINK that in the trees, the dryads, the leaf-haunters invisible, so sad in childlessness, ceased their swinging to look upon the boy and girl so enviable in their innocence and happiness. Gilian kneled and gathered up the flowers. It was, perhaps, more to hide his vexation than from courtesy that he did so, but the act was so unboylike, so deferring in its manner, that it restored to Nan as much of her good humour as her laughter had not brought back with it. As he lifted the flowers and put them together, there seemed to come from the fresh lush stalks of them some essence of the girl whose hands had culled and grasped them, a feeling of her warm palm. And when handing her the re-gathered flowers he felt the actual touch of her fingers, his head for a second swam. He wondered. For in the touch there had been something even more potent and pleasing than in the mother-touch of Miss Mary's hand that day when first he came to the town, the mother-touch that revealed a world not of kindness alone—for that was not new, he had it from the little old woman whose face was like a nut—but of understanding and sympathy.

"Have you any more wonders to show?" said Nan, now all in the humour of adventure.

"Nothing you would care for," he said. "There are lots of places just for thinking at, but—"

"I would rather them to be places to be seeing at," said Nan. Gilian reflected, and "You know the Lady's Linn?" he said. She nodded.

"Well," said he. "Do you know the story of it, and why it is called the Lady's Linn?"

Nan confessed her ignorance; but a story—oh! that was good enough!

"Come to the Linn and I'll show you the place, then," said Gilian, and he led her among the grasses, among the tall commanding brackens, upon the old moss that gave no whisper to the footfall, so that, for the nymphs among the trees, the pair of them might be comrades too, immortal. A few moments brought them to the Linn, a deep pool in the river bend, lying so calm that the blue field of heaven and its wisps of cloud astray like lambs were painted on its surface. Round about, the banks rose steep, magnificent with flowers.

"See," said Gilian, pointing to the reflection at their feet. "Does it not look like a piece of the sky tumbled among the grasses? I sometimes think, to see it like that, that to fall into it would be to tangle with the stars."

Nan only laughed and stooped to lift a stone.

She threw it into the very midst of the pool, and the mirror of the heavens was shattered.

"I never thought I could throw into the sky so far," she said mischievously, pleased as it seemed to spoil the illusion in so sudden and sufficient a manner.

"Oh!" he cried, pained to the quick, "you should not have done that, it will spoil the story."

"What is the story?" she said, sitting and looking down upon the troubled pool.

"You must wait till the water is calm again," said he, seating himself a little below her on the bank, and watching the water-rings subside. Then when the pool had regained its old placidity, with the flecked sky pictured on it, he began his Gaelic story.

"Once upon a time," said he, in the manner of the shealing tales, "there was a lady with eyes like the sea, and hair blowing like the tassel of the fir, and she was a daughter of the King in Knapdale, and she looked upon the world and she was weary. There came a little man to her from the wood and he said, 'Go seven days, three upon water and four upon land, and you will come to a place where the moon's sister swims, and there will be the earl's son and the husband.' The lady travelled seven days, three upon water and four upon land, and she came to the Linn where the sister of the moon was swimming. 'Where is my earl's son that is to be my husband?' she asked: and the moon's sister said he was hunting in the two roads that lie below the river bed. The lady, who was the daughter of the King of Knapdale, shut her eyes that were like the sea, and tied in a cushion above her head her hair that was like the tassel of the fir, and broke the crystal door of dream and reached the two hunting roads in the bed of the river. 'We are two brothers,' said the watchers, standing at the end of the roads, 'and we are the sons of earls.' She thought and thought. 'I am Sir Sleep,' said the younger. 'And will you be true?' said she. 'Almost half the time,' he answered. She thought and thought. 'I am very weary,' she said. 'Then come with me,' said the other, 'I am the Older Brother.' She heard above her the clanging of the door of dream as she went with the Older Brother. And she was happy for evermore."

"Oh, that is a stupid story," said Nan. "It's not a true story at all. You could tell it to me anywhere, and why should we be troubled walking to the Linn?"

"Because this is the Lady's Linn," said Gilian, "and to be telling a story you must be putting a place in it or it will not sound true. And Gillesbeg Aotram who told me the story—"

"Gillesbeg Aotram!" she said in amaze. "He's daft! If I thought it was a daft man's story I had to hear—"

"He's not daft at all," protested Gilian. "He's only different from his neighbours."

"That is being daft," said she. "But it is a very clever tale and you tell it very well. You must tell me more stories. Do you know any more stories? I like soldier stories. My father tells me a great many."

"The Cornal tells me a great many too," said Gilian, "but they are all true, and they do not sound true, and I have to make them all up again in my own mind. But this is not the place for soldier stories; every place has its own kind of story, and this is the place for fairy stories if you care for them."

"I like them well enough," she answered dubiously, "though I like better the stories where people are doing things."

They rose from their seat of illusion beside the Linn where the King of Knapdale's daughter broke the gate of sleep and dream. They walked into the Duke's flower garden. And now the day was done, the sun had gone behind Creag Dubh while they were sitting by the river; a grey-brown dusk wrapped up the country-side. The tall trees that were so numerous outside changed here to shorter darker foreign trees, and yews that never waved in winds, but seemed the ghosts of trees, to thickets profound, with secrets in their recesses. In and out among these unfamiliar growths walked Nan and her companion, their pathway crooking in a maze of newer wonders on either hand. One star peered from the sky, the faint wind of the afternoon had sunk to a hint of mingled and moving odours.

Gilian took the girl's hand, and thus together they went deeper into the garden among the flowers that perfumed the air till it seemed drugged and heavy. They walked and walked in the maze of intersecting roads whose pebbles grated to the foot, and so magic the place, there seemed no end to their journey.

Nan became alarmed. "I wish I had never come," said she. "I want home." And the tears were very close upon her eyes.

"Yes, yes," said Gilian, leading her on through paths he had never seen before. "We will get out in a moment. I know—I think I know, the road. It is this way—no, it is this way—no, I am wrong."

But he did not cease to lead her through the garden. The long unending rows of gay flowers stretching in the haze of evening, the parterres spread in gaudy patches, the rich revelation of moss and grass between the trees and shrubs were wholly new to him; they stirred to thrills of wonder and delight.

"Isn't it fine, fine?" he asked her in a whisper lest the charm should fly.

She answered with a sob he did not hear, so keen his thrall to the enchantment. No sign of human habitation lay around except the gravelled walks; the castle towers were hid, the boat-strewn sea was on their left no more. Only the clumps of trees were there, the mossy grass, the flowers whose beauty and plenteousness mocked the posie in the girl's hands. They walked now silent, expectant every moment of the exit that somehow baffled, and at last they came upon the noble lawn. It stretched from their feet into a remote encroaching eve, no trees beyond visible, no break in all its grey-green flatness edged on either hand by wood. And now the sky had many stars.

Their gravelled path had ceased abruptly; before them the lawn spread like a lake, and they were shy to venture on its surface.

"Let us go on; I must go home, I am far from home," said Nan, in a trepidation, her flowers shed, her eyes moist with tears. And into her voice had come a strain of dependence on the boy, an accent more pleasing than any he had heard in her before.

"We must walk across there," he said, looking at the far-off vague edge; but yet he made no move to meet the wishes of the girl now clinging to his arm.

"Come, come," said she, and pressed him gently at the arm; but yet he stood dubious in the dusk.

"Are you afraid?" she asked, herself whispering, she could not tell why.

He felt his face burn at the reflection; he shook her hand off almost angrily. "Afraid!" said he. "Not I; what makes you think that? Only—only—" His eyes were staring at the lawn.

"Only what?" she whispered again, seeking his side for the comfort of his presence.

"It is stupid," he confessed, shame in his accent, "but they say the fairies dance there, and I think we might be looking for another way."

At the confession, Nan's mood of fear that Gilian had conferred on her was gone. She drew back and laughed with as much heartiness as at his story of the heron's nest. The dusk was all around and they were all alone, lost in a magic garden, but she forgot all in this new revelation of her companion's strange belief. She turned and ran across the lawn, crying as she went, "Follow me, follow me!" and Gilian, all the ecstasy of that lingering moment on the edge of fancy gone, ran after her, feeling himself a child of dream, and her the woman made for action.

A sudden opening in the thicket revealed the shore, the highway, the quay with its bobbing lamps, the town with its upper windows lighted. At the gateway of the garden the Cornal met them. He was close on them in the dusk before he knew them, and seeing Gilian he peered closely in the girl's face.

"Who's this?" said he abruptly.

Gilian hesitated, vaguely fearing to reveal her identity, and Nan shrank back, all her memories of conversation in Maam telling her that here was an enemy.

Again the Cornal bent and looked more closely, lifting her chin up that he might see the better. She flashed a glance of defiance in his scarred old parchment face, and he drew his hand back as if he had been stung.

"Nan! Nan!" cried he, with a curious voice. "What witchery is this?" He was in a tremble. Then he started and laughed bitterly. "Oh no, not Nan!" said he. "Oh no, not Nan!" With the most rueful accent, almost chanting it as if it were a dirge.

"It *is* Nan," said Gilian.

"It is her breathing image," said the old man. "It is Nan, no doubt, but not the Nan I knew."

She turned and sped home by the seaside, without farewell, alarmed at this oddity, and Gilian and the Cornal stood alone, the Cornal looking after her with a wistfulness in his very attitude.

"The same, the same, the very same!" said he to himself, in words the boy could plainly hear. "Her mother to the very defiance of her eye." He clutched Gilian rudely by the shoulder. "What," said he, "were you wandering about with that girl for? Answer me that. They told me you were off after the soldiers, and I came up here hoping it true. It would have been the daft but likeable cantrip I should have forgiven in any boy of mine; it would have shown some sign of a sogerly emprise. And here you are, with a lass wandering! Where were you?"

Gilian explained.

"In the flower garden? Ay! ay! A lassie on the roadside met your fancy more than Geordie's men of war. Thank God, I was never like that! And Turner's daughter above all! If she's like her mother in her heart as she's like her in the face, it might be a bitter notion for your future."

He led the way home, muttering to himself. "Nan! Nan! It gave me the start! It was nearly a stroke for me! The same look about her! She is dead, dead and buried, and in her daughter she defies us still!"

XIV

THE CORNAL'S LOVE STORY

MISS MARY, in great tribulation, was waiting on them at the stair-foot, her face, with all its trouble in dark and throbbing lines, lit up by the lamp above the merchant's door. When she saw her brother coming with Gilian she ran forward on the footway, caught the boy by the hand and drew him in.

"I am very angry, oh, I am terribly angry with you!" she cried. "Do not speak a word to me." She pushed him into a chair and spread thick butter on a scone and thrust it in his hand. "To frighten us like this! The Captain is all over the town for you, and the General has sent men to drag for you about the quay."

Peggy the maid smiled over her mistress's shoulder at the youth. He ate his scone with great complacency, heartened by this token that something of Miss Mary's vexation was assumed. Not perhaps her vexation—for were her eyes not red as with weeping?—but her anger, if she had really been angry.

"You are a perfect heartbreak," she went on.

"The Cornal heard you had run off after the sogers, and—"

"Would that vex you?" asked Gilian.

"It would not vex Colin; he would give his only infant, if he had one, to the army; but I was thinking of you left behind in the march about the loch-head, and lost and starving somewhere about the wood of Dunderave."

"I would not starve in Dunderave so long as the nut and bramble were there," said Gilian, rejoicing in her kindly perturbation. "And I could not be lost anywhere—"

"—Except in the Duke's flower garden, wasting the time with—with—a woman's daughter," said the Cornal, putting his head in at the kitchen door. He frowned upon his sister for her too prompt kindness to the rover, and she hid behind her a cup of new-skimmed cream. "Come upstairs and have a talk with Dugald and me," he went on to the boy.

"Will it not do in the morning?" asked Miss Mary, all shaking, dreading her darling's punishment.

"No," said the Cornal. "Now or never. Oh! you need have no fears that I would put him to the triangle."

"Then I may go too?" said Miss Mary.

The Cornal put the boy in front of him and pushed him towards the stair-foot. "You stay where you are," he said to his sister. "This will be a man's sederunt."

They went up the stair together and entered the parlour, to find the General half-sleeping in his lug-chair. He started at the apparition of the entering youth.

"You are not drowned after all," said he, "and there's my money gone that I spent for a gross of stenlock hooks to grapple you."

"Sit down there," said the Cornal, pointing to the chair in which Gilian had first stood court-martial. The bottle was brought forth from the cupboard; the glasses were ranged again by the General. In the grate a sea-coal fire burned brightly, its glance striking golden now and then upon the polished woodwork of the room and all its dusky corners, more golden, more warm, more generous, than the wan disheartened rays of the candles that shook a smoky flame above the board. Gilian waited his punishment with more wonderment than fear. What could be said to him for a misadventure? He had done no harm except to cause an hour or two of apprehension, and if he had been with one whose company was forbidden it had never been forbidden to him.

"It's a fine carry-on this," said the Cornal, breaking the silence. "Ay! it's a fine carry-on." He stretched the upper part of his body over the low table with his arms spread out, and looked into the boy's eyes with a glance more judicial than severe. "Here are we doing our best to make a man of you, more in a brag against gentry that need not be named in this house than for human kindness, though that is not wanting I assure you, and what must you be at but colloguing and, perhaps, plotting with the daughter of the gentry in question? I will not exactly say plotting," he hastened to amend, remembering apparently that before him were but the rudiments of a man. "I will not say plotting, but at least you were in a way to make us a laugh to the whole community. Do you know anything of the girl that you were with?"

"I met her in the school before she got her governess."

"Oh, ay! they must be making the leddy of her; that was the spoiling of her mother before her. As if old Brooks could not be learning any woman enough schooling to carry on a career in a kitchen. And have you seen her elsewhere?"

"I heard her once singing on her father's vessel," said Gilian.

"She was singing!" cried the Cornal, standing to his feet and thumping the table till the glasses rang. "Has she that art of the devil too? Her mother had it; ay! her mother had it, and it would go to your head like strong drink. Would it not, Dugald? You know the dame I mean."

"It was very taking, her song," said the General simply, playing with the empty glass, his eyes upon the table.

"And what now did she sing? Would it be—"

"It was 'The Rover' and 'The Man with the Coat of Green'," said Gilian in an eager recollection.

"Man! did I not ken it?" cried the Cornal. "Oh! I kent it fine. 'The Rover' was her mother's trump card. I never gave a curse for a tune, but she had a way of lilting that one that was wonderful."

"She had, that," said the General, and he sighed.

The room, it seemed to Gilian, was a vault, a cavern of

melancholy, with only the flicker of the coal to light it up in patches. These old men sighing were its ghosts or hermits, and he himself a worldling fallen invisible among their spoken thoughts. To him the Cornal no longer spoke directly; he was thinking aloud the thoughts alike of the General and himself—the dreams, the actions, the joys, the bitterness of youth. He sat back in his chair, relaxed, his hand wrinkled and grey, with no lusty blood rushing any more under the skin; upon the arms his fingers beating tattoo for his past.

"You'll be wondering that between the Turners and us is little love lost, though no doubt Miss Mary with her clinking tongue has given you a glisk of the reason. He'll be wondering, Dugald, he'll be wondering, I'll warrant. And, man, there's nothing by-ordinar wonderful in it, for are we not but human men? There was a woman in Little Elrig who took Dugald's fancy (if you will let me say it, Dugald), and he was willing to draw in with her and give her a name as reverend as any in the shire, for who are older than the Campbells of Keils? It's an old story, and in a way it was only yesterday: sometimes I think it must be only a dream. But, dream or waking, I can see plainly my brother Dugald there, home on leave, make visitation to Glen Shira. I have seen him ambling up there happy on his horse (it was Black Geordie, Dugald—well I mind him), and coming down again at night with a glow upon his countenance. Miss Mary, she would be daffing with him on his return, with a 'How's her leddyship today, Dugald?' and he would be in a pleasant vexation at this guessing of what he thought his secret. It was no secret: was ever such a thing secret in the shire of Argyll? We all knew it. She was Mary's friend and companion, she would come to our house here on a Saturday; I see her plainly on that chair at the window."

The General turned with a gasp, following his brother's glance. "I wish to God you would not be so terribly precise," was what he said. And then he fingered at his glass anew.

"Many a time she sat there with our sister, the smell of the wallflower on the sill about her, and many a time she sang 'The Rover' in this room. In this very room, Dugald: isn't every word

I'm saying true? Of course it is. God! as if a dream could be so fine! Well, well! my brother, who sits there all bye with such affairs, went away on another war. She was vexed. The woods of Shira Glen were empty for her after that, I have no doubt, now that their rambles were concluded; she was lonely on the Dhu Loch-side, where many a time he convoyed her home in the summer gloaming. He came back a tired man, a man hashed about with wounds and voyaging, cold nights, wet marches, bitter cruel fare, not the same at all in make or fashion, or in gaiety, that went away. The girl—the girl was cold. I hate to say it, Dugald, but what is the harm in a story so old? She came about Miss Mary in this house as before, no way blate, but it was 'Hands off!' for the man who had so liked her."

He paused and stretched to fill his glass, but as he seized the bottle the hand shook so that he laid the vessel down in shame. The boy stood entranced, following the story intimately, guessing every coming sentence, filling up its bald outline with the pictures of his brain; riding with the General, almost in his prime and almost handsome, and hearing the woman sing in the window chair; feeling the soldier's return to a reception so cruel. The General said nothing, but sat musing, his eyes, wide and distant, on the board. And out in the street there was the traffic of the town, the high calls of lads in their boisterous evening play, the laugh of a girl. From the kitchen came the rattle of Peggy's operations, and in a low murmur Miss Mary's voice as she hummed to herself, her symptom of anxiety, as she was sieving the evening milk in the pantry.

The Cornal gulped the merest thimbleful of spirits and resumed in a different key.

"Then, then," said he, "then I became the family's fool. Oh! ay!"—and he laughed with a crackle at the throat and no merriment—"I was the family fool; there was aye a succession of them in our house, one after another, dancing to this woman's piping. For a while nobody saw it; Dugald never saw it, for he was sitting moping, wearying for some work anywhere away from this infernal clime of rain and sleep and old sorrows; Mary never noticed it—at least not for a little; she could not easily fancy her companion the character she was. But I would be meeting the girl here and there about the country, in the glen, in the town, as well as here in this very parlour where I had to sit and look indifferent, though—though my heart stounded, and I never met her but I felt a traitor to my brother. You will believe that, Dugald?" said he, recognition for a moment flashing to his eye.

And the General nodded, stretching himself weary on the chair.

"Oh, ay! even then I wished myself younger, for she was not long beyond her teens, and walking beside her I would be feeling musty and old, though I was not really old, as my picture there above the chimney-piece will show. I was not old, in heart—it pattered like a bairn's steps to every glimpse and sentence of her. I lost six months at this game, my corps calling me, but I could not drag myself away. Once I spoke of going, and she sang 'The Rover'—by God! it sealed me to her footsteps. I stayed for very pity of myself, seeing myself a rover indeed if I went, more distressed than ever gave the key to any song. The woods, the woods in spring; the country full of birds; Dhu Loch lap-lapping on the shore; the summer with hay filling the field, and the sky blue from hill to hill, the nights of heather and star—oh, yes, she led me a pretty dance, I'm thinking, and sometimes I will be wondering if it was worth the paying for."

The Paymaster's house was grown very still. Gilian ceased to make the pictures in his mind.

"I met her ghost up there on the road this very night, and I had a hand below her chin," said the Cornal with a gulp.

"You did not dare, you did not dare!" cried his brother, an apple-red upon his cheek, and half rising in his chair.

"Surely, surely—in a ghost," said the Cornal. "I would never have mentioned it had it been herself. Sit down, Dugald. It was her daughter. I never saw her so close before, and the look of her almost gave me a stroke. It was what I felt when I first saw her mother with a younger man than you or I. Just like that I met them in the gloaming, with Turner very jaunty at her side, rapping his leg with his riding-cane, half a head higher than myself, a generation less in years. It was a cursed bitter pill, Dugald! Then I understood what you had meant and what Mary meant by her warnings. But I was cool—oh yes! I think I was cool. I only made to laugh and pass on, and she stopped me with her own hand. 'I kept it from you as long as I could,' she said: 'it was cruel, it was the blackest of sins, but this is the man for me.' "

"That was the man for her," echoed the General, his sentence stifled in a sigh.

" 'This is the man for me.' Turner stood beside her, looking with an admiration, but to do him justice, ill at ease, and with some—with some—with some pity for me. Oh! that stunned me! 'Is it so indeed?' I said in a little when I came to myself, feeling for the first time old. 'And must it be farewell with me as with my brother Dugald?'

"You should not have said that at all," said the General. "I would not have said it."

"I daresay not; I daresay not," said the Cornal slowly, pondering on it. "But, mind you, I was in a curious position, finding myself the second fool of a family that had got fair warning. She birked up and took her gallant's arm. Said I then, 'We'll maybe get you yet; I have a younger brother still.' It was a stupid touch of bravado. 'Jock!' said she, laughing, all her sorrow for her misdoing gone; 'Jock! Not the three of you together; give me youth and action.' Then she went away with her new fancy, and I was left alone. I was left alone. I was left alone."

His voice, that had risen to a shout as he gave the woman's words, declined to a crackle, a choked harsh utterance that almost failed to cross the table.

Up got the General. "Never mind, never mind, Colin," said he as it were to a vexed child. "We took our scuds gamely, and there was no more to do. God knows we have had plenty since—made wanderers for the King, ill fed for the King, wounded and blooded for the King. What does it matter for one that was a girl and is now no more but a clod in Kilmalieu? I'm forgetting it all fast. I would never be minding it at all but for you and Miss Mary there, and that picture of the man I was once, on the wall. I mind more of Badajos and San Sebastian—that was the roaring, the bloody, the splendid time!—than of the girl that played us on her string—three brothers at a single cast—a witch's fishing. What nonsense is this to be bringing up at our time of life? In the hearing of a wean too."

A cough choked him and he stopped. At Gilian, sitting still and seemingly uncomprehending, the Cornal looked as at a stranger. "So it is," said he; "just a wean! I forgot, some way. How old are you—sixteen? Nonsense! By the look of you I would say a hundred. Oh, you're an old-farrent one, sitting there with your lugs cocked. And what do you think is the moral of my story? Eh?—the moral of it? The lesson of it? What? What? What?"

Gilian had the answer in a flash. "It is to be younger than the other man; it is—"

"What?" cried the Cornal. "That's the moral? To be younger than the other man. No more than that? To be young? Old Brooks never put you to your Æsops when that's all you can make of it."

The General sat back and folded his soft thick hands upon his lap. He drew in his breath and blew it out again with the gasp of the wearied emerging from water. "Do you know, Dugald," said he, "there's something in that view of it? We were not young enough. We had too sober an eye on life. Youth is not in the straight back or the clear eye; there is something more, and—the person you mentioned had it, and has it yet."

"That's all havers," said the Cornal; "all havers. I was as jocular at the time as Jiggy Crawford himself. It did not come natural, but I could force myself to it. The blame was not with us. She was a wanton hussy first and last, and God be with her!"

He gripped the boy by the jacket collar. "Up and away!" said he. "If my tale's in vain, there's no help for it. I cannot make it plainer. Do not be a fool, wasting the hours that are due to your tasks in loitering with the daughter of a woman who has her mother's eye and her mother's songs, and maybe her mother's heart."

He pushed the boy almost rudely out at the parlour door.

XV

ON BOARD THE *JEAN*

GILIAN went up to his attic, stood looking blankly from the window at the skylights on the other side of the street, his head against the camceil of the room. He was bewildered and pleased. He was bewildered at this new candour of the Cornal that seemed to rank him for the first time more than a child; he was pleased to have his escapade treated in so tolerant a fashion, and to be taken into a great and old romance, though there was no active feud in it as in Marget Maclean's books. Besides, the sorrow of the old man's love story touched him. To find a soft piece in that old warrior so intent upon the past and a splutter of glory was astonishing, and it was pitiful too that it should be a tragedy so hopeless. He listed once more on the Cornal's side in the feud against Maam, even against Nan herself for her likeness to her mother, forgetting the charm of her song, the glamour at the gate, and all the magic of the garden. He determined to keep at a distance if he was to be loyal to those who had adopted him. There was no reason, he told himself, why he should vex the Paymaster and his brothers by indulging his mere love of good company in such escapades as he had in the ship and in the Duke's garden. There was no reason why— His head unexpectedly bumped against the camceil of the room. He was startled at the accident. It revealed to him for the first time how time was passing and he was growing. When he had come first to the Paymaster's that drooping ceil was just within the reach of his outstretched hand; now he could touch it with his brow.

"Gilian! Gilian!" cried Miss Mary up the stair.

He went down rosy red, feeling some unrest to meet a woman so soon after the revelation of a woman's perfidy, so soon indeed after a love-tale told among men. The parlour, as he passed its slightly open door, was still; its candles guttered on the table. The fire was down to the ash. He knew, without seeing it, that the old men were seated musing as always, ancient and moribund.

Miss Mary gave him his supper. For a time she bustled round him, with all her vexation gone, saying nothing of his sederunt with her brothers. Peggy was at the well, spilling stoup after stoup to make her evening gossip the longer, and the great flagged kitchen was theirs alone.

"What—what was the Cornal saying to you?" at last she queried, busying herself as she spoke with some uncalled-for kitchen office to show the indifference of her question.

"Oh, he was not angry," said Gilian, thinking that might satisfy.

"I did not think he would be," she said. Then in a little again, reluctantly: "But what was he talking about?"

The boy fobbed it off again. "Oh, just about—about—a story about a woman in Little Elrig."

"Did you understand?" she said, stopping her fictitious task and gasping, at the same time scrutinising him closely.

"Oh, yes—no, not very well," he stammered, making a great work with his plate and spoon.

"Do not tell *me* that," she said, coming over courageously and laying her hand upon his shoulder. "I know you understand every word of the story, if it is the story I mean."

He did not deny it this time. "But I do not know whether it is the same story or not," he said, eagerly wishing she would change the subject.

"What I mean," said she, "is a story about a woman who

was a friend of mine—and—and she quarrelled with my brothers. Is that the one?"

"That was the one," said he.

Miss Mary wrung her hands. "Oh!" she cried piteously, "that they should be thinking about that yet! wiser-like would it be for them to be sitting at the Book. Poor Nan! Poor Nan! my dear companion! Must they be blaming her even in the grave? You understand it very well. I know by your face you understand it. She should not have all the blame. They did not understand; they were older, more sedate than she was; their merriment was past; there was no scrap left of their bairnhood that even in the manliest man finds a woman's heart quicker than any other quality. I think she tried to—to—to—like them because they were my brothers, but the task beat her for all her endeavour. It is an old, daft story. I am wondering at them bringing it up to you. What do you think they would bring it up to you for?" And she scrutinised him shrewdly again.

"I think the girl the Cornal saw me with put him in mind of her mother," said Gilian, pushing the idea no further.

She still looked closely at him. "The girl cannot help that," said she. "She is very like her mother in some ways—perhaps in many. Maybe that was the Cornal's reason for telling you the story."

There was not, for once, the response of understanding in Gilian's face. She could say no more. Was he not a boy yet, perhaps with the impulse she and the Cornal feared, all undeveloped? And at any rate she dare not give him the watchword that all their remembrances led up to—the word Beware.

But Gilian guessed the word, and his assumption of ignorance was to prevent Miss Mary from guessing so much. Only he misunderstood. He looked upon the desire to keep him from the company of the people of Maam as due to the old rancours and jealousies, while indeed it was all in his interest.

But in any case he respected the feelings of the Paymaster's family, and thereafter for long he avoided as honestly as a boy might all intercourse with the girl, whom circumstance the mischievous, the henchman of the enemy, put in his way more frequently almost than any of her sex. He must be meeting her in the street, the lane, the marketplace, in the highway, or in walks along the glen. He kept aloof as well as he might (yet ever thinking her for song and charm the most interesting girl he knew), and the days passed; the springs would be but a breath of rich brown mould and birch, the summers but a flash of golden days growing briefer every year, the winters a lessening interlude of storm and darkness.

Gilian grew like a sapling in all seasons, in mind and fancy as in body. Ever he would be bent above the books of Marget Maclean, getting deeper to the meaning of them. The most trivial, the most inadequate and common story had for him more than for its author, for under the poor battered phrase that runs through book and book, the universal gestures of bookmen, he could see history and renew the tragedies that suggested them at the outset. He was no more Brooks' scholar though he sat upon his upper forms, for, as the dominie well could see, he was launching out on barques of his own; the plain lessons of the school were without any interest as they were without any difficulty to him. He roamed about the woods, he passed precious hours upon the shore, his mind plangent like the wave.

"A droll fellow that of the Paymaster's," they said of him in the town. For as he aged his shyness grew upon him, and he went about the community at ease with himself only when his mind was elsewhere.

"A remarkable young gentleman," said Mr Spencer one day to the Paymaster. "I am struck by him, sir, I am struck. He has an air of cleverness, and yet they tell me he is—"

"He is what?" asked the Paymaster, lowering his brows suspicious on the innkeeper's hesitation.

"They tell me he is not so great a credit to old Brooks as he might expect," said the innkeeper, who was not lacking in boldness or plain speaking if pushed to it.

"Ay, they say that?" repeated the Paymaster, pinching his snuff vigorously. "Maybe they're right too. I'll tell you what. The lad's head is stuffed with wind. He goes about with notions swishing round inside that head of his, as much the plaything of nature as the reed that whistles in the wind at the riverside and fancies itself a songster."

Mr Spencer tilted his London hat down upon his brow, fumbled with his fob-chain, and would have liked to ask the Paymaster if his well-known intention to send Gilian on the same career he and his brothers had followed was to be carried into effect. But he felt instinctively that this was a delicate question. He let it pass unput.

Bob MacGibbon had no such delicacy. The same day at their meridian in the Abercrombie he broached the topic.

"I'll tell you what it is, Captain: if that young fellow of yours is ever to earn salt for his kail, it is time he was taking a crook in his hand."

"A crook in his hand?" said the Paymaster. "Would you have nothing else for him but a crook?"

"Well," said MacGibbon, "I supposed you would be for putting him into Ladyfield. If that is not your notion, I wonder why you keep it on for."

"Ladyfield!" cried the Paymaster. "There was no notion further from my mind. Farming, for all Duke George's reductions, is the last of trades nowadays. I think I told you plain enough that we meant to make him a soger."

MacGibbon shrugged his shoulders. "If you did I forgot," said he. "It never struck me. A soger? Oh, very well. It is in your family: your influence will be useful." And he changed the subject.

At the very moment that thus they discussed him, Gilian, a truant from school, which now claimed his attention, as Brooks sorrowfully said, "when he had nothing else to do and nowhere else to go", was on an excursion to the Waterfoot, where the Duglas in a sandy delta unravels at the end into numerous lesser streams, like the tip of a knotless fishing-line. It was a place for which he had an exceeding fondness. For here in the hot days of summer there was a most rare seclusion. No living thing shared the visible land with him except the sea-birds, the white-bellied, the clean and wholesome and free, talking like children among the weeds or in their swooping essays overhead. A place of islets and creeks, where the mud lay golden below the river's peaty flow; he had but to shut his eyes for a little and look upon it lazily, and within him rose the whole charm and glamour of oceans and isles. Swimming in the briny deeps that washed the rocks, he felt in that solitude so sufficient, so much in harmony with the spirit of the place, its rumination, its content, its free and happy birds, as if he were Ellar in the fairy tale. The tide caressed; it put its arms round him; it laughed in the sunshine and kissed him shyly at the lips. Into the swooping concourse of the birds he would send, thus swimming, his brotherly halloo. They called back; they were not afraid, they need not be—he loved them.

Today he had come down to the Waterfoot almost unknowing where he walked. Though the woods were bare there was the look of warmth in their brown and purple depths; only on the upper hills did the snow lie in patches. Great piles of trunks, the trunks of old fir and oak, lay above high-water mark. He turned instinctively to look for the ship they were waiting for, and behind him, labouring at a slant against the wind, was the *Jean* coming from the town to pick her cargo from the narrow estuary.

He was plucked at the heart by a violent wish to stay. At the poop he could see Black Duncan, and the seaman's histories, the seaman's fables all came into his mind again, and the sea was the very highway of content. The ship was all alone upon the water, not even the tan of a fisher's lug-sail broke the blue. A bracing heartening air blew from French Foreland. And as he was looking spellbound upon the little vessel coming into the mouth of the river, he was startled by a strain of music. It floated, a rumour angelic, upon the air, coming whence he could not guess—surely not from the vessel where Black Duncan and two others held the deck alone? It was for a time but a charm of broken melody in the veering wind, distinct a moment, then gone, then back a faint echo of its first clearness. It was not till the vessel came fairly opposite him that the singer revealed herself in Nan sitting on a waterbreaker in the lee of the companion hatch.

For the life of him he could not turn to go away. He rebelled against the Paymaster's service, and remained till the ship was in the river mouth beside him.

"Ho 'ille 'ille!" Black Duncan cried upon him, leaning upon his tarry gunnle, and smiling to the shore like a man far-travelled come upon a friendly face in some foreign port. The wooded rock gave back the call with interest. Round about turned the seaman and viewed the southern sky. A black cloud was pricked upon the spur of Cowal. "There's wind there," said he, "and water too! I'm thinking we are better here than below Otter this night. Nan, my dear, it is home you may get today, but not without a wetting. I told you not to come, and come you would."

She drummed with her heels upon the breaker, held up a merry chin, and smiled boldly at her father's captain. "Yes, you told me not to come, but you wanted me to come all the time. I know you did. You wanted songs, you wanted all the songs, and you had the ropes off the pawl before I had time to change my mind."

"You should go home now," said the seaman anxiously. "Here is our young fellow, and he will walk up to the town with you."

She pretended to see Gilian for the first time, staring at him boldly, with a look that made him certain she was thinking of the many times he had manifestly kept out of her way. It made him uneasy, but he was more uneasy when she spoke.

"The Paymaster's boy," said she. "Oh! he would lose himself on the way home, and the fairies might get him. When I go I must find my own way. But I am not going now, Duncan. If it will rain, it will rain and be done with it, and then I will go home."

"Come on board," said Duncan to the boy. "Come on board, and see my ship, then; she is a little ship, but she is a brave one, I'm telling you; there is nothing of the first of her left for patches."

Gilian looked longingly at the magic decks confused with

ropes, and the open companion faced him, leading to warm depths, he knew by the smoke that floated from the funnel. But he paused, for the girl had turned her head to look at the sea, and though he guessed somehow she might be willing to have him with her for his youth, he did not care to venture.

Then Black Duncan swore. He considered his invitation too much of a favour to have it treated so dubiously. Gilian saw it and went upon the deck.

Youth, that is so long (and all too momentary), and leaves for ever such a memory, soon forgets. So it was that in a little while Gilian and Nan were on the friendliest of terms, listening to Black Duncan's stories. As they listened, the girl sat facing the den stair, so that her eyes were lit to their depths, her lips were flaming red. The seaman and the boy sat in shadow. The seaman, stretched upon a bunk with his feet to the Carron stove, the boy upon a firkin, could see her every wave of fancy displayed upon her countenance. She was eager, she was piteous, she was laughing, in the right key of response always when the stories that were told were the straightforward things of a sailor's experience—storms, adventures, mishaps, passion, or calm. She had grown as Gilian had grown, in mind as in body; and thinking so, he was pleased exceedingly. But the tales that the boy liked were the tales that were not true, and these, to Gilian's sorrow, she plainly did not care for; he could see it in the calmness of her features. When she yawned at a tale of Irish mermaidens he was dashed exceedingly, for before him again was the sceptic who had laughed at his heron's nest and had wantonly broken the crystal of the Lady's Linn. But by and by she sang, and oh! all was forgiven her. This time she sang some songs of her father's, odd airs from English camp-fires, braggart of word, or with the melodious longings of men abroad from the familiar country, the early friend.

"I wish I was a soldier," he found himself repeating in his thought. "I wish I was a soldier, that such songs might be sung for me."

A fury at the futility of his existence seized him. He would give anything to be away from this life of ease and dream, away where things were ever happening, where big deeds were possible, where the admiration and desire were justified. He felt ashamed of his dreams, his pictures, his illusions. Up he got from his seat upon the firkin, and his head was in the shadows of the smoky timbers.

"Sit down, lad, sit down," said the seaman, lazy upon his arm upon the shelf. "There need be no hurry now; I hear the rain."

A moan was in the shrouds, the alarm of a freshening wind. Some drops trespassed on the cabin floor, then the rain pattered heavily on the deck. The odours of the ship passed, and in their place came the smell of the cut timber on the shore, the oak's sharpness, the rough sweetness of the firs, all the essence, the remembrance of the years circled upon the ruddy trunks, their gatherings of storm and sunshine, of dew, showers, earth-sap, and the dripping influence of the constant stars.

"I cannot stay here, I cannot stay here! I must go," cried the lad, and he made to run on deck.

But Duncan put a hand out as the lowest step was reached, and set him back in his place.

"Sit you there!" said he. "I have a fine story you never heard yet. And a fighting story too."

"What is it? What is it?" cried Nan. "Oh! tell us that one. Is it a true one?"

"It is true—in a way," said the seaman. "It was a thing that happened to myself."

Gilian delayed his going—the temptation of a new story was too much for him.

"Do you take frights?" Black Duncan asked him. "Frights for things that are not there at all?"

Gilian nodded.

"That is because it is in the blood," said the seaman; "that is the kind of fright of my story."

And this is the story Black Duncan told in the Gaelic.

XVI

THE DESPERATE BATTLE

"BLACK darkness came down on the wood of Creag Dubh, and there was I lost in the middle of it, picking my way among the trees. Fir and oak are in the wood. In the oak I could walk straight with my chin in the air, facing anything to come; in the fir the little branches scratched at my neck and eyes, and I had to crouch low and go carefully.

"I had been at a wedding in the farmhouse of Leacann. Song and story had been rife about the fire; but song and story ever have an end, and there was I in the hollow of the wood after song and story were by, the door-drink still on my palate, and I looking for my way home. It was nut-time. I had a pouch of them in my jacket, and I cracked and ate them as I went. Not a star pricked the sky; the dark was the dark of a pot in a cave and a snail boiling under the lid of it. I had cracked a nut and the kernel of it fell on the ground, so I bent and felt about my feet, though my pouch was so full of nuts that they fell showering in the fir dust. I swept every one with a shell aside, hunting for my cracked fellow, and when I found him never was nut so sweet!

"Then came to me the queerest of notions, that some night before in this same wood I had lost a nut, and the darkness was the dark of a pot in a cave and a snail under the lid of it. And yet the time or season that ever I cracked nuts in Creag Dubh was what I could never give name to.

" 'Where was it? When was it?' said I to myself, bent double creeping under the young larch with my plaid drawn up to fend my eyes, and the black fright crept over me. An owl's whoop would have been cheery, or the snort of a hind—and Creag Dubh is in daytime stirring with bird and beast—but here was I stark lonely in the heart of it, never a sound about, far from the hunting road, and my mind back among the terrors of a thousand years ere ever the Feinne were sung.

"In this dreamy quirk of the mind I felt I was a hunter and a man of arms. I was searching for something here in this ghostly wood. The cudgel and knife of folks I could not understand were coming on me! Fast, fast, and hard I crunched my nuts, chewing shell and meat fiercely between my teeth to fill the skull of my head with noise and shut out the quietness. Never a taste of what I ate, sour or sweet. But so hard and fast I crunched that soon my store of nuts was done and there I was helpless with my ears open to the roaring wave of sound that we call silence. I stood a little, and though my back grewed at the chill of the dreadful spaces behind me, I held my breath to study the full fright of the hour. Something was coming to me; I knew it. When this thing happened before, when a skin was my kilt and my shanks were bare, whatever I had to meet had met me in the round space among the candle-wood roots. The hair on my wrists stirred, a cry came to my throat and was over the edge of it and into the dark night like a man's heart scurrying craven to the door.

"Through the wood went that craven roar, the wood all its own and, a stranger, I listened to my own voice wake up Echo far off on Ben Dearg.

"The doors of Echo shut on the only thing I knew and was half friendly with in the Duke's wood, and down on me again came the quietest quietness.

" 'Be taking thy feet from here,' said I to myself, taking out my sailor-knife and scrugging my bonnet well on my brow. And there was no wind, not a breath, on Creag Dubh. The stars black out, the rough ground broken to my foot, the branches scraping unfriendly, I went on through the trees.

"When one goes up from the Leacann hunting road into the farmlands he comes in a while on a space among the trees, clean shorn like the shearing of a hook but for white hay that lies there thick and rustling in the spring of the year. 'Black Duncan,' said I, 'be pulling thyself together, gristle and bone, for here's the fright that stirs about the dark with fingers and claws.' I was the first man (said my notion) who ever set foot on the braes of Argyll, newly from Erin and Argyll thick with ghosts; daytime or dark the woods were full of things that hate the stranger. Under my feet the rotting dust of the fir-trees felt soft and clogging, like the banks of new-delved graves. My back shivered again to the feel of the space behind me; in my bonnet stirred my hair. I went into the glade with a dry tongue rasping on the roof of my mouth.

"When the Terror came up against me, I could have laughed in my sudden ease of mind, for here at last was something to be sure of, in a way. And I gripped back as it gripped fast at me, feeling it hairy at the neck and the crook of the arms—a breathing and lusty body.

" 'What have I here?' I asked, but never an answer. At my throat went ten clawed fingers, and there was Duncan at dismal battle, fighting for life with what he could not see, in his own home woods, but they so strange and never a friend to help!

"For a time I had no chance with the knife; but at last 'Steel, my darling!' said I, and I struck low in the soft spaces. 'Gloop,' said the knife, and Death was twisting at my feet.

"Did Duncan put hurry on his heels and fly? The hurry was not in me but the deep heart's wonder. My first dead thing that in life had ever struck back held me till the morning with a girl's enchantment. I went down on a knee in the grass and felt him, a soft lump, freezing slowly from the heel to the knee, from the knee to the neck. Some rags of costume were on him, a kilt of coarse plaiding and a half-shirt of skin, soaked in sweat at the armpits and wet with blood at the end.

"I waited till the morning to see what I had. 'This,' said I, hunched on a mound, 'is all as it was before.' The first sound I heard was the squeal of a beast caught at the throat among the bracken, then a hind snored among the grass. The morning walked solemn among the trees, stopping at every step to listen; birds put their claws down and shook themselves free of sleep and dew; a polecat slinking past me started at my eye and went back to his hole. Began the fir-trees waving in the wind, and then the day was open wide and far.

"In the dark I had strained my eyes to see what was at my feet till my eyeballs creaked in their hollows, yet now I had no desire to turn about from the cheerful dawn and look behind, but I did it with my heart thudding.

"Nothing was there to see, lappered blood, nor mark of body on grass!

"My knife, without a stain on the steel of it, was still in my hand. I wiped it with a tuft of bracken, and I laughed with something of a bitterness.

" 'So!' said I, 'the old story, the old story! It happened me before, and in a hundred years from now Black Duncan will be at the killing again.' "

XVII

THE STORM

THE vessel, straining at the rope that bound her to the shore, lay with a clumsy shoulder over the bank that shelved abruptly into the great depths where slimy weeds entangled. Her sails were housed and snug, the men in the bows lay under the flapping corner of the jib and played at cards, though the noise of the raindrops on their canvas roof might well disturb them. Gilian made no pause; he ran up at the tale's conclusion, at a bound he was on the shore, staggering upon the rocks and slipping upon the greasy weeds till he came to the salt bent grass, and with firmer footing ran like a young deer for the shelter of the wood. The rain battered after him, the wind rose. In front, the wood, so still an hour before, in its winter slumber, with no birds now to mar its dreams, had of a sudden roused to the rumour of the storm. As by an instinct, the young trees on the edge seemed to shudder before the winds came to them. Their slim tips could not surely be bowing, even so little, to the gale that was yet behind Gilian. But he passed them and plunged under the tall firs, and he felt secure only when the ruddy needles of other years were a soft carpet underfoot. It was true he found shelter here from the rain that slanted terrifically, but it was not for sanctuary from the elements he sought the rude aisles, though now he appreciated the peace of them. It was for escape from himself, from his sense of hopeless, inexplicable longing, from some tremendous convulsion of his mind created by Black Duncan's fable.

The wood was all a wood of fir, not old nor very young, but at that mid age when it has to all of country blood an invitation to odorous dusks and pathless wanderings below laced branches. The sun never could reach the heart of it, except at the hour of setting, when it flamed bloody through the pillars. The rain never seemed to penetrate, for the fir-needles underfoot grew more dusty year by year. But when the rain beat as it did now, through the whole of it went a sound of gobbling and drumming, and the wind, striking upon the trunks as if they were the strings of Ossian, harped a great and tremendous tune, wanting start or ending. And by and by there came company for Gilian as he sheltered in the wood. Birds of all kinds beat hurriedly through the trees and settled upon the boughs with a shudder of the quill, pleased to be out of the inclement open and cosily mantled in.

The boy went into the very inmost part of the wood without knowing the reason why thus he should fly from the ship that so recently had enchanted him, from the tales he loved. But in the soothing presence of the firs and the content of the animals sheltering from the storm, he found a momentary peace from the agitation that had set up in him, roused at the song of the girl, the story of the mariner. The emotions, the fears, longings, discontents that jangled through him as they had never done before relapsed to a mood level and calm, as if they, too, had sheltered from the storm like the birds upon the trees.

But by and by he became ashamed of his action, that must seem so foolish to the friends he had left in the ship without a word of explanation. His face flamed hotly at the thought of his rude departure. He would give a world to be able to go back again as if nothing had happened and sit unchallenged in the cosy den of the *Jean*. And musing thus he went through the wood till he came upon the bank of the Duglas, roaring grey and ragged, a robber from the hills, bearing spoil of the upper reaches, the town-lands, the open and windswept plains. It carried the trunks of great trees that had lain since other storms upon its banks, and with a great chafing and cracking no less than the wooden bridge from Clonary which the children were wont to cross from those parts on their way to school.

"That will go battering on the vessel," he thought, looking amazed at its ponderous beams flicking through the water and over the little cascades as if they had been feathers blown by an evening breeze. "That will go battering on the *Jean*," he thought, and of a sudden it seemed his manifest duty to warn the occupants of the ship to defend themselves from the unexpected attack.

He followed the bridge for a little, fascinated, wondering what was to become of it next in the tumult of waters till he came to the falls, where he had looked for a check to it. But it stayed no more than a moment on the lip of the precipice, swung up a jagged edge above the deep, then crashed into the linn, where it seemed to swerve and turn, giddy with its adventure. Gilian stood spellbound on the banks looking at it so far down, then he turned, and cutting off the bend of the river, made for the shore.

He crashed through bracken and bramble and through the fir-wood again, startling the sheltering birds by his hurry, emerging upon the face of the brae in sight of the *Jean* and the sea. In his absence a great change had come upon the wave, upon the hilly distance, upon the whole countenance of nature. The rain was no longer in drumming torrents, but in a soft and almost imperceptible veil; but if the rain had lost the wind had gained. And as he passed from the edge of the wood, all the trees seemed to twang and creak, or cracked loudly, parting perhaps at some dear nerve where sap and beauty would no longer course. In every bush along the edge of the wood there seemed a separate chorus of voices, melodious and terrific, whistle and whoop, shriek and moan. Even the grass nodding in the wind lent a thin voice to the chorus, a voice such as only the sharp and sea-trained ear may comprehend, that beasts hear long before the wind itself is apparent, so that they remove themselves to the bieldy sides of the hills before tumult breaks.

But it was the aspect of the sea that most surprised the boy, for where before there had been but a dreaming plain of smiles there was the riot of waters. The black lips of the wave parted and showed the white fangs underneath, or spat the spume of passion into the face of the day. It looked as if every glen and every gully, every corry and *eas* on that mountainous coast was spending its breath upon the old sea, the poor old sea that would be let alone to dream and rest, but must suffer the humours of the mischievous winds.

It was but for a moment Gilian lent his eye to the open and troubled expanse. He saw there no sign of ship, but looking lower into shore he beheld the *Jean* in travail at the Duglas mouth. The tide had come fully in while he was absent, the delta that before had been so much lagoon and isle was become an estuary, where, in the unexpected tide and rush of the river, the logs of fir and oak were all adrift about the sides of the vessel. Every hand was busy. They poled off as best they might the huge trunks that battered at the carvel planks and pressed upon the twanging cable. Forward of the mast Black Duncan stood commanding in loud shouts that could not reach the boy through the wind's bellowing, and as he shouted, he lent, like a good seaman, vigour to a spar and pushed off the besieging timbers, all his weight aslant upon the wood, his arms tense, a great and wholesome figure of endeavour.

But not Black Duncan nor his striving seamen so busy in that confusion of wind and water were the first to catch the boy's eye. It was Nan, struggling by her captain's side at the unshipped tiller, and in the staggering ship seeking to send it home in the avoiding helm-head. Her hair blew round her with the vaunting spirit of a banner, her body in every move was rich with a sort of exaltation.

As yet the bridge had not reached them. It might have been checked altogether in the linn, or it might still be slowly grinding its way round the great bend of the river, that Gilian had cut off by his plunge through the wood. But at least he was there to alarm, for its assault, borne down on the spate, would be worse by far than that of the timber. He beat his way again, bent, through the wind, to the water-edge now so far in and separate from the ship, and cried out a loud warning. It seemed to himself as he did so the voice of an infant, so weak was it, so shrill and piping, buffeted about by heaven's large and overwhelming utterance. They paid no heed at first, but by and by they heard him.

"The bridge! God! do you tell me?" cried Black Duncan in a visible consternation. "Is it far up?"

Gilian put his hand to his mouth and trumpeted his response.

"The bend! My sorrow! she's as good as on us then. We must be at our departures."

The mariners scurried about the deck; Black Duncan threw off the prisoning cable; there were shouts, swift looks, and a breathless pause; the *Jean* swung round before the corner of her jib, laboured clumsily for a moment unbelieving of her release, then drifted slowly from the river mouth, her little boat and her tiller left behind, the first caught by the warring tree-trunks, the latter dashed from Nan's hands by the swing of an unfastened boom. As helpless as the logs she had been encountering, she was loose before the wind that drove her parallel with the shore at no safe distance from its fringe of rocks.

Gilian, scarcely knowing what he did, ran along the shore, following her course, looking at her with a wild eye. The men were calling to him, waving, pointing, but what they meant he could not surmise; all his interest was in the girl who stood motionless, seemingly aghast at her mishap, with her hair still blowing about her.

To the north where he was running, black masses of clouds were piling, and the sea, so far as the eye could reach, was weltering more cruelly than before. Seagulls screamed without ceasing, and the human imitation of their calls roused uncanny notions that they welcomed the vessel to her doom. She seemed so helpless, so hopeless, dashed upon by the spume of those furious lips, bit by the grinding teeth.

But yet he ran on and on over the salt grass or the old wrack that the sea-spray wet to a new slime, never pausing but for a moment now and then to try and understand what the men on deck were shouting to him.

Off the shore north of the Duglas is a rock called Ealan Dubh, or the Black Island, a single bare and rounded block without a blade of grass on it, that juts out of the sea in all weathers and tides and is grown on thickly with little shellfish. Today it could not be seen, but the situation of it was plain in the curling crest of the white waves that bent constantly over it. Straight for this rock the *Jean* was driving, and a great pity came over Gilian, a pity for himself as he anticipated the sickening crash upon the rock, the rip of the timber, the gurgle at the holes, the sundering of the bolted planks, the collapse of the mast, the ultimate horrible plunge. He was Black Duncan, the swimmer, fighting hard for life between the ship and the shore; he was the girl, with wet hair flapping blindly at the eyes, clinging with bleeding fingernails to the rough shells that clustered on the rock. It was horrible, horrible! And then many tales from the shelves of Marget Maclean came to his memory where one in such circumstances had done a brave thing. To save the girl and bring her from the rock ashore—that was the thing to be done—but how? Even the sea fairy, as he had said, might be worth drowning for. Helplessly he looked up and down the shore. There was nothing to see but the torn fringe of the tide, the waving branches of the coast.

He had no more than grasped the solitude of the countryside (feeling himself something of God's proxy thus to be watching the destruction of the ship) when the *Jean* went upon the rock. Her shock upon it was not to be heard from the shore, and she did not break up all at once as he had anticipated; she paused as it might seem, quite willingly, in her career before the wind and slewed round a tarry broadside to the crested wave. She began to settle in the water by her riven quarter, but Gilian did not see that, for it came about slowly. All he could see was that Black Duncan and his men upon the higher part of the slanted deck were calling to him more loudly than before and pointing with frenzied gestures back in the direction whence they had come.

He looked back, he could not comprehend.

More loudly yet they called. They clustered, the three of them on the shrouds, and in one voice tried to bellow down the gale.

He could not understand. He turned a pitiful figure on the shore, his mind tumultuous with wrestling thoughts and dreads, with images of the rough depths where the girl's hair would sway like weed in a green haze in an everlasting stillness.

Again the seamen called, and it seemed, as he looked at their meaningless gesticulations, that the bowsprit of the vessel now pointed higher than before. The appalling story thus told to him had barely got home when he saw a change in the conduct of the seamen. They ceased to cry and wave; they looked no longer at him but in the direction whence he had come, and turning, he saw the vessel's little boat bobbing in the sea-troughs. It had an occupant too, a lad not greatly older than himself, using only a guiding oar, who so was directing the boat in the drifting waves towards the Ealan Dubh and the counter of the *Jean*.

Then the whole folly of his conduct, the meaning of the sea-men's cries, the obvious and simple thing he should have done came to Gilian—he discovered himself the dreamer again. A deep contempt for himself came over him and he felt inclined to run back to the solace of the woods with a shame more burdensome than before, but the doings of the lad who had but to wade to pick up the lost boat and was now bearing down on the doomed vessel prevented him. He watched with a fascination the things being done that he should have done himself, he made himself, indeed, the lad who did them. It was as if in a dream, looking upon himself with a stranger's admiration, he saw the little boat led dexterously beside the vessel in spite of the tumbling waves, and Black Duncan, out upon her bowsprit, board her, lift his master's daughter in, and row laboriously ashore. Then Gilian turned and made a poor, contemptuous retreat.

XVIII

DISCOVERY

THE town was dripping at its eaves and glucking full of waters at rone-mouths and syvers when he got into it after his disgraceful retreat. He was alone in the street as he walked through it, a wet woebegone figure with a jacket collar high up to the ears to meet the nip of the elements. Donacha Breck, leaning over his counter and moodily looking at the hens sheltering their windblown feathers under his barrow, saw him pass and threw over his shoulder to his wife behind a comment upon the eccentricity of the Paymaster's boy.

"He's scarcely all there," said he, "by the look of him. He's wandering about in the rain as if it was a fine summer day and the sun shining."

Crossing from the school to his lodging, an arm occupied by a great bundle of books, the other contending with an umbrella, was the dominie, and he started at the sight of his errant pupil who nearly ran against him before his presence was observed.

"Well, Gilian?" said he, a touch of irony in his accent, himself looking a droll figure, hunched round his books and turning like a weathercock jerkily to keep the umbrella between him and the wind that strained its whalebone ribs till they almost snapped.

Gilian stopped, looked hard at the ground, said never a word.

And old Brooks, over him, gazed at the wet figure with puzzlement and pity.

"You beat me; you beat me quite!" said he. "There's the making of a fine man in you; you have sharpness, shrewdness, a kind of industry, or what may be doing for that same; every chance of a paternal kind—that's to say a home complete and comfortable—and still you must be acting like a wean! You were not at the school today. I'm keeping it from Miss Campbell as long as I can, but I'll be bound to tell her of your truancy this time."

He risked the surrounding hand a moment from his books, bent a little and tapped the boy's jacket pocket.

"Ay! A book again!" said he slyly. "What is it this time? But never mind; it does not matter. I'll warrant it is not Mr Butter's Spellings nor Murray the Grammarian, but some trash of a no-velle. Any exercise for *your* kind but the appointed task! I wish—I wish—Tuts! laddie, you are wet to the skin, haste ye home and get a heat."

Gilian did not need a second bidding, but ran up the street, without slacking his pace till he got to the foot of the Paymaster's stair, where the wind from the pend-close was howling most dismally. He lingered on the stair, extremely loth to face Miss Mary with a shame so plain upon his countenance as he imagined it must be. No way that he could tell the story of the *Jean*'s disaster would leave out his sorry share in it. A quick ear heard him on the stair; the door opened.

"Oh, you rascal!" cried Miss Mary, her anxious face peering down at him. "You were never in the school till this time." She put her hand upon his bonnet and his sleeve and found them soaking. "Oh, I knew it! I knew it!" she cried. "Just steeping!"

He found an unexpected relief in her consternation at his condition and in her bustle to get him into dry clothing. After the experience he had come through, the storm and the spectacle he had seen as in a dream from the shore, he indulged in the cordiality and cosiness of the warm kitchen for a little with self-ish gladness. But it was only for a little; the disaster to the vessel and the consciousness that his own part in the business would certainly come to light, overwhelmed him again, and it was a most dolorous face that looked at Miss Mary over the viands she had just put before him.

"What ails the callant?" she demanded in a tremble, staring at him.

He burst into tears, the first she had seen on his face since ever he had come to her house, and all her mother's heart was sore.

"What mischief were you in?" she asked, putting an arm about his neck, and her troubled face down upon his hair as he shook in his chair. "I am sure you were not to blame. It could not have been much, Gilian. Tuts! tuts!" And so she went on in a ludicrous way, coaxing him to indifference for the sin she fancied.

At last he told her the beginnings of his tragedy, that he had seen the *Jean* wrecked on Ealan Dubh, and the girl Nan on board of her. She was for a moment dumb with horror, believing the end had come to all upon the vessel, but on this Gilian speedily assured her, and "Oh, amn't I glad!" said she with a simple utterance and a transport on her visage that showed how deep was her satisfaction.

"How did they get ashore?" she asked.

"In the small boat," said Gilian uncomfortably. "It caught on the logs at the mouth of the river when she drifted off, and—and—"

"And a boy went out in it and brought them help!" she cried, finely uplifted in a delight that she had guessed the cause of his trepidation. "Oh, you darling! And not to say a word of it! Am not I the proud woman this day? My dear companion Nan's girl!"

She caught him fervently as he rose ashamed from his seat to explain or to make an escape from the punishment that was in her error, a punishment more severe than if he had been blamed. She was one never prone to the displays of love and rapture, but this time her joy overcame her and she kissed him with something of a redness on her face. It was to the boy as if he had been smitten on the mouth. He drew back almost rudely in so great a confusion that it but confirmed her guess.

"You must come and tell my brothers," said she, "this very moment. Don't say anything about the lass, but they'll be keen to hear about the vessel. They sit there hearing nothing of the world's news, unless it comes to the fireside for them, and then I've noticed they're as ready to listen as Peggy would be at the Cross well."

She had him halfway to the parlour before he thought of a protest, he had found such satisfaction in being relieved from her mistaken pride in him. Then he concluded it was as well to go through with it, thinking that if the rescue of the girl was not to be in the story, his own shortcomings need not emerge. She pushed him before her into the room; her brothers were seated at the fire, and they only turned when her voice, in a very unaccustomed excitement, broke the quietness of the chamber.

"Do you hear this?" she cried, and her hand on Gilian's shoulder; "a vessel's sunk on the Ealan Dubh."

"I knew there would be tales to tell of this," said the General. "The wind came too close on the frost. I mind at Toulouse—"

"And Gilian was down at the Waterfoot and saw it all," she broke in upon the reminiscence.

"Was he, faith?" said the Cornal. "I like my tales at first hand. Tell us all about it, laddie; what vessel was she?"

He wheeled his chair about as he spoke, and roused himself to attention. It was a curious group, too much like his old courtmartial to be altogether to the boy's taste. For Miss Mary stood behind him, with an air of proud possession of him that was disquieting, and the two men seemed to expect from him some very exciting history indeed.

"Well, well!" said the Cornal, drumming with his fingers on his chair-arm impatiently, "you're in no great hurry with your budget. What vessel was it?"

"It was the *Jean*," said Gilian, bracing himself up for a plunge.

"Ye seem to be a wondrous lot mixed up with the fortunes of that particular ship," said the Cornal sourly. "What way did it happen?"

"She was in the mouth of the river," said Gilian, "and the

spate of the river brought down the wooden bridge at Clonary. I saw it coming, and I cried to them, and Black Duncan cast off leaving boat and tiller. She drove before the wind and went on Ealan Dubh, and sunk, and—that was all."

The story, as he told it, was as bald of interest as if it were a page from an old almanack.

"What came of the men?" said the Cornal. "The loss of the *Jean* does not amount to muckle; there was not a plank of her first timbers left in her."

"They got ashore in the small boat," said Gilian.

"Which was left behind, I think you said at first," said the Cornal, annoyed at some apparent link a-missing in the chain of circumstance. "If the boat was left behind as well as the tiller— I think you mentioned the tiller—how did they get ashore in it? Did you see them get ashore?"

"I saw Black Duncan and the girl, but not the others," answered Gilian, all at once forgetting that some caution was needed here.

Up more straightly sat the Cornal, and fixed him with a stern eye.

"Oh, ay!" said he; "she was in the story too, and you fancied you might hide her. I would not wonder now but you had been in the vessel yourself."

Gilian was abashed at his own inadvertence, but he hastened to explain that he was on the shore watching the vessel when she struck.

"But you were on the vessel some time?" said the Cornal, detecting some reservation.

"Oh, Colin, Colin, I wonder at you!" cried Miss Mary, now in arms for her favourite, and utterly heedless of the frown her brother threw at her for her interference. "You treat the boy as if he was a vagabond and—"

"—Vagabond or no vagabond," said the Cornal, "he was where he should not be. I'm wanting but the truth from him, and that, it seems, is not very easy to get."

"You are not just at all," she protested. Then she went over and whispered something in his ear. His whole look changed; where had been suspicion came something of open admiration, but he gave it no expression on his tongue.

"Take your time, Gilian," said he; "tell us how the small boat got to the vessel."

"The boy went down to the river mouth," said Gilian, "and—"

"—The boy?" said the Cornal. "Well, if you must be putting it that idiotic way, you must; anyway, we're waiting on the story."

"—The boy went down to the river mouth and got into the small boat. She was half full of water and he baled her as well as he could with his bonnet, then pushed her off. She went up and down like a cork, and he was terrified. He thought when he went in first she would be heavy to row, but he found the lightness of her was the fearful thing. The wind slapped like a big open hand, and the water would scoop out on either side—"

"Take it easy, man, take it easy; slow march," said the Cornal. For Gilian had run into his narrative in one of his transports and the words could not come fast enough to his lips to keep up with his imagination. His face was quivering with the emotions appropriate to the chronicle.

"—Then I put out the oar astern—"

"—Humph! *You* did; that's a little more sensible way of putting it."

"—I put the oar astern," said Gilian, never hearing the comment, but carried away by his illusion; "and the wind carried us up the way of Ealan Dubh. Sometimes the big waves would try to pull the oar from my hands, wanting fair play between their brothers and the ship. ("Havers!" muttered the Cornal.) And the spindrift struck me in the eyes like hands full of sand. I thought I would never get to the vessel. I thought she would be upset every moment, and I could not keep from thinking of myself hanging on to the keel and my fingers slipping in weariness."

"A little less thinking and more speed with your boat would be welcome," said the Cornal impatiently. "I'm sick sorry for them, waiting there on a wreck with so slow a rescue coming to them."

Gilian hesitated, with his illusion shattered, and, all unnerved, broke for the second time into tears.

"Look at that!" cried Miss Mary pitifully, herself weeping; "you are frightening the poor laddie out of his wits," and she soothed Gilian with numerous Gaelic endearments.

"Tuts! never mind me," said the Cornal, rising and coming forward to clap the boy on the head for the very first time. "I think we can guess the rest of the story. Can we not guess the rest of the story, Dugald?"

The General sat bewildered, the only one out of the secret, into which Miss Mary's whisper to the Cornal has not brought him.

"I am not good at guessing," said he; "a man at my time likes everything straightforward." And there was a little irritation in his tone.

"It's only this, Dugald," said his brother, "that here's a pluckier young fellow than we thought, and good prospects yet for a soger in the family. I never gave Jock credit for discretion, but, faith, he seems to have gone with a keen eye to the market for once in his life! If it was not for Gilian here, Turner was wanting a daughter this day; we could hardly have hit on a finer revenge."

"Revenge!" said the General, a flash jumping to his eyes, then dying away. "I would not have said that, Colin; I would not have said that. It is the phrase of a rough, quarrelsome young soldier, and we are elders who should be long by with it."

"Anyhow," said the Cornal, "here's the makings of a hero." And he beamed almost with affection on Gilian, now in a stupor at the complexity his day's doings had brought him to.

The Paymaster's rattan sounded on the stair, and "Here's John," said his sister. "He'll be very pleased, I'm sure."

It was anything but a pleased man who entered the room, his face puffed and red and his eyes searching around for his boy. He pointed a shaking finger at him.

"What, in God's name, do you mean by this?" he asked vaguely.

"Don't speak to the boy in that fashion," said the Cornal in a surprising new paternal key. "If he has been in mischief he has got out of it by a touch of the valiant—"

"Valiant!" cried the Paymaster with a sneer. "He made an ass of himself at the Waterfoot, and his stupidity would have let three or four people drown if Young Islay, a callant better than himself, had not put out a boat and rescued them. The town's ringing with it."

The scar on the Cornal's face turned almost black. "Is that true that my brother says?" said he.

Gilian searched in a reeling head for some answer he could not find; his parched lips could not have uttered it, even if he had found it, so he nodded.

"Put me to my bed, somebody," said the General, breaking in suddenly on the shock of the moment, and staggering to one side a little as he spoke. "Put me to my bed, somebody. I am getting too old to understand!"

XIX

LIGHTS OUT!

AS he spoke he staggered to the side, and would have fallen but for his sister's readiness. About that tall rush of a brother she quickly placed an arm and kept him on his feet with infinite exertion, the while uttering endearments long out of fashion for her or him, but come suddenly, at this crisis, from the grave of the past—the past where she and Dugald had played as children, with free frank hearts loving each other truly.

"Put me to my bed," said he again thickly and his eyes blurred with the utmost weariness. "Put me to my bed. O God! what is on me now? Put me to my bed."

"Dugald! Dugald! Dugald!" she cried. "My darling brother, here is Mary with you; it is just a turn." But as she said the flattering thing her face was hopeless. The odour of the southern-wood on the windowsill changed at once to laurel, rain-drenched, dark, and waving over tombs for the boy spellbound on the floor. All his shameful perturbation vanished, a trifling thing before the great Perturber's presence.

The brothers went quickly beside their sister, and took him to his bedroom, furnished sparsely always by his own wish that denied indulgence in anything much beyond a soldier's campaign quarters.

Dr Anderson came, and went, shaking hands with Miss Mary

in the lobby and his eyes most sternly bent upon the inside of his hat. "Before morning, at the very most," he said in his odd low-country voice. No more than that, and still it thundered at her soul like an infernal doom. Up she gathered her apron, up to her face, and fled in among her pots and pans, and loudly she moved among them to drown her lamentation.

Dr Colin came later and prayed in the two languages over a figure on the bed, and then went home to write another sermon than the one already started. The room he left was silent for a while, till of a sudden the eyes of the General opened and he looked upon the sorry company.

"Bring me MacGibbon," said he in a voice extremely sensible.

Gilian ran up the street and fetched the old comrade, who put his hand upon the General's head.

"Dugald, do you ken me?" said he.

"Do I ken you?" said the General with an unpractised smile. "You're the laddie that burned the master's cane. I would know your voice if you were in any guise, and what masquerade is this that you should be so old? . . . We're to be the first to move in the morning, under arms at scream of day. . . . Lord, but I'm tired! Bob, Bob, they're not thinking of us at home in the old place I'll warrant, and tomorrow we may be stricken corpses for the king without so much as Macintyre's stretching-board to give us a soger's chest and shoulders."

"Was there anything I could do, Dugald?" said the comrade, a ludicrous man with his paunch now far beyond the limit of the soldier's belt he used to buckle easily, wearing in a clownish notion of deference to this soldier's passing a foolish small Highland bonnet he had donned in old campaigns.

"There was something running in my mind," said the man in the bed. "I think I would be wanting you to take word home in case anything happened. I was thinking of—of—of—what was her name, now? You know the one I mean—her ladyship in Glen Shira. Am I not stupid to forget it? that's the worst of the bottle! What was her name, now? . . . *Battalion will form an hollow square.* . . . The name, the name, what was it? . . . *On the centre companies 'kwards wheel. . . .* I'm wearied to the marrow of my bones, all but the right arm, that's like a feather, that's like a . . . *By the right angle of the front face; sub-divisions to the right and left half wheel. Re-form the square. Halt! Dress!* . . . What's that piper doing out there? MacVurich, come in! This is not a reel at a Skye wedding. . . . Let me see, I have the name on the tip of my tongue—what could it be, now? *Steady, men!*"

The door of the chamber was pushed in a little, and to Gilian's mouth his heart rose up at the manifestation, for what was this with no footstep on the wooden stair? About him he felt of a sudden cold airs waft, and the door ajar with no one entering glued his gaze upon its panels. The others in the room had not perceived it. Miss Mary, grown of a sudden plain and old, looked up in the Cornal's face, craving there for something for the ease of sorrow, as if he that had wandered so far and seen the Enemy so often and so ugly had some secret to share with her whereby this ancient trouble could be marred. There she found no consolation. No magician but only the brother looked over an untidy scarf and a limp high collar at the delirious man in bed. The Paymaster stood at the window frowning out upon the street; MacGibbon coughed in short dry jerky coughs, patted with a bony hand upon the coverlet, turned his head away. A stillness that was like a swoon came over all.

"Is that you, mother?" It was the General who broke the quiet, and his eyes were on his sister. A flush had fallen like a sunset on his face, his eyes were very clear and full, and, with his shaven cheeks, he might in the mitigate light of the chamber have been a lad new waked from an unpleasant dream. His sister put her head upon the pillow beside him and an arm about his shoulders.

"Oh, Dugald. Dugald!" said she, "it is not mother yet, but only Mary." And the bedstead shook with the stress of her grief.

"Mary, is it?" said he, shutting his eyes again. "What are you laughing at? I was not up there at all; I never saw her today, upon my word; I was just giving Black George an exercise no further than the Boshang Gate. . . . I'm saying, though, you need not let on about it to Colin . . . Colin, Colin, Colin, I wish we were home; the leaf must be fine and green upon Dunchuach. . . . They're over the river at Aldea Tajarda, and we push on to Cieudada. . . . What's that, Mackay? let go the girl! And you the Highland gentleman! *Lo sien—sien—siento mucho, Señora.*"

"I am at your shoulder, Dugald, do you not know me?" asked the Cornal, gently putting his sister aside. His brother looked and smiled again, but did not seem to see him.

"What was her name? and I'll send her my love and duty, for, man, between us, I was fond of her, too. . . . There was a song she had:

> The Rover went a-roving far upon the foreign seas,
> Oh, hail to thee, my dear, and fare-ye-weel.

Only it was in the Gaelic she sung it."

His voice, that was very weak and thin now, cracked, and no sound came though his lips moved.

Miss Mary took a cup and wet his lips. He seemed to think it a Communion, for again he shut his eyes, and "God," said he, "I am a sinful man to be sitting at Thy tables, but Thou knowest the soldier's trade, the soldier's sacrifice, and Thou art ready to forgive."

And still Gilian was in his bewilderment and fear about the open door. Had anything come in that was there beside them at the bed? Down in the kitchen Peggy poked the fire with less than her customary vigour, but between her cheerful and worldly occupation and this doleful room, felt Gilian, lay a space—a stairway full of dreads. All the stories he had heard of Death personified came to him fast upon each other, and they are numerous about winter fires in the Highland glens. He could fancy almost that he saw the plaided spectre by the bedside, arms akimbo, smiling ghastly, waiting till his prey was done with earthly conversation. It was horrible to be the only one in that chamber to know of the terrific presence that had entered at the door, and the boy's mouth parched with old, remote, unreasonable fears.

They did not disappear, those childish terrors, even when a kitten moved across the floor and began to toy with the vallance of the bed, explaining at once the door's opening. For might not the kitten, he thought, be more than Peggy's foundling, be the other Thing disguised? He watched its gambols at the feet of that distressed household, watched its pawing at the fringe, turning round upon itself in playfulness, emblem surely of the cruel heedlessness of nature.

MacGibbon moved to the window and stood beside the Paymaster, saying no word, but looking out at the vacant street, its causeway still shining with the rain. They were turning their backs, as it were, on a sorrow irremediable. Miss Mary and the Cornal stood alone by the dying man. He lay like a log but that his left hand played restlessly on the coverlet, long in the fingers, sinewy at the wrist. Miss Mary took it in hers and put palm to palm, and caressed the back with her other hand with an overflowing of affection that murmured at her throat. And now that MacGibbon did not see and the Cornal had blurred eyes upon his brother's boyish countenance, she felt free to caress, and she laid the poor hand against her cheek and coyly kissed it.

The General turned his look upon her wet face with a moment's comprehension. "Tuts! never mind, Mary, my dear," said he, "it might have been with Jamie yonder on the field, and there—there you have a son—in a manner—left to comfort you." Then he began to wander anew. "A son," said he, "a son. Whose son? Turner threw our sonlessness in our Jock's face, but it was in my mind there was a boy somewhere we expected something of."

Miss Mary beckoned on Gilian to come forward to the bedside. He rose from the chair he sat on in the furthest corner with his dreads and faltered over.

"What boy's this?" said the General, looking at him with surmising eyes. "He puts me in mind of—of—of—of an old tale somewhere with a sunny day in it. Nan! Nan! Nan!—that's the name. I knew I would come on it, for the sound of it was always like a sunny day in Portugal or Spain—*He estado en España.*"

"This is the boy, Dugald," said Miss Mary; "this is just our Gilian."

"I see that. I know him finely," said the General, turning upon him a roving melancholy eye: "Jock's recruit. . . . Did you get back from your walk, my young lad? I never could fathom you, but perhaps you have your parts. . . . Well, well . . . what are ye dreaming on the day? . . . Eh? Ha! ha! ha! Aye dreaming, that was you; you'll be dreaming next that the lassie likes you. Mind, she jilted Jock, she jilted Colin, she jilted me; were we not the born idiots? yet still-and-on. . . . Sixty miles in twenty-four hours; good marching, lads, good marching, for half-starved men, and not the true heather-bred at that."

The voice was becoming weaker in every sentence, the flush was paling on the countenance. Standing by the bedside, the Cornal looked upon his brother with a most rueful visage, his face hoved up with tears.

"This beats all!" said he, and he turned and went beside the men at the window, leaving Miss Mary caressing still at the hand upon the coverlet, and with an arm about the boy.

"He was a strong, fine, wiry man in his time," said MacGibbon, looking over his shoulder at this end of a stormy life. "I mind him at Talavera; I think he was at his very best there."

The Paymaster looked, too, at the figure upon the bed, looked with a bent head, under lowered eyebrows, his lip and chin brown with snuffy tears.

"At sixteen he threw the cabar against the champion of the three shires, and though he was a sober man a bottle was neither here nor there with him," said the Cornal.

Miss Mary was upon her knees.

"The batteries are to open fire on San Vincent; seven eighteen-pounders and half a dozen howitzers are scarcely enough for that job. Tell Mackellar to move up two hundred yards further on the right." The General babbled again of his wars in a child's accent, that rose now and then stormily to the vehemence of the battlefield. "*Columns deploy on the right centre company. . . . No, no, close column on the rear of the Grenadiers. . . .* I wish, I wish. . . . Jock, Jock, where's your boy now? I cannot see him, I'm sore feared he's hiding in the sutler's vans. I knew him for a dreamer from the first day I saw him. . . . That's Williams gone and my step to Major come. God sain him! we could have better spared another man. . . . *Halt, dress!*"

He opened his eyes again and they fell upon Gilian. "You mind me of a boy I once knew," said he. "Poor boy, poor boy, what a pity of you! My sister Mary would have liked you. I think we never gave her her due, and indeed she had a generous hand."

"Here she's at your side, dear Dugald," said his sister, and her head went down upon his breast.

"So she is," said he, arousing to the fact; "I might be sure she would be there!" He disengaged the hand she had in hers, and wearily placed it for a moment on her hair with an awkward effort at fondling. "Are you tired, my dear?" he said, repeating it in the Gaelic. "It's a dreich dreich dying on a feather bed." He smiled once more feebly, and Gilian screamed, for the kitten had touched him on the leg.

"Go downstairs, this is no place for you, my dear," said Miss Mary; and he went willingly, hearing a stertorous breathing in the bed behind him.

PART II

XX

THE RETURN

WHEN the General died, the household in the high burgh
land suffered a change marvellous enough considering how
little that old man musing in his parlour had had to do for years
with its activities. Cornal Colin would sit of an evening with
candles extravagantly burning more numerous than before to
make up for the glowing heart extinguished; the long winter
nights, black and stifling and immense around the burgh town,
and the wind with a perpetual moan among the trees, would
find him abandoned to his sorry self, looking into the fire,
the week's paper on his knees unread, and him full of old
remembrances and regrets. It had become for him a parlour full
of ghosts. He could not, in October blasts, but think of Jamie
yonder on the cold foreign field with no stone for his memorial;
Dugald, so lately gone, an old man, bent and palsied, would
return in the flicker of the candle, remitted to his prime, the very
counterpart of the sturdy gallant on the wall. Sometimes he would
talk with these wraiths, and Miss Mary standing still in the lobby,
her heart tortured by his loneliness, would hear him murmuring
in these phantom visitations. She would, perhaps, venture in now
and then timidly, and take a seat unbidden on the corner of a
chair near him, and embark on some topic of the day. For a
little he would listen almost with a brightness, but brief, brief

was the mood; very soon would he let his chin fall upon his breast, and with pouted lips relapse into his doleful meditation.

All life, all the interests, the activities of the town seemed to drift by him; folk saw him less and less often on the plain stones of the street; children grew up from pinafores to kilts, from kilts to breeches, never knowing of his presence in that community that at last he saw but of an afternoon in momentary glimpses from the window.

On a weekend, perhaps, the veterans would come up to cheer him if they could; tobacco that he nor any of his had cared for in that form would send its cloud among Miss Mary's dear naperies, but she never complained: they might have fumed her out of press and pantry if they brought her brother cheer. They talked loudly; they laughed boisterously; they acted a certain zest in life: for a little he would rouse to their entertainment, fiddling heedlessly with an empty glass, but anon he would see the portrait of Dugald looking on them wondering at their folly, and that must daunten him. It would not take long till some extravagance of these elders made him wince, and there was Cornal Colin again in the dolours, poor company for them that would harbour any delusion of youth. It was pitiful then to see them take their departures, almost slinking, ashamed to have sounded the wrong note in that chamber of sober recollections. Miss Mary, lighting them to the door with one of her mother's candlesticks, felt as she had the light above her head and showed them down the stair as if she had been the last left at a funeral feast. Her shadow on the wall, dancing before her as she returned, seemed some mockery of the night.

Only Old Brooks could rouse the Cornal to some spirit of liveliness. In a neighbourly compassion the dominie would come in of a Sunday or a Friday evening, leaving for an hour or two the books he was so fond of that he must have a little one in his pocket to feel the touch of when he could not be studying the pages. Seated in the Cornal's chair, he had a welcome almost blithe. For he was a man of great urbanity, sobered by thought upon the complexities of life, but yet with sparkling courage.

He found the brothers now contemptuous of the boy who showed no sign of adaptability or desire for that gallant career that had been theirs. These, indeed, were the cold days for Gilian in a household indifferent to him save Miss Mary, who grew fonder every day, doting upon him like a lover for a score of reasons, but most of all because he was that rarity the perpetual child, and she must be loving somewhere.

"I have not seen the lad at school for a week now," Brooks said, compelled at last by long truancies.

"So?" said the Cornal, showing no interest. "It is not my affair. John must look after his own recruit, who seems an uncommon tardy one, Mr Brooks—an uncommon tardy."

"But I get small satisfaction from the Captain."

"I daresay, I daresay; would you wonder at that in our Jock? He's my brother, but some way there is wanting in him the stuff of Jamie and of Dugald. Even in his throes upon his latter bed Dugald could see what Jock could never see—the doom in this lad's countenance. As for me, I was done with the fellow after the trick he played us in his story of the wreck on Ealan Dubh. I blame him, in a way, for my brother Dugald's stroke."

The dominie looked in a startled remonstrance. "I would not blame him for that, Cornal," he said: "that was what the Sheriff calls *damnum fatale*. Upon my word, though Gilian has been something of a heartbreak to myself, I must say you give him but scant justice among you here."

"I can see in him but youth wasted, and the prodigal of that is spendthrift indeed."

"I would not just say wasted," protested the dominie. "There's the makings of a fine man in him if we give him but a shove in the right direction. He baffles me to comprehend, and yet"—this a little shamefacedly—"and yet I've brought him to my evening prayers. I would like guidance on the laddie. With him it's a spoon made or a horn spoiled. Sometimes I feel I have in him fine stuff and pliable, and I'll be trying to fathom how best to work it, but my experience has always been with more common metal, and I am feared, I'm feared, we may be botching him."

"That was done for us in the making of him," said the Cornal.

"I would not say that either, Cornal," said the dominie firmly. "But I'm wae to see him brought up on no special plan. The Captain seems to have given up his notion of the army for him."

"You can lead a horse to the water but you cannot make him drink. What's to be made of him? Here's he sixteen or thereabouts, and just a bairn over lesson-books at every chance."

Brooks smiled wistfully. "It is not the lesson-books, Cornal, not the lesson-books exactly. I wish it was, but books of any kind—come now, Cornal, you can hardly expect me to condemn them in the hands of youth." He fondled the little Horace in his pocket as a man in company may squeeze his wife's hand. "They made my bread and butter, did the books, for fifty years, and Gilian will get no harm there. The lightest of novelles and the thinnest of ballants have something precious for a lad of his kind."

The Cornal made no response; the issue was too trivial to keep him from his meditation. His chin sunk upon his chest as it would not have done had the dominie kept to the commoner channels of his gossip that was generally on universal history, philosophy of a rough and ready rural kind, and theology handled with a freedom that would have seriously alarmed Dr Colin if he could have heard his Session Clerk in the operation.

"Eh? Are you hearing me, Cornal?" he pressed, eager to compel something for the youth whose days were being wasted.

"Speak to Miss Mary," was all the Cornal would say. "I have nothing to do with him, and John's heedless now, for he knows his plan for the army is useless."

The dominie shook his head. "Man!" he cried. "I cannot even tell of his truancy there, for her heart's wrapped up in the youth. When she speaks to me about him her face is lighted up like a day in spring, and I dare not say cheep to shatter her illusion."

Gilian, alas! knew how little these old men now cared for him. The Cornal had long since ceased his stories; the Paymaster, coming in from his meridian in the Sergeant More, would pass him on the stair with as little notice as if he were a stranger in the street. Miss Mary was his only link between his dreams, his books, and the common life of the day, and it was she who at last made the move that sent him back to Ladyfield to learn with Cameron the shepherd—still there in the interests of the Paymaster who had whimsically remained tenant—the trade that was not perhaps best suited for him, but at least came somehow most conveniently to his practice. But for the loss of her consoling and continual company there would have been almost joy on his part at this returning to the scene of his childhood. He went back to it on a summer day figuring to himself the content, the carelessness that had been his there before and thinking, poor fool, they were waiting where he had left them.

Ladyfield was a small farm of its kind with four hundred sheep, seven cows, two horses, a goat or two and poultry. When the little old woman with a face like a nut was alive she could see the whole tack at one sweep of the eye from the rowan at the door, on the left up to the plateau where five burns were born, on the right to the peak of Drimfern. A pleasant place for meditation, bleak in winter for the want of trees, but in other seasons in a bloom of colour.

Though he was there 'prentice to a hard calling, Gilian's life was more the gentle's than the shepherd's. He might be often on the hill, but it was seldom to tend his flock and bring them to fank for clip or keeling, it was more often to meditate with a full pagan eye upon the mysteries of the countryside. A certain weeping effect of the mists on the ravines, one particular moaning sound of the wind among the rocks, had a strange solace for his ear, chording with some sweet melancholy of his spirit. He loved it all, yet at times he would flee from the place as if a terror were at his heels and in a revolt against the narrowness of his life, hungering almost to starvation for some companionship, for some salve to an anxious mind, and, in spite of his shyness, bathe in the society of the town—an idler. The people as he rode past would indicate him with a toss of the head over their shoulders, and say, "The Paymaster's boy," and yet the down was showing on his lip. He would go up the street looking from side to side with an expectancy that had no object; he stared almost rudely at faces, seeking for he knew not what.

It was not the winters with their cold, their rain, their wind and darkness, that oppressed him most in his banishment, but the summers. In the winter the mists crowded so close about, and the snow so robbed the land of all variety, that Ladyfield house with its peats burning ceaselessly, its clean paven court, its store of books he had gathered there, was an enviable place for compactness and comfort, and he could feel as if the desirable world was in his immediate neighbourhood. Down in the street he knew the burgh men were speeding the long winter nights with song and mild carousal; the lodges and houses up the way, each with its spirit keg and licence, gave noisiness to the home-returning of tenants for Lochow from the town, and as they went by Ladyfield in the dark they would halloo loudly to the recluse lad within who curled, nor shot, nor shintied, nor drank, nor did any of the things it was youth's manifest duty to do.

But the summer made his station there in Ladyfield almost intolerable. For the roads, crisp, yellow, straight, demanded his going on them; the sun-dart among distant peaks revealed the width and glamour of the world. "Come away," said the breezes; passing gipsies all jangling with tins upon their backs awoke dreams poignant and compelling. When the summer was just on the turn at that most pitiful of periods, the autumn, he must go more often down to town.

XXI

THE SORROWFUL SEASON

IT was on a day in a month of August he went to town to escape the lamentation of the new-weaned lambs, that made the glen sorrowful from Carnus to Kincreggan. A sound pleasant in the ears of Cameron the shepherd, who read no grief in it, but the comfortable tale of progress, growth, increasing flocks, but to Gilian almost heart-rending. The separation for which the ewes wailed and their little ones wept, seemed a cruelty; that far-extending lamentation of the flocks was part of some universal coronach for things eternally doomed. Never seemed a landscape so miserable as then. The hills, in the morning haze, gathered in upon his heart and seemed to crush it. A poor farmer indeed to be thus affected by short brute sorrows, but so it was with Gilian, and on some flimsy excuse he left Ladyfield in the afternoon and rode to town. He had grown tall and slim in those latter days; his face would have seemed—if not handsome altogether—at least notable and pleasant to any other community than this, which ever preferred to have its men full-cheeked, bronzed, robust. He had an air of gentility oddly out of place with his immediate history; in his walk and manner men never saw anything very taking, but young women of the place would feel it, puzzle themselves often as to what the mystery of him was that made his appearance on the street or on the highway put a new interest in the day.

The Paymaster was standing gossiping at the inn door with Mr. Spencer, Rixa, and General Turner himself—no less, for the ancient rancour at the moment was at rest.

"Here he comes," said old Mars sourly, as Gilian turned round the Arches into the town. "He's like Gillesbeg Aotram, always seeking for something he'll never find."

"Your failure!" said Turner playfully, but with poor inspiration, as in a moment he realised.

The Paymaster bridled. He had no answer to a truth so manifest to himself. In a lightning-flash he remembered his boast in the schoolroom at the dregy, and hoped Turner had not so good a memory as himself. He could only vent his annoyance on Gilian, who drew up his horse with a studied curvet—for still there was the play-actor in him to some degree.

"Down again?" said he with half a sneer. There is a way of leaning on a stick and talking over the shoulder at an antagonist that can be very trying to the antagonist if he has any sense of shyness.

"Down again," agreed Gilian uncomfortably, sorry he had had the courtesy to stop. The others moved away, for they knew the relations of the man and his adopted son were not of the pleasantest.

"An odd kind of farm training!" said the old officer. "I wish I could fathom whether you are dolt or deep one."

Gilian might have come off the horse and argued it, for he had an answer pat enough. He sat still and fingered the reins, looking at the old man with the puffed face, and the constricted bull neck, and self-satisfaction written upon every line of him, and concluding it was not worth while to explain to a nature so shallow. And the man, after all, was his benefactor: scrupulous about every penny he spent on himself, he had paid, at Miss Mary's solicitations, for the very horse the lad bestrode.

"Do you know what Turner said there?" asked the Paymaster, still with his contemptuous side to the lad. "He called you our failure. God, and it's true! Neither soldier nor shepherd seems to be in you, a muckle bulrush nodding to the winds of heaven! See that sturdy fellow at the quay there?"

Gilian looked and saw Young Islay, a smart ensign home on leave from the county corps that even yet was taking so many fine young fellows from that community.

"There's a lad who's a credit to all about him, and he had not half your chances; do you know that?"

"He seems to have the knack of turning up for my poor comparison ever since I can mind," said Gilian, good-humouredly. "And somehow," he added, "I have a notion that he has but half my brains as well as half my chances." He looked up to see Turner still at the inn door. "General Turner," he cried, his face reddening and his heart stormy, "I hear that in your frank estimate I'm the Paymaster's failure; is it so bad as that? It seems if I may say it, scarcely fair from one of your years to one of mine."

"Shut your mouth!" said the Paymaster coarsely, as Turner came forward. "You have no right to repeat what I said and show the man I took his insolence to heart."

"I said it; I don't deny," answered the General, coming forward from the group at the door and putting his hand in a friendly freedom on the horse's neck and looking up with some regret in Gilian's face. "One says many things in an impetus. Excuse a soldier's extravagance. I never meant it either for your ear or for unkindness. And you talk of ages: surely a man so much your senior has a little privilege?"

"Not to judge youth, sir, which he may have forgotten to understand," said Gilian, yet very red and uneasy, but with a wistful countenance. "If you'll think of it I'm just at the beginning of life, a little more shy of making the plunge perhaps than Young Islay there might be, or your own son Sandy, who's a credit to his corps, they say."

"Quite right, Gilian, and I ask your pardon," said the General, putting out his hand. "God knows who the failures of this life are; some of them go about very flashy semblances of success. In these parts we judge by the external signs, that are not always safest; for my son Sandy, who looks so thriving, and so douce when he comes home, is after all a scamp whose hands are ever in his simple daddy's pockets." But this he said laughing, with a father's reservation.

The Paymaster stared at this encounter, in some ways so much beyond his comprehension. "Humph!" he ejaculated; and Gilian rode on, leaving in the group behind him an uncomfortable feeling that somehow, somewhere, an injustice had been done.

Miss Mary's face was at the window whenever his horse's hooves came clattering on the causeway—she knew the very clink of the shoes. "There's something wrong with the laddie today," she cried to Peggy; "he looks unco dejected;" and her own countenance fell in sympathy with her darling's mood.

She met him on the stair as if by accident, pretending to be going down to her cellar in the pend. They did not even shake hands; it is a formality neglected in these parts except for long farewells or unexpected meetings. Only she must take his bonnet and cane from him and in each hand take them upstairs as if she were leading thus two little children, her gaze fond upon the back of him.

"Well, auntie!" he said, showing at first no sign of the dejection she had seen from the window. "Here I am again. I met the Captain up at the inn door, and he seems to grudge me the occasional comfort of hearing any other voice than my own. I could scarcely tell him as I can tell you, that the bleating of the lambs gave me a sore heart. The very hills are grieving with them. I'm a fine farmer, am I not? Are you not vexed for me?" His lips could no longer keep his secret, their corners trembled with the excess of his feeling.

She put a thin hand upon his coat lapel, and with the other picked invisible specks of dust from his coat sleeve, her eyes revealing by their moisture a ready harmony with his sentiment.

"Farmer indeed!" said she with a gallant attempt at badinage; "you're as little for that, I'm afraid, as you're for the plough or the army." She led him into her room and set a chair for him as if he had been a prince, only to have an excuse for putting an arm for a moment almost round his waist. She leaned over him as he sat and came as close as she dared in contact with his hair, all the time a glow in her face.

"And what did you come down for?" she asked, expecting an old answer he never varied in.

He looked up and smiled with a touch of mock gallantry wholly new. "To see you, of course," said he, as though she had been a girl.

She was startled at this first revelation of the gallant in what till now had been her child. She flushed to the coils above her ear. Then she laughed softly and slapped him harmlessly on the back. "Get away with you," she said, "and do not make fun of a douce old maiden!" She drew back as she spoke and busily set about some household office, fearing, apparently, that her fondness had been made too plain.

"Do you know what the Captain said?" he remarked in a tone less hearty, moving about the room in a searching discontent.

"The old fool!" she answered irrelevantly, anticipating some unpleasantness. "He went out this morning in a tiravee about a button wanting from his waistcoat. It's long since I learned never to heed him much."

It was a story invented on the moment; in heavenly archives that sin of love is never indexed. Her face had at once assumed a look of anxiety, for she felt that the encounter had caused Gilian's dejection as he rode down the street.

"What was he saying?" she asked at last, seeing there was no sign of his volunteering more. And she spoke with a very creditable show of indifference, and even hummed a little bar of song as she turned some airing towels on a winter-dyke beside the fire.

"Do you think I'm a failure, auntie?" asked he, facing her. "That was what he called me."

She was extremely hurt and angry.

"A failure!" she cried. "Did anyone ever hear the like? God forgive me for saying it of my brother, but what failure is more notorious than his own? A windy old clerk-soger with his name in a ballant, no more like his brothers than I'm like Duke George."

"You do not deny it!" said Gilian simply.

She moved up to him and looked at him with an affection that was a transfiguration.

"My dear, my dear!" said she, "is there need for me to deny it? What are you yet but a laddie?"

He fingered the down upon his lip.

"But a laddie," she repeated, determined not to see. "All the world's before you, and a braw bonny world it is, for all its losses and its crosses. There is not a man of them at the inn door who would not willingly be in your shoes. The sour old remnants—do I not know them? Grant me patience with them!"

"It was General Turner's word," said Gilian, utterly unconsoled, and he wondered for a moment to see her flush.

"He might have had a kinder thought," said she, "with his own affairs, as they tell me, much ajee, and Old Islay pressing for his loans. I'll warrant you do not know anything of that, but it's the clavers of the Cross well." She hurried on, glad to get upon a topic even so little away from what had vexed her darling. "Old Islay has his schemes, they say, to get Maam tacked on to his own tenancy of Drimlee and his son out of the army, and the biggest gentleman farmer in the shire. He has the ear of the Duke, and now he has Turner under his thumb. Oh my sorrow, what a place of greed and plot!"

"That Turner said it, showed he thought it!" said Gilian, not a whit moved from bitter reflection upon his wounded feelings.

"Amn't I telling you?" said Miss Mary. "It's just his own sorrows souring him. There's Sandy, his son, a through-other lad (though I aye liked the laddie and he's young yet), and his daughter back from her schooling in Edinburgh, educated, or polished, or finished off as they call it—I hope she kens what she's to be after next, for I'm sure her father does not."

Gilian's breast filled with some strange new sense of sudden relief. It was as if he had been climbing out of an airless, hopeless valley, and emerged upon a hill-crest, and was struck there by the flat hand of the lusty wind and stiffened into hearty interest in the rolling and variegated world around. In a second, the taunt of the General of Maam was no more to him than a dream. A dozen emotions mastered him, and he tingled from head to foot, for the first time man.

"Oh, and *she's* back, is she?" said he with a crafty indifference, as one who expects no answer.

Miss Mary was not deceived. She had moved to the window and was looking down into the street where the children played, but the new tone of his voice, and the pause before it, gave her a sense of desertion, and she grieved. On the ridges of the opposite lands, seagulls perched and preened their feathers, pigeons kissed each other as they moved about the feet of the passers-by. A servant lass bent over a window in the dwelling of Marget Maclean and smiled upon a young fisherman who went up the middle of the street, noisily in knee-high boots. The afternoon was glorious with sun.

XXII

IN CHURCH

IF the lambs were still wailing when Gilian got back to
Ladyfield he never heard them. Was the glen as sad and empty
as before? Then he was absent, indeed! For he was riding through
an air almost jocund, and his spirit sang within him. The burns
bubbled merrily among the long grasses and the bracken, the
myrtle cast a sharp and tonic sweetness all around. The mountain bens no more pricked the sky in solemn loneliness, but
looked one to the other over the plains—companions, lovers,
touched to warmth and passion by the sun of the afternoon. It
was as if an empty world had been fresh tenanted. Gilian, as he
rode up home, woke to wonder at his own cheerfulness. He
reflected that he had been called a failure—and he laughed.

Next day he was up with the sun, and Cameron was amazed
at this new zeal that sent him, crook in hand, to the hill for
some wanderers of the flock, whistling blithely as he went. Long
after he was gone he could see him, black against the sky, on the
backbone of the mountain, not very active for a man in search
of sheep. But what he could not see so far was Gilian's rapture
as he looked upon the two glens severed by so many weary miles
of roadway, but close together at his feet. And the chimneys of
Maam (that looks so like an ancient castle at Dhu Loch head)
were smoking cheerily below. Looking down upon them he made

a pretence to himself after a little that he had just that moment remembered who was now there. He even said the words to himself, "Oh! Nan—Miss Nan is there!" in the tone of sudden recollection, and he flushed in the cold breeze of the lonely mountain, half at the mention of the name, half at his own deceit with himself.

He allowed himself to fancy what the girl had grown to in her three years' absence among Lowland influences, that, by all his reading, must be miraculous indeed. He saw her a little older only than she had been when they sat in the den of the *Jean* or walked a magic garden, the toss of spate-brown hair longer upon her shoulders, a little more sedateness in her mien. About her still hung the perfume of young birch, and her gown was still no lower than her knees. He met her (still in his imagination upon the hill-top) by some rare chance, in the garden where they had strayed, and his coolness and ease were a marvel to himself.

"Miss Nan!" he cried. "They told me you were returned and . . ." What was to follow of the sentence he could not just now say.

She blushed to see him; his hand tingled at the contact with hers. She answered in a pleasant tone of Edinburgh gentility, like Lady Charlotte, and they walked a little way together, conversing wondrously upon life and books and poems, whose secrets they shared between them. He was able to hold her fascinated by the sparkle of his talk; he had never before felt so much the master of himself, and his head fairly hummed with high notions. They talked of their childhood—

Here Gilian dropped from the clouds, at first with a sense of some unpleasant memory undefined, then with shivering, ashamed, as his last meeting with the girl flashed before him, and he saw himself again fleeing, an incapable, from the sea-beach at Ealan Dubh.

If she should remember that so vividly as he did! The thought was one to fly from, and he sped down the hill furiously, and plied himself busily for the remainder of the day with an industry Cameron had never seen him show before. Upon him had obviously come a change of some wholesome and compelling kind. He knew it himself, and yet—he told himself—he could not say what it was.

Sunday came, and he went down to church in the morning as usual, but dressed with more scruples than was customary. Far up the glen the bell jangled through the trees of the Duke's policies, and the road was busy with people bound for the sermon of Dr Colin. They walked down the glen in groups, elderly women with snow-white piped caps, younger ones with sober hoods, and all with Bibles carried in their napkins and southernwood or tansy between the leaves. The road was dry and sandy; they cast off their shoes, as was their custom, and walked barefoot, carrying them in their hands till they came to the plane-tree at the crossroads, and put them on again to enter the town with fit decorum. The men followed, unhappy in their unaccustomed suits of broad-cloth or hodden, dark, flat-faced, heavy of foot, ruminant, taming their secular thoughts as they passed the licensed houses to some harmony with the sacred nature of their mission. The harvest fields lay half-garnered, smoke rose indolent and blue from cot-houses and farm-towns; very high up on the hills a ewe would bleat now and then with some tardy sorrow, for her child. A most tranquil day, the very earth breathing peace.

The Paymaster and Miss Mary sat together in Keils pew, Gilian with them, conscious of a new silk cravat. But his mind almost unceasingly was set upon a problem whose solution lay behind him. Keils pew was in front, the Maam pew was at least seven rows behind, in the shadow of the loft, beneath the cushioned and gated preserve of the castle. One must not at any time look round, even for the space of a second, lest it should be thought he was guilty of some poor worldly curiosity as to the occupants of the ducal seat, and today especially, Gilian dared not show an unusual interest in the Turner pew. His acute ear had heard its occupants enter after a loud salutation from the elder at the plate to the General, he fancied there was a rustle of garments such as had not been heard there for three years. All other sounds in the church—the shuffle of feet, the chewing of sweets with which the worshippers in these parts always induce wakefulness, the noisy breathing of Rixa as he hunched in his corner beside the pulpit—seemed to stop while a skirt rustled. A glow went over him, and unknowing what he did he put forward his hand to take his Bible off the book-board.

Miss Mary from the corners of her eyes, and without turning her face in the slightest degree from the pulpit where Dr Colin was soon to appear, saw the action. It was contrary to every form in that congregation; it was a shocking departure from the rule that no one should display sign of life (except in the covert conveyance of a lozenge under the napkin to the mouth, or a clearance of the throat), and she put a foot with pressure upon that of Gilian nearest her. Yet as she did so, no part of her body seen above the boards of the pew betrayed her movement.

Gilian flushed hotly, drew back his hand quickly, without having touched the book, and bent a stern gaze upon the stairs by which Dr Colin would descend to his battlements.

It was a day of stagnant air, and the church swung with sleepy influences. The very pews and desks, the pillars of the loft and the star-crowned canopy of the pulpit, seemed in their dry and mouldy antiquity to give forth soporific dry accessions to that somnolent atmosphere, and the sun-rays, slanted over the heads of the worshippers, showed full of dust. Outside, through the tall windows, could be seen the beech-trees of the Avenue and the crows upon them busy at their domestic affairs. Children in the Square cried to each other, a man's footsteps passed on the causeway, returned, and stopped below the window. Everybody knew it was Black Duncan the seaman, of an older church and reluctant, yet anxious, to share in some of the Sabbath exercises.

Gilian, with the back of the pew coming up near his neck, wished fervently it had been built lower, for he knew how common and undignified his view from the rear must thus be made. Also he wished he could have had a secret eye that he might look unashamed in the direction of his interest. He tingled with feeling when he fancied after a little (indeed, it was no more than fancy) that there was a perceptible odour of young birch. Again he was remitted to his teens, sitting transported in the *Jean*, soaring heavenward upon a song by a bold child with spate-brown hair. He put forward his hand unconsciously again, and this time he had the Bible on his knee before Miss Mary could check him.

She looked down with motionless horror at his fingers fever-ishly turning over the leaves, and saw that he had the volume upside down. Her pressure on his foot was delayed by astonish-ment. What could this conduct of his mean? He was disturbed about something; or perhaps he was unwell. And as she saw him still holding the volume upside down on his knee and continuing to look at it with absent eyes she put her mittened hand into the pocket of her silk gown, produced a large peppermint lozenge, and passed it into his hand.

This long unaccustomed courtesy found him awkwardly un-prepared, and his fingers not closing quickly enough on the sweet it fell on the floor. It rolled with an alarming noise far to the left, and stirred the congregation like a trumpet. Though little movement showed it, every eye was on the pew from which this disturbance came, and Miss Mary and Gilian knew it. Miss Mary did not flinch; she kept a steadfast eye straight in front of her, but to those behind her the sudden colour of her neck betrayed her culpability. Gilian was wretched, all the more because he heard a rustle of the skirts behind in Turner's pew, and his imagination saw Miss Nan suppressing her laughter with shak-ing hair and quite conscious that he had been the object of Miss Mary's attention. He felt the blood that rushed to his body must betray itself behind. All the gowk in him came uppermost; he did not know what he was doing; he put the Bible awkwardly on the book-board in front of him, and it, too, slid to the floor with a noise even more alarming than that of the rolling sweet.

The Paymaster, clearing his throat harshly, wakened from a dover to the fact that these disturbances were in his own terri-tory, and saw the lad's confusion. If that had not informed him the mischievous smile of Young Islay in Gilian's direction would have done so. He half turned his face to Gilian, and with shut lips whispered angrily:

"Thumbs! thumbs!" he said. "God forgive you for a gomeral!" And then he stared very sternly at Rixa, who saw the movement of the swollen neck above the 'kerchief, knew that the Paymaster was administering a reproof, and was comforted exceedingly by this prelude to the day's devotions.

Gilian left the book where it lay to conceal from those behind that he had been the delinquent. But he felt, at the same time, he was detected. What a contrast the lady behind must find in his gawkiness compared with the correct and composed deportment of the Capital she had come from! He must be the rustic indeed to her, handling lollipops yet like a child, and tumbling books in a child's confusion. As if to give more acuteness to his picture of himself he saw a foil in Young Islay so trim and manly in the uniform old custom demanded for the Sunday parade, a shrewd upward tilt of the chin and lowering of the brow, his hand now and then at his cheeks, not so much to feel its pleasing roughness, as to show the fine fingers of which he was so conscious. It demanded all his strength to shake himself into equanimity, and Miss Mary felt rather than saw it.

What ailed him? Something unusual was perturbing him. An influence, an air, a current of uneasiness flowed from him and she shared his anxiety, not knowing what might be its source. His every attitude was a new and unaccustomed one. She concluded he must be unwell and a commotion set up in her heart, so that Dr Colin's opening prayer went sounding past her a thing utterly meaningless like the wind among trees, and love that is like a high march wall separated her and her favourite from the world.

She surrendered even her scruples of kirk etiquette to put out a hand timidly as they stood together at the prayer, and touched Gilian softly on the sleeve with a gush of consolation in the momentary contact.

But he never felt the touch, or he thought it accidental, for he was almost feverishly waiting till that interminable prayer was ended that he might have the last proof of the presence of the girl behind him. The crimson hangings of the canopy shook in the stridor of Dr Colin's supplication, the hollows underneath the gallery rumbled a sleepy echo; Rixa breathed ponderously and thought upon his interlocutors, but no other life was apparent; it was a man crying in the wilderness, and outside in the playground of the world the children were yet calling and laughing content, the rooks among the beeches surveyed, carelessly, the rich lush policies of the Duke.

Gilian was waiting on the final proof, that was only in the girl's own voice. He remembered her of old a daring and entrancing vocalist, in the harmony one thread of gold among the hodden grey of those simple unstudied psalmodists.

The prayer concluded, the congregation, wearied by their long stand, relapsed in their hard seats with a sense of satisfaction, the psalm was given out, the precentor stuck up on the desk before him the two tablets bearing the name of the tune, "Martyrs", and essayed at a beginning. He began too high, stopped and cleared his throat. "We will try it again," said he, and this time led the voices all in unison. Such a storm was in Gilian's mind that he could not for a little listen to hear what he expected. He had forgotten his awkwardness, he had forgotten his shame; his erratic and fleet-winged fancy had sent him back to the den of the *Jean*, and he was in the dusk of the ship's interior listening to a girl's song, moved more profoundly than when he had been actually there by some message in the notes, some soothing passionate melancholy without relation to the words or to the tune, some inexplicable and mellow vibration he had felt first as he stood, a child, on the road from Kilmalieu, and a bird solitary in the winds, lifting with curious tilt of feathers over the marshy field, had piped dolorously some mystery of animal life man must have lost when he ceased to sleep stark naked to the stars. In his mind he traced the baffling accent, failing often to come upon it, anon finding it fill all his being with an emotion he had never known before.

Miss Mary was now more alarmed than ever. For he was not singing, and his voice was for wont never wanting in that stormy and uncouth unison of sluggish men's voices, women's eager earnest shrilling. It was as if he had been absent, and so strong the illusion that she leaned to the side a little to touch him and assure herself he was there.

And that awakened him! He listened with his workaday ears to separate from the clamour, as he once had done, the thread of golden melody. For a moment he was amazed and disappointed; no unusual voice was there. If Miss Nan was behind him, she was taking only a mute part in the praise, amused mildly perhaps—he could not blame her—by this rough contrast with the more tuneful praise she was accustomed to elsewhere.

And then—then he distinguished her. No, he was wrong; no, he was right, there it was again, not so loud and clear as he had expected, but yet her magic, unmistakably, as surely as when first it sounded to him in "The Rover" and "The Man with the Coat of Green". A thrill went through him. He rose at the close of the psalm, and trod upon clouds more airily, high-breastedly, uplifted triumphantly, than Ronaig of Gaul who marched, in the story, upon plunging seas from land to land.

"He has been eating something wrong," concluded Miss Mary, finding ease of a kind in so poor an excuse for her darling's perturbation. It accounted to her for all his odd behaviour during the remainder of the service, for his muteness in the psalmody, his restless disregard of the sermon, his hurry to be out of the straight-backed, uncomfortable pew.

As he stood to his feet to follow the Paymaster she ventured a hand from behind upon his waist, pretending to hasten the departure, but in reality to get some pleasure from the touch. Again he never heeded; he was staring at the Maam pew, from which the General and his brother were slowly moving out.

There was no girl there!

He could scarcely trust his eyes. The aisle had a few women in it, moving decorously to the door with busy eyes upon each other's clothes; but no, she was not there, whose voice had made the few psalms of the day the sweetest of his experience. When he got outside the door and upon the entrance steps the whole congregation was before him; his glance went through it in a flash twice, but there was no Miss Nan. Her father and his brother walked up the street alone. Gilian realised that his imagination, and his imagination only, had tenanted the pew. She was not there!

XXIII

YOUNG ISLAY

"THE clash in the kirkyard is worth half a dozen sermons," say the unregenerate, and though no kirkyard is about the Zion of our parish, the people are used to wait a little before home-going and talk of a careful selection of secular affairs; not about the prices of hoggs and queys, for that is Commerce, nor of Saturday night's songs in the tavern, for that (in the Sabbath mind) is Sin. But of births, marriages, courtships, weather, they discourse. And Gilian, his head dazed, stood in a group with the Paymaster and Miss Mary, and some of the people of the glens, who were the ostensible reason for the palaver. At first he was glad of the excuse to wait outside, for to have gone the few yards that were necessary down the street and sat at Sunday's cold viands even with Peggy's brew of tea to follow would be to place a flight of stairs and a larch door between him and— And what? What was he reluctant to sever from? He asked himself that with as much surprise as if he had been a stranger to himself. He felt that to go within at once would be to lose something, to go out of a most agreeable atmosphere. He was not hungry. To sit with old people over an austere table with no flowers on it because of the day, and see the Paymaster snuff above his tepid second day's broth, and hear the Cornal snort because the mince-collops his toothlessness demanded on other days of the week were not available today, would be, somehow, to bring a sordid, unable, drab and weary world close up on a vision of joy and beauty. He felt it in his flesh, in some flutter of the breast. It was better to be out here in the sun among the chattering people, to have nothing between him and Glen Shira but a straight sweep of windblown highway. From the steps of the church he could see the Boshang Gate and the hazy ravines and jostling elbows of the hills in Shira Glen. He saw it all, and in one bound his spirit vaulted there, figuring her whose psalm he had but heard in the delusion of desire.

The Duke came lazily down the steps, threw a glance among his clan and tenantry, cast his plaid, with a fine grace, about his shoulders, touching his bonnet with a finger as hat or bonnet rose in salutation, and he went fair up in the middle of the street.

The conversation ceased, and people looked after him as on an Emperor.

"He's going to London on Tuesday, I hear," said Major Hall to Mr Spencer. It was the Major's great pride to know the prospective movements at the Castle sooner than anyone else, and he was not above exchanging snuff-mulls with Wat Thomson, the ducal boot-brusher, if ducal news could only be got thereby.

"London, London; did you say, London, sir?" said the innkeeper, looking again with an envy after his Grace, the name at once stirring in him the clime from which he was an exile. And the smell of peaty clothes smote him on the nostril for the first time that day. He had been so many Sundays accustomed to it that as a rule he no longer perceived it but now it rose in contrast to the beefy, beer-charged, comfortable odours of his native town.

"Ah! he's going on Tuesday," said the Paymaster, "but when Duke George's gone, there are plenty of Dukes to take his place. Every officer in his corps will be claiming a full command, quarrelling among themselves. There'll be Duke Islay—"

"Hus—s—sh!" whispered Major Hall discreetly from the corner of his mouth. "Here's his young fellow coming up behind." Then loudly, "It's a very fine season indeed, Captain Campbell, a very fine season."

Young Islay came forward with a salute for the Captain and his sister. He was Gilian's age and size, but of a different build, broader at the shoulder, fuller at the chest, black of hair, piercing of eye, with just enough and no more of a wholesome conceit of himself to give his Majesty's uniform justice. When he spoke it was with a clear and manly tone deep in the chest.

He shook hands all round, he was newly come home from the lowlands, his tunic was without speck or crease, his chin was smooth, his strong hands were white; as Gilian returned his greeting he felt himself in an enviable and superior presence. Promptly, too, there came like a breath upon glass a remembrance of the ensign of the same corps who kissed his hand to Nan on just such another day of sunshine at Boshang Gate.

"Glad to see you back, Islay," said the Paymaster, proffering his Sabbath snuff-mull. "Faith, you do credit to the coat!" And he cast an admiring eye upon the young soldier.

Young Islay showed his satisfaction in his face.

"But it's a smaller coat than yours, Captain," said he, "and easier filled nowadays than when fighting was in fashion. I'm afraid the old school would have the better of us."

It was a touch of Gaelic courtesy to an elder, well-meant, pardonable; it visibly pleased the old gentleman to whom it was addressed, and he looked more in admiration than before upon this smart young officer.

"Up the glen yet, Gilian?" said Islay, with the old schoolboy freedom, and Gilian carelessly nodded, his eyes once more roving on the road to Boshang Gate. Young Islay looked at him curiously, a little smile hovering about the corners of his lips, for he knew the dreamer's reputation.

The Paymaster gave a contemptuous "Humph!" "Up the glen yet. You may well say it," said he. "And like to be. It's a fine clime for stirks."

Gilian did not hear it, but Miss Mary felt it sting to her very heart, and she moved away, pressing upon her favourite's arm to bring him with her. "We must be moving," said she; "Peggy will be scolding about the dinner spoiled with waiting."

But no one else seemed willing to break up the group. Young Islay had become the centre of attraction. MacGibbon and Major Hall, the Sheriff, Mr Spencer and the dominie, listened to his words as to a sage, gratified by his robust and handsome youth, and the Turners had him by the arm and questioned him upon his experience. Major MacNicol, ludicrous in a bottle-green coat with abrupt tails and an English beaver hat of an ancient pattern, jinked here and there among the people, tip-toeing, round-shouldered, with eyes peering and alarmed, jerking his head across his shoulder at intervals to see that no musket barrel threatened, and at times, for a moment or two, he would hang upon the outskirts of Young Islay's *levée*, with a hand behind an ear to listen to his story, filled for a little space with a wave of vague and bitter recollection that never broke upon the shore of solid understanding, enchanted by a gleam of red and gold, the colours of glory and of youth.

"Let us go home," whispered Miss Mary, pulling gently at Gilian's coat.

"Wait, wait, no hurry for cold kail hot again," said the Paymaster, every instinct for gossip alert and eager.

"And you showed him the qualities of a Highland riposte! Good lad! Good lad! I'm glad that Sandy and you learned something of the art of fence before they tried you in the Stirling fashion," General Turner was saying. "You'll be home for a while won't you? Come up and see us at Maam; no ceremony, a bird, a soldier's jug, and—"

"And a soldier's song from Miss Nan, I hope," continued the young officer, smiling. "That would be the best inducement of all. I hear she's home again from the low country, and thought she would have been in church today."

"City ways, you know, Islay, city ways," said Turner, tapping the young fellow playfully on the shoulder with his cane. "She did not come down because she must walk! I wonder what Dr Colin would say if he found me yoking a horse to save a three miles Sabbath daunder to the kirk. Come up and have your song, though, any day you like; I'll warrant you never heard better."

"I'm certain I never did," admitted Young Islay heartily.

"And when I think," said the General softly, more closely pressing the young fellow's arm, "that there might be no song now at all but for your readiness with an oar, I'm bound to make a tryst of it: say Tuesday."

"Certainly!" said Young Islay. "About my readiness with an oar, now, that was less skill than a boy's luck. I can tell you I was pretty frightened when I baled—good heavens, how long ago!—the water from the punt, and felt the storm would smother me!" He was flushing to speak of a thing so much to his credit, and sought relief from his feelings by a random remark to the Paymaster's boy.

"You mind?" said he, with a laughing look at Gilian, who wished now that he were in the more comfortable atmosphere of the Paymaster's parlour for he was lamentably outside the interests of this group. "You mind?" he pressed again, as if the only victim of that storm and stranding could ever forget!

"I remember very well," said Gilian in an Anglified accent that renewed all Miss Mary's apprehension, for it showed an artificial mood. "I came out of that with small credit," he went on, sparing himself nothing. "I suppose I would have risked my life half a dozen times over to be of any service; what was wanting was the sense to know what I should do. There you had the advantage of me. And did you really bail the boat with your bonnet?"

"Faith I did!" said Young Islay, laughing.

"I knew it," said Gilian. "I knew your feelings and your acts as well as if it had been myself that had been there. I wish my comprehension of the act to be done was as ready as my imagination. I wish—"

A shyness throttled the words in his mouth when he found all the company looking upon him, all amused or a little pitiful except the dominie, whose face had a kindly respect and curiosity, and Miss Mary, who was looking wistfully in his eyes.

"There are two worlds about us," said Brooks; "the manifest, that is as plain as a hornbook from A to Ampersand; the other, that is in the mind of man, no iota less real, but we are few that venture into it further than the lintel of the door." And he had about his eyes an almost fatherly fondness for Gilian, who felt that in the words were some justification for him, the dreamer.

The street was emptying, one by one the people had dispersed. Young Islay's group broke up, and went their several ways. The Paymaster and Miss Mary and Gilian went in to dinner.

"What's the matter with you, my dear?" whispered Miss Mary at the turn of the stair when her brother had gone within.

"Matter?" said Gilian, surprised at her discovery. "Nothing that I know of. What makes you think there is anything the matter with me?"

She stopped him at the stair-head, and here in the dusk of it she was again the young companion. "Gilian, Gilian," said she, with stress in her whisper and a great affection in the face of her. " Do you think I can be deceived ? You are ill; or something troubles you. What were you eating?"

He laughed loudly; he could not help it at so prosaic a conclusion.

"What carry-on is that on the stair on a Lord's day?" cried the Paymaster angrily and roughly from his room as he tugged short-tempered at the buckle of his Sabbath stock.

"Then there's something bothering you, my dear," said Miss Mary again, paying no heed to the interruption. And Gilian could not release his arm from her restraint.

"Is there, auntie?" said he. "Perhaps. And still I could not name it. Come, come, what's the sense of querying a man upon his moods?"

"A man!" said Miss Mary.

"On the verge at least," said he, with a confidence he had never had in his voice before, taking a full breath in his chest.

"A man!" said she again. And she saw, as if a curtain had fallen from before her eyes, that this was no more the fair-haired, wan-faced, trembling child who came from Ladyfield to her heart.

"I wish, I wish," said she all trembling, "the children did not grow at all!"

XXIV

MAAM HOUSE

MAAM HOUSE stands mid-way up the glen, among pasture and arable land that seems the more rich and level because it is hemmed in by gaunt hills where of old the robber found a sequestration and the hunter of deer followed his kingly recreation. The river sings and cries, almost at the door, mellow in the linns and pools, or in its shallow links cheerily gossiping among grey stones; the Dhu Loch shines upon its surface like a looking-glass or shivers in icy winds. Round about the bulrush nods; old great trees stand in the rains knee-deep like the cattle upon its marge pondering, and the breath of oak and hazel hangs from shore to shore.

To her window in the old house of Maam would Nan come in the mornings, and the beauty of Dhu Loch would quell the song upon her lips. It touched her with some melancholy influence. Grown tall and elegant, her hair in waves about her ears, in a rich restrained tumult about her head, her eyes brimming and full of fire, her lips rich, her bosom generous—she was not the Nan who swung upon a gate and wished that hers was a soldier's fortune. This place lay in her spirit like a tombstone— the loneliness of it, the stillness of it, the dragging days of it, with their dreary round of domestic duties. She was not a week home, and already sleep was her dearest friend, and to open her eyes in the morning upon the sunny but silent room and miss the clangour of Edinburgh streets was a diurnal grief.

What she missed of the strident town was the clustering round of fellow creatures, the eternal drumming of neighbour hearts, the feet upon the pavement and the eager faces all around that were so full of interest they did not let her seek into the depths of her, where lay the old Highland sorrows that her richest notes so wondrously expressed. The tumult for her! Constant touch with the active, the gay! Solitude oppressed her like a looming disease. Sometimes, as in those mornings when she looked abroad from her window upon the glen, she felt sick of her own company, terrified at the pathetic profound to which the landscape made her sink. Then she wept, and then she shook the mood from her angrily and flashed about the house of Maam like a sunbeam new-washed by the rain.

Her father used to marvel at those sudden whims of silence and of song. He would come in on some poor excuse from his stable or cunningly listen above his book and try to understand; but he, the man of action, the soldier, the child of undying ambitions, was far indeed from comprehension. Only he was sure of her affection. She would come and sit upon his knee, with arms around his neck, indulgent madly in a child's caresses. Her uncle James, finding them thus sometimes, would start at an illusion, for it looked as if her mother was back again, and her father, long so youthful of aspect, seemed the sweetheart husband once more.

"Ah! you randy!" he would say to his niece, scowling upon her; "the sooner you get a man the better!"

"If there is one in the world half so handsome as my father—yes," she would answer merrily, nestling more fondly in the General's breast, till he rose and put her off with laughing confusion.

"Away! away!" he would cry in pretended annoyance. "You make my grey hairs ridiculous."

"Where are they?" she would say, running her white fingers over his head and daintily refastening the ribbon of that antiquated queue that made him always look the chevalier. She treated him, in all, less like a father than a lover, exceedingly proud of him, untiring of his countless tales of campaign and court, uplifted marvellously with his ambitious dreams of State preferment. For General Turner was but passing the time in Maam till by favour promised a foreign office was found for him elsewhere.

"And when the office comes," said he, "then I leave my girl. It is the one thing that sobers me."

"Not here! not here!" she cried, alarm in eye and tone. So he found, for the first time, her impatience with the quiet of Maam. He was, for a little, dumb with regret that this should be her feeling.

"Where better, where safer, my dear?" he asked. "Come up to the bow-window." And he led her where she could see their native glen from end to end. The farm-towns, the cots were displayed; smoke rose from their chimneys in the silent air, grey blue banners of peace.

"Bide at home, my dear," said he softly, "bide at home and rest. I thought you would have been glad to be back from towns among our own kindly people in the land your very heart-blood sprang from. Quiet, do you say? True, true," and still he surveyed the valley himself with solemn eyes. "But there is content here, and every hearth there would make you welcome if it was only for your name, even if the world was against you."

She saw the reapers in the fields, heard their shearing songs that are sung for cheer, but somehow in this land are all imbued with melancholy. Loud, loud against that sorrow of the brooding glen rose up in her remembrance the thoughtless clamour of the lowland world, and she shivered, as one who looks from the window of a well-warmed room upon a night of storm.

Her father put an arm about her waist.

"Is it not homely?" said he, dreading her reply.

"I can bear it—with you," she answered pitifully. "But if you go abroad, it would kill me. I must have something that is not here; I must have youth and life—and—life."

"At your age I would not have given Maam and the glen about it for my share of Paradise."

"But now?" said she.

He turned hastily from the window and nervously paced the room.

"No matter about me," he answered in a little. "Ah! you're your mother's child. I wish—I wish I could leave you content here." He felt at his chin with a nervous hand, muttered, looked on her askance, pitied himself that when he went wandering he must not have the consoling thought that she was safe and happy in her childhood's home.

"I wish I had never sent you away," he said. "You would have been more content today. But that's the manner of the world, we must pay our way as we go, in inns and in knowledge."

She ran up with tripping feet and kissed him rapturously.

"No lowland tricks!" he cried, pleased and yet ashamed at a display unusual in these parts. "Fancy if someone saw you!"

"Then let them look well again," she said, laughingly defiant, and he had to stoop to avoid the assault of her ripe and laughing lips. The little struggle had brought a flame to her eye that grew large and lambent; where her lower neck showed in a chink of her kerchief-souffle it throbbed and glowed. The General found himself wondering if this was, indeed, his child, the child he had but the other day held in the crook of his arm and dandled on his knee.

"I wish," said he again, while she neatly tied the knot upon his queue, "I wish we had a husband for you, good or—indifferent, before I go."

"Not indifferent, father," she laughed. "Surely the best would not be too good for your daughter! As if I wanted a husband of any kind!"

"True, true," he answered thoughtfully. "You are young yet. The best would not be too good for you; but I know men, my dear, and the woman's well off who gets merely the middling in her pick of them. And that minds me, I had one asking for you at the kirk on Sunday. A soldier, no less. Can you guess him?"

"The Paymaster's Boy," said she promptly, curiosity in her countenance.

Her father laughed.

"Pooh!" he exclaimed. "Is that all you have of our news here that you don't know Gilian's farming, or making a show of farming, in Ladyfield? He never took to the army after all, and an old brag of Mars is very humorous now when I think of it."

"I told him he never would," said Nan, with no note of triumph in the accuracy of her prediction. "I thought he could play-act the thing in his mind too well ever to be the thing itself."

"It was Young Islay I mean," said her father. "A smart fellow; he's home on leave from his corps, and he promises to come some day this week to see the girl whose father has some reason to be grateful to him."

She flushed all at once, overtaken by feelings she could not have described—feelings of gratitude for the old rescue, of curiosity, pleasure, and a sudden shyness. Following it came a sudden recollection of the old glamour that was about the ensign—such another, no doubt, as Young Islay—who had given her the first taste of gallantry as he passed with the troops in a day of sunshine. She looked out at the window to conceal her eyes, and behold! the glen was not so melancholy as it was a little ago. She wished she had put on another gown that afternoon, the rustling one of double tabinet that her Edinburgh friends considered too imposing for her years, but that she herself felt a singular complacence in no matter what her company might be.

"A smart fellow," repeated her father musingly, flicking some dust from his shoes, unobserving of her abstraction. "I wish Sandy took a lesson or two from him in application."

"Ah!" she cried, "you're partial just because—" And she hesitated.

"—Just because he saved my lassie's life," continued Turner, and seized by an uncommon impulse he put an arm round her and bent to kiss her not unwilling lips. He paused at the threshold, and drew back with a half-shamed laugh.

"Tuts!" said he. "You smit me with silly lowland customs. Fancy your old Highland daddie kissing you! If it had been the young gentleman we speak of—"

A loud rap came to the knocker of the front door, and Nan's hands went flying to her hair in soft inquiries; back to her face came its colour.

It was Young Islay. He came into the room with two strides from the stair-head and a very genteel obeisance to the lady, a conceit of fashion altogether foreign to glens, but that sent her back in one dart of fancy to the parlour of Edinburgh, back to the warm town, back to places of gaiety, and youth, and enterprise, back to soft manners, the lip gossiping at the ear, shoes gliding upon waxen floors, music, dance, and mirth. Her heart throbbed as to a revelation, and she could have taken him in her arms for the sake of that brave life he indicated.

His eyes met hers whenever he entered, and he could not draw them away till hers, wavering before him, showed him he was daring. He turned and shook hands with the General, and muttered some commonplace, then back again he came to that pleasant face so like and yet so unlike the face he had known when a boy.

"You'll hardly know each other," said the father, amused at this common interest. "Isn't she a most elderly person to be the daughter of so young and capable a man?"

Young Islay ranged his mind for a proper compliment, but for once he was dumb; in all the oft-repeated phrases of his gallant experiences there was no sentiment to do justice to a moment like this. "I am delighted to meet you again," he said slowly, his mind confused with a sense of the inadequacy of the thing and the inexplicable feelings that crowded into him in the presence of a girl who, three years ago, would have no more disturbed him than would his sister. She was the first to recover from the awkwardness of the moment.

"I was just wishing I had on another gown," she said more frankly than she felt, but bound to give utterance to the last clear thought in her mind. "I had an idea we might have callers."

"You could have none that became you better," said the lad boldly, feasting upon her charms of lip and eye. And now he was the soldier—free, bold, assured.

"What? In the way of visitors," laughed her father, and she flushed again.

"I spoke of the gown," said Young Islay (and he had not yet seen it, it might have been red or blue for all he could tell). "I spoke of the gown; if it depends on that for you to charm your company, you should wear no other."

"A touch of the garrison, but honest enough to be said before the father!" thought General Turner.

Nan laughed. She courtesied with an affected manner taught in Edinburgh schools.

"Sir," she said, "you are a soldier, and of course the gown at the moment in front of you is always the finest in the world. Don't tell me it is not so," she hastened to add, as he made to protest, "because I know my father and all the ways of his trade, and—and—and if you were not the soldier even in your pleasantries to ladies I would not think you the soldier at all."

The General smiled and nudged the young fellow jocosely. "There," said he, "did I not tell you she was a fiery one?"

"I hope you did not discuss me in that fashion," said Nan, pausing with annoyance as she moved aside a little, all her pride leaping to her face.

"Your father will have his joke," said Young Islay quickly. "He barely let me know you were here."

The General smiled again in admiration of the young fellow's astuteness, and Nan recovered.

They went to the parlour. Through the window came the songs of the reapers and the twitter of birds busy among the seeds at the barn-door. Roses swinging on the porch threw a perfume into the room. Young Islay felt, for the first time in his life, a sense of placid happiness. And when Nan sang later—a newer, wider world, more years, more thoughts, more profound depths in her song—he was captive.

To his aid he summoned all his confidence; he talked like a prince (if they talk head-up, valiantly, serene and possessing); he moved about the room studiously unconscious and manly; he sat with grace and showed his hand, and all the time he claimed the girl for his. "You are mine, you are mine!" he said to himself over and over again, and by the flush on her neck as she sat at the harpsichord she might be hearing, through some magic sense, his bold unspoken thought.

Evening crept, lights came, the father went out to give some orders at the barn; they were left alone. The instrument that might have been a heavenly harp at once lost its dignity and relapsed to a tinkling wire, for Nan was silent, and there crowded into Young Islay's head all the passion of his people. He rose and strode across the room; he put an arm round her waist and raised her, all astounded, from the chair.

She turned round and tried to draw back, looking startled at his eyes that were wide with fire.

"What do you mean?" she gasped.

"Need you ask it?" he said in a new voice, raising an arm round her shoulder. His fingers unexpectedly touched her warm skin beneath the kerchief-souffle. The feeling ran to his heart, and struck him there like an earthquake. Down went his head, more firm his hold upon the lady's waist; she might have been a flower to crush, but yet he must be rude and strong; he bent her back and kissed her. Her lips parted as if she would cry out against this outrage, and he felt her breath upon his cheek, an air, a perfume maddening. "Nan, Nan, you are mine, you are mine!" said he huskily, and he kissed her again.

Out in the fields, a corncrake raised its rasping vesper and a shepherd whistled on his doings. The carts rumbled as they made for the sheds. The sound of the river far off in the shallows among the saugh-trees came on a little breeze, a murmur of the sad inevitable sea that ends all love and passion, the old Sea beating black about the world.

In the room was an utter silence. She had drawn back for a moment stupefied, checking in her pride even the breathing of her struggle. He stood bent at the head a little, contrite, his hat, that he had lifted, in his hand. And they gazed at each other—people who had found themselves in some action horribly rude and shameful.

"I think you must have made a mistake, or have been drinking," she said at last, her breast now heaving stormily and her eyes ablaze with anger. "I am not the dairy-maid."

"I could not help it," he answered lamely. "You—you—you made me do it. I love you!"

She drew back shocked.

He stepped forward again, manly, self-possessed again, and looked her hungrily in the eyes. "Do you hear that?" he said. "Do you hear that? I love you! I love you! There you look at me, and I'm inside like a fire. What am I to do? I am Highland; I am Long Islay's grandson. I am a soldier. I am Highland, and if I want you I must have you."

She drew softly towards the door as if to escape, but heard her father's voice without, and it gave her assurance. A pallor had come upon her cheek, only her lips were bright as if his kiss had seared them.

"You are Highland, you are Highland, are you?"' she said, restraining her sobs. "Then where is the gentleman? Do you fancy I have been growing up in Maam all the years you were away among canteens for you to come home and insult me when you wished?"

He did not quail before her indignation, but he drew back with respect in every movement.

"Madame," he said, with a touch of the ballroom, "you may miscall me as you will; I deserve it all. I have been brutal; I have frightened you—that would not harm a hair of your head for a million pounds; I have disgraced the hospitality of your father's house. I may have ruined myself in your eyes, and tomorrow I'll writhe for it, but now—but now—I have but one plea: I love you! I'll say it, though you struck me dumb for ever."

She recovered a little, looked curiously at him, and "Is it not something of a liberty, even that?" she asked. "You bring the manners of the Inn to my father's house." The recollection of her helplessness in his grasp came to her again, and stained her face as it had been with wine.

He turned his hat in his hand, eyeing her dubiously but more calmly than before.

"There you have me," he said, with a large and helpless gesture, "I am not worth two of your most trivial words. I am a common rude soldier that has not, as it were, seen you till a moment ago, and when I was at your—at your lips, I should have been at your shoes."

She laughed disdainfully a little.

"Don't do that," said he, "you make me mad." Again the tumult of his passion swept him down; he put a foot forward as if to approach her, but stopped short as by an immense inward effort. "Nan, Nan, Nan," he cried so loudly that a more watchful father would have heard it outside. "Nan, Nan, Nan, I must say it if I die for it: I love you! I never felt—I do not know—I cannot tell what ails me, but you are mine!" Then all at once again his mood and accent changed. "Mine! What can I give? What can I offer? Here's a poor ensign, and never a war with chances in it!"

He strode up and down the room, throwing his shadow, a feverish phantom, on the blind, and Nan looked at him as if he had been a man in a play. Here was her first lover with a vengeance! They might be all like that; this madness, perhaps, was the common folly. She remembered that to him she owed her life, and she was overtaken by pity.

"Let us say no more about it," she said calmly. "You alarmed me very much, and I hope you will never do the like again. Let me think I myself was willing"—he started—"that it was some—some playful way of paying off the score I owe you."

"What score?" said he, astonished.

"You saved my life," she answered, all resentment gone.

"Did I?" said he. "It would be the last plea I would offer here and now. That was a boy's work, or luck as it might be; this is a man before you. I am not wanting gratitude, but something far more ill to win. Look at me," he went on; "I am Highland, I'm a soldier, I'm a man. You may put me to the door (my mother in heaven would not blame you), but still you're mine."

He was very handsome as he stood upon the floor resolute, something of the savage and the dandy, a man compelling. Nan more ill to win. Look at me," he went on; "I am Highland, I'm a soldier, I'm a man. You may put me to the door (my mother in heaven would not blame you), but still you're mine."

He was very handsome as he stood upon the floor resolute, something of the savage and the dandy, a man compelling. Nan felt the tremor of an admiration, though the insult was yet burning on her countenance.

"Here's my father," she said, quickly sitting at the harpsichord again, with her face away from it and the candlelight.

Into the room stepped the General, never knowing he had come upon a storm. Their silence surprised him. He looked suspiciously at the lad, who still stood on the floor with his hat in his hand.

"You're not going yet, Islay?" said he, and there was no answer.

"Have you two quarrelled?" he asked, again glancing at his daughter's averted face.

Young Islay stammered his reply. "I have been a fool, General, that's all," said he. "I brought the manners of the Inn, as your daughter says, into your house, and—"

The father caught him by the sleeve and bent a most stern eye.

"Well, well?" he pushed.

"And—the rest, I think, should be between yourself and me," said Young Islay, looking at Nan now with her back to them, and he and the father went out of the room.

XXV

THE EAVESDROPPER

THERE was no moon, but the sky hung thick with stars, and the evening was a rare dusk where bush and tree stood half revealed, things sinister, concealing the terrific elements of dreams. Over the hills came Gilian, a passionate pilgrim of the night. The steeps, the gullies, the hazel thickets he trod were scarcely real for him, he passed them as if in a swoon, he felt himself supreme, able to step from ben to ben, inspired by the one exaltation that puts man above all toils, fears, weariness and doubts, brother of the April eagle, cousin-german of the remote and soaring star.

He approached the house of Maam by a rough sheep-path along the side of the burn, leaped from boulder to boulder to keep the lights of the house in view, brushed eagerly through the bracken, ran masterfully in the flats. When he came close to the house, caution was necessary lest late harvesters should discover him. He went round on the outside of the orchard hedge, behind the milk-house wall, and stood in the concealment of a little alder planting. The house was lit in several windows, it struck—thought he—warm upon a neck and flashed back in a melting eye within; his heart drummed furiously.

In the farmyard the workers were preparing to depart for the night from their long day of toil. All but the last of the horses had been stabled; the shepherds were returning from the fanks; two women, the weariness of their bodies apparent in their attitudes even in the dusk, stood for a little in the yard, then with arms round each other's waists went towards the cot-house, singing softly as they went. The General's voice in Gaelic rose over all but the river's murmur, as he called across the wattle gate to a herd-boy bearing in peat for the night and morning fires. And the night was all wrapt in an odour of bog myrtle and flowers.

That outer world, for once, had no interest for Gilian; his eyes were on the windows, and though the interior of Maam was utterly unknown to him from actual sight, he was fancying it in every detail. He knew the upper room where Nan slept; he had watched the light come to it and disappear, every night since she had returned, though he could not guess how in that eminent flame she was reading the memorials, the letters, the diaries of her lost lowland life and weeping for her solitude.

The light was not there now; it was too early in the evening, so she must be in the room whose two windows shone on the grass between the house and the barn. He could see them plainly as he stood in the planting, and he busied himself, forgetting all the outside interests of the house, in picturing its interior. Nan, he told himself, sat sewing or reading within, still the tall lady of his day-dreams, for he had not yet seen her since her return.

And then he heard her harpsichord, its unfamiliar music amazing him by its relation to some world he did not know, the world from which she had just returned. She was playing the prelude of the simplest song that ever had been taught in an Edinburgh academy, yet these ears, accustomed only to rough men's voices, the song of birds, now and then a harsh fiddle grating for its life about the countryside, or the pipe of the hills, imbued the thin and lonely symphony with associations of life genteel and wide, rich and warm and white-handed. Never seemed Miss Nan so far removed as then from him, the home-staying dreamer. Up rose his startled judgment and called him fool.

But hark! her voice came in and joined the harpsichord—surely this time he was not mistaken? Her voice! it was certainly her voice! He held his breath to listen for fear he should lose the softest note as it came from her lips. Now he was well repaid for his nights of traverse on the hills, his watching, his disappointment! The very night held breath to listen to that song, not the song that had been sung in the *Jean*, but another, the song of a child no more, but of a woman, full of passion, antique love and sorrow, of the unsatisfied and yearning years.

The music ceased; the night for a space swooned into a numb and desolate silence. Then in the field behind, the last corncrake harshly called; a shepherd whistled on his dogs; a cart rumbled over the cobbles, making for the shed. The sound of the river as it came to him among the alder-trees seemed the sound the wave makes in the ears of the sinking and exhausted swimmer.

Gilian turned over in his pocket a lucky flint arrowhead, and wished for a glimpse of Nan.

He had no sooner done so than her shadow showed upon the blind, hurried and nervous as in some affright.

His heart leaped; he made a step forward as if he would storm that citadel of his fancy, but he checked himself on a saner thought that he was imbuing the shadow with fears that were not there. He drew a deep breath and turned his lucky arrowhead again. For a second or two there was no response. Then another shadow came upon the blinds—a man's, striding for a little back and forward, as if in perturbation. Who could it be? the trembling outsider asked himself. Not the father; there was no queue to the shadow, and a vague suggestion of the General's voice had come but a moment before from another part of the steading. Not the uncle? This was no long, bent, bearded apparition, but the figure of youth. Gilian promptly fancied himself the substance of the shadow in that envied light and presence, seeing the glow of fire and candle in Nan's eyes as she turned to the accepted lover. "Nan, Nan!" he whispered, "I love you! I love you!"

A faint breath from a new point came through the trees, the

dryads sighing for all this pitiful illusion. It struck chill upon his face; he shivered and prepared to set off for home across the hill. A last reluctant glance was thrown at the window, and he had turned towards the milk-house wall when a sound of opening doors arrested him. Now he could not escape unobserved; he withdrew into the shadow of the trees again.

The General and another came out and stood mid-way between the house and the planting. There they spoke in constrained words that did not at first reach him. Against the grey dun of the sky he could separate their figures, but he could not guess the identity of the General's companion.

In a second or two they moved nearer and he was an unwilling listener, though a keenly interested one.

"Come, come," said the General, in a tone of some annoyance, "you had me out to hear your explanation, and now I'm to be kept chittering in the night air till you range your inside for words."

The other murmured something in a voice that did not intelligently reach the planting.

"Ay, you did, did you?" said the General in reply, very dryly, and then he paused. "I'll warrant you found a tartar," he said in a little.

The other answered softly in a word or two.

There was another pause, and then the General laughed, not with much geniality. "That was all the news you brought me out here for?" said he. "Come, come, the lady can look after herself so far as that goes. Either that or she's not her mother's child. And yet—and yet, I would not be saying. Edinburgh and all their low-country notions make some difference; I see them in her. This is not the girl I sent off south on a mail-gig—just like a parcel. Curse the practice that we must be risking the things of our affection among strangers!"

There was no more than the brief and muffled answer, like that of a man ashamed.

"I've seen that before," said the General stiffly. "It's not uncommon at the age, but it's unusual to take the old gentleman into the garden at night without his bonnet to tell him so little as that."

The answer, still muffled to the listener in the planting, poured forth quickly.

"Highland," said the General, "queer Highlands! And it must be now or never with us, must it? Well, young gentleman, you have nerve at least," and he quoted a Gaelic proverb. He put his hand on the shoulder of the other and leaned to whisper. Gilian could make the action out against the sky. Then "Good-night" and the father's footsteps went back to the door and the unknown proceeded down the glen.

On an impulse irresistible, Gilian followed at a discreet distance keeping on the verges of the grass beside the road, so that his footsteps might not betray him. All the night was tenantless but for themselves and some birds that called dolefully in the woods. The river, broadened by the burns on either hand that joined it, grew soon to a rapid and tumultuous current washing round the rushy bends, and the Dhu Loch when they came to it had a ripple on its shore, so that they were at the bridge and yet the one who led was not aware that he was followed. He leaned upon the crenellated parapet and hummed a strain of song as Gilian came up to him with a swinging step, now on the footway.

Young Islay started at this approach without warning, but he was not afraid. He peered into Gilian's face when he had come up to him.

"Oh, you!" said he. "I got quite a start, I thought at first it was Drimmin dorran's ghost." This, laughingly, of a shade with a reputation for haunting these evening solitudes.

"You're late on the road?" he went on curiously.

"No later than yourself," answered Gilian, vaguely grieving to find that this was the substance of his shadow on the blind and the audience for Miss Nan's entertainment.

"Oh! I was—I was on a visit," said Young Islay. He went closer up to Gilian and added eagerly, as one glad to unbosom, "Man! did you ever hear—did you ever hear Miss Nan sing?"

"Long ago," said Gilian; "it's an old story."

"Lucky man!" said Young Islay enviously, "to be here so long to listen when I was far away."

"She was away herself a good deal," said Gilian, "but when we heard her we quite appreciated our opportunities, I assure you."

"Did you, faith?" said Young Islay, with a jealous tone. "You seem," he went on, "to have made very little use of them. I wonder where the eyes of you could be. I never saw her, really, till an hour or two ago. I never heard her sing before, but yet, some way—" He hesitated in embarrassment.

Gilian made no answer. He felt it the most natural thing in the world that anyone seeing and hearing Nan should appreciate herself and her singing. There was no harm in that.

The night was solemn with the continual cry of the owls that abound in the woody shoulder of Duntorvil; a sweet balmy influence loaded the air, stars gathered in patches between drifts of cloud. For some distance the young men walked together silent, till Young Islay spoke.

"I've been away seeing the world," said he hurriedly, like a man at a confession, "not altogether with my father's wish, who would sooner I stayed at home and farmed Drimlee; moving from garrison to garrison, giving my mind no hearth to stay at for more than a night at a time, and I've been missing the chance of my life. I went up the way there an hour or two since—Young Islay, a soldier, coarse, ashamed of sentiment, and now I go down another man altogether. I would not say it to anyone but yourself; you're a sort of sentimental person in a wholesale way; you'll understand. Eh, what? You'll understand!" He threw out his chest; breathed fully. "I'm a new man, I'm telling you. I wonder where the eyes of you fellows were?"

Even yet Gilian did not grudge Young Islay the elation that was so manifest.

"You understand, we did not see much of her in these parts lately, much more than yourself. I have not seen her myself since she returned. Has she changed much?"

"Much!" exclaimed Young Islay, laughing. "My son! she is not the girl I knew at all. When I went in there—into the room up there, you know, I was—I was—baffled to know her. I think I expected to see the same girl I had—I had—you mind, brought the boat out to, the same loose hair, the same—you know, I never expected to see a princess in Maam. A princess, mind you, and she looked all the more that because her uncle met me at the stair-foot as I was going in. A sour old scamp yon! He was teasing out his beard, and, 'A nice piece there,' said he, nodding at the door, 'and I'm sure her father would be glad to have her off his hands.' I laughed and—"

"I would have struck him on the jaw," said Gilian with great heat.

"Oh!" said Young Islay, astonishment in his voice. He said no more for a little. Then, "I was not very well pleased myself with the remark when I went into the room and saw the lady it referred to. You're not—you're not chief in that quarter, are you?"

"Chief!" repeated Gilian. "You're ahead of me even in seeing the lady."

"Oh well, that's all right," said Young Islay, seemingly relieved. "Look here; I'm gone, that's the long and the short of it! I'm seeing a week or two of hard work before me convincing her ladyship that a young ensign in a marching regiment is maybe worth her smiling on."

Gilian turned cold with apprehension. This, indeed, was a revelation of love-making in garrison fashion.

"You don't know the girl at all," he said.

"So much the better," said Young Islay; "that means that she does not know me, and that's all the better start for me, perhaps. It's a great advantage, for I've noticed that they're all the most interested—the sex of them—in a novelty. I have a better chance than the best man in these parts, that has been under her eye all the time I was away. I'll have stiff work, perhaps, but I want her, and between ourselves, and not to make a brag of it, I'll have her. You'll not breathe that," he added, turning in apprehension, stopping opposite Gilian and putting his hand on his coat lapel. "I am wrong to mention it at all even to you, but

208

I must out with what I feel to somebody. The thing is dirling in my blood. Listen, do you hear that?" He threw out his chest again, held his breath, and Gilian could almost swear he heard his heart throb with feeling.

"Does she want you? That's the question, I suppose," said Gilian weakly.

"That is not the question at all, it's do I want her? There must be a beginning somewhere. Look at me; I'm strong, young, not very ugly (at least they tell me), I'm the grandson of Long Islay, who had a name for gallantry; the girl has no lover—Has she?" he asked eagerly, suddenly dropping his confidence.

"Not that I'm aware of," said Gilian.

"Well, there you are! What more is to be said? In these things one has but to wish and win—at least that's been my training and my conviction. Here she's lonely—I could see it in her; the company of her father is not likely to be long for her, and her Uncle Jamie is not what you would call a cheerful spark. Upon my soul, I believe I could get her if I was a hunchback. . . . Mind, I'm not lightlying the lady; I could not do that in this mood, but I'm fair taken with her; she beats all ever I saw. You know the feeling? No, you don't; you're too throng at book notions. God! God! God! I'm all ashake!"

He looked at Gilian, trying in the dark to make out how he was taking this, to make sure he was not laughing at him. Gilian, on the contrary, was feeling very solemn. He felt that this was a dangerously effective mood for a lover, and he knew the lad before him would always bring it to actual wooing if it got that length. He had no answer, and Young Islay again believed him the abstracted dreamer.

"I have this advantage," he went on, unable to resist. "She likes soldiers; she said as much; it was in her mother and in her; she likes action, she likes spirit. She has them herself in faith! she almost boxed my ears when—when—but I could swear she was rather tickled at my impudence."

"Your impudence!" repeated Gilian, "were you in that mood?"

"Oh, well, you know—I had the boldness to—"

"To what?" said Gilian; apprehending some disaster.

"Just a trifle," said Young Islay, shrewdly affecting indifference. "A soldier's compliment; we are too ready with them in barrack-yards, you know." And he sighed as he remembered the red ripe lips, the warm breath on his face, and the tingling influence of the skin he touched under the kerchief.

They walked on in silence again for a while. The night grew dark with gathering clouds. Lights far out at sea showed the trailing fishers; a flaring torch told of a trawler's evening fortune made already. And soon they were at the Duke's lodge and Gilian's way up Glen Aray lay before him. He was pausing to say good-night, confused, troubled by what he had heard, feeling he must confess his own regard for the girl and not let this comparative stranger so buoyantly outdo him in admiration.

"Now," said he, hesitating, "what would you think I was in Glen Shira myself for?"

"Eh?" said Young Islay, scarcely hearing, and he hummed the refrain of the lady's song.

"In Glen Shira; what was I doing there?" repeated Gilian. He wanted no answer. "It was on the odd chance that I might see Miss Nan. We are not altogether without some taste in these parts, though wanting the advantage of travel and garrison gallantry. I was in the garden when you were inside. I heard her singing, and I think I got closer on herself and her song than you did."

"My dear Gilian," said Young Islay, "I once fought you for less than that." He laughed as he said it. "If you mean," he went on, "that you are in love with Miss Nan, that's nothing to wonder at, the miracle would be for you to be indifferent. We're in the same hunt, are we then? Well, luck to the winner! I can say no fairer than that. Only you'll have to look sharp, my boy, for I'm not going to lose any time, I assure you. If you're going to do all your courtship of yon lady from outside her window, you'll not make much progress, I'm thinking. Good-night; good-night!" He went off laughing, and when he had gone away a few yards Gilian, walking slowly homewards, heard him break whistling into the air that Nan had sung in the parlour of Maam.

XXVI

AGAIN IN THE GARDEN

ONLY for a single sleepless night was Gilian dashed by this evidence that the world was not made up of Miss Nan and himself alone. Depressions weighed on him as briefly as the keener joys elated, and in a day or two his apprehension of Young Islay had worn to a thin gossamer, and he was as ardent a lover as anyone could be with what still was no more than a young lady of the imagination. And diligently he sought a meeting. It used to be the wonder of Mr Spencer of the Inns, beholding this cobweb-headed youth continually coming through the Arches and hanging expectant about the town-head, often the only figure there in these hot silent days to give life to the empty scene. There is a stone at Old Islay's corner that yet one may see worn with the feet of Gilian, so often he stood there turning on his heel, lending a gaze to the street where Nan might be, and another behind to the long road over the bridge whence she must sometime come. Years after he would stop again upon the blue slab and recall with a pensive pleasure those old hours of expectation.

For days he loitered in vain, the wonder of the Inns and its frequenters. Nan never appeared. To her father a letter had come; the Duke had come up on the back of it; there had been long discourse and a dram of claret wine in the parlour; the General came out when his Grace's cantering horse had ceased its merry hollow sound upon the dry road to Dhu Loch, and breathed fully like one relieved from an oppression. Later Old Islay had come up, crabbed and snuffy, to glower on Nan as he passed into the house behind her father, and come out anon smiling and even joco with her, mentioning her by her Christian name like the closest friend of the family. Then for reasons inscrutable her father would have her constant in his sight, though it was only, as it seemed, to pleasure an averted eye.

By and by Gilian turned his lucky flint one morning in a fortunate inspiration, and had no sooner done so than he remembered a very plausible excuse for going to a farm at the very head of Glen Shira. He started forth with the certainty, somehow, that he should meet the lady at last.

He had transacted his business and was on his way to the foot of the glen when he came upon her at Boshang Gate. Her back was to him; she was looking out to sea, leaning upon the bars as if she were a weary prisoner.

She turned at the sound of his footstep, a stranger utterly to his eyes and imagination, but not to his instinct, her hair bound, her apparel mature and decorous, her demeanour womanly. And he had been looking all the while for a little girl grown tall, with no external difference but that!

She took an impulsive step towards him as he hesitated with his hand dubious between his side and his bonnet, a pleasant, even an eager smile upon her face.

"You are quite sure you are you?" she said, holding out her hand before he had time to say a word. "For I was standing there thinking of you, a little white-faced fellow in a kilt, and here comes your elderly wraith at my back like one of Black Duncan's ghosts!"

"I would be the more certain it was myself," he answered, "if you had not been so different from what I expected."

"Oh! then you had not forgotten me altogether?" she said, waiting her answer, a mere beginner in coquetry emboldened to practice by the slightly rustic awkwardness of the lad.

"Not—not altogether," said he, unhappily accepting the common locution of the town, that means always more than it says.

A spark of humour flashed to merriment in her eyes and died to a demure ember again before he noticed it. "Here's John Hielan'man," she said to herself, and she recalled, not to Gilian's credit in the comparison, the effrontery of Young Islay.

The situation was a little awkward, for he held her hand too long, taking all the pleasure he could from a sudden conviction that in all the times he had seen Glen Shira it had never seemed fully furnished and habitable till now. This creature, so much the mistress of herself, and dainty and cheerful, made up for all its solitude; she was the one thing (he felt) wanting to make complete the landscape.

Her blush and a feeble effort to disengage her hand brought him to himself.

"I am pleased to see you back," said he shyly, as he released her. "I had not forgotten—oh no, I had not forgotten you. It would be easy to convince you of that, I think, but in all my recollection of Miss Nan I had more of the girl in the den of the *Jean* in my mind than the Edinburgh lady."

"You'll be meaning that I am old and—and pretty no longer," said she. "Upon my word, you are honestly outspoken in these parts nowadays." She pouted, with lines of annoyance upon her brow, which seriously disturbed him, and so obviously that she was compelled to laugh.

Not a word could he find to say to raillery which was quite new to him, and so for the sake of both of them as they stood at the gate Miss Nan had to ply an odd one-sided conversation till he found himself at his ease. By and by his shyness forsook him.

The sun was declining; the odours of the traffic of peace blew from the land; one large and ruddy star lit over Strone. The fishers raised their sails, and as their prows beat the sea they chanted the choruses of the wave.

A recollection of all this having happened before seized them together; she looked at him with a smile upon her lips, and he was master of her thought before she had expressed it.

"I know exactly what you are thinking of," he said.

"It was the odd thing about you that you often did," she replied. "It's a mercy you do not know it always, John Hielan'man," she thought.

"You are remembering the evening we walked in the Duke's garden," he said. "It looks but yesterday, and I was a child, and now I'm as old—as old as the hills." He looked vaguely with half-shut eyes upon the looming round of Cowal, where Sithean Sluaidhe was tipped with brass. "As old as the hills," he went on, eager to display himself, and also to show he appreciated her advantages. "Do you know I begin to find them irksome? They close in and make a world so narrow here! I envy you the years you have been away. In that time you have grown, mind and body, like a tree. I stunt, if not in body, at least in mind, here in the glens."

She looked at him covertly with her face still half averted, and found him now more interesting than she had expected, touched with something of romance and mystery, his eyes with that unfathomed quality that to some women makes a strange appeal.

"One sees much among strangers," she confessed. "I thought you had been out of here long ago. You remember when I left for Edinburgh they talked of the army for you?"

"The army," he said, wincing imperceptibly. "Oh! that was the Paymaster's old notion. Once I almost fell in with it, and as odd a thing as you could imagine put an end to the scheme. Do you know what it was?" He glanced at her with a keen scrutiny.

"No, tell me," she said.

"It was the very day we were here last, when the county corps moved off to Stirling. I was in the rear of them very much a soldier indeed, shouldering a switch, feeling myself a Major-General at the very least, when a girl sitting on the gate there, waving a tiny shoe, caught my eye, drew me back from the troops I was following, and extinguished my martial glory as if it were a flambeau thrown in the sea. I think that was the very last of the army for me."

"I don't understand it," she said.

"Nor I," he confessed frankly; "only there's the fact! All I know is that you cut me off from every idea of the army then and there. I forgot all about it, and it had been possessing my mind for a week before, night and day."

"I think I remember now that I told you, did I not, that you were not likely to be a soldier because you could pretend it too well ever to be the thing in actuality."

"I remember that too. *Dhe!* how the whole thing comes back! I wonder—"

"Well!" she pressed.

"I wonder if we walked in the Duke's garden again, if we could restore the very feelings of that time—the innocence and ignorance of it?"

"I don't know that I want to do so," said she, laughing.

"Might we not—" He paused, afraid of his own temerity.

"Try it, you were going to say," she continued.

"You see I have little of your own gift. I'm willing. I am going to the town, and we might as well go through the grounds as not."

Something in his manner attracted her; even his simple deference, though she was saying "John Hielan'man, John Hielan'man!" to herself most of the time and amused if not contemptuous. He was but a farmer—little more, indeed, than a shepherd, yet something in his air and all his speech showed him superior to his circumstances. He was a godsend to her dreariness in this place Edinburgh and the noisy world had made her fretful of, and she was in the mood for escapade.

They walked into the policies, that were no way changed. Still the flowers grew thick on the dykes; the tall trees swayed their boughs: still the same, and yet for Gilian there was, in that faint tinge of yellow in the leaves, some sorrow he had not guessed in the day they were trying to recall.

"It is all just as it was," said she. "All just as it was; there are the very flowers I plucked," and she bent and plucked them again.

"We can never pluck our flowers twice," said he. "The flowers you gathered then are ghosts."

"Not a bit," said she. "Here they are re-born," and she went as before from bush to bush and bank to bank, humming a strain of sailor song.

They went under the trees on which he had fancied his heron's nest, and they looked at each other, laughing.

"Wasn't I a young fool?" he asked. "I was full of dream and conceit in those days."

"And now?" she asked, burying her face in the flowers and eyeing him wonderingly.

"Oh, now," said he, "I have lost every illusion."

"Or changed them for others, perhaps."

He started at the suggestion. "I suppose you are right, after all," he said. "I'm still in a measure the child of fancy. This countryside moves me—I could tenant it with a thousand tales; never a wood or thicket in it but is full of song. I love it all, and yet it is my torture. When I was a child the Paymaster once got me on the bridge crying my eyes out over the screech of a curlew—that has been me all through life—I must be wondering at the hidden meanings of things. The wind in the winter trees, the gossip of the rivers, the trail of clouds, waves washing the shore at night—all these things have a tremendous importance to me. And I must laugh to see my neighbours making a to-do about a mercantile bargain. Well, I suppose it is the old Highlands in me, as Miss Mary says."

"I have felt a little of it in a song," said Nan.

"You could scarce do otherwise to sing them as you do," he answered. "I never heard you yet but you had the magic key for every garden of fancy. One note, one phrase of yours comes up over and over again that seems to me filled with the longings of a thousand years."

He turned on her suddenly a face strenuous, eyes filled with passion.

"I wish! I wish!" said he all fervent, "I wish I could fathom the woman within."

216

"Here she's on the surface," said Nan, a little impatiently, arranging her flowers. And then she looked him straight in the eyes. "Ladyfield seems a poor academy," she said, "if it taught you but to speculate on things unfathomable. I always preferred the doer to the dreamer. The mind of man is a far more interesting thing than the song of the river I'm thinking, or the trailing of mist. And woman—" she laughed and paused.

"Well?—" He eyed her robust and wholesome figure.

"Should I expose my sex, John Hielan'man, or should I not?" she reflected with an amused look in her face yet. "Never bother to look below the surface for us," she said. "We are better pleased, and you will speed the quicker to take us for what we seem. What matters of us is—as it is with men too—plain enough on the surface. Dear, dear! what nonsense to be on! You are far too much of the mist and mountain for me. As if I had not plenty of them up in Maam! Oh! I grow sick of them!" She began to walk faster, forgetting his company in the sudden remembrance of her troubles; and he strode awkwardly at her heels, not very dignified, like a menial overlooked. "They hang about the place like a menace," said she. "No wonder mother died! If she was like me she must have been heartbroken when father left her to face these solitudes."

"It is so, it is so," confessed the lad. "But they would not be wearisome with love. With love in that valley it would smile like an Indian plain."

"How do *you* ken?" said she, stopping suddenly at this.

"It would make habitable and even pleasant," said he, "a dwelling where age and bitterness had their abode."

"Faith, you're not so blate as I thought you!" she said, setting aside the last of her affected shy simplicity.

"Blate!" he repeated, "I would not have thought that was my failing. Am I not cracking away to you like an old wife?"

"Just to hide the blateness of you," she answered. "You may go to great depths with hills and heughs and mists—and possibly with women too when you get the chance, but, my dear Gilian, you're terribly shallow to any woman with an eye in her head."

"Did you say 'Gilian'?" he asked, stopping and looking at her with a high colour.

"Did I?" she repeated, biting her lips. "What liberty!"

"No, no," he cried—

"I thought myself young enough to venture it; but, of course, if you object—"

He looked at her helplessly, realising that she was making fun of him, and she laughed. All her assurance was back to her, she knew the young gentleman was one she could twist round her little finger.

"Well, well," she went on after a silence, "you seem poorly provided with small talk. In Edinburgh, now, a young man with your chances would be making love to me by this time."

He stared at her aghast. "But, but—"

"But I would not permit it, of course not! We were brought up very particularly in Miss Simpson's, I can assure you." This with a prim tightening of her lips and a severity that any other than our dreamer would have understood. To Nan there came a delight in this play with an intelligence she knew so keen, though different from her own. It was with a holiday feeling she laughed and shone, mischievously eyeing him and trying him with badinage as they penetrated deeper into the policies.

They reached the Lady's Linn, but did not repeat old history to the extent of seating themselves on the banks, though Gilian half suggested it in a momentary boldness.

"No, no," said she. "We were taught better than that in Miss Simpson's. And fancy the risks of rheumatism! You told me one of Gillesbeg Aotram's stories here; what was it again?"

He repeated the tale of the King of Knapdale's daughter. She listened attentively, sometimes amused at his earnestness, that sat on him gaukily, sometimes serious enough, touched with the poetry he could put into the narrative.

"It is a kind of gruesome fable," she said when he was done, and she shuddered slightly. "The other brother was Death, wasn't he? When you told it to me last I did not understand."

They walked on through the intersecting paths whose maze

had so bewildered them before: "After all, it is not a bit like what it was," said she. "I thought it would take a wizard to get out of here, and now I can see over the bushes and the sea is in sight all the time."

"Just so," he answered, "but you could see over no bushes in those days, and more's the pity that you can see over them now, in the Duke's garden as well as in life, for it's only one more dream spoiled, my dear Nan."

"Oh! there is not much blateness there! You are coming on, John Hielan'man." But this was to herself.

"Then to you this is just the same as when we lost our way?"

"The same and not all the same," he admitted. "I can make it exactly the same if I forgot to look at you, for that means sensations I never knew then. I cannot forget the place has been here night and day, summer and winter, rain and sun, since we last were in it, and time makes no difference; it is the same place. But it is not the same in some other way, some sad way I cannot explain."

The night was full of the fragrance of flowers and the foreign trees. There was no breath of wind. They were shades in some garden of dream compelled to stand and ponder for ever in an eternal night of numerous beneficent stars. No sound manifested except the lady's breathing, that to another than the dreamer would have told an old and wholesome Panic story, for her bosom heaved, that breath was sweeter than the flowers. And the dryads, no whit older as they swung among the trees, still all childless, must have laughed at this revelation of an age of dream. Than that sound of maiden interest, and the far-off murmur of the streams that fell seaward from the woody hills, there was at first no other rumour to the ear.

"Listen," said Gilian again, and he turned an anxious ear towards that grey grassy sea. His hand grasped possessingly the lady's arm.

"Faith, and you are *not* blate," said she whimsically, but indifferent to remove herself from a grasp so innocent.

She listened. The far bounds of the lawn were lost in gloom, in its midst stood up vague in the dusk a great druidic stone. And at last she could distinguish faintly, far-away, as by some new sense, a murmur of the twilight universe, the never-ending moan of this travailing nature. A moment, then her senses lost it, and Gilian yet stood in his rapt attention. She withdrew her arm gently.

"Hush, hush!" he said. "Do you not fancy you hear a discourse?"

"I do?" she answered a little impatiently, but not without a kindly sense of laughter as at a child. "Bees and midges, late things like ourselves. You are not going to tell me they are your fairies."

"They are, of course they are," he protested, laughing. "At least a second ago I could have sworn they were the same that gave me my dread on the night the Cornal met us. Even yet"—his humour came back—"even yet I fear to interrupt their convocations. Let us go round by the other path."

"What, and waste ten minutes more!" she cried. "Follow me, follow me!"

And she sped swiftly over the trim grass, bruising the odours of the night below her dainty feet. He followed, chagrined, ashamed of himself, very much awake and practical, realising how stupid if not idiotic all his conversation must seem to her. Where was the mutual exchange of sentiments on books, poetry, life? He had thrown away his opportunity. He overtook her in a few steps, and tore the leaves from his story book again to please or to deceive the Philistine.

"I thought we could bring it all back again—that was the object of my rhapsody, and you seem to have kept good memory of the past."

They were under the lamps of the lodge gates. She eyed him shrewdly.

"And you do not believe these things yourself? So? I have my own notions about that. Do you know I begin to think you must be a poet. Have you ever written anything?"

He found himself extremely warm. Her question for the first

time suggested his own possibilities. No, he had never made poetry, he confessed, though he had often felt it, as good as some of the poetry he had read in Marget Maclean's books that were still the favourites of his leisure hours.

"It'll be in that like other things," she said with some sense of her own cruelty. "You must be dreaming it when you might be making it."

"I never had the inspiration—"

"What, you say that to a lady who has been talking fair to you!" she pointed out.

"But now, of course—"

"Just the weather, Gilian," she hastened to interject. "A bonny night with stars, the scent of flowers, a misty garden—I could find some inspiration in them myself for poetry, and I make no pretence at it."

"There was a little more," he said meaningly; "but no matter, that may wait," and he proceeded immediately to the making of a poem as he went, the subject a night of stars and a maiden. They had got into the dark upper end of the town overhung by the avenue trees, the lands were spotted with the lemon lights of the evening candles, choruses came from the New Inns where fishermen from Cowal met to spend a shilling or two in the illusion of joy. Mr Spencer saw them as he passed and was suffused by a kindly glow of uncommon romance. He saw, as he thought, a pair made for each other because they were of an age and of a size (as if that meant much); what should they be but lovers coming from the gardens of Duke George in such a night and the very heavens twinkling with the courtship of the stars? He looked and sighed. Far off in the south was an old tale of his own; the lady upstairs eternally whining because she must be banished to the wilds away from her roaring native city was not in it. "Lucky lad!" said he to himself. "He is not so shy as we thought him." They came for a moment under the influence of the swinging lamp above his door, then passed into the dusk. He went into his public room, and "Mary," he cried to a maid, "a little drop of the French for Sergeant Cameron and me. You will allow me, Sergeant? I feel a little need of an evening brace." And he drank, for the sake of bygone dusks, with his customer.

Nan and Gilian now walked on the pavement, a discreet distance apart. She stopped at the mantua-maker's door. He lingered on the parting, eager to prolong it. The street was deserted; from the Sergeant More's came the sound of song; some fallen leaves ran crisp along the stones, blown by an air of wind. He had her by the hand, still loth to leave, when suddenly the door of the mantua-maker's opened and out came a little woman, who, plunging from the splendour of two penny dips into the outer mirk, ran into his arms before she noticed his presence. She drew back with an apology uttered in Gaelic in her hurried perturbation. It was Miss Mary.

"Auntie," he said, no more.

She glanced at his companion and started as if in fear, shivered, put out a hand and bade her welcome home.

"Dear me! Miss Nan," said she, "amn't I proud to see you back? What a tall lady you have grown, and so like—so like—" She stopped embarrassed. Her hand had gone with an excess of kindness upon the girl's arm ere she remembered all that lay between them and the heyday of another Nan than this. Of Gilian she seemed to take no notice, which much surprised him with a sense of something wanting.

At last they parted, and he went up with Miss Mary to the Paymaster's house.

XXVII

ALARM

NAN'S uncle, moving with hopeless and dragging steps about the sides of Maam hill, ruminating constantly on nature's caprice with sheep and crop, man's injustice, the poverty of barns, the discomforts of seasons, nourishing his sour self on reflections upon all life's dolours, would be coming after that for days upon the girl and Gilian gathering berries or on some such childish diversion in the woods behind the river. A gaunt, bowed man in the decline of years, with a grey tangle of beard—a fashion deemed untidy where the razor was on every other man's face— he looked like a satyr of the trees, when he first came to the view of Gilian. He saw those young ones from remote vistas of the trees, or from above them in cliffs as they plucked the boughs. In lanes of greenwood he would peer in questioning, and silent, and there he was certain to find them as close as lovers, though, had he known it, there was never word of love. And though Gilian was still, for the sake of a worn-out feud with the house of the Paymaster, no visitor to Maam, that saturnine uncle would say nothing. For a little he would look, they uncomfortable, then he would smile most grim, a satyr, as Gilian told himself, more than ever.

He came upon them often. Now it would be at the berries, now among the bulrushes of Dhu Loch. They strayed like children.

Often, I say, for Gilian had no sooner hurried through his work in these days than he was off in the afternoon, and, on some pretence, would meet the girl on a tryst of her own making. She was indifferent—I have no excuse for her, and she's my poor heroine—about his wasted hours so long as she had her days illumined by some flicker of life and youth. He never knew how often it was from weeping over a letter from Edinburgh, or a song familiar elsewhere, upon the harpsichord, she would come out to meet him. All she wanted was the adventure, though she did not understand this herself. If no one else in a bonnet came to Maam—and Young Islay was for reasons away in the Lowlands—this dreamer of the wild, with the unreadable but eloquent face and the mysterious moods would do very well. I will not deny that there might even be affection in her trysts. So far as she knew they were no different from trysts made by real lovers elsewhere since the start of time, for lovers have ever been meeting in the woods of these glens without saying to each other why.

Gilian went little to town in that weather, he was getting credit with Miss Mary, if not with her brothers, for a new interest in his profession. Nor did Nan. Her father did not let her go much without himself, he had his own reasons for keeping her from hearing the gossip of the streets.

A week or two passed. The corn, in the badger's moon, yellowed and hung; silent days of heat haze, all breathless, came on the country; the stubble fields filled at evening with great flights of birds moving south. A spirit like Nan's, that must ever be in motion, could not but irk to share such a doleful season; she went more than ever about the house of Maam sighing for lost companions, and a future not to be guessed at. Only she would cheer up when she had her duties done for the afternoon and could run out to the hillside to meet Gilian if he were there.

She was thus running, actually with a song on her lips, one day, when she ran into the arms of her uncle as he came round the corner of the barn.

"Where away?" said he shortly, putting her before him, with his hands upon her shoulders.

She reddened, but answered promptly, for there was nothing clandestine in her meetings on the bare hillside with Gilian.

"The berries again," she said. "Some of the people from Glen Aray are coming over."

"Some of the people," he repeated ironically; "that means one particular gentleman. My lassie, there's an end coming to that."

He drew a large-jointed coarse hand through his tangled beard and chuckled to himself.

"Are you aware of that?" he went on. "An end coming to it. Oh! I see things; I'm no fool: I could have told your father long ago, but he's putting an end to it in his own way, and for his own reasons."

"I have no idea what you mean," she said, surprised at the portentous tone. She was not a bit afraid of him, though he was so little in sympathy with her youth, so apparently in antagonism to her.

"What would you say to a man?" he asked cunningly.

"It would depend, uncle," she said readily and cheerfully, though a sudden apprehension smote her at the heart. "It would depend on what he said to me first."

The old man grinned callously as the only person in the secret.

"Suppose he said: 'Come away home, wife, I've paid a bonny penny for ye'?"

"Perhaps I would say, if I was in very good humour at the time, 'You've got a bonny wife for your bonny penny.' More likely I would be throwing something at him, for I have my Uncle Jamie's temper they say, but I'm nobody's wife, and for want of the asking I'm not likely to be."

"Well, we'll see," said the uncle oracularly. Then abruptly, "Have you heard that your father's got an appointment?"

"I—I heard just a hint of it, of course he has not told me all about it yet," she answered with a readiness that surprised herself when she reflected on it later, for the news now so unexpectedly given her in the momentary irritation of the old man was news indeed, and though she was unwilling to let him see that it was so, a tremendous oppression seized her; now she was to be lonely indeed. Half uttering her thoughts she said, "I'll sooner go with him than stay here and—"

"Oh, there's no going yonder," said the uncle. "Sierra Leone is not a healthy clime for men, let alone for women. That's where the man comes in. He could hardly leave you alone to stravaige about the hills there with all sorts of people from Glen Aray."

"The white man's grave!" said she, appalled.

"Ay!" said he, "but he's no ordinary white man; he's of good stock."

"And—and—he has found a man for me," she said bitterly. "Could I not be left to find one for myself?"

Her uncle laughed his hoarse rude laugh again, and still combed his tangled beard.

"Not to his fancy," he answered. "It's not every one who would suit." He smiled grimly—a wicked elder man. "It's not every one would suit," he repeated—as if he was anxious to let the full significance of what he meant sink to her understanding. And he combed his rough beard with large-jointed knotted fingers, and looked from under his heavy eyebrows.

"Seeing the business is so commercial," said she, "I'm sure that between the two of you you will make a good bargain. I am not sure but I might be glad to be anywhere out of this if father's gone and I not with him." She said it with outer equanimity, and unable to face him a moment longer without betraying her shame and indignation, she left him and went to the cornfield where Black Duncan was working alone.

That dark mariner was to some extent a grieved sharer of her solitude in Maam. The loss of the *Jean* on Ealan Dubh had sundered him for ever from his life of voyaging. The distant ports in whose dusks wild beasts roared and spices filled the air were far back in another life for him; even the little trips to the Clyde were, in the regrets of memory, experiences most precious. Now he had to wear thick shoes on the hill of Maam or sweat like a common son of the shore in the harvest-fields. At night upon his pillow in the barn loft he would lie and mourn for unreturning days and loud and clamorous experience. Or at morning ere he started the work of the day he would ascend the little tulloch behind the house and look far off at a patch of blue—the inner arm of the ocean.

Nan found him in one of his cranky moods, fretful at circumstances, and at her father who kept him there on the shore, and had no word of another ship to take the place of the *Jean*. Of late he had been worse than usual, for he had learned that the master was bound for abroad, and though he was a sure pensioner so long as Maam held together, it meant his eternal severance from the sea and ships.

Nan threw herself upon the grass beside him as he twisted hay-bands for the stacks, and said no more than "Good afternoon" for a little.

He gloomed at her, and hissed between his teeth a Skye pibroch. For a time he would have her believe he was paying no attention, but ever and anon he would let slip a glance of inquiry from the corner of his eyes. He was not too intent upon his own grievances to see that she was troubled with hers, but he knew her well enough to know that she must introduce them herself if they were to be introduced at all.

He changed his tune, let a little more affability come into his face, and it was an old air of her childhood on the *Jean* he had at his lips. As he whistled it he saw a little moisture at her eyes; she was recalling the lost old happiness of the days when she had gone about with that song at her lips. But he knew her better than to show that he perceived it.

"Have you heard that father's going away, Duncan?" she asked in a little.

"I have been hearing that for five years," said he shortly. He had not thought her worries would have been his own like this.

"Yes, but this time he goes."

"So they're telling me," said Black Duncan.

He busied himself more closely than ever with his occupation.

"Do you think he should be taking me?" she asked in a little.

He stopped his work immediately, and looked up startled.

"The worst curse!" said he in Gaelic. "He could not be doing

227

that. He goes to the Gold Coast. Do I not know it—the white man's grave?"

"But this Glen Shira," said she, pretending merriment, "it's the white girl's grave for me, Duncan. Should not I be glad to be getting out of it?" And now her eyes were suffused with tears though her lips were smiling.

"I know, I know," said he, casting a glance up that lone valley that was so much their common grief. "And could we not be worse? I'm sure Black Duncan, reared in a bothy in Skye, who has been tossed by the sea, and been wet and dry in all airts of the world, would be a very thankless man if he was not pleased to be here safe and comfortable, on a steady bed at night, and not heeding the wind nor the storm no more than if he was a skart."

"Oh! you're glad enough to be here, then?" said she.

"Am I?" said he. And he sighed, so comical a sound from that hard mariner that she could not but laugh in spite of the anxieties oppressing her.

"I'm not going with him," she proceeded.

"I know," said he. "At least I heard—I heard otherwise, and I wondered when you said it, thinking perhaps you had made him change his mind."

"You thought I had made him change—what do you mean?" she pressed, feeling herself on the verge of an explanation, but determined not to ask directly.

Black Duncan became cautious.

"You need not be asking me anything: I know nothing about it," said he shortly. "I am very busy—I—" He hissed at his work more strenuously than ever.

Then Nan knew he was not to be got at that way.

"Oh, well, never mind," said she; "tell me a story."

"I have no time just now," he answered.

Nan's uncle came round the corner of the dyke, no sound from his footsteps, his hands in his pockets, his brows lowering. He looked at the two of them and surmised the reason of Nan's discourse with Black Duncan.

"Women—" said he to himself vaguely. "Women—" said he, pausing for a phrase to express many commingled sentiments he had as to their unnecessity, their aggravation, and his suspicion of them. He did not find the right one. He lifted his hand, stroked again the tangled beard, then made a gesture, a large animal gesture—still the satyr—to the sky. He turned and went down to the riverside. Mid-way he paused and stroked his beard again, and looked grimly up at where the maid and the manservant were blue-black against the evening sky. He shrugged his shoulders. "Women," said he, "they make trouble. I wish—I wish—" He had no word to finish the sentence with, he but sighed and proceeded on his way.

Nan seemed to be lazily watching his figure as she sat in the grass, herself observed by Black Duncan. But she really saw him not.

"Ah well! never mind the story, Duncan," she said at last; "I know you are tired and not in the mood for *sguŭlachd*, and if you like I will sing you my song."

"You randy!" he said to himself, "you are going to have it out of me, my dear." And he bent the more industriously to his task.

"Stop, stop!" he cried before she had got halfway through the old song of "The Rover". "Stop! stop!" said he. He threw the binding bands from him and faced the crimson west, with his back to her.

"Any port but that, my dear! If you are grieving because you think you are going abroad you need not be anything of the kind, my leddy. This is the place for you, about your father's door and him away where the fevers are—aye and the harbours too with diversions in every one of them."

"And Uncle Jamie's going to keep me, is he?" said she. "Lucky me! I was aye so fond of gaiety, you mind."

"Whoever it is that's to keep you it might be worse," said he.

"Then there's somebody."

"Somebody," he repeated; "the cleverest young—"

"Stop! stop!" she cried, rising suddenly to her feet; "do not dare to mention a name; spare me that."

He looked at her in amazement.

"Do you think I'm a stone, Duncan?"

"You would not be asking me that twice if I was younger myself," he said redly, looking at her fine figure, the blush like a sunset on her neck, the palpitation of her bosom, the flash and menace of her eyes.

"Well, well, well, go on, tell me more," she cried when she had recovered herself. "What more is there?"

"You are the one that should know most," said he.

"I know nothing at all," she answered bitterly. "It seems that nowadays the lady is the last to be taken into confidence about her own marriage."

"Are you telling me?" he asked incredulously.

"I'm swearing it down your throat!" she cried. "If I had a friend in this countryside he would be pitying my shame that I must be bargained for like a beast at a fair and not have a word in the bargain."

"My name's what my name may be," said he, putting out an arm and addressing the world, "and you are my master's daughter; I would cut off that hand to save you a minute's vexation. What did Black Duncan know but that you had the picking of the gentleman yourself—and you might have picked worse, though I tell you I did not care to hear about the money in it."

"The money," she exclaimed, turning pale to the lips; "then— then—then there's money in it?"

"He's a smart young fellow—"

"No name, no name, or you are no friend of mine! Money, you say?"

"I could have picked no better for you myself."

"Did you say money?"

"I thought once there might be something."

"Money, money," she repeated to herself.

"A tocher should not be all on one side," said he, "and I know the gentleman would be glad to have you—"

"Perhaps the whole countryside knows more about it than I do; it could scarcely know less. I wondered why they were looking at me in the church on Sunday. Oh! I feel black burning shame—shame—shame!"

She put her hands to her face to hide her tears; she trembled in every part.

"They know; the cries are in at least," said Duncan.

"The cries! the cries!" she repeated. "Is my fate so near at hand as that?"

"You'll be a married woman before the General takes the road," said he.

She took her hands from her face; her eyes froze and snapped, cold as ice, the very redness of her weeping cooling pale in her passion. She had no words to utter; she left him hurriedly, and ran fast into the house.

XXVIII

GILIAN'S OPPORTUNITY

HER father was at the door when she went in. Now for the first time she knew the reason for his change of manner lately, for that bustle about trivial affairs when she was near, that averted eye when she was fond and humorous. She went past him, unable to speak more than an indifferent word, and great was his relief at that, for he had been standing there bracing his courage to consult her on what she must be told of sooner or later. He looked after her as she sped upstairs. "I wonder how she'll take it?" he said to himself, greatly perplexed. "A father has some unco' tasks to perform, and here's a father not very well fitted by nature for the management of a daughter." He took off his hat and dried a clammy brow that showed how much the duty postponed had been disturbing him. "It's for the best, but it's a vulgar business even then. If it was her uncle, now, he would wake her out of her sleep to tell her the news. Poor girl, poor girl! I wish she had her mother."

He went into the barn, where corn was piling up, the straw filling the gloomy gable-ends with rustling gold. Loud he stormed among some workers there; loud he stormed, for him a thing unusual; and they bent silent to their work and looked at one another knowingly, sensible that he was ashamed of himself.

Sitting dry-eyed on the edge of her bed, Nan reflected upon her next step. At a cast of her mind round all the countryside she could think of no woman to turn to in this trouble, and only with a woman could she share it. Her pride first, and then the fear of her father's anger, left her only certain limits in which to operate. Her pride would not let her even show curiosity in the identity of the man who was to be her doom, nor confess to another that she did not know his name. And the whole parish, if it was acquainted with her sale (as now she deemed it), must be her enemy. Against any other outrage than this she would have gone straight to her father. He that she loved and caressed, on whose knees sometimes even yet she sat, would not be deaf to any ordinary plea or protest of hers. She would need but to nestle in his arms, and loose and tie the antique queue, and perhaps steal a kiss willingly surrendered, and all would be well. But this, all her instincts, all her knowledge of her father told her, was no ordinary decision of his. He had gone too far to draw back. The world knew it; he feared to face her because for once to please her he could not cancel what was done. There was no hope, she told herself, in that direction; even if there was she would not have gone there, for the sordid horror of this transaction put a gulf between them. Feverishly she turned over her lowland letters, and there she found but records of easy heart and gaiety; no sacrificing friends were offering themselves in the pages she had mourned over in her moods of evening loneliness. And again she brought her mind back to her own country, and sitting still dry-eyed, with a burning skin, upon her bed, reviewed her relatives and friends, weighing which would be most like to help her.

She almost laughed when she found she had reduced all at last to one eligible—Elasaid, her old Skye nurse, and the mother of Black Duncan, who was in what was called the last of the shealings, by the lochs of Kames. Many a time her mother had gone to the shealing a young matron for motherly counsel, but Nan herself had never been there, though Elasaid had come to Nan to nurse her when her mother died. In the shealing, she felt sure, there was not only counsel, but concealment if occasion demanded that.

But how was she to get there, lost as it was somewhere miles beyond the corner of the Salachary hill, in the wild red moors between the two big waters?

First she thought of Young Islay—first and with a gladness at the sense of his sufficiency in such an enterprise. His was the right nature for knight-errantry in a case like hers, but then she reflected that he was away from home—her father had casually let that drop in conversation at breakfast yesterday; and even if he had been at home, said cooler thought, she would hesitate to enlist him in so sordid a cause.

Then Gilian occurred—less well adapted, she felt, for the circumstances; but she could speak more freely to him than to any other, and he was out there in the hazel-wood, no doubt, still waiting for her. Gilian would do, Gilian would have to do. If he could have seen how unimpassioned she was in coming to this conclusion he would have been grieved.

She went out at once, leisurely and with her thoughts constrained upon some unimportant matter, so that her face might not betray her tribulation when she met him.

In the low fields her uncle was scanning the hills with his hands arched above his eyes to shield them from the glare of the westering sun, groaning for the senselessness of sheep that must go roaming on altitudes when they are wanted specially in the plains. She evaded his supercilious eyes by going round the hedges, and in ten minutes she came upon Gilian, waiting patiently for her to keep her own tryst. His first words showed her the way to a speedy explanation.

"Next week," said he, "we'll try Strongara; the place is as full of berries as the night is full of stars. Here they're not so ripe as on the other side."

"Next week the berries might be as numerous as that at the very door of Maam," said she, "and I none the better for them."

"What's the matter?" he cried, appalled at the omen of her face.

"My father is going abroad at once," she answered.

"Abroad?" he repeated. He had a branch of bramble in his

hand, plucked for the crimson of its leafage. He drew it through his hands and the thorns bled the palms, but he never felt the pain. She was going too! She was going away from Maam! He might never see her again! These late days of tryst and happiness in the woods and on the hills were to be at an end, and he was again to be quite alone among his sheep with no voice to think on expectantly in slow-passing forenoons, and no light to shine like a friendly eye from Maam in evening dusks!

"Well," she said, looking curiously at him. "My father is going abroad, have you heard?"

"I have not," he answered; and she was relieved, for in that case he had not learned the full ignominy of her story.

"Can you not say so little as 'good luck' to us?" she asked in her lightest manner.

"You—you are going with him, then?" said Gilian, and he delighted in the sharp torture of the thorns that bled his hands.

"No," she answered, "it's worse than that, for I stay. You have not heard? Then you are the only one in the parish, I am sure, so ignorant of my poor business. They're—they're looking for a man for me. Is it not a pretty thing, Gilian?" She laughed with a bitterness that shocked him. "Is it not a pretty thing, Gilian?" she went on. "I'm wondering they did not lead me on a halter round the country and take the best offer at a fair! It was throwing away good chances to give me to the first offerer, was it not, Gilian?"

"Who is it?" he asked, every nerve jarring at the story.

"Do you think I would ask?" she said sharply. "It does not matter who it is and it is the last thing I would like to know, for then I would know who knew my price in the market."

"Your father would never do it!"

"My father would not do but what he thought he must. He is poor, though I never thought him so poor as this; and I daresay he would like to see me settled before he goes. It is the black settling when I'm cried in the kirk before I'm courted."

"They can never marry you against your will," said Gilian in a dull, lifeless way, as if he had no great belief in what he laid forth.

"And that would be true," she said, "if I had a friend in the whole countryside. I have not one except—"

He flushed and waited, and so did she expectantly, thinking he would make the fervent protest most lads would do under the same circumstances. But in the moment's pause he could not find the words for his profound feeling.

"—Except old Elasaid, the nurse on the Kames moor," she continued.

"Oh, her!" said he lamely.

"There's none else I could think of."

"Look at me," he cried; "Look at me; am I not your true friend? I will do anything in the world for you." But he still went on torturing himself with his bramble branch, the most insensible of lovers.

She was annoyed at his want of the commonest courage or tact. "John Hielan'man! John Hielan'man!" she said inwardly, trying a little coquetry of the downcast eyes to tempt him. For now she was so desolate that she almost loved this gawky youth throbbing in sympathy with her tribulation.

"I believe you are my true friend, I believe you are my true friend, and there is no one else," she said, blushing now with no coquetry, and if he had not been a fool and his fate against him, he might at a hand's movement or a word have had her in his arms. The word to say was sounding loud and strong within him; he took her (only, alas! in fancy) to his breast, but what was she the wiser?

"And I can do nothing?" he said pitifully.

"Nothing!" said she; "you can do everything."

"Show me how, then," he said eagerly.

She had been gazing away from him with her eyes on Maam, that looked so sombre a home, and was certainly now so cruel a home, and she turned then, almost weeping, her breath rising and falling, audible to his ear, the sweetest of sounds.

"Will you take me away from here?" she asked in entreaty. "I must go away from here."

"I will take you anywhere you wish," said he. He held out his hands in a gesture of sudden offering, and she felt a happiness as one who comes upon a familiar and kind face all unexpectedly in a strange country. Her face betrayed her gladness.

"I will take you, and who would be better pleased?" said Gilian.

She explained her intention briefly. She must leave Maam at the latest tomorrow night without being observed, and he must show her the way to Elasaid's shealing.

"Ah! give me the right," he said, "and I will take you to the world's end." He put out his hands and nigh encircled her, but shyness sent him back to a calmer distance.

"John Hielan'man!" she repeated to herself, annoyed at this tardiness, but she outwardly showed no knowledge of it.

They planned what only half in fun she called their elopement. He was to come across to Maam in the early morning.

XXIX

THE ELOPEMENT

HE had ideas of his own as to how this enterprise should be
conducted, but on Nan's advice he had gone about it in
the fashion of Marget Maclean's novels, even to the ladder. It
was not a rope ladder, but a common one of wood that Black
Duncan was accustomed to use for ascent to his sleep in the loft.

Gilian, apprised by Nan of its exact situation, crept breath-
lessly into the barn, left his lantern at the door, and felt around
with searching fingers. The place was all silent but for the seaman's snores as he slept the sleep of a landsman upon his coarse
pallet. Outside a cock crew; its sudden alarm brought the sweat
to Gilian's brow; he clutched with blind instinct, found what he
wanted, turned and hastened from the dusty barn.

The house of Maam was jet-black among its trees, no light
peeped even in Nan's room.

Carefully he put the ladder against the wall beneath her window, and as he did so he fancied he heard a movement above.
He stood with his hand on one of the rungs, dubious, hesitating.
For the first time a sense of the risks of the adventure swept into
that mind of his, always the monopoly of imagination and the
actor. He was ashamed to find himself half-wishing she might
not come. He tried to think it was all a dream, and he pinched
his arm to try and waken himself. But the blank black walls of

Maam confronted him; the river was crying in its reeds; it was a real adventure that must be gone on with.

He lit the lantern. Through the open door of it as he did so the flood of light revealed his face anxious and haggard, his eyes uncertain. He closed the lantern and looked around.

Through the myriad holes that pierced the tin, pin-points of fire lanced the night, streaming in all directions, throwing the front of the house at once into cold relief with a rasping, harled, lime surface. The bushes were big masses of shade; the trees, a little more remote, seemed to watch him with an irony that made him half ashamed. What an appalling night! Over him came the sentiments of the robber, the marauder, the murderer. As he held the lantern on his finger a faint wind swung it, and its lances of light danced rhythmic through the gloom. He put it under his plaid, and prepared to give the signal whistle. For the life of him he could not give it utterance; his lips seemed to have frozen, not with fear, for he was calm in that way, but with some commingling of emotions where fear was not at all. When he gave breath to his hesitating lips, it went through inaudible.

What he might have done then may only be guessed, for the opening of the window overhead brought an end to his hesitation.

"Is it you?" said Nan's voice, just a little revealing her anxiety in its whisper. He could not see her now that his lantern was concealed, but he looked up and fancied her eyes were shining more lambent than his own lantern that smelled unpleasantly.

He wet his lips with his tongue. "The ladder is ready; it's up against your window, don't you see it?" he said, also whispering, but astounded at the volume of his voice.

"Tuts!" she exclaimed impatiently, "why don't you show a light? How can I see it without a light?"

"Dare I?" he asked, astonished.

"Dare! dare! Oh dear!" she repeated. "Am I to do the daring and break my neck perhaps?"

Out flashed the lantern from beneath his plaid and he held it up to the window. Nan leaned over and all his hesitation fled.

He had never seen her more alluring. Her hair had become somehow unfastened, and, without untidiness, there lay a lock across her brow; all her blood was in her face, her eyes might indeed have been the flames he had fancied, for to the appeal of the lantern they flashed back from great and rolling depths of luminousness. Her lips seemed to have gathered up in sleep the wealth of a day of kissing. A screen of tartan that she had placed about her shoulders had slipped aside in her movement at the window and showed her neck, ivory pale and pulsing.

"Come along, come along!" he cried in an eager whisper, and he put up his arms, lantern and all, as if she were to jump. Something in his first look made her pause.

"Do you really want to go?" he asked, and she was drawing her screen by instinct across her form. An observer, if there had been such, might well have been amused to see an elopement so conducted. There was still no sound in the night, except that the cock crew at intervals over in the cottars. The morning was heavy with dew; the scent of bog myrtle drugged the air.

"Do I really want?" she repeated. "Mercy! what a question. It seems to me that yesterday would have been the best time to ask it. Are you rueing your bargain?" She looked at him with great dissatisfaction as he stood at the foot of the ladder, by no means a handsome cavalier, as he carried his plaid clumsily. He was made all the more eager by her coldness.

"Come, come!" he cried; "the house will be awake before you are ready, and I cannot be keeping this lantern lighted for fear someone sees it."

"We are safe for an hour yet, if we cared to waste the time," she said composedly, "and if you're sure you want it—"

"Want you, Nan," he corrected.

"That's a little more like it," she said to herself, and she dropped the customary bundle at his feet. He picked it up gingerly, as if it were a church relic; that it was a possession of hers, apparel apparently, made him feel a slight intoxication. No swithering now; he would carry out the adventure if it led to the end of the world! He hugged the bundle under his arm, as if it were a woman, and felt a fictional glow from the touch of it. "Well?" said she impatiently, for he was no longer looking at her, no longer, indeed, conceding her so little as the light of the lantern, which he had placed on the ground, so that its light was dissipated around, while none of it reached the top of the ladder.

"Well," she repeated sharply, for he had not answered.

He looked up with a start. "Are you not coming?" he said, with a tone to suggest that he was waiting impatiently.

She had the window wide open now; she leaned out on her arms ready to descend; the last rung of the ladder was a foot lower than the sill of the window; she looked in perplexity at her cavalier, for it was impossible to put much of grace into an emergence and a descent like this.

"I am just coming," she said, but still she made no other move, and he held up the lantern for her to see the better.

"Well, be careful!" he advised, and he thought how delightful it was to have the right to say so much.

"O Gilian!" she said helplessly, "you are far from gleg."

He gazed ludicrously uncomprehending at her, and in his sense of almost conjugal right to the girl failed to realise her delicacy.

"Go round to the barn and make sure that Duncan is not moving; he's the only one I fear," she said. "Leave the lantern."

He did as he was told; he put the lantern on the ground; he went round again to the barn, put his head in, and satisfied himself that his seaman was still musical aloft. Then he hurried back. He found the lantern swinging on Nan's finger, and her composed upon the ground, to which she had made a speedy descent whenever he had disappeared.

"Oh! I wanted to help you," said he.

"Did you?" said she, looking for a sign of the humorist, but he was as solemn as a sermon.

They might have been extremely sedate in Miss Simpson's school in Edinburgh, but at that moment Miss Nan would have forgiven some apparent appreciation of her cleverness in getting him out of the way while she came feet first through a window.

They stood for a moment in expectancy, as if something was going to happen, she still holding the lantern, trembling a little, as it might be with the cold, he with her bundle under his arm pressed affectionately.

"And—and—do we just go on?" she asked suggestively.

"The quicker the better," said he, but he made no movement to depart, for his mind was in the house of Maam, and he felt the father's sorrow and alarm at an empty bed, a daughter gone.

She put out an arm, flushing in the dark as she did so, as if to place it on his neck, but drew back and put the lantern fast behind her, lest her fervour had been noticed by the ironic and jealous night. He, she saw, could not notice; the thing was not in his mind.

"In the stories they just move off, then?" said she shyly. "There was the meeting, the meeting—no more, and they just went away?"

"And the sooner the better," said he, again leading the way at last, after taking the lantern from her, and "John Hielan'man, John Hielan'man!" she cried vexatiously within.

She followed, pouting her lips in the darkness. "It's quite different from what I expected," she said, whispering as they passed the front door and down by the burn.

"And with me too," he confessed. "I had it made up in my mind all otherwise. There should have been moonlight and a horse, and many other things."

"It seems to me you are not making so much as you might of what there is," she suggested. "Are you sure it is not a trouble to carry the lantern and the bundle too?"

"Oh! no, no!" he cried softly, but eagerly, every chivalric sentiment roused lest she should deprive him of the pleasure of doing all he could for her.

She sighed.

"Are you vexed you have come?" he asked, stopping and turning on her his yet wan face full of regret and of dubiety too.

"The thing is done," she answered abruptly, and they were stepping carefully over the burn that ran about its boulders in the dark, gurgling. "Are you sure you are not sorry yourself?"

"I am not a bit sorry," he said, "but—but—"

"Your 'buts' are too late, Gilian," she went on firmly. "If you rued the enterprise now, I would go myself." But she relaxed some of the coldness of her mood as he shifted his lantern to the other hand and put a bashful but firm and supporting hand below her arm to secure her footing in the rough ascent. This was a little more like what she had expected, she told herself, though she missed something of warmth in the action. How could she tell that the hand that held her was trembling with passion, that her shawl fringe as it was blown across his face by the breeze was something he could have kissed rapturously?

And now they were well up the hillside. The house of Maam, the garden, the plantings, the noisy river, were down in the valley, all surrendered to the night. Their lantern, swinging on the lad's finger, threw a path of light before them, showing the short cropped grass, the rushy patches, or the gall they trod odorously, or the heather in its rare clumps. No sound came louder than the tumbling waters; their voices, as they spoke even yet guardedly as people will in enterprises the most solitary when their consciences are unresting, seemed strange and unfamiliar to each other.

Soon they were on the summit of the hill range and below them lay the two glens, and the first breath of the morning came behind from Strone, where dawn threw a wan grey flag across the world. They plunged into the caldine trees of Strongara, sped fast across Aray at Three Bridges, and the dawn was on Balantyre, where the farm-touns high and low lay like thatched forts, grey, cold, unwelcoming in the morning, with here and there a stream of peat reek from the *greasach* of the night's fires. They became, as it might be, children again as they hastened through the country. He lost all his diffident dubiety and was anew the bold adventurer, treading lover-like upon the very stars. A passion of affection was on him; he would take her unresisting hand and lead her as though she were his, really, and before them was their moated castle. And Nan forgot herself in the fresh zest of the dewy morning that now was setting the birds to their singing in the dens that hang above the banks of the Balantyre burn.

A rosy flush came to the hills where on the upper edges spread the antlers of deer sniffing the wind, rejoicing in the magnificence of the fine highland country in its autumn time. Nan hummed and broke into a strain of the verse of Donacha Ban that chants the praise of day and deer-hunting; she charmed her comrade; he felt the passion of the possessor and stopped and turned upon her and made to kiss. She laughed temptingly, drew back, warding her lips with the screen that now she had arranged in a new and pleasing fashion on her shoulders so that she looked some Gaelic huntress of the wilds. "So, so, Gilian!" said she, "you have found that there might be more in the books than simply to take the girl away with not so much as 'Have you a mouth?' when she stepped out at the window."

"What a fool I was!" he cried. "I was thinking of it all the time, but did not dare." But awakened to the actuality of what he now had dared, he was ashamed to go further.

Nan laughed. He looked odd indeed standing facing her with the lantern burning yet in his hand though the day was almost wide-awake. He was a poet bearing his own light about the world extravagantly while the sun was shining for common mortals.

"Out with your light!" said she. And then she added: "If you dared not do it in the dark when you met me first, you cannot do it now," and he was dashed exceedingly. He puffed out the flame.

"That's aye me!" he said as they resumed their journey up the second hill of their morning escapade. "I am too often a day behind the fair. I was—I was—kissing you a score of times in fancy and all the time you were willing in the actual fact."

"Was I indeed?" she retorted shortly, with a movement to bring her shawl more closely round her. "Do not be so flattering. I like you little over-blate, Gilian, but I like you less over-bold. If you could see yourself you would know which suits you best."

He had no answer. He must face his brae with lacerated feelings, now a step removed from the girl who walked with him. But only for a little was he depressed. She saw she had vexed him, and soon she was humming again, and again they were children of illusion and content.

They reached the pass that led to the lochs, and now Gilian had to confess himself in a strange country, but he did not reveal the fact to his companion. They talked of their coming sojourn in these lovely wilds that her mother had known and loved. The sun would shine constantly for them; the lakes—the little and numerous lakes—would be fringed with dreams and delight, starshine would find them innocent among the heather, remitted to the days of old when they were happy and careless, when no trouble marred their sky. Only now and then, as they sped on their way, Gilian wished fervently he knew more of where he was going, and was certain that life in the wilds would be so pleasant and easy as they pictured it.

When they came at last upon the slope of Cruach-an-Lochain that revealed the great valley of the lakes, they stood raptured by the spectacle before them. Far off, the great hollow among the hills was hazy and mysterious, but spread before them was the moor, tangled with grass and heather, all vacant in the morning dream. A tremor of wind was in the grass about their feet, a little mist tarried about the warm side of Ben Bhreac, caught among the juniper bushes the hunters had put there for shelter. All over brooded calm, a land forgetful of its stormy elements, of the dripping nights, the hail-beat, shrewd frost and hurricane. They could not, the pair of them, flying from a world of anxieties, but stop and look at the spectacle, when they came on the face of the Cruach. For a little they did not speak.

"My God!" said Gilian at last, a lump somewhere at his throat. "It seems as if this place had been waiting on us tenantless since the start of time. Where have we been to be so long and so far away from it? *Mo chridhe, mo chridhe!*"

"Now that I see it," said she doubtfully, "it seems melancholy enough. I wish——" She hung upon her sentence, with a rueful gaze out of her eyes at the scene.

"Melancholy!" he repeated. "Of course, of course," he quickly came to her reflection, "what could it be but melancholy with all the past unrecoverable behind it? It must be brooding for its people gone. Empty, empty, but I see all the old peoples roaming in bands over it, the sun smiting them, the rain drenching, I cannot but be thinking of shealing huts that spotted the levels, of bairns crying about the doors, of nights of *ceilidh* round peat fires dead and cold now, but yet with the smoke of them hanging somewhere round the universe."

He stopped, and turned away from her, concealing his perturbation.

She shivered at the thought and partly from weariness and hunger, with a little sucking in of the breath his ear caught, and he turned, a different man.

"You are tired; will we rest before we go further?"

"Is it far?" she asked.

He reddened. He cast a fast glance round the country as if to look for some familiar landmark, but all was strange to him.

"I do not know," he confessed humbly. "I was never on the moor before."

"Mercy!" she said. "I thought there was never a lad from town but had fished here."

"But I was different," he replied. "The woods and waters about the door were enough for me. But we'll get to Elasaid's very soon, I'm sure, and find fire, food, and rest."

She bit her nether lip in annoyance at a courtier so ill-prepared for their adventure. She turned to look back to the familiar country they were leaving behind them, and for a moment wished she had never come.

"I wish we could have them now," she said at last; the words drawn from her by her weariness.

"And so we can," said he eagerly, with a delight at a reflection that sprung into his mind like a revelation. "We can go down to the water there and build a fire, and rest and eat. It will be like what I fancied, a real adventure of hunters, and I will be the valet, and you will be the—the queen."

So they went down to the lakeside. Heathery braes rose about it, reflected in its dark water; an islet overgrown with scrub lay in the middle of it, the very haunt of possible romance; Gilian straight inhabited the same with memories and exploits. Nan sat her down on the springy heather that swept its scents about her, she leaned a tired shoulder on it, and the bells of the ling blushed as they swayed against her cheek. Gilian put down his lantern, a ludicrous companion in broad sunshine, and was dashed by the sudden recollection that though he had talked of something to eat, he had really no means of providing it!

The girl observed his perturbation and shrewdly guessed the reason.

"Well?" she said maliciously, without a smile; "and where are we to get the food you so nicely spoke of?"

He stood stupefied, and so dolorous a spectacle that she could not but laugh.

"You have got none at all, but imagined our feast—as usual," she said, unfolding her bundle. "It was well I did not depend on your forethought, Gilian," and she took a flask of milk and some bread from within. He was as much vexed at the spoiling of his illusion about the contents of the bundle as at the discovery of his thoughtlessness. What he had been so fervently caressing against his side had been no more romantic than bread and cheese and some more substantial augmentation for the poor table of the old woman they were going to meet!

The side of the loch bristled with dry heather roots; he plucked them and placed them on the side of a boulder beside Nan, and set fire to them, and soon a cheerful blaze competed with the tardy morning chill. They sat beside it singularly uplifted by this domestic hearth among the wilds; he felt himself a sort of house-holder, and to share as he did the fare of the girl was a huge delight. Her single cup passed between them; at first he was shy to touch at all the object her lips had kissed; he showed the feeling in his face, and she laughed again.

He joined in the merriment, quite comprehending. Next time the cup came his way he boldly turned it about so that where last she had sipped came to his lips, and there he lingered—just a shade too long for the look of the thing. What at first she but blushed and smiled at, she frowned upon at last with a sparkle of the eye her Uncle Jamie used to call in the Gaelic the torch of temper. Gilian missed it; that touch of his lip upon her cup had recalled the warmth of her hand upon the flowers he had gathered when she had let them fall in the Duke's garden, but this was closer and more stirring. As he kneeled on the heather he felt himself a worshipper of ancient days, and her the goddess of long-lost times. An uplifting was in his eyes; it would have been great and beautiful to anyone that could have understood, but her it only vexed.

When he handed back the cup she tossed it from her. It broke—sad omen!—on their first hearthstone. "That'll do," said she shortly, "it's time we were going." And she gathered hastily the remains of their breakfast and made for a departure.

He surveyed her dubiously, wondering why she so abruptly checked the advances he could swear she had challenged.

"I am sorry I vexed you," he stammered.

She brought down her brows questioningly. There was something pleasant and tempting though queen-like and severe in her straightened figure standing over him curved and strong and full, her screen fallen to her waist, a strand of her hair blown about her cheek by a saucy wind.

"Vexed?" she queried, and then smiled indifferent. "What would I be vexed at? We are finished, are we not? Must we be burdening ourselves unnecessarily going on a road you neither know the length or nature of?"

And without a word more they proceeded towards the shealing that was to be the end of their adventure.

XXX

AMONG THE HEATHER

OLD Elasaid met them at the door. She was a woman with eyes profound and piercing under hanging brows, a woman grey even to the colour of her cheeks and the checks of the gown that hung loosely on her gaunt figure. It was with no shealing welcome, no kind memory of the old nurse even, she met them, but stood under her lintel looking as it were through them to the airt of the country whence they had come. She passed the time of day as if they had been strangers, puckering her mouth with a sort of unexpressed disapproval. They stood before her very much put out at a reception so different from what they had looked for, and Gilian knew that there must be something decisive to say but could not find it in his head.

"Well," said the old woman at last, "this'll be the good man, I'm thinking?" But still she had that in her tone, a sour dissatisfaction that showed she had her doubts.

Gilian was not unhappy at the assumption, but felt warm, and Nan reddened.

"Not at all," she answered with some difficulty. "It's just a friend who convoyed me up."

"Well I kent it," said the old woman, who spoke English to show she was displeased, and there was in her voice a tone of satisfaction with her own shrewdness. "When I saw you coming up the way there I thought there was something very unlike the thing about this person with you. The other one would have been a little closer on your elbow, and a lantern's a very queer contrivance to be stravaiging with on a summer day."

All her contempt seemed to be for Gilian, and he felt mightily uncomfortable.

"Tell me this," she went on, suddenly taking Nan by the arm and bending a most condemnatory face on her; "tell me this: did you run away from the other one?"

"Mercy on me!" cried the girl. "Is the story up here already?"

"Oh, we're not so far back," said the dame, who did not add that her son the seaman had told her the news on his last weekly visit.

"Then I'll need the less excuse for being here," said Nan, trying to find in the hard and unapproving visage any trace of the woman who in happier days used to be so kind a nurse.

"No excuse at all!" said old Elasaid. "If it's your father's wish you're flying from, you need not come here." She stepped within the house, pulled out the wattle door and between it and the fir post stuck a disapproving face.

"Go away! go away!" she cried harshly, "I have no room for a baggage of that kind." Then she shut the door in their faces; they could hear the bar run to in the staples.

For a minute or two they stood aghast and silent, and Nan was plainly close on tears. But the humour of the thing struck her quick enough—sooner than Gilian saw it—and she broke into laughter, subdued so that it might not reach the woman righteous within, and her ear maybe at the door chink. It was not perhaps of the heartiest merriment, but it inspired her companion with respect for her spirit in a moment so trying. She was pale, partly with weariness, partly with distress at this unlooked-for reception; but her lips, red and luscious, smiled for his encouragement.

"Must we go back?" he asked, irresolute, as they made some slow steps away from the door.

"Back!" said Nan, her eyes flashing. "Am I mad? Are you

speaking for yourself? If it must be back for you let me not be keeping you. After all you bargained for no more than to take me to old Elasaid's, and now that I'm here and there's none of the Elasaid I expected to meet me, I'll make the rest of my way somewhere myself." But her gaze upon that rolling and bleak moorland was far less confident than her words.

Gilian made no reply. He only looked at her reproaching for her bitterness, and humbly took up step by her side as she walked quickly away from the scene of the cold reception.

They had gone some distance when Elasaid opened her door again and came out to look after them. She saw a most touching helplessness in the manner of their uncertain walk across the heather, with no fixed mind as to which direction was the best, stopping and debating, moving now a little to the east, now a little to the west, but always further into the region of the lochs. She began to blame herself for her hastiness. She had expected that, face to face with her disapproval, the foolish young people would have gone back the road they came; but here they were going further than ever away from the father in whose interest she had loyally refused her hospitality. She cried loudly after them with a short-breathed Gaelic halloo, too much like an animal's cry to attract their attention. Nan did not hear it at all; Gilian but dreamed it, as it were, and though he took it for the call of a moor-fowl, found it in his ready fancy alarmingly like the summons of an irate father. But now he dared betray no hesitancy; he did not even turn to look behind him.

Elasaid cried again, but still in vain. She concluded they were deliberately deaf to her, and "Let them go!" she said crabbedly, flaunting an eloquent arm to the winds, comforting herself with the thought that there was no other house in all that dreary country to give them the shelter she had denied.

The sun by this time was pouring into the moor from a sky without a speck of cloud. Compared with the brown and purple of the moor and the dull colour of Ben Bhreac—the mount away to the south-east—the heavens were uncommonly blue, paling gradual to their dip. In another hour than this distressed and perplexed one, our wanderers would have felt some jocund influence in a forenoon so benign and handsome.

And now, too, the country began to show more its true character. Its little lochs—a great chain of them—dashed upon their vision in patches of blue or grey or yellow. The valley was speckled with the tarns. Gilian forgot the hazards of the enterprise and the discomforts to be faced; he had no time to think of what was to be done next for them in their flight, so full was he with the romance of those multitudinous lakelets lost in the empty and sunny wilds, some with isle, all with shelving heathery braes beside them, or golden bights where the little wave lapped. He turned to his companion with an ecstasy.

"Did you ask me if I rued it?" he said. "Give me no better than to stay here for ever—with you to share it."

She met his ardour with coolness. "I wish you had been so certain of that a little ago," she said; "you seem very much on the swither. Have you thought of what's to be done next? It is all very well to be putting our backs to the angry Elasaid behind us there, but all the time I'm wondering what's to be the outcome."

He confessed himself at a loss. She eyed him without satisfaction. This young gentleman, who seemed so enchanting in circumstances where no readiness of purpose was needed, looked very inadequate in the actual stress of things, in the broad daylight, his flat bonnet far back on his brow, his face wan, his plaid awry. And there was something in his carriage of the ridiculous lantern that made her annoyed at herself for some reason.

She stopped, and they hung hesitating, with the lapwings crying about them, and no other sound in the air.

"I'm going back," said she, as if she meant it.

His face fell. This time there was no mistaking his distress.

"No, no, you cannot, Nan," he said. "We will get out of it somehow; you cannot return, and what of me? It would be ill to explain."

"We're neither whaup nor deer," said she, shrugging her shoulders, "to live here wild the rest of our days."

Gilian looked about him rather helplessly, and he started at the sight of a gable wall, with what in a shealing might pass for a window in it, and he knew it for a relic of the old days, when the moor in its levels here would be spotted with happy summer homes, when the people of Lochow came from the shores below and gave their cattle the juicy grazing of these untamed pastures, themselves living the ancient life, with singing and spinning in the open, gathering at nights for song or dance and tale in the fine weather.

"There's something of shelter at least," he said, pointing to it. She looked dubiously at the dry-stone walls almost tumbling, the cabars of what had been a byre fallen over half the interior, and at the rank nettles—head-high almost—about the rotten door.

"Is this home-coming?" she said whimsically, forcing a smile, but she was glad to see it. By this time she was master of her companion's mind, and could guess that it would be to him a palace for them both. But they went up towards the abandoned hut, glad enough, both of them, to see an edifice, even in decay, showing man had once been there, where now the world about seemed given over to vacant sunshine or the wild winds of heaven, the rains, and doleful birds. It stood between two lochs that were separated from each other by but a hundred yards of heather and rush, its back-end to one of the lochs, the door to Ben Bhreac.

Gilian went first and trod down the nettles, making a path that she might the more comfortably reach this sanctuary so melancholy. She gathered up her gown close round her, dreading the touch of these kind plants that hide the shame of fallen lintels and the sorrow of cold hearths, and timidly went to the door, her shawl fallen from one of her shoulders and dragging at the other. She put her head within, and as she did so, the lad caught the shawl, unseen by her, and kissed the fringe, wishing he could do so to her lips.

A cold damp air was in the dwelling, that had no light but from the half-open door and the vent in the middle of the roof.

She drew back shuddering in spite of herself, though her whole desire was to seem content with any refuge now that she had brought him so far on what looked like a gowk's errand.

He ventured an assuring arm around her waist and they went slowly in together, and stood silent in the middle of the floor where the long-dead fire had been, saying nothing at all till their eyes had grown accustomed to the gloom.

What she felt beyond timidity she betrayed not, but Gilian peopled the house at an instant with all its bygone tenants, seeing the peats ruddy on the stones, the smoke curling up among the shining cabars, hearing ghosts gossiping in muffled Gaelic round the fire.

Yet soon they found even in this relic of old long-gone people the air of domesticity; it was like a shelter even though so poor a one; it was some sort of an end to her quest for a refuge, though the more she looked at its dim interior the more content she was with the outside of it. Where doubtless many children had played, on the knowe below a single shrub of fir-wood beside the loch, Nan spread out the remains of her breakfast again and they prepared to make a meal. Gilian gathered the dry heather tufts, happy in his usefulness, thinking her quite content too, while all the time she was puzzling as to what was next to be done. Never seemed a bleak piece of country so lovely to him as now. As he rose from bending over the heather and looked around, seeing the moor in its many colours stretch in swelling waves far into the distance, the lochans winking to the day and over all a kind soft sky, he was thrilling with his delight.

She summoned him in a little to eat. He looked at her scanty provender, and there was as much of truth as self-sacrifice in his words as he said: "I do not care for eating; I am just satisfied with seeing you there and the world so fine." And still exulting in that rare solitude of two he went further off by Little Fox Loch and sought for white heather, symbol of luck and love, as rare to find among the red as true love is among illusion. Searching the braes he could hear, after a little, Nan sing at the shealing hut. A faint breeze brought the strain to him faintly so that it might be the melody of fairydom heard at eves on grassy hillocks by the gifted ear, the melody of the gentle other world, had he not known that it had the words of "The Rover". Nan was singing it to keep up her heart, far from cheerful, tortured; indeed with doubt and fear, and yet the listener found in the notes content and hope. When he came back with his spray of white heather he was so uplifted with the song that he ran up to her for once with no restraint and made to fasten it at her neck. She was surprised at his new freedom but noway displeased. A little less self-consciousness as he fumbled at the riband on her neck would have satisfied her more, but even that disappeared when he felt her breath upon his hair and an unconscious touch of her hand on his arm as he fastened the flower. She let her eyes drop before his bold rapture, he could have kissed her there and then and welcome. But he only went halfway. When the heather was fastened he took her hand and lifted it to his lips, remembering some inadequate tale in the books of Marget Maclean.

"John Hielan'man! John Hielan'man!" she said within herself, and suddenly she tore the white spray from her bosom and threw it passionately at her feet, while tears of vexation ran to her eyes.

"Forgive me, forgive me, I have vexed you again," said Gilian, contrite. "I should not be so bold."

She could not but smile through her tears.

"If you will take my heather again and say nothing of it, I will never take the liberty again," he went on, eager to make up for his error.

"Then I will not take it," she answered.

"It was stupid of me," said he.

"It is," she corrected meaningly.

"I never had any acquaintance with—with—girls," he added, trying to find some excuse for himself.

"That is plain enough," she agreed cordially, and she followed it with a sigh.

For a minute they stood thus irresolute and then the lad bent and lifted the ill-used heather. He held it in his hand for a moment tenderly as if it was a thing that lived, and sighed over it, and then, fearing that, too, might seem absurd to her and vexatious, he made an effort and twirled it between a finger and thumb by its stem like any casual wildflower culled without reflection.

"What are you going to do with it now?" she asked him, affecting indifference, but eyeing it with interest; and he made no answer, for how could he tell her he meant to keep it always for remembrance? "Give it to me," she said suddenly, and took it from his fingers. She ran into the house and placed it in the only fragment of earthenware left by the departed tenants. "It will do very well there," she said.

"But I meant it for you," said Gilian ruefully. "It is a sign of good luck."

"It is a sign of more than that, I've heard many a time," she replied, and he became very red indeed for he knew that as well as she, though he had not said it. "I'll take it for the luck," she went on.

"And for mine too," said Gilian.

"That's not so blate, John Hielan'man!" said she: again to herself. "And for yours too," she conceded, smiling. "When you find that I have taken it away from there you will know it is for your luck too."

"And it will be at your breast then?" he cried eagerly.

She laughed and blushed and laughed again, most sweetly and most merrily. "It will be at—at—at my heart," she said.

"Ah," said he, in an instinct of fear that quelled his rapture; "ah, if they take you from me!"

"When I take your heather," said she, "it will be for ever at my heart."

Oh! then that savage moorland was Paradise for the dreamer, and he was a coquette's slave, fettered by a compliment. The afternoon passed, for him at least, in a delirium of joy; she, though she never revealed it, was never at a moment's rest from her plans of escape from her folly. Late in the afternoon she came to a lame conclusion.

"You will go down to the town tonight," she said, "and—"

"And you!" he cried, alarmed at the notion of severance.

"I'll stay here, of course. You'll tell Miss Mary that we—that

256

I am here, and she will tell you what we—what I, must do."

"But—but—" he stammered, dubious of the plan.

"Of course I can go home again to Maam now," she broke in coldly, and she was vexed for the alarm and grief he showed at the alternative.

"I will go; I will go at once," he cried, but first he went far down on Blaraghour for wood for a fire to cheer her loneliness, and the dusk was down on them before he left her.

She gave him her hand at the door, a hand for once with helpless dependence in the clinging and the confidence of it, and he held it long without dissent from her. Never before had she seemed so beautiful or so affable, so necessary to his life. Her trials had paled the colour of her face and her eyes had a hint of tears. Over his shoulder she would now and then cast a glance of apprehension at the falling night and check a shudder of her frame.

"Good-night!" he said.

"Good-night!" she answered, and yet she did not loose her prisoned hand.

He sighed, and brought, in spite of her, an echo from her heart.

Then he drew her suddenly to his arms and scorched her face with lips of fire.

Nan released herself and fled within. The door closed; she dared not make her trial the more intense by seeing the night swallow up her only living link with the human world beyond the vague selvedge of the moor.

And Gilian, till the dawn came over Cruach-an-Lochain, walked by the side of Little Fox Loch, within view of the hut that held his heart.

XXXI

DEFIANCE

THAT there was some unusual agitation in the town Gilian
could gather as soon as he had set foot within the Arches
in the early morning. It was in the air, it was mustering many
women at the well. There they stood in loud and lingering
groups, their stoups running over extravagantly while they kept
the tap running, unconscious what they were about. Or they
had a furtive aspect as they whispered in the closes, their aprons
wrapping their folded arms. At the door of the New Inns, Mr
Spencer was laying forth a theory of abduction. He had had
English experience, he knew life; for the first time since he had
come to this place of poor happenings he had found something
he could speak upon with authority and an audience to listen
with respect. What his theory was, Gilian might have heard fully
as he passed; but he was thinking of other things, and all that
came to him were two or three words, and one of the errant
sentences was seemingly about himself. That attracted all his
attention. He gave a glance at the people at the door—the
innkeeper, MacGibbon, with an unusual Kilmarnock bonnet on
that seemed to have been donned in a hurry; Rixa, in a great
perturbation, having just come out of a shandry-dan with
which he had been driving up Glen Shira; Major Paul, and
Wilson the writer. The innkeeper, who was the first to see the

lad, stopped his speech with confusion and reddened. They gave him a stare and a curt acknowledgment of his passage of the time of day as the saying goes, looked after him as he passed round Old Islay's corner, and found no words till he was out of sight.

"That puts an end to that notion, at any rate," said the Sheriff, almost pleased to find the Londoner in the wrong with his surmises. And the others smiled at Mr. Spencer as people do who told you so. Two minutes ago they were half inclined to give some credit to the plausibility of his reasoning.

The innkeeper was visibly disturbed. "Dear me! I have been doing the lad an injustice after all; I could have sworn he was the man in it if it was anybody."

"Pooh!" said Rixa, "the Paymaster's boy! I would as soon expect it of Gillesbeg Aotram."

They went into the hostelry, and Gilian, halfway round the factor's corner, was well-nigh ridden down by Turner on a roan horse spattered on the breast and bridle with the foam of a hard morn's labour. He had scoured the countryside on every outward road, and come early at the dawn to the ferry-house and rapped wildly on the shutter. But nowhere were tidings of his daughter. Gilian felt a traitor to this man as he swept past, seeing nothing, with a face cruel and vengeful, the flanks of his horse streaked with crimson. The people shrunk back in their closes and their shop-doors as he passed all covered upon with the fighting passion that had been slumbering up the glen since ever he came home from the Peninsula.

It was the breakfast hour in the Paymaster's. Miss Mary was going in with the Book and had but time to whisper welcome to her boy on the step of the door, for the brothers waited and the clock was on the stroke. Gilian had to follow her without a word of explanation. He was hungry; he welcomed the little respite the taking of food would give him from the telling of a confidence he felt ashamed to share with Miss Mary.

The Paymaster mumbled a blessing upon the vivours, then fed noisily, looking, when he looked at Gilian at all, but at the upper buttons of his coat as if through him, and letting not so little as the edge of his gaze fall upon his face. That was a studious contempt, and Gilian knew it, and there were many considerations that made him feel no injury at it. But the Cornal's utter indifference—that sent his eye roaming unrecognising into Gilian's and away again without a spark of recognition—was painful. It would have been an insufferable meal, even in his hunger, but for Miss Mary's presence. The little lady would be smiling to him across the table without any provocation whenever her brothers' eyes were averted, and the faint perfume of a silk shawl she had about her shoulders endowed the air with an odour of domesticity, womanhood, maternity.

For a long time nobody spoke, and the pigeons came boldly to the sill of the open window and cooed.

At last said the Paymaster, as if he were resuming a conversation: "I met him out there on horseback; the hunt is still up, I'm thinking."

"Ay?" said the Cornal, as if he gripped the subject and waited the continuance of the narrative.

"He'll have ranged the country, I'm thinking," went on his brother. "I could not but be sorry for the man."

Miss Mary cast upon him a look he seldom got from her, of warmth more than kinship, but she had nothing to say; her voice was long dumb in that parlour where she loved and feared, a woman subjugate to a sex far less worthy than her own and less courageous.

"Humph!" said the Cornal. He felt with nervous inquiry at his ragged chin, inspired for a second by old dreads of untidy morning parades.

"I had one consolation for my bachelordom in him," went on the younger brother, and then he paused confused.

"And what might that be?" asked the Cornal.

"It's that I'm never like to be in the same scrape with a child of mine," he answered, pretending a jocosity that sat ill on him. Then he looked at Miss Mary a little shamefaced for a speech so uncommonly confidential.

The Cornal opened his mouth as if he would laugh, but no sound came.

"I'm minding," said he, speaking slowly and in a muffled accent he was beginning to have always; "I'm minding when that same, cast in your face by the gentleman himself, greatly put you about. Jock, Jock, I mind you were angry with Turner on that score! And no child to have the same sorrows over! Well—well—" He broke short and for the first time let his eyes rest with any meaning on Gilian sitting at the indulgence of a good morning's appetite.

Miss Mary put about the breakfast dishes with a great hurry to be finished and out of this explosive atmosphere.

"There was an odd rumour—" said the Paymaster. He paused a moment, looking at the inattentive youth opposite him. He saw no reason to stay his confidences, and the Cornal was waiting expectingly on him. "An odd rumour up the way; I heard it first from that gabbling man Spencer at the Inns. It was that a young gentleman of our acquaintance might have had a hand in the affair. I could not say at the fi-rst whether the notion vexed or pleased me, but I assured him of the stupidity of it." He looked his brother in the eyes, and fixing his attention, cunningly dropped a lid to indicate that the young gentleman was beside them.

The Cornal laughed, this time with a sound.

"Lord," he cried. "As if it was possible! You might go far in that quarter for anything of dare-deviltry so likeable. What's more, is the girl daft? Her mother had caprice enough, but to give her her due she took up with men of spirit. There was my brother Dugald— But this one, what did Dugald call him— ay! on his very death-bed? The dreamer, the dreamer! It will hold true! Him, indeed!" And he had no more words for his contempt.

All the time, however, Gilian was luckily more or less separate from his company by many miles of fancy, behind the hills among the lochs watching the uprising of Nan, sharing her loneliness, seeing her feet brush the dew from the scented gall. But the Cornal's allusion brought him to the parlour of his banishment, away from that dear presence. He listened now but said nothing. He feared his very accent would betray his secret.

"I'll tell you what it is," said the Cornal again, "whoever is with her will rue it; mind, I'm telling you. It's like mother like child."

"I'm glad," said the Paymaster, "I had nothing to do with the sex of them." He puffed up as he spoke it; there was an irresistible comedy in the complacence of a man no woman was ever like to run after at his best. His sister looked at him; his brother chuckled noiselessly.

"You—you—you—" said the elder brother grimly, but again he did not finish the sentence.

The meal went on for a time without any speech, finished, and Miss Mary cried at the stair-head for her maid, who came up and sat demurely at the chair nearest the door while the Cornal, as hurriedly as he might, ran over the morning's sacred exercise from the Bible Miss Mary laid before him. The Paymaster took his seat beside the window, looking out the while and heedless of the Scriptures, watched the fishermen crowding for their mornings into the house of Widow Gordon the vintner. Miss Mary stole glances at her youth, the maid Peggy fidgeted because she had left the pantry door open and the cat was in the neighbourhood. As the old man's voice monotonously occupied the room, working its way mumblingly through the end of Exodus, conveying no meaning to the audience, Gilian heard the moor-fowl cry beside Little Fox. The dazzle of the sunshine, the sparkle of the water, the girl inhabiting that solitary spot, seemed very real before him, and this dolorous routine of the elderly in a parlour no more than a dream from which he would waken to find himself with the girl he loved. Upon his knees beside his chair while the Cornal gruffly repeated the morning prayer he learned from his father, he remained the remote wanderer of fancy, and Miss Mary knew by the instinct of affection as she looked at the side of his face through eyelids discreetly closed but not utterly fastened.

The worship was no sooner over than Gilian was for off after

Miss Mary to her own room, but the Paymaster stayed him with some cold business query about the farm, and handed him a letter from a low-country wool merchant relative to some old transaction still unsettled. Gilian read it, and the brothers standing by the window resumed their talk about the missing girl: it was the subject inspired by every glance into the street where each passer-by, each loiterer at a close-mouth, was obviously canvassing the latest news.

"There's her uncle away by," said the Paymaster, straining his head to follow a figure passing on the other side of the street. "If they had kept a stricter eye on her from the first when they had her they might have saved themselves all this."

"Stricter eye!" said the Cornal. "You ken as much about women as I ken about cattle. The veins of her body were full of caprice, that's what ailed her, and for that is there any remede? I'm asking you. As if I did not ken the mother of her! Man, man, man! She was the emblem and type of all her sex, I'm thinking, wanting all sobriety, hating the thought of age in herself and unfriendly to the same in others. A kind of a splash on a fine day upon the deep sea, laughing over the surface of great depths. I knew her well, Dugald knew her—"

"You had every chance," said the Paymaster, who nowadays found more courage to retort when his brother's shortness and contempt annoyed him.

"More chance, of course I had," said the Cornal. "I'm thinking you had mighty little from yon lady."

"Anyway, here's her daughter to seek," said the Paymaster, feeling himself getting the worst of the encounter; "my own notion is that she's on the road to Edinburgh. They say she had aye a crave for the place; perhaps there was a pair of breeches there behind her. Anyway, she's making an ass of somebody!"

Gilian threw down the letter and stood to his feet with his face white. "You're a liar!" said he.

No shell in any of their foreign battles more astounded the veterans he was facing with wide nostril and a face like chalk.

"God bless me, here's a marvel!" cried the Cornal when he found voice.

"You—you—you damned sheep!" blurted the Paymaster. "Do you dare speak to me like that? For tuppence I would give you my rattan across the legs." His face was purple with anger; the stock that ran in many folds about his neck seemed like a garotte. He lifted up his hand as if to strike, but his brother caught his arm.

"Let the lad alone," said he. "If he had a little more of that in his make I would like him better."

Together they stood, the old men, facing Gilian with his hands clenched, for the first time in his life the mutineer, feeling a curious heady satisfaction in the passion that braced him like a sword and astounded the men before him.

"It's a lie!" he cried again, somewhat modifying his accusation. "I know where she is, and she's not in Edinburgh nor on her way to it."

"Very well," said the Paymaster, "ye better go and tell Old Islay where she is; he's put about at the loss of a daughter-in-law he paid through the nose for, they're saying."

The blow, the last he had expected, the last he had reason to look for, struck full and hard. He was blind then to the old men sneering at him there; his head seemed charged with coiling vapours; his heart, that had been dancing a second ago on the wave of passion, swamped and sank. He had no more to say; he passed them and left the room and went along the lobby to the stair-head, where he stood till the vapours had somewhat blown away.

XXXII

AN OLD MAID'S SECRET

MISS MARY bustled about her kitchen with a liveliness that might have deceived anyone but Gilian, who knew her to be in a tremendous perturbation. She clattered among pans, wrestled with her maid over dishes and dusters, and kept her tongue incessantly going on household details. With a laughable transparency she turned in a little to the lad and said something about the weather. He sat down in a chair and gloomed into the fire, Miss Mary watching his every sigh, but yet seemingly intent upon her duties.

"Donacha Breck's widow was over before we were up today, for something for her hoast," she said. "She had tried hyssop and pennyroyal masked in two waters, but I gave her sal prunelle and told her to suck it till the cough stopped. There's a great deal of trouble going about just now: sometimes I think—" She stopped incontinent and proceeded to sweep the floor, for she saw that Gilian was paying no attention to her. At length he looked at her and then with meaning to Peggy bent over her jaw-box.

"Peggy," said Miss Mary, "go over and tell the mantua-maker that she did not put the leavings in the pocket of my jacket, and there must have been a good deal."

Peggy dried her arms, tucked up the corner of her apron, and

265

departed, fully aware of the stratagem, but no way betraying the fact. When she was gone, Miss Mary faced him, disturbed and questioning.

"We had a quarrel in there," said he shortly. "I am not going to put up with what they said about any friend of mine."

She had no need to ask who he spoke of. "Is it very much to you?" said she, turning away and busy with her brush that she might be no spectator of his confusion. A great fear sprang up in her; the boy who had grown up a man for her in the space of a Sunday afternoon was capable of new developments even more rapid and extraordinary.

"It should be very much to anybody," said he, "to anybody with the spark of a gentleman, when the old and the soured and the jealous—"

"I'm thinking you are forgetting, Gilian," said she, facing him now with a flush upon her face.

"What? what?" he asked, perplexed. "You think I should be grateful. I cannot help it; you were the kind one and—"

"I was not thinking of that at all," she rejoined. "I was just thinking you had forgotten that I was their sister, and that I must be caring much for them. If my brothers have said anything to vex you, and that has been a too common thing—my sorrow!—in this house, you should be minding their years, my dear. It is the only excuse I can offer, and I am willing to make up for their shortcomings by every kindness." And she smiled upon the lad with the most wonderful light of affection in her eyes.

"Oh," he cried, "am I not sure of that, auntie? You are too good to me. What am I to be complaining—the beggarly orphan?"

"Not that, my dear," she cried courageously, "not that! In this house, when my brothers' looks were at their blackest for you, there has always been goodwill and motherliness. But you must not be miscalling them that share our roof, the brothers of Dugald and of Jamie." Her voice broke in a gasp of melancholy; she stretched an arm and dusted from a corner of the kitchen a cobweb that had no existence, her eyesight dim with unbrimming tears. At any other time than now Gilian would have been smitten by her grief, for was he not ever ready to make the sorrows of others his own? But he was frowning in a black-browed abstraction on the clay scroll of the kitchen floor, heartsick of his dilemma and the bitterness of the speeches he had just heard.

Miss Mary could not be long without observing, even in her own troubles, that he was unusually vexed. She was wise enough to know that a fresh start was the best thing to put them at an understanding.

"What did you come to tell me today?" she asked, composing herself upon a chair beside him and taking up some knitting, for hers were the fingers that were never idle.

"Come down to tell you? Come down to tell you?" he repeated, in surprise at her penetration, and in some confusion that he should so sharply be brought to his own business.

"Just so," she said. "Do you think Miss Mary has no eyes, my dear, or that they are too old for common use? There was something troubling you as you came in at the door; I saw it in your face—ay, I heard it in your step on the stair."

He fidgeted and evaded her eyes. "I heard outside that—that Turner's daughter had not been got, and it vexed me a little."

"Turner's daughter!" she said. "It used to be Miss Nan; it was Miss Nan no further gone than Thursday, and for what need we be so formal today? You are not heeding John's havers about your name being mixed up with the affair in a poor Sassanach innkeeper's story? Eh, Gilian?" And she eyed him shrewdly, more shrewdly than he was aware of.

Still he put her off. He could not take her into his confidence so soon after that cold plunge into truth in the parlour. He wanted to get out of doors and think it all over calmly. He pretended anger.

"What am I to be talked to like this for? All in this house are on me. Is it wonderful that I should have my share in the interest the whole of the rest of the parish has in this young lady lost?"

He rose to leave the room. Miss Mary stopped him with the

least touch upon the arm, a lingering, gentle touch of the finger-tips, and yet caressing.

"Gilian," she said softly, "do you think you can be deceiving me? *M'eudail, m'eudail!* I know there is a great trouble in your mind, and is it not for me to share?"

"There is something, but I cannot tell you now what it is, though I came here to tell you," he answered, making no step to go.

"Gilian," said she, standing before him, and the light from the window touching her ear so that, beside the darkness of her hair (for she had off her cap), it looked like a pink flower, "Gilian, can you not be telling me? Do you think I cannot guess what ails you, nor fancy something for its cure?"

He saw from the shyness of her face that she had an inkling of at least the object of his interest.

"But I cannot be mentioning it here," he said, feebly enough. "It's a matter a man must cherish to himself alone, and not be airing before others. I felt, in there, to have it in my mind before two men who had worked and fought and adventured all their lives, and come to this at last, was a childish weakness."

She caught hold of his coat lapel, and fingered it, and looked as she spoke, not at the face above her, but at some vision over his shoulder. "Before them, my dear," she said. "That well might be, though even they have not always been the hard and selfish veterans. What about me, my dear? Can I not be understanding, think you, Gilian?"

"It is such a foolish thing," said he weakly, "a thing of interest only to the very young."

"And am I so old, my dear," she said, "not to have been young once? Do you think this little wee wife with her hair getting grey—not so grey either, though—was always in old maid dolours in her garret thinking of hoasts and headaches and cures for them, and her brothers' slippers and her own rheumatics on rainy days? Oh, my dear, my dear! you used to understand me as if it had been through glass—ay, from the first day you saw me, and my brother's sword must be sending me to my weeping;

can you not understand me now? I am old, and the lowe of youth is down in its ember, but once I was as young—as young—as—as—as the girl you are thinking of."

He drew back, overwhelmed with confusion, but she found the grip of his coat again and followed up her triumph.

"Did you think I could not guess so little as that, my dear? Oh, Gilian, sometimes I'll be sitting in there all my lone greeting my eyes out over darning hose, and minding of what I have been and what I have seen, and the days that will never come any more. The two upstairs will be minding only to envy and to blame—me, I must be weeping as much for my sin as for my sorrow. Do I look so terrible old, Gilian, that you cannot think of me as not so bad-looking either, with a bonny eye, they said, and a jimp waist, and a foot like the honey-bee? It was only yesterday; ah, it was a hundred years ago! I was the sisterly slave. No dancing for me. No romping for Mary at hairst or Hogmanay. My father glooming and binding me motherless to my household tasks, so that Love went by without seeing me. My companions, and she the dearest of them all, enjoying life to the full, and me looking out at this melancholy window from year to year, and seeing the traffic of youth and all the rest of it go by."

She released his lapel and relapsed, all tears, upon her chair.

"Auntie, auntie!" he cried, "do not let my poor affairs be vexing you." He put, for the first time in his life, an arm about her waist, bending over her, with all forgotten for the moment save that she had longed for love and seemingly found it not. At the touch of his arm she trembled like a maiden in her teens and forced a smile upon her face. "Let me go," she said, and yet she gloried in that contact as she sat in the chair and he bent over her.

"And was there no one came the way?" he asked.

"Was I not worth it, do you think?" she replied, yet smiling in her tears. "Oh, Gilian, not this old woman, mind you, but the woman I was. And yet—and yet, it is true, no one came; or if they came, they never came that I wanted."

"And he?" said Gilian.

She paused and sighed, her thin little hands, so white for all their toil in that hard barracks, playing upon her lap. "He never had the chance. My father's parlour had no welcome, a soldier's household left no vacant hours for an only daughter's gallivanting. I had to be content to look at him—the one I mean—from the window, see him in the church or passing up and down the street. They had up Dr Brash at me—I mind his horn specs, and him looking at my tongue and ordering a phlebotomy. What I wanted was the open air, a chance of youth, and a dance on the green. Instead of that it was always 'Ho, Mary!' and 'Here, Mary,' and 'What are you wasting your time for, Mary?'" She was all in a tremble, moist no more with tears, but red and troubled at her eyes. "And then—then—then he married her. If he had taken anyone else it would not have seemed so hard. I think I hated her for it. It was long before I discovered they were chief, for my brothers that were out and in kept it from me for their own reasons, and they never kent my feeling. But when she was cried and married and kirked, each time it was a dagger at my heart. Amn't I the stupid old *cailleach*, my dear, to be talking of such a thing? But oh! to see them on the street together; to see him coming home on his furloughs—I am sure I could not be but unfond of her then! I mind once I wished her dead, that maybe he might—he might see something in me still. That was when Nan was born and—"

"What," cried Gilian, "and was he Nan's father? I—I did not know."

She turned upon him an old face spoiled by the memories of the moment. "Who else would it be, my dear?" said she, as if that settled it. "And you are the first in the world I mentioned it to. He has never seen me close in the face to guess it for himself, before or since. It might have happened if I wished, after, but that was the punishment I gave myself for my unholy thought about my friend his wife."

"Ah, little auntie, little auntie," said he in Gaelic. "Little auntie, little auntie!" No more than that, and yet his person was stormy with grief for her old sorrow. He put his arm about her neck now—surely never Highland lad did that before in their position, and tenderly, as if he had practised it for years, he pressed her to his breast and side.

"And is it all by now but a recollection?" said he softly.

"All by long syne," said she, dashing the tears from her face and clearing herself from that unusual embrace. "Sometimes I'll be thinking it was better as it was, for I see many wives and husbands, and the dead fire they sit at is less cheery than one made but never lighted. You mustn't be laughing at an old lady, Gilian."

"I would never be doing that, God knows," he answered solemnly.

"And I am sure you would not, my dear," she said, looking trustfully at him; "though sometimes I must be laughing at myself for such a folly. Lads and lasses have spoken to me about their courtships and their trials, and they never knew that I had anything but an old maid's notion of the thing. And that's the way with yourself, is it not, Gilian? Will you tell me now?"

Still he hung hesitating.

"Do you—are you fond of the girl?" said she and now it was he who was in the chair and she was bending over him.

"Do I not?" he cried, sudden and passionate lest his confidence should fail. "Ay, with all my heart."

"Poor Gilian!" said she.

"Yes, poor Gilian!" he repeated bitterly, thinking on all that lay between him and the girl of his devotion. Now, if ever, was the time to tell the real object of his visit, how that those old surmisers upstairs were wider of the mark than the innkeeper, and that the person for whom the hunt was up through half the shire was sequestered in the lonely shealing hut on the moor of Kames.

"I am sorry," she went on, and there was no mistake about it, for her grief was in her face. "I am sorry, but you must forget, my dear. It is easy—sometimes—to forget, Gilian; you must be just throng with work and duty, and by and by you'll maybe wonder at yourself having been in the notion of Nan Gordon's daughter, made like her mother (and God bless her!) for the vexation of youth, but never for sober satisfaction. I am wae for you, Gilian, and I cannot help you, though I would tramp from here to Carlisle in my bauchles if it would bring her to you."

"You maybe would not need to go so far," he answered abruptly. "There is a hut behind the hill there, and neither press nor fire nor candle nor companion in it, and Nan—Miss Nan, is waiting there for me to go back to her, and here I'm wasting precious hours. Do you not see that I'm burning like a fire?"

"And you have the girl in the moor?" she cried incredulously.

"That I have!" he answered, struck by the absolute possession her sentence suggested. "I have her there. I took her there. I took her from her father's home. She came willingly, and there she is, for me!"

He held out his arms with a gesture indescribable, elate, nervous with his passion. "Auntie, think of it: you mind her eyes and her hair, yon turn of the neck, and her song? They're mine, I'm telling you."

"I mind them in her mother," said the little lady, stunned by this intelligence. "I mind them in her mother, and they were not at all, in her, for those who thought they were for them. This— this is a terrible thing, Gilian," she said piteously.

He rose, and "What could I do?" he asked. "I loved her, and was I to look at her father selling her to another one who never had her heart?"

"Are you sure you have it yourself, Gilian?" she asked, and her face was exceedingly troubled.

"It's a thing I never asked," he confessed carelessly. "Would she be where she is without it being so?"

"Where her mother's daughter might be in any caprice of spirit I would not like to guess," said Miss Mary, dubious. "And I think, if I was the man, it would be the first thing I would be making sure about."

"What would she fly with me for if it was not for love?" he asked.

"Ask a woman that," she went on. "Only a woman, and only some kinds of women, could tell you that. For a hundred reasons good enough for herself, though not for responsibility."

He bit his lips in perplexity, feeling all at sea, the only thing clear to his mind being that Nan was alone on the moor, her morning fire sending a smoke to the sky, expectation bringing her now and then to the door to see if her ambassador was in view.

For the sake of that sweet vision he was bound to put another question to Miss Mary—to ask her if the reference by her brother to Old Islay bore the import he had given it. He braced himself to it—a most unpleasant task.

"It's true," she said. "Do you mean to tell me you did not know he was the man?"

"I did not. And the money?"

"Oh, the money!" said Miss Mary oddly, as if now a great deal was explained to her. "Did Nan hear anything of that?"

"She knows everything—except the man's name. She was too angry to hear that."

"Except the man's name," repeated Miss Mary. "She did not know it was Young Islay." She turned as she spoke, and busied herself with a duster where there was no need for it. And when she showed him her face again, there were tears there, not for her own old trials, but for his.

"You must go back there," she said firmly, though her lips were trembling, "and you will tell Miss Nan that whatever Old Islay would do, his son would never put that affront on her. At the worst, the money was no more than a tocher with the lad; it was their start in Drimlee and Maam that are now together for the sake of an old vanity of the factors. . . . You must tell all that," she went on, paying no heed to the perplexity in his face. "It would be unfair to do less, my dear; it will be wiser to do all. Then you will do the other thing—if need be—what you should have done first and foremost; you'll find out if the girl is in earnest about yourself or only indulging a cantrip like her mother's daughter. Ask her—ask her—oh! what need I be telling you? If you have not the words in your heart I need not be putting them in your mouth. Run away with you now!" and she pushed him to the door like a child that had been caressed and counselled.

He was for going eagerly without a word more, but she cried him back. For a moment she clung to his arm as if she was reluctant to part with him.

"Oh!" she cried, laughing, and yet with tears in her voice, "a bonny-like man to be asking her without having anything to offer."

He would have interrupted her, but she would not let him.

"Go your ways," she told him, "and bring her back with you if you can. Miss Mary has something in a stocking foot, and no long need for it."

XXXIII

THE PROMISE

WHEN Gilian came down the stair and to the mouth of the
pend-close, he stood with some of the shyness of his childhood that used to keep him swithering there with a new suit on,
uneasy for the knowledge that the colour and cut of it would be
the talk of the town as soon as it was seen, and that someone
would come and ask offhand if Miss Mary was still making-
down from the Paymaster's waistcoats. It was for that he used at
last to show a new suit on the town by gentle degrees, the first
Sunday the waistcoat, the next Sunday the waistcoat and trousers,
and finally the complete splendour. Now he felt kenspeckle, not
in any suit of material clothes but in a droll sense of nakedness.
He had told his love and adventure in a place where walls heard
and windows peered, and a rumour out of the ordinary went on
the wind into every close and soared straight to the highest
tenement—even to the garret rooms. He felt that the women at
the wells, very busy, as they pretended, over their boynes and
stoups, would whisper about him as he passed, without looking
up from their occupation.

Down the street towards the church there was scarcely anyone to be seen except the children out for the midday airing
from Brooks' school, and old Brooks himself going over to Kate
Bell's for his midday waters with a daundering step as if he had

no special object, and might as readily be found making for the quay or the coffee-house. The children were noisy in the play-ground, the boys playing at port-the-helm, a foolish pastime borrowed in its parlance and its rule from the seafarers who frequented the harbour, and the girls more sedately played peeveral-al and I dree I dree I dropped it, their voices in a sweet unison chanting, yet with a sorrow in the cadence.

Up the street some men sat on the Cross steps waiting the coming of the ferry-boat from Kilcatrine, for it was the day of the weekly paper. Old Islay went from corner to corner, looking eager out to sea, his hands deep in the pockets of his long coat. Major McNicol put his head cautiously out at his door that his servant lass held open and scanned the deadly world where Frenchmen lay in ambush. He caught a glimpse of Gilian spying from the pend-close and darted in trembling, but soon came out again, with the maid patting him kindly and assuringly on the back. From close to close he made a tactical advance—swift dashes between on his poor bent old limbs, and he drew up by Gilian's side.

"All's well!" said he with a breath of relief. "Man! but they're throng today; the place is fair hotching with them."

Gilian expressed some commonplace and left the shelter of the pend-close and went up the street round the factor's corner. He looked behind him there. The ferry-boat from Kilcatrine was in; Young Islay had stepped the first off the skiff and was speak-ing—not to his father, but to General Turner, whose horse, spat-tered with foam and white with autumn dust, a boy held at the quay head. The post-runner took a newspaper from his pocket and handed it to the men waiting at the Cross; they hastened into the vintners, and one of them read aloud to the company with no need to replenish his glass. Against the breast wall the tide at the full lapped with a pleasant sound. Mr Spencer came out to the front of the Inns, smoking a segar, very perjink with a brocade waistcoat and a collar so high it rasped his ears.

Everything visible impressed itself that day acutely on Gilian as he went out of the town; not only as if he were naked but as if he were raw and feeling flesh, and he was glad when the turn of the road at the Arches hid this place from his view.

A voice cried behind him, and turning around he found Peggy running after him with a basket, Miss Mary's afterthought for the fugitive girl on the moor.

Very quickly he sped up the hills; Nan ran out to meet him as he came up the brae from Little Fox. She had been crying in the morning till tears would come no longer, but now she was composed; at least her eyes were calm and her cheeks lost the pallor they had from a night almost sleepless in that lonely dwelling. As he saw her running out to meet him he filled with elation and with apprehension. She was so beautiful, so airy, so seemingly his alone as she ran out thus from their refuge, that he grudged the hours he had been gone from her.

"Oh," she cried, "the spring was no more welcome to the wood. I hope you have brought good news, Gilian." And up she went to him and linked an arm through his with some of the composure of the companion and some of the ardour of the sweetheart.

"I think it's all well," said he, putting his arm round her as they went up towards the hut together.

"Is it only thinking?" she asked with disappointment in her voice, all the ardour gone from her face, and her arm withdrawn. "I was so certain it would be sureness for once. Will Miss Mary not help me? I am sorry I asked her. It was not right, perhaps, that my father's daughter should be expecting anything from the sister of the Campbells of Keil." She was all tremulous with vexed pride and disappointment.

"Miss Mary is your very kind friend, Nan," he protested, "and she will help you as readily as she will help me."

"I am to go down then?" she cried, uplifted again.

"Well, yes—that is, it is between ourselves."

"That's what I would be thinking myself, John Hielan'man," she thought. And still with all her contempt for his shrinking uncertainty there was a real fondness that might in an hour have come to full blossom in that solitude where they so depended on each other.

"I was to ask you something," he said.

"My wise Miss Mary!" said Nan to herself. "Women have all the wits." But she said nothing aloud, waiting for his explanation.

"I thought there was no need of it myself, but she said she knew better."

"Very likely she was right too," said Nan. "And now you must tell me all about what is going on down-by. Are they looking for me? What is my father saying? Do they blame me?"

Gilian told her all he knew or thought desirable, as they went up to the hut and prepared for the first meal Nan had that day. It was good that the weather favoured them. No sign of its habitual rain and wind hung over the moorland. Soft clouds, white like the wool of lambs new-washed in running waters, hung motionless where the sky met the moor, but over them still was the deep blue, greying to the dip.

They lit a fire in the hut with scraps of candle-fir Gilian had picked up on the way from the town, and a cheerful flame illumined the mean interior, but in a while they preferred to go outside and sit by the edge of Little Fox. In a hollow there the wilds seemed more compact about them; the sense of solitude disappeared; it was just as if one of their berrying rambles in the woods behind Maam had been prolonged a little further than usual. Lazily they reclined upon the heather, soft and billowy to their arms; the kind air fanned them, a melody breathed from the rippling shore.

All the reading in Marget Maclean's books, the shy mornings, the pondering eves, the ruminations lonely by wood and shore, had prepared Gilian for such an hour, and now he felt its magic. And as they sat thus on the bank of the little lake, Nan sung, forgetting herself in her song as she ever must be doing. The waves stilled to listen; the birds on the heather came closer; the clouds, like wool on the edge of Ben Bhreac, tarried and trembled. And Gilian, as he heard, forgetting all that ancient town below of unable elders and stagnant airs, illusion gone and glory past, its gossip at well and close, its rancours of clan and family, knew the message now of the bird that cried across the swampy meadowland at Kilmalieu. Love, love, love—and death. It was the message of bird and flower, of wave and wind, the deep and constant note in Nan's song, whatever the words might be. No more for a moment the rustic, the abashed shepherd, but with the secret of the world filling his heart, he crept closer to Nan's side as she leaned upon the heather, and put an arm around her waist.

"Nan, Nan," he cried, "could we not be here, you and I alone together for ever?"

The gaudy bubble of her expectation burst; she released herself from his grasp with "John Hielan'man! John Hielan'man!" in her mind.

"And was that Miss Mary's question? I thought she was a more sensible friend to both of us."

"Never a better," said he. "She offered her all and—"

"What!" cried Nan, anger flaring in her face, "are you in the market too?"

He stammered an excuse.

"It was not a gift," said he, "but to you and me; and that, indeed, was as much as Old Islay meant, to give him his due."

"Old Islay, Old Islay!" she repeated, turning her face from him to hide its sudden remorse. "Islay, Islay," she repeated to herself. He noticed the hand she leaned upon, so soft, so white, so beautiful, trembled in its nest among the heather. He was so taken up with it there among the heather, so much more beautiful than the fairest flower, that he did not notice how far he had given up his secret.

He caught the hand and fondled it, and still she repeated to herself like a coronach, "Islay, Islay." For once more the rude arm was round her waist in Maam, and the bold soldier was kissing her on the lips.

Gilian stood up and "Oh!" he cried, as he looked from her to the landscape, and back from the landscape to her again, "Oh!" he cried, "I wondered, when you were gone in Edinburgh, what was wanting here. When Miss Mary told me you were come home, I felt it was the first time the sun had shone, and the birds had found a song."

"Young Islay!" she still was thinking, hearing the dreamer but to compare him with the practitioner she knew.

And then the dreamer, remembering that his question was still unput, uttered it shyly and awkwardly. "Do you love me?" said he.

It was for this she had fled from Young Islay, who knew his mind and had no fear to speak it!

"Do I love you?" she repeated. "Are you not too hasty?"

"Am I?" he said, alarmed.

And she sighed.

"Oh yes, of course you are! You know so little of me. You have taken me from my father's house by a ladder at night, and share a moor with me, and you know I have no friend to turn to in the world but yourself. You have eyes and ears, and still you must be asking if it is not hasty to find out if I love you. It is a wonder you have the boldness to say the word itself."

"Well," he pursued gawkily, though he perceived her drift clearly, "here I am, and I do love you. Oh, what a poor word it is, that love, for the fire I feel inside me. There is no word for that, there is nothing but a song for it that some day I must be making. Love, quo' she; oh, I could say that truly of the heather kissing your hand, ay, of the glaur your feet might walk on upon a wet day!"

"My best respects to you, Master Gilian!" said Nan. "You have the fine tongue in your head after all. What a pity we have been wasting such a grand opportunity for it here!" and there was an indulgence in her eye, though now and then the numb regret of a blunder made came upon her spirit.

"Will you come down with me?" he went on, far too precipitate for her fancy.

"When?" she asked, thoughtlessly robbing a heather-tuft bell by bell with idle fingers.

"Now; Miss Mary expects us this evening."

"Miss Mary!" said she, a little amused and annoyed. "You would never have come to the bit but for her."

"Perhaps not," he confessed, "but here I am, and God bless her for bringing me to it! Will you—will you take my white heather now?" And he stood, something of a lout, with nervous hands upon his hips.

"It looks very pretty where it is," she answered playfully. "And for what should I be decking myself in the wilderness?"

She wanted the obvious compliment, but this was a stock from a kail garden, and "Oh, John Hielan'man!" she cried aloud for the first time.

"You promised, you know," he said lamely.

"That was yesterday, and this is today, and—" she could not finish for thinking of Young Islay.

"Must I be taking it to you?" he went on, making to move to the door of the hut where lay the symbol of his love and the token of her surrender.

"Wait! wait!" she cried, standing to her feet and approaching him. "Is that all there is in the bargain? Are there no luck-pennies at this sort of market?"

He understood her and kissed her with a heart furious within but in his movement hesitating, shy and awkward.

For her life she could not but recall the other—the more confident and practised one she had fled from. She drew off, red, to give her no more than her due, for the treachery of her mind.

"Leave it," she said to him. "I will get it myself. Does anyone besides Miss Mary know we are here?"

"No."

"Then she will tell nobody our secret. You will go down now. We could scarcely go together. You will go down now, and tell her I will follow in the dusk."

"You have given me no answer, Nan," he pleaded; "the heather!"

"The heather will be at my heart!" she cried hurriedly.

It was a promise that sang in his head as he went on his way, the herald of joy, the fool of illusion.

XXXIV

CHASE

WHEN he had gone and was no further than the shoulder of the brae lying between the hut and Little Fox, and there was no longer any chance of his turning to repeat his wild adieux, Nan went into the old hut and put the sprig of white heather at her bosom, and gave way to a torrent of tears. She could not have done so in the sunshine outside, but in that poor interior, even with the day spying through the roof, she had the sense of seclusion. She cried for grief and bitterness. No folly she had ever committed seemed so great as this her latest, that she should blindly have fled from a danger unmeasured into a situation that abounded with difficulties. She blamed herself, she blamed her father, she blamed Gilian for his inability to be otherwise than God had made him. In contrast to his gawky shyness—the rusticity of the farm and hill, rose up constant in her remembrance the confident young gentleman she had run away from without so much as a knowledge of his name. She cried, and the afternoon came, a blush of fire and flowing gold upon the hills, the purple of the steeps behind her darkened; upon Big Fox behind, some wild duck floated and gossiped.

She was still at her crying, a maiden altogether disconsolate, with no notion of where next she should turn, afraid to go home yet never once thinking of going to Miss Mary's refuge as she had promised, and the world was all dolorous round her, when a step bounded near the door. She started in terror and shrank into the darkest corner of the hut. The footstep came not quite close to the door; it was as if the stranger feared to find a house empty and hesitated before setting foot on the threshold. From where she stood she could not see him, though his breath was to be heard, short and panting. The square of the open door was filled with green and purple—the green of the rank nettle, the purple of the bell-heather she had been always careful to spare as she had gone in and out.

Who could it be? Her first thought was of some fisherman or sportsman late upon the hill and attracted by the smoke of the hut that had so long known no fire. Then she thought of her father, more kindly and more contrite to him than she had ever felt before. If it was her father, what should she do? Would she run out and dare all for his forgiveness of her folly, and take his terms if that were possible now that her name and his were ridiculous through all the shire? But it could not be her father. Her father would not be alone and—

Into the square of light stepped Young Islay! He was all blown with the hurry of his ascent after hearing from Black Duncan (who had heard from Elasaid) that Nan had been there in the morning, and now there was no sign of life about the silent hut except the blue reek that rose over the mouldering thatch. He was a brave youth, but for once he feared to try his fate.

As he stood in the doorway and looked into the dark interior, where a poor fire smouldered in the centre of the floor, he seemed so woebegone that Nan could not but smile in spite of her trepidation. He but looked a second, then turned to seek her elsewhere.

As he turned away she called faintly, all blushing and all tears, but yet with a smile on her face that never sat so sweetly there as when her feelings mingled. He started as at the voice of a ghost, and hung hesitating on the threshold till she stepped from her gloomy corner into the light of the afternoon. As he saw her where a moment before was a vacancy he could scarcely believe

283

his eyes. But he did not hesitate long. In an instant, encouraged by her tears and smiles, he had an arm round her.

"Nan! Nan!" he cried, "I have found you! I never was so happy in my life!"

For a moment she did not put him off; and he took her hesitation for content.

"What did it mean? Were you flying from me?" he asked.

All her hardships, all the wrong and degradation leaped into her recollection. She withdrew herself firmly from that embrace that might be the embrace of love and possession or of simple companionship in trial.

"I would never have been here but for you," said she. "Did you—did you pay much?"

"Ah!" he cried ruefully, "there's where you do me injustice! Did you know me so little—and indeed you know me but little enough, more's my sorrow—did you know me so little that you must believe me a savage to be guilty of a crime like that? Must I be saying that before God I did not know that my father and—and—"

"—And my father."

"—And your father, though I would be the last to charge him, were scheming in any commercial way on my behalf? Come, come, I was not blate, was I? the last time we were together; my impudence was not in the style of a man who would go the other way about a wooing, was it?"

"Then you did not know?" She blushed and paused.

"I knew nothing," he protested. "I knew nothing but that I loved you, and you know that too if telling can inform you. I told my father that, and he was well enough pleased, and I could not guess he would make a fool of me and a victim of you in my absence."

She stood trembling to this revelation of his innocence, and, once more the confident lover, Young Islay tried to take her in his arms.

She ran from him, not the young lady of Edinburgh but a merry-hearted child, making for the side of Little Fox, the air as she went flapping her gown till it beat gaily like a flag. She ran light-footed, laughing in her sudden ease of mind, and on the more distant of the two slopes of Cruach-an-Lochain, antlers rose inquiring; then a red deer looked and listened, forgetting to crop the poor grass at his feet.

For a second or two Young Islay paused, wondering at her caprice; then he caught the spirit of it and followed with a halloo. A pleasant quarry—the temptation of it made his blood tingle as no sport in the world could do; his halloo came back in echoes from the hill, jocund and hearty echoes, and Sir Deer at a bound went far to the rear among the bracken.

Nan sped panting yet laughing. Then she heard his cry. "I am coming, I am coming," he called. It might have been the pibroch of the dawn, the hopeful conquering dawn on valley rims. She put more vigour into her flight; her lips set hard; she thought if he caught her before she reached the spot where Gilian last had kissed her, she must be his for good.

"Run as you like, I am coming," cried her pursuer, and he was easily overtaking her. Then he saw how hard and earnestly she strove. With a grimace to himself, he slackened his pace and let her gain ground.

"I must be doing my best for Gilian," she thought; but as she risked a glance over her shoulder and saw the pursuit decline, saw his face handsome and laughing and eager, full of the fun of the adventure, across a widening space, saw him kiss his hand to her as he ran leisurely, she forgot that she had meant to run for fair play and Gilian, and she, too, slackened her pace.

A moment more and he caught her, and she relapsed in his arms with a sigh of exertion and surrender.

"Faith, you are worth running for!" said he, turning her to him to see into her eyes. For a little he looked at the flushed and beautiful countenance. Her bosom throbbed against his breast; her head thrown back, showed the melting passion of her eyes like slumbering lakes only half hid by her trembling lids, her lips red and full, tempting, open upon pearls. She was his, he told himself, all his, and yet—and yet, he had half a regret that now he had caught he need chase no more—the regret of the hunter when the deer is home, of the traveller who has reached the goal after pleasant journeyings.

His pause was but for a moment, then on her lips he pressed his; on all her glowing face fell the fever of his kisses.

"Nan, Nan!" he whispered, "you are mine, did I not tell you?"

"I suppose I am," she whispered faintly. Then to herself, "Poor Gilian!"

"And yet," said he, "I'm not worth it."

"I daresay not," she confessed, nestling the more closely in his arms. "But you won me when you saved my life."

"Did I?" said he. "How very wise of me! Give me a kiss, then!"

She tried to free herself, and the white heather at her neck fell between them. She stooped for it and he to get her kiss, but she was first successful. To him she held out the twig of pale bells.

"The kiss or that; you can have either," she said. "One is love and the other is luck."

"Then, sweetheart, I'll have both," said Young Islay.

XXXV

AN EMPTY HUT

THE town bell rang, the little shops were shuttered. Miss Mary, with a new cap on to do justice to the occasion, had sat for hours with Gilian at the window, waiting; the Cornal was in bed, and the Paymaster, dubious but not unpleased, was up at MacGibbon's telling the story over a game of dambrod. And still Nan did not appear. There was a sign of changing weather above Strone, and Gilian was full of sorrow to think of the girl travelling to him through darkness and rain, so he started out to meet her by the only path on which she must come.

He reached the lochs as the night was drawing in. The moor was sounding loud and eerie with the call of large birds. Very cold and uncharitable, a breeze came from Cruach-an-Lochain, and in the evening dusk the country seemed most woefully poor and uninhabitable. So it appeared to Gilian for a moment when at last he came to the head of the brae where he should have his first sight of the light that could make that wild as warm and hospitable and desirable as a king's court. There was no light now! At first he doubted his eyesight; then he thought he was not at the right point of view; then he was compelled to confess to himself that darkness was assuredly where before had been a bright spot like one of the stars that shine in murky heavens in the midst of storms to prove that God does not forget.

She had been kept, the dear heart, he told himself; she had been kept by her modesty waiting for the dusk, and fallen asleep for weariness.

He went awkwardly off the customary track so that he might reach the shealing the quicker by a short cut that led through boggy grass. He stumbled in hags and tripped on ancient heather-tufts; the birds wheeled and mocked over him, something in their note most melancholy and menacing to his ear.

The loch with the islet was muttering in its sleep, and woke with the shriek of a thousand frightened birds when this phantom stumbled on its solitude. The tiny island even in the dusk rose black like a hearse plume in the water. At his feet he felt upon a stone the tinkle of broken glass, and he stooped to feel. His finger came upon the portions of the broken cup, and he remembered, with shame for his own share in the scene, how Nan had punished his awkwardness by casting from her the vessel of which this was the fragment. She had had her lips to this, her fingers had touched it; it was a gem to put in his pocket, and he put it there. He searched round again as he repeated in his mind all the incidents of that first morning in the moor, and a little further on he came upon the ashes of their dead fire. Poor dead fire, grey old ashes, flame quenched, warmth departed, loneli- ·ness come—the reflections made him shiver.

As he stood there in what was now the dark night, he might have been a phantom mourning for the unrecoverable, the ghost of old revelries, the shade of pleasant bygone hearths and love the ancient.

He shook himself into the present world, and left behind the ashes of their fire and made for the shealing hut, all the way solacing himself with fancy. The girl was his, but he never let his mind linger on the numerous difficulties that lay inevitably be-tween the present hour and his possession of her. He projected himself into the future with a blank unexplained behind, and saw them at unextinguishable hearths, love accompanying them through generations. Through the heather he brushed eagerly now, his eyes intent upon the dim summits of the brae from which again he should see the light of the shealing if it was there. Loch Little Fox, and Great Fox, and all the black and sobbing pools among the heather he passed on the light feet of love, and when he came to the brae top and still found no beacon there, he was exceedingly dashed.

"I hope, I hope there is nothing wrong," he said aloud. And he hurried the faster.

The sky was full of clouds, all but a patch star-sown over Ben Bhreac, and all through the hollows and hags ran a wail of rain-wind most mournful. The birds that had been crying over the pools departed, and there was no sound of animal life. The wind moaned and the pools sobbed. About the black edifice in which he thought was all he prized most dear on earth, blackness hung like a terror. Breathless he stood at the door. It was wide open! It was wide open! It was wide open to the night wind! As if a hand of ice had clutched him at the heart he shook and staggered back.

"God of Grace!" he cried in his mother tongue, then "Nan! Nan!" he called to the dark within. There was no answer, and a bird flew out above his head.

He cried no more there, but out he ran into the vacant moor and loudly he called to the night, "Nan! Nan!" till his voice seemed to himself some terrific chant of long-dead peoples come first to this strange land and crying for each other in the wilderness where they were lost.

"Nan! Nan!" he cried, sometimes entreating, sometimes peremptory, as though she might be hiding in the dark in some childish caprice. "Nan! Nan!" he called plaintively, and he called sharply too and loudly, the possessor. The sides of Ben Bhreac woke to answer "Anan," as people reply in dreams; and the stars of heaven in their little garden over the hill had no interest whatever in his crying; they hung out cool and imperturbable, and the wind wailed, but not for his anxieties, on the reeds of Little Fox.

Then he pressed his hand upon his heart to still its uproar and strained his ears to listen. No sound of a girl's voice, no foot upon the heather. He could scarcely believe his senses. In his mind, as he approached the house she had seemed as essential a part of it as the sky was portion of the universe, and here she was gone!

"After all, she may be in the house asleep," he thought, cheating himself into a moment's comfort; and back he went again. He listened at the threshold for a breath: no sound came to him; the fire was all out, the air was the air of a dungeon. "Nan!" he called timidly. He got no reply.

Timidly now he stepped into that chamber that had been sacred to him before—the holy of holies—and fumbled with a steel. The sparks showed him his hands trembling, but at first he did not dare to look behind him for fears intangible. The dried heather stems caught the flame of the tinder; there was but a handful of them; they flared up in a moment's red glare on the interior, then died out crackling. It was enough to show him the place was empty. It showed him, too, his lantern, the poor companion of his adventure, lying on the floor as if it had been tumbled there in some hasty escape; he picked it up and lit it, the gleam lighting a ghastly face. And then he went out again, not knowing why or what he might do there, but bound to be moving and away from that empty shell where had been his kernel untasted. The wind had risen and was rising higher still. On Little Fox side he stood, a ludicrous object, with the pinpoints of light pricking the darkness. He was there the dreamer and the hesitator, his eyes vacant. He wore a short ill-fitting jacket; his vest had come unbuttoned in the haste of his clamber up the moor; his bonnet was drawn low upon his brow. As he cherished the lantern from the wind with his back bent he was no figure of the ideal lover, but yet some tragedy was in the look of him—some great and moving fate that might have made the night pity him. Down again to their little knowe he went, and cast himself upon it and surrendered to emotion. It was for him the grave of love, the new-reared mound of his affection. Even yet he could see where she had pressed down the heather as she reclined. Looking at the heather he remembered the white spray of his affection that she had said would be the sign of his fate. He went back quickly to the hut, the wind still puffing at his foolish lantern, and he found the heather gone. It comforted him exceedingly. She had gone, why or where he could not guess, but she had taken with her the token of his love and thereby left him her capitulation. His heather was at her heart!

Wearied utterly, as much by the stress of his passions as by the ardours of the day, he took possession of her couch and slept till morning.

XXXVI

CONCLUSION

FAIR day in the town, and cattle roved about the street,
bellowing, the red and shaggy fellows of the moors, mourning in Gaelic accent and with mild large eyes pondering on the
mysteries of change. Behind them went the children, beating them
lightly on the flanks with hazel wands, imagining themselves
travellers over the markets of the world, and others, the older
ones, the bolder ones, went from shop to shop for farings, eating,
as they went, the parley-man and carvey-cake of the Fair day.
Farmers and shepherds gossiped and bargained on the footpaths
or on the grass before the New Inns; the Abercrombie clattered
with convivial glass and sometimes rose the chorus to a noisy
ditty of Lorn. Old Brooks, with his academy shut for holiday,
stood at the church corner with a pocket full of halfpence for his
bairns, and a little silver in his vest for the naughty ones he had
thrashed with the ferule and grieved for. "To be good and clever
is to be lucky enough," he said; "I must be kind to my poor
dunces." Some of them, he saw, went with his gift straight to
Marget Maclean's. "Ah," he said, smiling to himself, "they're
after the novelles! I wish Virgil was so much the favourite, or
even the Grammarian."

All in the pleasant sunshine the people walked abroad on the
plain-stones; a piper of the company of Boboon the wanderer,

with but two drones to his instrument, played the old rant of the clan as Duke George went past on a thoroughbred horse.

"Do you hear yon?" asked the Paymaster, opening the parlour window to let in that mountain strain his brother loved so truly.

The Cornal cocked an ear, drew down shaggy brows on his attention, and studied, musingly, the tune that hummed from the reeds below.

" 'Baile Inneraora'!" said he. "I wish it was 'Bundle and Go'. That's the tune now for Colin Campbell, for old Colin Campbell, for poor Colin Campbell who once was young and wealthy. I've seen the day that rant would set something stirring here"—and he struck a bony hand upon his breast. "Now there's not a move"—and he searched still with fingers above his heart. "Not a move! There's only a clod inside where once there was a bird."

He stood with his head a little to the side, listening to the piper till the tune died, half accomplished, at a tavern door. Then the children and the bellowing kine had the world to themselves again. The sound of carriage wheels came from the Cross, and of the children calling loud for bridal bowl-money.

"What's that?" asked the Cornal, waking from his reverie; and his brother put his head out at the window. He drew back at once with his face exceeding crimson.

"What is't?" said the Cornal, seeing his hesitation.

"A honeymoon pair," said the brother, and fumbled noisily with the newspaper he had in his hand.

"Poor creatures! And who is it? Though I never get over the door you'll tell me nothing."

The Paymaster answered shortly. "It's the pair from Maam," said he, and back to his paper again.

Up to his brow the Cornal put a trembling hand and seemed amazed and startled. Then he recollected, and a sad smile came to his visage. "Not a clod altogether yet!" said he, half to himself and half to his brother. "I felt the flutter of a wing. But it's not your grief or mine this time, Jock; it's your poor recruit's."

"He's down in Miss Mary's room, and that's the place for the like of him."

"Is it?" said the Cornal. "Dugald understood him best of any of us; he saw this coming, and I mind that he grieved for the fellow."

"He's grieving plenty for himself, and let him!" said the Paymaster, setting aside his journal. "Look what he dropped from his pocket this morning. Peggy thought it was mine and she took it to me. Mine! Fancy that! I'm jalousing she was making a joke of me." He produced, as he spoke, a scrap of paper with some verses on it and handed it to his brother.

The Cornal held the document far from his failing eyes and perused the writing. It was the first of those heart-wrung fancies that went to the making of the volume that lies before me as I write—the familiar lament for the lost "Maid of the Moor" that shepherds still are singing on his native hills.

"A ballant!" said he, wondering, and with some contempt.

"That's just what it is," said his brother. "There was never the like broke out in this family before, I'm glad to say."

The Cornal screwed his lips firmly. "It's what I would call going altogether too far," he said. "I'm feared your recruit will affront us again. A song, now! did you ever know the like of it? I'll not put up with it! Did you say he was down with Miss Mary?"

"I saw her laying the corner of the table," said the Paymaster, "and I'll warrant it was not to feed herself at this time of day."

The Cornal looked again at the verses, clearing his eyes with his hand, as if he might happily be mistaken. But no, there were the foolish lines, and some sentiments most unmanly frank of love and idleness among the moor and heather. He growled; he frowned below his shaggy brows: "Come down this instant and put an end to it," said he.

"He's with Mary," his brother reminded him, hesitating.

"I don't care a curse if he was with the Duke," said the Cornal. "I'll end this carry-on in an honest and industrious family."

He led the way downstairs, the Paymaster following softly, both in their slippers. Noiselessly they pushed open the door of Miss Mary's room and gazed within. She and her darling were

294

looking over the window at the tumultuous crowd of children scrambling for Young Islay's bowl-money scattered by Black Duncan in the golden syver sand. Miss Mary in that position could not but have her arm about his waist, and her hand unconsciously caressed the rough home-spun of his jacket. The brothers, unobserved, stood silent in the doorway.

"That's the end of it!" said Gilian bitterly, as he came wholly into the room. His face, shone on by the sun that struck above the tall lands opposite from fiery clouds, was white to the lips. Miss Mary looked up into his eyes, mourning in her very inmost for his torture.

"I would say 'fair wind to her,' my dear, and a good riddance," said she, and yet without conviction in her tone.

"I will say 'fair wind' readily," he answered, "but I cannot be forgetting. I know she likes—she loves me still."

Miss Mary showed her pity in her face, but nothing at all had she to say.

"You are not doubting it, are you?" he cried eagerly; and, still unnoticed in the doorway, the Paymaster grimaced his contempt, but his brother, touched by some influence inexplicable, put the poem in his pocket and delayed the entry.

"Are you doubting?" again cried the lad, determined on his answer but dreading a denial.

"It is not your bowl-money the bairns are gathering at the Cross," said Miss Mary simply.

"True," he acknowledged; "but she went because she must. She loves me still, I'm telling you; she has my heather at her heart!"

Miss Mary understood. She looked at her dreamer and stifled a sigh. Then she saw her brothers in the doorway, silent, and her hand went down and met his and fondled it for his assurance as on the day he first stood, the frightened stranger, on that floor, and she had sheltered his shyness in the folds of her bombazine gown.